DURT

THE COPERNICUS QUESTION

JAMES SLATER

JAMESSLATERBOOKS.COM

ACKNOWLEDGMENTS

Eternal thanks to my Beta Readers, especially the ones who took the time to mark up and send back the beta books. Mike, Bill, Harrold, Tony, and of course, Mom and Dad. The storyline is stronger because of you, and the full 31 chapters are now included. To Gary, thanks for the always entertaining conversations; and to Sarah for the cover design, thank you for bringing to life a vision that existed only in my mind.

- NO, THEY HADN'T TAMED ALASKA AS MANY OF THEM HAD SET OUT TO DO. ALASKA WOULDN'T PUT UP WITH THAT.

[1]
ALASKA

BUZZ YELPED. Durt shivered against the cold and looked up. The young husky, aside from serving as his best friend, was also his early warning system. October in Alaska was betraying signs of winter, and while first snow hadn't shown its face yet, he knew it wouldn't be too far off. The log cabin wasn't exactly a modern, energy-efficient house, and he supposed that's why they called it a cabin. Weather had been fine for the previous couple of weeks of his stint here, and he loved nature and the solitude—for a time. It beat the hell out of city living. That's what Dad said, anyway. The people and the mess and the fighting and the...well, there *was* quite a list. In fact, it was one of a number of lists that Dad would rant about in the evenings at Harry's. The evils of modern society. The dangers of the big city. The criminal weapon problem. There were more, too. There were times like these when he agreed with his father, even if those times were becoming a rare occurrence. But he could change his mind. He did it all the time.

The fire in the retro Franklin stove was almost out, and it was time to replenish his supply from the woodpile on the porch. It seemed stupid to him that it was almost the year 3000, and he was still building fires for warmth. He laughed to himself. That was one thing that didn't get mentioned at Harry's. If you were cold in the city, you didn't have to do anything. The house knew it and made its own comfort adjustments. There was something to be said for that.

He buzzed down to the city now and again. That was the beauty of being a pilot. Mobility. Freedom. And this, a place to call his own—even if it didn't actually belong to him. Still, it was just him with nobody else around for hundreds of kilometers. Rare in today's world. Access to the parks or the farms? That was something special. He had here what was the envy of almost everyone he met. He had space. In the city, and what wasn't the city by this time? he thought, you could drive surface streets from Seattle to Santiago. Pretty much anything that wasn't forest preserve or food production farms was city. But some days he loved the adventure, the risk, the conveniences, and the girls—of course the girls—of the city.

A creaking plank on the porch evoked a warning whine from Buzz.

"Dad, is that you?" he called out.

He wasn't expecting a visit today, but Dad's responsibilities took him all over the region, so the occasional drop-by visit wasn't uncommon, either.

"Can you grab an armful of wood?" he called out, rising from his three-legged stool near the stove. "I'm almost out in here."

He grabbed his jacket from a peg on the wall behind the stove. Buzz was instantly at his heels, his whining now constant.

"C'mon, puppy. Let's go get some wood," he said to Buzz, his constant shadow.

"Dad? I'll give you a hand."

He opened the door and stepped into the chilly Alaska fall. His heart stopped. He stood frozen. Staring. It wasn't Dad.

A bear stared back at him. And not just any bear, he realized. A grizzly. The animal was up on its hind legs, one giant paw on the woodpile, the other by his side. If bears could have surprised expressions, this bear would have one. *This was bad.* If there were a hundred rules in the forest, the one you didn't want to forget was not to surprise a grizzly. You never knew how they would react. Mentally, they were not the kings of the forest, but physically? Durt knew he could never win a bear fight.

He stared at the bear, afraid to move a muscle.

The bear tilted its head as if curious as to what type of odd-looking bear had just emerged to confront him. Was this a threat? Did he need to exert his dominance? The beast opened its mouth wide as fear coursed through Durt. But it wasn't to take a bite. It was to yawn, a giant, slow bear yawn. Apparently, the animal had made its decision. No threat here, just another skinny, curious animal in the forest.

Then Buzz screwed it up. Stupid dog. It wasn't his fault. Buzz was a puppy. He barked suddenly.

Durt was wholly surprised at the speed at which it happened. The bear reacted much faster than he did, not out of aggression, but surprise, and that *other* paw, the not-on-the-woodpile paw, swiped out in a sudden flash. Durt moved as quickly as he could to avoid contact, but his speed was no match for the king of the forest. The blow from the paw knocked him sideways, the giant claws raking his face and the force launching his slender form easily against the sturdy log walls of the cabin.

He let out a scream of pain that was cut sharply on impact. He reeled and stumbled, falling back onto the woodpile and taking some of the sawn logs with him as he tumbled onto the porch.

Buzz was barking incessantly now, and as he raised his head, the pain and dizziness overwhelming him, he sensed the bear's retreat from the falling wood, a dark mass of fur and teeth and claws rumbling away from the cabin and back into the Alaskan forest.

Then everything went black.

* * *

He pushed the dog away. Buzz was licking his face as it throbbed. He wasn't sure how long he'd been out, but he felt weak, and a lot of his blood was now on the porch. His head was pounding, and he could feel the open wounds on his face. Jesus. Was this his destiny? His ultimate contribution to life? To bleed to death in a cold cabin in the forest? He went to stand up, but dizziness forced him back to the porch. This was crazy. Gathering his strength a second time, he didn't try to stand. Instead, he crawled back inside the cabin, barely able to close the door before collapsing in a heap again.

"Buzz, get me a cigarette," he said to the Husky.

Yeah, that would happen.

If Buzz were a bot dog, it might happen, he thought, but he wasn't. He was a real live, fur and slobber dog that wasn't going to be talked into anything but chasing squirrels and tripping over himself and his best friend in the cabin. Where the hell were his cigarettes, anyway? He could barely think through his pounding dizzy head. With a deep breath, he crawled toward the bathroom. There had to be one in there. All other things considered, a smoke was probably a best first move. Get the mind back in working order and focus. He was supposed to be the rescuer, not someone who needed rescuing.

The dog thought he was playing again.

"Not helping, Buzz," he told his dog through gritted teeth. "I need something you can't give me."

Buzz dropped to the floor. He'd heard his name, and that meant some kind of a game. On his knees on the floor was not a position Durt regularly assumed, and Buzz was curious and happy to learn the rules of the new game. Eager and waiting.

He looked back at the dog for a moment and stopped short.

There, under the wood-burning stove, he saw the red corner of the cigarette pack that had probably found its new hiding place after dropping out of his pocket on one of his fire-tending chores. Now he remembered. He was out of cigarettes, with the exception of the pack in the medkit he kept in the can. He'd fished them out yesterday and promptly lost track of them. He didn't smoke that often, but that was another rule of the forest. Be prepared. You never knew what was going to happen. Because something always happens.

He smiled with a sudden realization, and the pain from the bear wound on the side of his face made him gasp. Buzz *had* found his cigarettes, whether he'd intended to or not. A bit of luck and a bit of who-knows-what-else just might get him by.

The fire was out in the stove, but a few embers remained. He scooped out a small pile with the ash shovel that leaned against the stove and felt the heat of the coals on his sensitive face as he lit the cigarette.

As the healing smoke made its way into his lungs and his bloodstream, he turned over slowly onto his back. He felt Buzz beside him, the Husky now sensing all was not right, and he felt the buzz within him as the cigarette began to have its effect. He exhaled and watched the smoke gather above him as he stared at the cabin's wooden ceiling. In its infancy, he knew, tobacco had been a health hazard. But a compromise between biotechnology and human beings who couldn't seem to give up the habit resulted in a new generation of health cigarette. Manipulation at the molecular level transformed tobacco from a hazard into a benefit. Cellular regeneration or some crap like that. He didn't know how it all worked, but here in 30th-century living, smoking could save your life. Like it was saving his right now.

He smoked slowly and realized he must have dozed off when an alien sound awoke him. At least it was alien to the woods here in Alaska.

"Durt you there?" came the crackling voice from the cabin wall. "Durt, it's CJ. Come back."

Fucking CJ. On the radio.

It was the last thing he needed this morning. He and CJ worked at opposite ends of the same industry—tourism. There wasn't a lot of tourism work in their neck of the woods, as only a select few could afford to make the necessary donations to the Forest Service that could warrant a trip into reserved park service lands. They called them extreme vacations, and they, like the

Forest Service elite, were restricted to what they could bring into the parks. None of the new field technology was allowed. Tourists had to survive here like people survived here a thousand years ago. And yes, sometimes they got into trouble. CJ would fly them to wherever they needed to go, and invariably, they'd get in over their heads, and CJ would call him to get them out. CJ was much better at selling those extreme options than he was at dealing with the consequences of his sales.

Another of Alaska's rules he kept in mind, and this one wasn't just for extreme guests. It was for everyone. Alaska could be a nasty bitch when she turned cold.

He tried standing up and succeeded, making his way the few feet to the radio.

"Durt, it's CJ. I need some help," came the voice again.

He could hear the tension and the fear in CJ's voice. Not that he could ever really tell if CJ was serious or not, and he wasn't sure CJ could either. He got regular radio calls asking for help for things like finding his underwear or taking a leak. That was CJ. He read a different tone in CJ's voice today.

He thumbed the radio and replied. "CJ. Durt here. It's not underwear again, is it? Because I just don't have time for your crap today."

CJ came back with a two-word reply. "Glacier jumping."

He closed his eyes and swore to himself. He was going to need another cigarette.

* * *

He shook his head. It was something he always did when he talked to CJ. His best—and worst—friend.

"And why in the hell would I pull one of your high-dollar clients out of the jam that you put them in in the first place?" His tone was harsh. He sounded demanding as he listened to himself. But he was sure CJ deserved it.

The radio was silent.

"You cheap son-of-a-bitch. Did you run out of money for your oil burner? Again?"

The silence continued.

He already knew the answer. Either he was lying or he wasn't. If he was lying, it meant that this was a jam that left a tourist stranded beyond the edge of CJ's capabilities as a pilot, and he needed Durt's skill. If he wasn't lying, then he'd gotten himself into another gambling jam and couldn't afford the fuel to run his plane. He ran what he called the quintessential extreme vacation. It was like stepping back in time to the 20th century. He had a fuel-burning plane with an internal combustion engine. Problem was, with his lifestyle, he couldn't always plan on having money to pay for the fuel when he needed it. Which was a problem if something like this happened. He spent a lot of time in Vegas and more in Michigan. He was actually a competent gambler and made big money on a fairly regular basis. When he was there, he lived the big life as did everyone around him. No better friend to have than CJ, flush with a win. Problem was, he couldn't keep it, and by the time he made it home, he'd often have little or nothing left. He'd been too cheap to buy a grav drive for his plane. He regretted it once in a while. Durt figured this was one of those whiles.

Finally, the radio spoke. "C'mon, man. You know I'm good for it."

He probably was, too. Not that it mattered, Durt thought. As rescue pilots for the region, they were obligated to respond. And today, if it wasn't CJ, it had to be him. It was OK. He didn't need to share the fact he'd been stupid enough to stand that close to a grizzly and get his face sliced up like he did.

"Alright, man. I'll cover you this time. But you're gonna pay for this one."

CJ, his voice a little more upbeat this time, replied. "You know I always do. Coordinates are in your navunit."

There were a few exceptions to the retro rules inside the Park boundaries, and mostly they had to do with search and rescue.

The Park service liked its donations and wanted to make sure they didn't lose any of their big donors. Donors got special access, sometimes off the books. He knew the donations helped the service. Well, the service's senior directors, anyway, he corrected himself. The problem for him was, on trips like these, if they weren't registered with the official rescue units, the flight took on a whole new dimension of risk. He had no idea where the navunit and the plane would take him.

What he did know was that he loved to fly. He'd admitted both to his father and himself that he was something of a daredevil, but his record stood for itself. He'd never failed a rescue mission, and he wasn't going to start today.

The cigarette had stabilized the wound, and he taped some gauze in place to cover the hideous open slash left by the surprised grizzly. He worked quickly but awkwardly, the reflection in the mirror fooling his sense of right and left.

"Aw, fuck it," he said to himself as the tape left a less-than-perfect dressing on his cheek. It didn't matter anyway, he'd probably lose it on the run to the plane. He had a fully stocked med kit there. Maybe he'd do some touch up once he got airborne.

Buzz was right beside him, tongue out and ears pointed at the cabin's ceiling above. Buzz was ready for anything. He smiled. Yep, he was, too.

"Let's go, Buzz. Time to fly."

He grabbed the radio and threw his ditch bag over his shoulder. Buzz was scratching impatiently at the door and whining. He knew where they were going, and he was always the first one to get there.

The crisp October air stung his eyes, but in a good way. It had been a while since they'd been on a rescue call, and the cigarette and the adrenaline worked together to give him that sense of invincibility. By the time he'd vaulted off the rough-hewn cabin's porch, Buzz had already reached the edge of the clearing and disappeared down the path that led into the woods. At a walking pace, the plane was a few minutes' walk. Buzz would be there in less than a minute, and he'd be there, right on the husky's tail. Blood pumped through his veins as he entered the woods himself. The familiar evergreen trunks guided his footsteps, and their scent reminded him how few people on Earth ever actually saw these trees. Some days he cared nothing about the whole benefit of these wide open spaces, but today as he strained forward into the biting air, it was all magic. Certainly, lives were on the line. And his responsibility as a pilot was at the forefront of his thoughts. He wouldn't fail. He couldn't. He smiled to himself and immediately regretted it as the sharp sting of the bear wound ripped across his face.

Even in Alaska's partially overcast day, the water reflected the filtered sun through the trees. Spruce and western hemlock fared well in this climate, offering protection from the winds and beckoning the inevitable snow to decorate their extended branches. Beauty and desolation went hand-in-hand here. It was an unforgiving environment that didn't take kindly to missteps. Misjudge climate or wildlife, and you'd be pulled out after the spring thaw —or not.

Green hills stood watch on either side of the long lake that came into view as he broke out of the forest and into the open. He ignored the zig-zag trail that offered a mild incline and a gentle slope to his float plane. He'd take it on the way back when his time schedule was not quite so compressed. He chose instead the direct downhill shortcut Buzz usually took to his ride, the plane's bright red reflection a stark contrast to the forest's greens and the lake's watery blues. It bobbed expectantly on its mooring, its first passenger sitting now, tongue out, urging Durt forward with his eyes.

Not two minutes after he'd left the cabin behind, he was preflighting in the cockpit, double-checking his systems and inventory. This was not the place for short-cutting. Were something missing or broken, he'd have a contingency for pretty much everything, but airborne, options quickly narrowed to mostly undesirable choices. No, he double and triple-checked everything.

Up there, he was his own flight crew, mechanic, and pilot, and each day it seemed, he took turns playing each of these roles. It was a good system, and he stuck to it.

Preflight told him he'd done his job well, his systems were ready and functioning. Buzz sat in his co-pilot seat, the panting now replaced by an expectant gaze out the window. He was ready. He gave the dog a head pat for good luck.

He was missing one thing. It had nothing to do with his plane. It had to do with the navunit. Without coordinates, he wasn't going anywhere. But that didn't stop him. He was going flying today, rescue or not. It might be a shorter trip than expected. He was pretty sure he knew the general area where CJ's clients would be found. Damn glacier surfers. And the navunits didn't always get great reception here in the middle of nowhere. But once he got to elevation, they should pick it up.

The wind had ruffled up the surface of the lake, and that would give them a few bumps on take-off, but a facing breeze would give them a nice bit of lift, too.

"Here we go, Buzz."

Buzz whined in anticipation. The dog loved to fly. They both did.

[2]
NEVADA

IT WAS ANOTHER WORLD. A world of freedom and flight. Adventure. Buzz, as always, sat transfixed at the window as the pair got airborne. It was a bumpy ride, but the thrill of takeoff and the lightness inside of him made him think of smiling before his bandaged face thought the better of it. Beneath them, the ruffled surface of the lake made a better landscape than it had a runway, and as the plane climbed above the October evergreens, Alaska's vast beauty and strength opened up before them. If he did nothing else today, this vista in itself would make it a great day. Few people ever got this view. He ran his fingers through Buzz's warm fur then reached to adjust the environmental controls. There might be better days for flying, but not many.

Data now streamed across the flight display before him, and he switched to audio mode, drinking in the Alaskan landscape ahead with his eyes.

"What does it look like out there today, Nev?" he asked.

Nev was the name he'd chosen for his navunit. It was a female voice, and he'd chosen the name Nevada, partly because, like Alaska, he was captivated by the extreme environment of that state to the south. The Americas were packed with billions of people living on top of one another with few exceptions. Parts of

Nevada were in that category, too. But Nevada was mostly wild and untamed, much like their current environment. The second reason for his choice of names was much simpler. Nevada was the name of the Moon-based manufacturing company that made these navunits. The name *Nevada* was emblazoned in chrome letters across the front of the unit.

"You're not going to like it."

Durt shook his head. It was October in Alaska. There wasn't much that was going to surprise him.

"Spill it, Nev."

"Storm system moving in over the Gulf of Alaska."

"Details." He didn't mean to bark, but that was how it came out.

Nev's reply was not in her standard programmed voice, but direct digital monotone from the Ocean Rescue service. She was miffed at his response.

"Coastal weather forecast for the northern Gulf of Alaska up to 100 nautical miles out, including Kodiak Island and Cook Inlet," droned the flat machine response, spewing its automated forecast.

He rolled his eyes. Nev's voice kept him company in the air. He'd spent the extra cash to have the enhanced emotional response programming installed. It made her sound more like a human being, and she was a pretty good conversationalist. Usually a good traveling companion, too. But she was sometimes sensitive, and this was one of those times. Were there an actual girl there in the plane, she probably would have done the same thing. Then he'd have to apologize. As he did now.

"Sorry Nev. Started my day on the wrong side of the cabin."

The voice switched abruptly in mid-sentence from the machine-speak to Nev's pleasant programmed voice.

"A 910 millibar low 75 nautical miles northwest of Yakutat will move into the northern panhandle this afternoon," she continued.

Durt vectored the plane in an easterly direction, heading for glacier country as he mentally inventoried wind and weather conditions. He didn't have the specific coordinates, but they should be in the system by now. As if on cue, the incoming chime of updated information joined Nev's ongoing weather forecast.

"Sorry," she said, with apparent annoyance that the chime had interrupted the personal touch of her weather delivery.

"Is that our destination message with coordinates?"

"Yes. But you're not going to like it."

This time he couldn't help it. He smiled. And winced at the pain. She was playing with him. But he kept his mouth shut and said nothing.

"You need to turn the plane around and go the other way, Durt. We're not going slip-sliding around on glaciers today. These coordinates put our destination on the far side of Kodiak Island."

She was right. He didn't like it.

"Is that a joke? If CJ's messing with us, I will put this plane down on top of his pointed little head and dance all over his face. If it *is* a joke, it's not a funny one."

"No joke, Durt. I've confirmed coordinates with Ocean Rescue. They have the same distress call, but they've got their hands full."

He shook his head. "No," he said, as much to himself as to Nev. "We're not doing it. They're on the island. They can just sit tight until OR gets to them. I can't be risking everything just to allow some big shot to come in out of the cold.

"I told you that you wouldn't like it."

As usual, she was right. He now understood why CJ had passed along the rescue assignment and lied about the location. Had CJ told the truth, he'd still be sitting in the cabin. This was both beyond CJ's expertise and tolerance for risk. His, too. Not to mention it was also at the very edge of the flying range of CJ's fragile oil burner. He listened for subsequent details, but Nev was uncharacteristically silent.

"What is it Nev? What aren't you telling me? Why'd they call us?"

"It's a life-threatening injury, Durt. It's in OR's queue, but they can't get there in time. We're their only hope of making it home alive."

Now it made sense. The problem was, and they all knew it, flying a floatplane on an over-ocean mission—into the eye of an approaching storm? Even on his liberal scale of risk assessment, it wasn't on the chart. By all standards, he knew it was a suicide mission. Pilot school? Not a chance. They'd sit tight and hand off to the OR and hope for the best. Landing and takeoff? There were a shitload of variables. But somewhere out there was a guy slowly dying, praying for a rescue. He heard his father's voice. Alaska was in their blood. Alaska could never kill them because they *were* Alaska. They were in Alaska, and Alaska was in them. Only if they surrendered would they fail. Big words. Would they apply here? He had to decide. If he re-vectored for the relative safety of the lake and the cabin, no one could blame him. No one would blame him. *Wrong,* he contradicted himself. He would blame himself. Shit, if a bear couldn't kill him, a little wind and water couldn't do much worse.

Buzz whined as the wings dipped, and they flew west. Into the coming storm.

* * *

He couldn't be sure. And that was why he'd banked the float plane again and retreated from the blackness of the storm front advancing over the Gulf of Alaska. Screw CJ's clients, he thought. They should have known what they were getting into.

"I wondered if you might do that," came Nev's voice from the console.

He ignored the comment and kept his eye on the stretch of ocean below them that gave Kodiak Island its last name. Farther east the Alaska coast extended a welcoming gesture.

He'd turned the plane around and was heading home. All things considered, his enthusiasm and established rescue routine habit had him breaking, on a regular basis, pretty much every safety protocol in the book. Ocean rescues belonged to Ocean Rescue. And while technically Kodiak Island wasn't the ocean, he'd have to cross the ocean, make a beach landing—and a beach takeoff.

It wasn't something that was done every day. In fact, to the best of his knowledge, it wasn't something that had ever been done. He was sure he'd remember that tale of rescue from the multitude he'd heard at Harry's bar. Lots of service rescues over the years, but only the hairiest of them were repeated as legends at Harry's Bar. They might as well call the place Hairies, for the kinds of tales they told. After years, and not too many he had to admit in his case, it was hard to distinguish the fact from the fiction. But he could repeat the ones he'd heard word-for-word. Service training flew in the face of pretty much every one of these. Had they observed the safety and training policies outlined in their service standards, few of these rescues should have been undertaken in the first place. The service's most important assets were its rescue pilots and crew. Their mission was not to respond to every single rescue call that came in, but to fly the missions they knew they could complete.

Drink and stories flowed way too freely at Harry's most of the time, but when push came to shove, there was only one case where service rescue teams launched without a second thought. And that was if one of their own was in trouble. That wasn't in the service standards. That was in the team's standards. If you believed the stories, they hadn't lost one of their own in more than a century. He was a believer.

That was not the case here. This was just some dumbass. Two dumbasses actually, according to the distress call, with too much money and too much time out for a thrill. He, himself, could be the third dumbass, he thought, if he flew his non-ocean certified plane into what looked to be one of the worst storms of the year—maybe a decade—for a rescue attempt. But still. If he could do it, that would be something else. It might be him they would—.

Nev cut him off in mid-thought. "I know what you're thinking."

Not likely. He hadn't installed any extended logic programming from ThirdEye. He'd considered the expense and benefit and opted out of the rather pricey option. Nev's unique logic was that of a pilot program, though, so he never knew what to expect. It was some experimental brain emulation. Rather than coding from existing bot libraries, it went the other way. It mapped human thought and speech patterns, then added on navigational and bot programming after. She was first generation. He'd thought it was funny that he was a pilot testing a pilot program on a navigational pilot. And the price, because of the first-generation status, was something he could afford.

"I don't think you do."

"It's not difficult."

"Difficulty is not the question. It's a question of your programming."

"You want to bet?"

He laughed. "What would you pay me with?"

"It doesn't matter. I won't lose."

"You will."

"Alright, a gentleman's bet then."

"But you're not a gentleman."

He heard what he took to be a sniffing sound.

"Well," she said shortly. "based on this conversation, neither are you."

In this case, she wasn't wrong. His emotions bled over into his speech. He was being an immature little bitch. He rolled his eyes.

"Alright, smart guy. Tell me what I'm thinking."

"I'm not a guy, Durt. If you want a male interface, you could have asked for one. That was an option. I can make those arrangements if that's what you want."

That was more like it. That was Nev's quirkiness that revealed itself on a semi-regular basis.

"No, I don't want a male interface. I like you fine. I apologize. Let me back up and start again." He paused and took a breath. "Alright smart girl, tell me what I'm thinking."

It didn't have the same ring to his ears as the smart guy question had. It sounded a bit awkward, but it was working fine for Nev's programming.

"You're thinking about discarding your service safety standards and making a rescue attempt, not because you care about human safety, but because you think you might become a hero at Harry's bar.

Damn. How was that possible? How did she even know about Harry's bar? She was a damn nav system.

He realized he'd probably mentioned it fairly frequently on previous flights; him talking because he was bored, and her listening, and apparently, absorbing everything.

She wasn't wrong. Again.

"You're right, Nev. On both counts. That's what I was thinking, and on second thought, I changed my mind. You're much more of a gentleman than me. Sorry about that. Do you think it's wrong to think about that?"

"I don't know right or wrong. That has to be your call. I only know actions and consequences."

Wasn't that the truth? he thought. Consequences. No one would think worse of him for following standard policy. By the book. He was a good pilot and a smart rescue responder. If he decided not to do it, there was going to be a pretty good reason. But on the other hand, he didn't want to stay here forever. He loved to fly, but what was the point of flying if the only one you were flying with was a damn machine? And your dog, of course. But neither filled his desire to do something more.

He was his father's son, but he wasn't. Dad was the senior and most respected serviceman in Alaska. "We are Alaska," he'd say on a regular basis; "You can't run away from what you are." And Dad paid for what he was on a daily basis. He was a by-the-book guy who killed when killing was needed, and who drank to help him deal with who he was, and who he'd become.

Durt always felt he'd needed something more. The son had the opportunity, no, the responsibility, to go beyond what the father had become. There were a lot of things out there inviting him to go beyond. The world. The Moon. Beyond. But by-the-book rescue pilots didn't go beyond. They made their rescues. They listened to hairy rescue tales. They lived. They flew. They died. But they didn't go beyond. He thought of himself as a by-the-book pilot. But was it true?

Again, the small plane banked. Beside him, Buzz perked up and gazed at the angled panorama of Kodiak Island as it came into view again. His tail wagged, then stopped suddenly. He whined as they both stared out into a black horizon.

No, this wasn't by-the-book. This was so far beyond the book, it wasn't funny. Their unwritten future lay in the sky before them. They might call him foolhardy. They might call him an idiot, but they would call him *something* tomorrow at Harry's.

In the meantime, time was running out. He caught his breath and put the plane into a steep descent toward the island. He didn't have a clue how he would pull it off, but he had an idea, and the edges of a plan were beginning to form.

* * *

When Buzz yowled, it meant excitement ahead. As the floatplane dove sharply toward the green carpet of Kodiak Island below, the husky's cry was that of a battle cry, shouting out instinctively to the other members of his pack that the hunt was on. Of course, thousands of feet above the Earth's surface, he had no pack, at least no canine pack. His pack consisted of one human and one robotic nav-system, both of whom were now well used to the dog's diving howl.

For Durt, the sound was the starting gun to his race with fate. If it was to be suicide, he knew he was killing Buzz, too. But it didn't cross his mind for more than an instant. Winds out of the south rushing northward into the gulf gave them a real challenge. The little plane itself was sturdy enough, but the winds would play havoc with their directional heading and progress. No way was he flying over this system. No, his plan was to use the island as a kind of windbreak. It would be something of a round-about course, but with Nev doing the vector math, his worst enemy was not the wind itself, but the wind's consistency. He could handle a good, strong steady blow, but rogue gusts could easily leave them, the rescuers, in the same position as their rescuees—stranded, putting out a mayday call of their own.

The island's surface revealed more detail as the plane descended. Trees growing on rocks in the ocean. It was wild and untamed and unpopulated by humans, with the exception, of course, of the two they were now after. A sudden flash of realization hit him, and he asked Nev for clarification.

"Nev. Review destination coordinates with the surface map. Confirm Pasagshak Beach."

"Confirmed," came the reply as quickly as he could finish his sentence.

He shook his head and silently cursed CJ. He'd ignored the reality until until now. He wished for a glacier-surfing rescue. Not today. No, today was ocean surfing. They 'd need to ride the big waves the Pacific was kicking up on the south side of the island if they were going to pull this off. Yes, he reasoned to himself, those should be pretty extreme. He had another thought. They must have been there for a while, too. CJ would only trek that far on a solid weather forecast. Or a big payday. Whichever it was, CJ was going to have to fork over for a really long time to make this one even.

Durt leveled the plane off and found some flying room on the north side of the island, picking his way as carefully as he could and relying on Nev to anticipate those venturi bursts of wind created by the island's topography. It was slow going, and Buzz looked up more than once from his standard traveling position, curled up in the co-pilot seat, as the plane took occasional solid hits that tossed it relentlessly northward, taking back their carefully won southing. It was a game of give and take, and what he needed was patience and a steady hand. His face was on fire again, and he lit another cigarette. Even though his state-of-the-art first aid kit lay only a few feet away, there was no way he was going to autopilot in this state. The wound was trying both his patience and his steady hand, but there would be plenty of time for healing and whining later. He breathed in deeply and braced for another wind buffet.

The width of the island was only about 60 miles across, maybe a 35-minute crossing on a sunny day. But they'd been at it an hour now, their extended game of cat and mouse with the wind making piss-poor passage time. They were making forward progress, however, and they were still airborne, and that was something.

Sneaking past Larsen Bay at about 2,000 feet, Durt nosed further into the island's interior, up Uyak Bay and north of the island's imposing Koniag Peak. Kodiak Island's range made a pretty good windbreak, but sooner or later, they had to crest the ridge and face down winds screaming out of the Gulf of Alaska. Nev calculated the quickest route, given their conditions, but even though he knew the impact would be brutal, he gritted his teeth, feeling the burn of his wounded face when the headwinds slammed into the tiny plane. The impact brought the plane to an almost full stop before the wind caught its dipped wing and wrenched it violently into a long-ranging arc that was to take them past their intended rescue destination. The forward progress into the wind shook the plane with a constant thumping that tested his pilot restraint and threatened to tear the plane to pieces.

At one time, that might have been easily possible. The plane was a 20th-century replica, but one of the benefits composite technology offered in the 30th century was superb tensile strength. The plane could take it. For Buzz, though, this was something new. If a dog could have a worried expression, he had one now. He watched Durt from his co-pilot perch, curled up, his nose on his paws and his eyes on his best friend.

Within 15 minutes, now back over the ocean, they'd made enough progress south into the gulf and turned their headwind into a tailwind. The banging in the plane suddenly quiet, Nev guided his approach, now using the local hand-held distress signal she was picking up from the island ahead.

Beside him, Buzz was alert. "Alright boy, this isn't what this plane was made for, but I'm pretty sure we can make it work. Hang on to your biscuits."

Again, he put the plane into a dive, although not nearly as steep as the previous one. It didn't matter.

Buzz raised his head and howled, energized again, an excited tail wagging them on.

"That's right, Buzz! Hang on tight because we're going surfing."

[3]
LUNASEC

Tuck was an addict. No question about it. The mug on the console before him read "LUNASEC" in big, bold letters, and the steaming hot coffee it contained was his drug of choice. It was imported and expensive and not a brand most cops on the Moon would presume to drink, especially in the afternoon, but he wasn't most cops.

The curved, semi-circular wall before him was a digital show of color and movement that he controlled with well-practiced fingers. He might have been a professional musician. The idea of creating and repeating the same songs for the rest of his professional life, however, didn't hold a strong appeal for his curious brain, but nimble fingers and a nimble mind found themselves right at home here in Copernicus, the Moon's giant manufacturing settlement.

His name was Marlin Tucker, but no one called him that. Not even he called himself that. He was Tuck, and Tuck was lead investigator on an odd case that had the rest of the more senior investigators scratching their heads and making excuses. Most carried the title of Investigator, but few of them actually earned it. He knew and told himself on a regular basis, that even if he found duty here intriguing, it wasn't for everyone. In fact, most of the

LUNASEC force were Earth dregs who found themselves here because they couldn't investigate their way out of an unlocked room.

That was just fine for him. Pretty easy to make a name for yourself when you're surrounded by mediocre colleagues. Not that they were bad. They were just average. They knew the security system regulations, and they knew the case protocols. To those outside of the LUNASEC organization, they were just cops. They did their time, filed their reports and went home. But to him, they were oafs. Few had the ability to synthesize the clues of a crime scene, be it actual or virtual, and conceptualize the actual event or events that created them.

He was different. That's what he lived for. The mystery. The challenge. They called him one of the young guns. He liked that, even if he didn't carry a gun. With this console and the security center at his disposal, he had no need for one. He had a million eyes and an army of drones to do his snooping and whatever enforcement might be necessary.

He was an anomaly in the security ranks, and sooner or later, everyone would come to him for help. They were all authorized to book time and use what they called the "Kick," the Central Information Center where he spent a good portion of his waking hours, but few did. Why invest months and years of practice and sweat when the young gun could do it for you in a few minutes? It didn't make sense to them, and that made perfect sense to him.

They brought him coffee and cigarettes and whatever else he had a desire for. It was amazing sometimes the variety of contraband cops would have in their evidence lockers. Funny, too, how a lot of it just disappeared. Based on his personal assessment of his fellow cops, it didn't really matter, anyway. Capital crimes weren't compromised by any lack of evidence in their inventory. No, capital crimes came to him, and none of his cases ever relied on anything inventoried and stored in any evidence security zone.

He was charming in his own way. He wore a light beard and kept his dark hair a bit longer than security standards allowed, but here, almost no one complained. His piercing gray eyes took in the rights, the wrongs, the crimes and the punishments of the Moon. They were a light shade of disarming gray that, for whatever reason, usually got him what he wanted. But his strength was more than just visual and mental. Time not spent in front of his wall was in the combat gyms or on the streets. He wasn't there often, but there was no substitute for it on a breaking case. Feet on the ground, he could feel the case breaking. That was the magic of being an investigator.

Of course, all of this was out if the races were on, he thought. On the Moon the racing standards made the Earth pastime look like kindergarten. Here, the races were outside Copernicus' manufactured metropolis. Rules were non-existent and mistakes were real and forever. Racers here were tough and inventive, and watching them jockey with one another, putting their respective lives on the line for little more than bragging rights and the lunar championship, made the contests personal and visceral. He liked to catch them when he could, but usually wound up catching them on the Net right here in the Kick.

He took a long whiff of the steaming coffee in the LUNASEC mug, and leaning his chair back, put his feet up on the console. He pushed racing to the back of his mind and concentrated on the continuous motion of surveillance visuals rushing across the curved wall in front of him. He considered them as he sipped slowly, watching nothing in particular and seeing everything. If nothing else, coffee was his edge. A cop sitting at his desk with his feet up and drinking coffee was not an unexpected sight, especially here in the heart of Copernicus where company policies pretty much policed themselves.

What *was* unusual was the coffee he drank. It wasn't cop coffee. No cop on a cop salary could afford to sip his actual organic Earthside blend. And that was the vision he used to illustrate to himself that things were not always what they seemed to be. He was a kid with longish hair and delusions of grandeur, or so they thought. Which was fine with him. He liked to be underestimated. He gave them what they wanted, not what they needed, and they were happy to get it.

This case was something else. It was clear to Tuck that nothing he'd put together on the case to date was anything that made sense. He could smell something here, and the cause and effect relationship that lay at the heart of every explanation of facts was still missing. He'd chased leads for weeks. Or was it months? He kept all of his regular channels open and watched for others as he walked his way through the various investigative and surveillance tasks that came in. Still nothing. Smoke. Vapor. Shit.

The heart of the case had to do with missing employees. And mutilations. As the Earth's primary location for manufacturing and remanufacturing, the volume of human traffic into and out of Copernicus, was regular. Bots did the actual hands-on manufacturing and assembly of products, but the business operations, the maintenance and shipping and programming and—. He stopped thinking about it. There were a shitload of people here, for one reason or another. And where you find humans, you find human problems. Jealousy, greed, revenge all manifested themselves in crimes. It was much worse down on the planet, but here, he found a different aspect. The crimes that he did latch onto were usually less physical and more cerebral. Hacking, conspiracy, espionage between rival corporations. Often they went higher than the criminals themselves. Things were never what they should be or seemed to be anywhere, and that was certainly true on the Moon.

The coffee would tell him. He didn't know how, but he was sure that unique aroma would bring his mind into focus. The steam from his cup engulfed his face with its divine aroma.

The slight hiss of the pressure door behind him interrupted his measured concentration.

"Oh, good. You're here, Tuck," came the voice.

He didn't turn around. What was the point? He kept his gaze on the wall and waited for the imminent request.

"Listen, I know you're busy, and you've got a queue a kilometer long, but I've got this thing that I think you could really help me out with."

Ever vigilant, Tuck's mind still focused on the wall. This was how they all started. He took another sip of his coffee, waiting for the actual request. He'd trained himself mentally to block out most of what they said.

The voice continued. "So, I'm following up on this break-in on the upper side of Newton. Guy says it happened while he was at work, and now he's got—"

The story went on, but he wasn't really listening. Newton was a Copernicus suburb that gave them a good portion of their cop work. If you were new to the Moon, you lived in Newton until you found someplace better or caught a ride back to Earth. Lots of transients. Plenty of dashed hopes. It was the Moon's giant waiting room, a community always in flux. He focused on and caught the last few scenes of his current surveillance routines, his hands dancing on and above the console, sliding scenes across the wall and popping them out into 3D rotations in front of the wall when he needed a closer look.

Without a word, the wall flashed and shifted. A darker, more squalid scene filled the wall before them. Newton.

Tuck shot a sideways glance, not to identify Ric Carter—Carter's walk and talk had already done that—but to see what offering he'd brought. He freely admitted his weaknesses, and let it be known that he was open to bribery as a way of temporarily changing his priorities. Never for money. What the hell did he want with money? But Carter had him pegged on this one. The package in his hand was not too big, but it bore a special circular imprint of green and black that immediately made his mouth water. Caribbean sugar cookies. Nuts and sugar and cookie and lime. He felt a twinge of anticipation in his mouth as he held out his hand. He hadn't even touched the bag, and he was eating the cookie already.

"You got me," he said with a smile, taking the bag and ripping open its sealed contents.

The resulting aroma mingled with its coffee counterpart and teased his nose. He inhaled slowly, savoring the treat before extracting a cookie and offering one to Carter beside him.

Carter obliged. Of all his cop co-workers, Carter was one of the least offensive. His shortcomings were not mental or motivational, but experiential. He was one of the younger cops on staff and was here by request, not by assignment. A skinny wisp of a kid, his baritone voice seemed out of place as it resonated from his thin chest. What hair remained of his regulation trim was fair, and his sharp blue eyes watched the wall, and Newton, with interest. He had a lot of potential, Tuck reasoned, with the sugar cookie as clear evidence of both good taste and a perceptive mind. Carter didn't visit nearly as often as some of the others, and when he did, it meant he'd hit a wall and needed a new perspective. Tuck was always liberal with his recommendations on approach, but few understood his insights and fewer made use of them. Carter was one of the few.

The northwest quadrant of Newton was the first likely search area. If there was an established section of the Newton suburb, they'd find it there. The residence was locked and secure and the resident was working, so this was a logical choice. Break-ins here were not uncommon, those residences being the closest target to what might as well be called the Moon's slum. You could find and buy anything in Newton. And often enough, the sale price was paid for with locally-lifted goods.

"Here, let me give you the specific coordinates," Carter told him, digging out his digi-tab from his uniform.

He never got there. He stood, frozen in mid-motion, his hand inside his uniform jacket, but his eyes locked on the video wall. He made an odd, surprised sound, and as Tuck turned, he saw a piece of cookie in Carter's open mouth, his frozen stare aligning with his now-pointing finger.

Tuck quickly raised both hands over the console, fingers extended, and all motion on the wall suddenly stopped.

Carter was still trying to say something while chewing the

cookie, but Tuck understood, moving both hands in a slow left-ward movement that invoked the universal reverse feature in the Kick. Vehicles slowly reversed, people walked backward as his eyes scanned the wall for the anomaly that had left Carter speechless.

And there it was.

On a Newton walkway, arms and legs outstretched, lay a body. Face-down. Only it wasn't face-down. There was no face. The body was headless.

"Shit," muttered Tuck. "Another one."

[4]
NEWTON

THEY CHECKED OUT A CRUISER, and Carter took pilot duties. Just because. It wasn't that Tuck couldn't drive, and he admitted to himself that seemed counterintuitive because of his fascination with racing, but he just didn't. Of all the talents he had, he figured his attention was always better spent applying his inquisitive mind than applying impatient hands to the navigation controls. Carter eased the vehicle out of the LUNASEC docking bay as Tuck settled in to continue his investigation. He pulled the passenger view screen into 3D virtual space before him and punched in his remote access code to the Kick. The big semi-circle view wall that he spent so much time at now appeared before him in miniature. To his brain, it was the same. Whether the images were meters away on a wall or centimeters away in space, he was plugged into the thousands of sensors and cameras placed across the populated areas of the Moon.

He smiled. There was something comfortable and something omniscient about this view. He was the all-seeing eye, and there was no escaping the truth from this view. Well, that was usually true, he told himself. It was true when there weren't dead bodies popping up without heads. And that was where he was headed now. He first took a look at the scene from the stationary cameras on the street. He knew the area. Commercial district a couple minutes walk from the center of Newton.

There was usually plenty of activity in this area, and today was no exception. Using his fingers to select the various views, he noted the high volume of foot traffic, a good portion of which, was backed up by a gathering crowd of curious on-lookers. The crowd now blocked a clear view of the prone corpse. He didn't care. There would be plenty of time for looking at the corpse. What he needed most now was an orientation tour of the area. The corpse was the end result and might lend some additional clues, he thought, but he needed the backstory. How had the corpse ended up on the walkway? Was it dumped? He was pretty sure it hadn't walked there by itself.

Tuck selected a bio-filter, and the human traffic on the street disappeared from view. The modified filter displayed an empty street. That's the view he needed. A couple restaurants, a tattoo place, a public communications center. Nothing industrial in this area. These were all service-based businesses that made money from the transient population. The businesses were always in flux. The transient tastes here emulated the ever-shifting fads on Earth, and new services and products popped up on a regular basis, scrambling to keep up with offerings that would keep them in the black. While the businesses changed, the owners usually didn't. Because of their Newton location, and the relative instability of its population, incidents were frequent, and he'd personally met with a number of the business owners. Question was, he thought, from which of them had the body come?

Satisfied with his area review and the local layout, he re-engaged with the crowd. As he did, his peripheral vision told him something was amiss.

"What the hell, Carter?"

Carter looked over at him and shook his head in curiosity, "What?"

"We're on our way to a crime scene. You have the full

authority of LUNASEC behind you. Some reason you're not using it?"

He hadn't realized until now that they weren't soaring above vehicle traffic but locked into remote traffic direction with what looked like every other vehicle on the Moon. Buses, construction vehicles, personal transportation of all shapes and sizes. All waiting patiently or otherwise to be vectored to their chosen destinations. There were no traffic accidents on the Moon, but there were also few enough throughways that remote transponder control made the decision for drivers on when they'd reach their destinations.

Carter gave him an embarrassed shrug. "I....ah." Then he regained his composure and tapped the cruiser's console. "New software push yesterday. I'm a bit behind in my certification. Which was fine," He paused for a second. "until—"

If Tuck had to characterize the look, sheepish would have been the word that came to mind, but that wasn't an unusual look with the company he kept. Once delegated to another, the requirement for deductive logic had a tendency to go into hibernation. The brain, just like every other muscle of the human body, needed to be exercised. In cases where it was not, its tendency was to retreat and to atrophy. That was a standard expression that usually accompanied the favors he was asked to perform, the magic he and only he seemed to be able to coax from the Kick.

The problem was, he had never, until this moment anyway, considered Carter to be on that level. Carter was sharper and more perceptive than that. A cut above. He shrugged as he tapped in his own override code into the cruiser's system, and the plodding pace of remotely directed lunar traffic dropped away below them.

Carter's expression was hard to read. Relief? Embarrassment? Something else? Carter resumed control of the vehicle, now on full manual. "Thanks, Tuck."

He acknowledged the comment in silence and returned his focus to Newton's commercial district and its current status. In the moments his attention had been diverted, the crowd had probably doubled. He had another look at the scene without its human distractions and reviewed again the most likely last exit for the headless body.

Restaurant? Had there been a last meal, maybe?

He knew he had the ability to just roll back the video, but he preferred to take in the scene and the evidence in his own particular order. Seeing the surveillance videos first often had a way of suggesting a quick, but potentially false conclusion. No, there would be plenty of time for video replays. Right now, he needed to be in the receive mode so that when he did review the video, the appropriate conclusion would present itself.

As was required on Copernicus, their flight elevation was moderate. The protective field that gave them the ability to live and work as humans without wearing a breathing apparatus extended a few thousand meters above the surface. Because the Moon itself had no atmosphere, and its days on the bright side were unending, the field-contained atmosphere was programmed to look and feel like Earth, with blue sky and some random cloud programming for daytime. Night reflected an accurate view of the Earth and stars visible from the moon at any given time, but because of its synchronous rotation, held only incidental alignment with the Moon's actual condition beyond the field. It was an incredible feat of engineering and programming, and a private joke in the scientific community, but its elegance was lost on the majority of Copernicus inhabitants. For them, it felt pretty much like they remembered Earth feeling. Days were hotter and longer in the programmed summer than in the winter. Styles changed, holidays came and went. As on Earth, so on the Moon. It wasn't by chance. No, the Moon had a mission and a purpose: to serve Earth's manufacturing needs. The more its inhabitants felt at home, the happier—and more productive—they were.

There was a difference, though. No storms on the Moon. That was one less variable to have to factor into workdays, travel, and in his case, flight planning, although he admitted to himself, he could go for a good storm now and again.

Yes, the Moon had its own personality.

They left the buildings and parks that made up the Copernicus' central governance and oversight district behind them, and the surface below changed from an official feel to a residential feel with homes giving way to the greens and blues of towering apartments with rooftop gardens and pools that dotted the landscape. And then there was Newton. Newton's practical shades of gray reflected its utilitarian nature. Newton was never really a destination. It was more of a place to stop on the way to someplace else. Newton was part commercial district, part transient residence. It was the frontier of the undecided. New arrivals. Imminent departures. You could find anything in Newton. Or, as he knew from previous experience, you might find nothing. It was easy to talk to people in Newton, but credibility was always suspect. Everyone ran his own game here. It was a quid-pro-quo kind of place.

He sometimes found it hard to believe that, with all the automation available in the 30th century, it took so many human hands to make it work, especially here on the Moon. He knew the answer, though. Repair and calibration and oversight and programming. The more complex it got, the more human touches it needed. Part of it was the manufacturing, but a huge part was design and prototyping, not pursuits left to the machines. They came, and they went, but they all passed through Newton.

Carter was a good pilot, even if unused to flying transponder-free. His motions were deft and sure, and they made good time on their way to Newton. "It's the Headhunter, isn't it?"

"Is that what they're saying?" The LUNASEC bullpen was as long on theories as it was short on investigative talent.

Carter nodded, his face locked on his screen and his Newton destination. "This is the first serial killer we've had here in as long as anyone can remember."

"Serial killer? Who said anything about a serial killer?"

"Not me. But that's what they are saying.

"They?"

"You know. The bullpen."

Of course, he knew who they were. They were the short-sighted, jump-to-conclusions cops he put up with every day.

"What about you?"

Carter shook his head. "What about me?"

"What's your take? Is that your theory? Serial killer?

"Nah. I don't think so, but I could be wrong."

There it was. Carter was his kind of investigator. Sometimes it was hard to tell. That was his take, too. The serial killer case was something hard to pin down just because this type of criminal didn't think like a logical human would. Brain wires were crossed. Something wasn't connected inside of them. It made it difficult to deduce elements when the fundamentals of logic were tossed into space. "What makes you doubt the theory?"

Tuck watched the facial expression of his pilot. His right eye squinted in thought. He could almost hear wheels turning inside Carter's mind. He'd ask himself the same question. How much to tell? How much speculation would make him look like a fool in front of Tuck?

Carter nodded as he spoke. "Two things, actually. First, based on what I know of the case, and I'm sure it's not everything, it seems way too random. Backgrounds of the victims have nothing in common as far as I can tell. They've been men and women, older and younger. All over the place." He paused, lost in thought for a moment, as if uncertain whether he wanted to actually share his second idea. He took one hand off the controls for a moment, rubbing his chin. "I guess the other thing that really gets me," he paused momentarily in thought, "and it's a big thing, not a weird little, overlooked clue, but with all the resources we have," he looked over now and smiled at Tuck. "You. The Kick. All this video surveillance and manipulation capability. I find it hard to believe that after all these deaths, we don't have some evidence—even a description of any perp. Doesn't that seem odd to you?"

He hadn't been wrong about Carter. Carter had hit on the

same odd missing piece that he'd mulled over himself. Whoever this killer was, presuming it was a killer. Whoever was behind this knew the ins and outs of LUNASEC. How it worked. How it didn't work. Its strengths and weaknesses.

Carter began his descent into Newton, the gathering crowd now massed into a black carpet of onlookers choking the main and adjoining streets. Carter put them down within about 50 meters of the body using the only viable landing point, the commercial rooftop. The businesses used the rooftops for supply and equipment storage, and it wasn't too difficult to identify and maneuver into a cruiser-sized spot.

They used the staff access door and made their way through a fusion restaurant. Tuck wasn't quite sure what foods were fused, but it certainly smelled delicious as they made their way to the ground level. Here and there a diner remained to eat. The rest, at least those who hadn't already made their way out into the street, were plastered against the street-side windows, wrestling with one another to get an in-person glimpse of what they'd no doubt all seen on their wristcomms minutes before.

Carter went ahead, pushing through the human barricade, his badge held high as he announced, "LUNASEC. Make way!"

A few made space, but just a few. Carter thumbed the badge into low and popped it off as he repeated himself, this time accompanied by a sound that was familiar to all Moon inhabitants. "LUNASEC. Make way!"

The badge's two-tone alternating sound belonged exclusively to law enforcement. At this volume, it did nothing but warn of impending pain. Usually, this cleared the decks. While it did a fair job today, the excitement surrounding the corpse interfered with usual behavior. Tuck watched Carter thumb the badge to medium and repeat himself again. "LUNASEC. Clear the area. *Now.*"

A good portion of the crowd came to their senses and scattered away from the crowd's vortex, but the buzz of the crowd and its mentality hid the warning from the those at the edge of the mob who quickly rushed forward to fill the void.

Carter looked back at Tuck, disbelief in his eyes. "This is crazy!"

Tuck raised his own badge above his head. "They're asking for it. Give them a taste." He had no intention of doubling the potency of the badge, but he armed it nonetheless. The aural properties of the badge would shield him from what was about to become a headache for the rest of the crowd.

Carter nodded and activated his badge.

The two-tone scream did exactly what it was designed to do. Three short bursts had the crowd with hands to their heads, screaming in pain, retreating up or down the street or back inside the local businesses. In ten seconds the street was clear. Almost.

Aside from the headless prone figure on the walkway, two figures remained. Tuck pocketed his badge. He had a few questions for them.

Carter put his hand on Tuck's shoulder. "I bet they're ME."

Tuck thought for a moment "ME?"

"You know, Medical Examiners."

"I know what ME stands for, Carter. But they shouldn't be here yet. We're supposed to call them."

Carter looked at him with a grin. "Yeah, I think they got the call already."

As much as he didn't like the disconnect, Tuck had a different issue to deal with now.

Carter saw the look and turned to see what Tuck was watching. "What?"

Tuck didn't say anything but nodded up.

Carter followed his gaze, then shook his head as if he'd forgotten something "Oh crap. You want me to call a Cleaner?"

Above the two MEs and the corpse, the air was dark with bugs. Insect-sized flying cameras had captured and continued to broadcast the entire event across the network, which meant anyone online on the Moon or on Earth now had a birds-eye view of their investigation.

Tuck shook his head. "Never seen so many. I figured there'd be a few, but this is a whole new level."

"Look, I can have someone here in half an hour. Clean it up like nobody's business."

"They won't be here in half-an-hour."

Carter was puzzled. "Why not?"

"Because they're just about to find another headless corpse."

"Another one? What are you talking about?"

Tuck smiled, removed his digi-tab from inside his LUNASEC vest and made a pair of finger movements before replacing it. "Just watch."

It was only a few at first, but within a minute, what was left of the bug swarm seemed to bunch, then take off at what seemed to be an unreasonable speed to the north.

Carter still didn't understand. "What just happened?"

Tuck shrugged. "Not sure, but I think there was a report just filed. Headless corpse. Just outside the Boer recycler."

"The big one?"

Tuck nodded. "And if this thing's any good," he said, patting the tablet inside his vest, "the timing should be perfect. They activate it twice a day, right?"

Carter nodded.

"I think orders will be up on new bugs here in the very near future. I'm afraid the coordinates of the body is pretty close to that thing's intake." He shrugged with a smile. "Oops."

Tuck returned his attention to the reason for their excursion. The body. The streets weren't empty, but after the badge flash, the crowd had dispersed, and locals now gave the body a wide berth. Behind them, the restaurant doors closed and the faces pressed up against the windows receded and returned to their meals. The business district of Newton had taken a step toward returning to its normal routine.

The thing that bothered him before now stared him directly in the face. The MEs. The reps, neither of whom could be older than 25 or so, were in the process of moving the body around the corner. He could now see the rear of the official vehicle, in the absence of the curious crowd, its unmistakeable rear-end poking out beyond the corner of the building.

"C'mon," he said to Carter, "I've got a couple of questions for these two."

Aside from official vests, the words Medical Examiner, emblazoned on their backs, they might have been a couple of dancers or accountants or pilots. But the vests made them official. "What's the rush?" Tuck called out as they approached. "You know you're breaking our investigative protocol."

The pair stopped what they were doing and turned to meet their law enforcement counterparts.

"LUNASEC. Agents Carter and Tuck," said Carter, making their introductions.

The women stepped forward. They offered no handshakes, but they did offer an explanation.

"Rhonda," said the dark-haired one, a mixed look of surprise and annoyance on her face. "And this is Kandi." Rhonda was clearly in charge. All business. Both women had deep blue eyes, and were it not for her clearly feminine assets, the younger one, Kandi, might be mistaken for a boy. Her auburn hair was tight, in a short cut.

"Sorry for the breach, boys," said Rhonda, "but we got an express request from the ME proper. Herself," she said, as if disobeying an order from the ME would have some unspoken consequence. "We were in the neighborhood, and, well, we're just trying to do our jobs."

"And keep them," piped up Kandi.

Both women wore a type of hat, something Tuck judged to be non-functional because of their location. No weather in Copernicus might require a hat; the protective field a few thousand meters above them was programmed to filter out any harmful rays. Not that it mattered. The hats were only about the size of his fist and had no discernible purpose as far as he could tell. He wondered if maybe they served as badge siren shields.

"Let us have a quick look, then we won't hold you up. And what's with all this up top?" asked Tuck, motioning to his head. "Is that a new addition to the uniform?"

The one called Rhonda smiled maybe a bit too sweetly for Tuck's taste. "No. It's style. All the rage on Earth. You haven't seen these yet? You should get out more."

Tuck ignored the comment and moved his focus toward the body now awaiting onward transportation. He examined the wound where the head should have been. Clothing was standard industrial wear. Victim had probably just finished work. Work boots rounded out the ensemble. The only other item of note was that, like previous victims, both hands were missing, too. He had a quick look at where the hands should have been, the wounds a pretty good match to that of the cranial removal, but he'd leave the final assessment to the ME. What was it the girl had called her? Yes, he remembered, ME Herself.

He'd done some business with ME Herself. Tough to work with, if he remembered correctly, and that was just incidentally. What must it be like to work for her on a daily basis? He didn't doubt their concern a bit, and with a good part of the known worlds now aware of the latest addition to what was being called the Headhunter case, it made sense that Herself would like to see the body in its least-molested condition.

He pulled Carter aside. "Look, I don't disbelieve their story, but I like to keep my eye on things. Do me a favor. Ride with them and make sure this evidence is delivered securely to the ME. Her review may turn out to be crucial to the case."

Carter nodded his understanding and was about to ask the question Tuck knew he thought he needed to ask.

"It's OK. I'll take the cruiser. And yes, I know how to pilot it. Just because I don't fly myself doesn't mean I'm not qualified."

Carter shot him an *I-knew-it* smile. He couldn't help his parting shot. "Oh, and Carter? *My* certs are current."

Carter rolled his eyes with a grin, apparently happy enough to serve as the latest addition to the ME team.

Tuck left the three of them to move the headless, handless evidence. He needed some street time to puzzle some things out. Boots on the street had a way of doing that. Street food and street people could change his perspective and tell him things the Kick couldn't, and since this case was one that just didn't want to solve itself, he figured he might be here in Newton for a while.

[5]
KODIAK

VISIBILITY WAS POOR. It got worse the closer they flew to the active ocean beneath them, but the actual surf landing went a lot smoother than Durt expected. The plane's pontoons bumped the surf tops a couple of times, but with their airspeed only a few knots faster than their tailwind, the approach and landing went off exactly as he'd planned. He thought about smiling, remembered his face, and thought better of it.

The wind continued to buffet the plane as Durt taxied to a stop above the surf line. Getting on to the beach had been the easy part of his plan. Getting off? That, he admitted to himself, would be a different story. But one thing at a time. He knew Nev could locate the emergency beacon, but he didn't ask her for directions. No need. This was Buzz's specialty.

He slipped into his service coat and felt the pounding surf thump in his chest as he opened the plane's doors, emergency medkit in hand. While the interior of the plane was spartan, its ambient temperature was a deceptive contrast to the local climate and conditions. Wind and salt and sand assaulted him, teared his eyes, and tore at his wound. The pain seared his face, and he climbed immediately back into the plane to properly bandage it it. He knew he couldn't focus on rescue tasks if he himself were so distracted by pain he couldn't even walk properly. Bandaged as best he could in the cramped quarters, he jumped back onto the beach, dragging the medkit behind him through the hatch. Instinctively, he turned his sensitive cheek away from the onslaught and walked backward up the beach, guided by Buzz's fresh tracks.

Durt was a much better pilot than he was a medic, but the medkit was self-contained and self-directed. The times he'd used it before were few, but when he did have to perform some stabilizing procedure, the doc-in-the-box was there to make the medical assessment and walk him through the appropriate procedure. Anything from dispensing pain medication to patching a wound to setting a broken bone. Gauging the force of the salty surf that sprayed him rhythmically, he wondered if he might be setting a bone today. He couldn't fathom what might be so life-threatening that they couldn't wait on Ocean Rescue.

His red plane stood in stark contrast to the extreme elements of Kodiak Island, a world of grey and black and white. He used its receding size to gauge his backward progress up the beach. He estimated now he'd backed about 300 meters and paused for a minute to see if he could discern Buzz's howl over the wind and surf. Nothing.

He plodded on, hiding his sensitive cheek on the leeward side of the wind behind the high protective collar of his coat. He was tempted to put up the hood to save his ears from the stinging sand, but he needed them both out and alert, focused on his canine beacon.

It was probably a full 600 meters before Buzz's signal came through. Turning his back to the wind, he scanned the beachhead before him as the velocity of the wind put up his hood for him. He felt relief and momentary warmth, his now-numb ears out of the barrage, his full attention now on what appeared to be three bodies before him.

Packs and equipment piled around them, the first was sitting up, a wild expression on his face, his right hand gripping his left wrist, and where his left hand should have been was nothing. Crap. His hand was off. No way he could reattach a hand. Might make this rescue a bit easier than he'd anticipated. The second, clothed only in a shirt, lay flat on his back. Durt shivered involuntarily and wondered if he might be dead, but realized his coat was draped over the handless one. He'd probably given his coat to the first to ward off shock before succumbing to hypothermia. Yes, he thought to himself as he made the emergency med assessment, this was certainly doable. The third person? The third person was not a person at all. It was the reason for Buzz's now constant barking.

It was a bear. A huge, dead bear. A Kodiak. It was stretched out on the beachhead next to the pair, a huge hunting knife in the sand beside it, its blade covered in what appeared to be blood of the dead bear.

A chill made its way down Durt's back as the realization came to him. These weren't extreme surfers. They were poachers. This guy without the hand had tried to saw off the bear's head as a trophy but hadn't made a whole lot of progress. Things were tough here in Alaska. Dead bear's necks included. He shook his head in disgust and considered leaving them to their own devices. But something deep inside him wouldn't allow it. It wasn't his call. This guy would face Park Service justice. That was his destiny. Durt was here to make sure he made it there in one piece to face those charges.

He moved quickly. He produced a thermal bag from the medkit, wrapping the prone figure into a giant silver package.

"One hot tamale," he said to the newly wrapped body. He'd sacrificed his body heat and consciousness for his partner, but the bag would put him right directly. He turned to the second and swore.

"Son-of-a-bitch," he said with an incredulous tone.

The guy was back at work with the knife, trying again to saw off the Kodiak's head.

"What in the hell do think you're doing?"

The guy kept sawing and stabbing, his handless arm at one side and not making much progress. He was trying to say something, but his words came out garbled and nonsensical. He was in shock, but for whatever reason, he didn't want to leave the bear head behind.

He closed his eyes in disgust and quickly retrieved a med belt from the kit and strapped it around the guy's middle. While he was at it, he found a pack of cigarettes and the emergency bandage pack. The good one. He sat back, leaning against a pile of their equipment, sheltered from the wind, and inhaled deeply, watching the med belt do its work. Movement slowed. The guy could no longer hold onto the knife, and it dropped again to the rocky sand. Within a minute all movement had ceased, and the belt's stasis mode took over.

He smoked another minute, listening to the howling wind, his now silent husky by his side. A good job, now partly done. Feeling the side of his face gingerly, he pulled his temporary bandage and placed the emergency bandage, letting it do its work. He'd saved it just in case he needed it for his medic duties, but now that his triage of the pair was complete, he was putting it to good use. It form-fitted to his face, cleaning, absorbing and sanitizing as it did. The pain that had dulled his senses subsided now somewhat, and at long last, he smiled without pain. Time to go. He took a last pull on the cigarette and stood, now facing the red swatch of the plane he'd just landed. It was time to re-trace his backward steps. It was time to get the hell out of there.

Time to pull off the least possible leg of his journey.

* * *

Durt left the Kodiak bear where it lay at the edge of the beachhead, its dead neck still intact, the wind screaming a song of sorrow for the wasted life of the great beast. He retraced his sandy footprints to the plane and taxied it back for his pick up. He shook off his emotions and focused on business. Loading passengers and equipment. The beach was probably long enough for a makeshift runway, he thought. It was the rock formation at the end of the point that looked a little too close for his own personal takeoff comfort as he slowly taxied the wind-rattled plane toward it. With two extra passengers and their gear now packed and stacked behind him, he wanted more room—some kind of margin for error. The rock formation would provide something of a windbreak, on their leeward side, he reasoned, and Nev confirmed that was the case.

With a little luck and a little more skill, he figured he should be able to get up enough speed behind the rocky point to lift him over those wicked looking surf breakers that pounded the point relentlessly. His grav-drive propeller strained against the side wind as he steered his red plane slowly back down the beach until it sighed with relief as he rounded the point and put the wind on his tail. An inlet of protected water opened up before them. Its surface was choppy, but he'd made takeoffs on worse before. This wouldn't be that bad.

"Well Durt, we'll see now if you're brilliant or a fool," said Nev as he pointed his all-terrain pontoons back into the wind and ran his pre-flight double check before take off.

"What do you think?"

"I don't think. You know that."

"No, I mean do the math. We can make it, right?"

"It is possible, but you've got very little margin of error, and the thing I can't calculate is variation in wind and waves. Those are critical risk factors that I can't help you with. You need—what do you call it—luck?"

Durt nodded to himself. Yes, he did need a bit of that. He closed his eyes for a moment before jamming the throttle forward.

It was a bumpy ride. Maybe his bumpiest yet. But he had the speed he needed. The rock formation on the point, his barrier and his salvation, looked different from this angle—an odd piece of earth sculpted by sea and wind into its surreal shape. But its natural beauty made it no less imposing. He needed to fly past it with as little margin as possible. He wanted to be able to reach out and touch it as he flew by to maximize his acceleration before facing down the brutal headwind.

The bumpy ride ended abruptly, the final wave from below serving as his ski jump. The plane went quiet, but he knew it wouldn't last long.

Nev was silent, and he was thankful for that. He needed every ounce of concentration he had to respond to the avalanche of wind just ahead.

Here and there, small evergreen trees had found a foothold in the rock formation, their short and twisted shapes revealing themselves as they closed the distance to the point. Like him, they held on to their existence, their piece of turf, straining against the odds and the elements in this inhospitable environment.

Even though he was prepared for it, the force of the oncoming wind shocked Durt. It slammed into the tiny speck of red trying to jump the rollers in front of it. He was sweating now, perspiration on his brow, his hands wet on the controls. Nev had been right, and he was lucky. He cleared the closest and largest wave with no margin and began to dip his wing, the slow return bank now underway.

Behind him, he heard motion. Buzz heard it, too, his furry ears skyward.

Must be the hot tamale.

"Are you there? Can you hear me?" he shouted over the wind's noise.

"Yes," came the barely audible rasping reply.

"Welcome back. Hang tight there. As soon as we can get a little more space between us and the ocean, I'll unwrap you. Just sit tight for now."

Not that the guy had any choice. He was wrapped up with no freedom of movement, now stored like the rest of his equipment. As much as he hated what these two were doing out here on the island, for now, he had to maintain his professional demeanor as an agent of the Park Service.

The wind now favored their return trip, and Durt banked his red plane and let the wind carry them north over the island. He was concerned for the passengers' safety and chose the same protected course they'd come. He didn't have the facilities to judge internal injuries, and though it made no difference to the guy without the hand, he'd try and minimize the turbulence on their return trip. He had more time now.

"Nev, I need the safest route back to a medical facility. Minimize risk. What are my options?"

Nev began spouting options, but she didn't get to the end of her option list before Durt mentally tuned her out. She'd pick the most practical, anyway, he knew. She picked a backward copy of the way he'd come. He asked Nev to set the coordinates, then engaged the autopilot and promptly switched her off, feeling the plane trace its low-elevation route that used the island's topography as a shelter against the season's first major storm. He felt a strange emotional mix of exhilaration and terror and a few other emotions he couldn't put his finger on, but none of them included the desire to talk with a smart-aleck navigation system. What he wanted to do was fly, and this was a rare occasion. He just needed a few minutes of mental and physical recovery.

The winds here, while more reasonable to fly in, were also insanely unpredictable. Beside him, Buzz watched the gray landscape and the pounding of rain. The dog loved it when the plane climbed and dove, but the erratic battering by the wind made him whimper. Durt figured if he were a flying husky, he'd do that and more.

The storm's constant rain and wind and a bit of ego persuaded him to disengage the autopilot after a few disturbing gusts dropped his heart onto the tiny plane's deck. Flying manually would take a lot more out of him physically, but he could feel the wind directly and respond more adeptly than the preprogrammed autopilot would. With a deep breath, he took the controls again.

Somehow, morning had worked its way into afternoon as he

threaded their shaky route across the island, carefully balancing their elevation in a screaming world of gray, the storm's gale above and the island's interior waterways, restless and agitated, just a few hundred feet below. He figured the plane's composite components would hold together. The question was, would he?

Could he count on himself to make the right decision? He'd be a lot more confident were this the standard glacier rescue that CJ had told him it would be. The plane was set up for that. He'd done quite a few of those, and the plane had performed flawlessly. Over the ocean? Unless he was landing, it should be pretty much the same, but as he made his way toward Larsen Bay and Shelikof Strait, his last major obstacle before Alaska's mainland, there was something there he feared. He didn't know what it was, but it was there still the same. A lurking fear that manifested itself as an unseen monster. It didn't matter, he decided abruptly. Whatever power that monster held, he would take it on. Hadn't he just landed—and taken off—from a Kodiak Island beach in the middle of a storm? If that wasn't legend material, he didn't know what was.

The trussed poacher in the back was making noise again. The wind had been reasonably steady for the past few minutes, and this might be the best chance he'd get to loosen the bound poacher. Aside from what they'd done and the problems they'd created, he had no idea who they actually were. His obligation was to serve in his capacity as a Park Service representative, and in spite of his personal feelings, he had to present a professional appearance. If he mistreated a VIP, should these guys turn out to be VIPs, and his action resulted in compromising a major donation, it would be his ass. His job.

He engaged the autopilot, unbuckled his harness and climbed between the cockpit seats into the back. Unsuccessful before because of the wind, he now released the unfrozen passenger from his cocoon, and even though he now had regained the warmth in his body, the poacher hugged himself as if to hug the cold out of his mind, too. Even his voice had a chill to it. "Where are we?"

He didn't look like a poacher. Now that he had the time to examine him as something more than a triage case, the sense of calm is what Durt saw reflected in the features. This was a man used to being in charge. Used to solving tough problems. You didn't get that way by being scared. Of anything. His handsome face was tired, but the eyes were bright as if excited to be in a life and death situation. Age was hard to judge with rich folks, and anyone who could afford to fund this kind of a trip fell into that category. What made him unique was his beard. It wasn't long and wild like some of the Park Service folk during the winter months. No, this was more of a decoration, a well-manicured style choice that clearly spelled power and money.

"Still over Kodiak Island. Approaching the Shelikof Strait." He kept it simple and direct. Professional.

The guy closed his eyes as if picturing their location in his mind. "ETA?"

Durt hadn't really thought about time at all. It wasn't a critical factor. He'd get there as fast as he could. The handless guy needed major medical, but he was in stasis. He ignored the question. "Look, move around a bit. Stretch out. We've got a few minutes before we hit the straits, and then you need to be strapped again. That wind is going to be something else, and I don't need any additional injuries thrown in on top of what we've already got. Then, after we're through that wind trap, we can talk ETA."

The man nodded and stood, still a little unsteady on his feet, and the motion of the plane wasn't helping.

Durt climbed back into the front seat. "Probably better if you do your stretching on the deck there. Then strap yourself in," he called over his shoulder.

He switched Nev on for a weather and wind advisory and promptly shut her off again. If he was to make this wind transition, he needed all of his senses focused. Automated safety and flight systems could distract him, and he knew, luck being what it was, the distraction would come when it would do the most damage. He wanted three things in the world now. He wanted himself, the plane and the storm. Man versus the elements. Durt versus Alaska.

He strapped Buzz in tightly. The husky wouldn't do well until they had a little more stability in their flight, and strapped in, the dog was one more potential distraction eliminated.

"Hang on," he called out, as much to himself as to his passengers, as he flew directly into the gray monster of wind and rain.

He had a little over 200 meters of elevation and figured that should be enough insurance to get him through to align with the prevailing winds. He counted on the plane's composite materials to hold together, and he wasn't disappointed. The little red plane held together as the wind slammed into it from the south. What he didn't count on was the force. He felt it in his chest. He felt it in his seat, and he felt it in the plane's manual controls as they were ripped from his hands. He'd never flown in anything like this. He'd survived downdrafts in the mountains before, but he was powerless to arrest the tremendous vice of wind pushing them toward the waves below.

Next to him, Buzz felt the motion of the dive and let out a half-hearted howl, but they weren't nose-down like they usually were, they were nose-up, and then they were all over the place. The plane wasn't responding as it should. He had no time. He fought for control and gripped the controls again, pulling back and locking them in place, praying the wind would abate, even a little bit, to allow a recovery.

At 50 meters, he felt it. The wings began to gain some purchase and then caught abruptly, the force cementing him to his seat. He smiled against the force as the plane returned to his control. He couldn't budge yet, but felt the pull and judged the distance. No margin of error whatsoever.

Then he remembered what he'd forgotten.

It happened in an instant, too quickly for him to flip the manual switch. If he could have turned it off with his mind, they would have made it. If he'd left Nev on and put up with her chatter, they would have made it. But he hadn't. He was sure he'd thought of everything. And he had. Almost. His grav-drive engine was set for mountain rescue. If the plane hit anything, the engine cut out, shifting its field energy to an exterior safety shield. If the plane slammed into a glacier, the plane and its occupants were protected. He'd used it a couple of times, and it had worked exactly as it was designed. It was an older system on the verge of becoming obsolete. Newer systems had overcome this weakness, but it was the system he could afford—the system that fell within the budget of his Park Service paycheck.

Over the ocean, he knew, it would work flawlessly, too. But the results would be markedly different. Below was water, and at this speed, slamming into a wave would be the same as slamming into a mountain. It would trigger the system, cut the engine, engage the field, and leave them bobbing in the ocean.

He was right.

Sometimes he hated being right. This was one of those times. The starboard wingtip caught a wave, and they went from crushing G-force to tossing and pitching. The plane's protection field was watertight, so they weren't wet, and it displaced enough water so they were buoyant. The real issue was that it was airtight as well. They only had a few hours of air left until they'd suffocate. The distress signal went out automatically with the engine cut-out, but he knew the odds of an Ocean Rescue response. They had their hands full, and that's why they'd called him in the first place. He had a choice. He could suffocate, or he could manually deactivate the field for more air—and lose both his watertight integrity and his buoyancy. A submarine, he thought, this plane was not.

Behind him, he heard cursing. He had one medkit which meant two medbelts. Of course, what he wanted to do was take the two medbelts, one each for himself and Buzz, and leave the poachers to the elements. But he couldn't. It wasn't in him, and it wasn't his sworn duty. He was certain his friends and colleagues would not blame him in the least, but that wasn't who he was. He felt a sickness inside of him when he thought that he was giving up his own life and that of his best friend for a couple of law-breakers. But if that's how it had to be, then so be it.

Buzz was still strapped in, and the ocean battering them from outside made maneuvering inside virtually impossible. He tried to time his move into the back as best he could and was thrown sideways as he made for the medkit stowed in the side equipment bin. He clawed his way back the few feet to remove the belt from the kit, then turned to face the bearded poacher. Surprisingly, the man's face was calm. Ready to help. "What do you need from me?" he asked as Durt strapped the belt around him and pressed the stasis switch.

The eyes started to fade immediately, and Durt wasn't sure if the poacher heard his answer or not. "Your oxygen."

Back in the pilot seat, he recorded a final message into his flight recorder, a curt, two-minute recap that started with his departure that morning from the lake and ended with his current decision. He switched the thing off, closed his eyes and felt the violence of the ocean as it tossed his tiny red plane about its surface.

He shook his head and cursed the ocean and his circumstances. He cursed the poachers for their crimes. He cursed CJ for collaborating with them and then passing on this ill-fated trip to him. Most of all, he cursed himself for the stupid pride that convinced him not to turn back when he'd had the chance.

"Sorry Buzz," he apologized to his best friend, the strapped-in husky in the seat next to him. "Things didn't go exactly as I planned."

[6]
HARRY'S

HARRY'S BAR wasn't fancy. It was more frontier. The walls of its rear corner, lined with every booze imaginable, stood behind a raised bar. A stage that sometimes hosted their local rock stars took up the other rear corner and a full-sized taxidermic bear watched Harry's patrons from its perch halfway up a red cedar trunk that served as beam support in the center of the bar's tables. The bear had some other stuffed animal friends, or at least parts of them, scattered around the back wall of the place. A moose head and a wolf helped the bear keep an eye on things. They were probably also what gave the place its unique frontier scent.

No one was quite sure who Harry was. He'd probably been some guy centuries ago who liked to drink more than he liked to hunt or to fish. The bar had been bought and sold probably a hundred times over the years. Plenty of folks like that around. The current Harry was a woman named Ida. She fit the profile well. A hard-headed woman with an easy name to pronounce. Hated to fish, but drank like one. She'd become as much a part of the service as the service itself. One thing was certain. If someone died in the Park Service line of duty, the gathering would be at Harry's. If a week had seven days, then days five, six and seven—

and sometimes even four—would have a gathering at Harry's. Today, there was definitely a gathering at Harry's.

The good news was that no one had to die to instigate it. Durt was as surprised as anyone to find himself at the table of honor with the Park Service royalty, his father included, together with his bearded rescue victim. Buzz was making the rounds as he usually did, and as another cold ale hit the table in front of him, he relaxed a bit.

Just a few days before, he'd said his final prayers and resigned himself to suffocation within his ironic field of protection. Now, he had a new perspective. Ocean Rescue did have their hands full, but what he underestimated was the reach and the influence of the Park Service crew. Jake Newman who sat next to him at the table had been his rescuing angel. His own personal Ocean Rescue. Jake was a fisherman who plied the Alaskan waters the old-fashioned way. There were still a few who risked their lives to scrape out a fisherman's living and avoided the less sportsman-like, more high-tech methods. Jake was one of them. He liked working for himself and hated the thought of debt.

When Durt's distress signal went out, it didn't just go out to OR, it went out to anyone with an appropriate receiver. And like Durt had done, when the call for help came in, Jake, who had just pulled his ship and his crew to safety, turned right around and headed back into the storm. The Park Service had rescued Jake's brother two years back, and Jake said he'd known the call would come someday—an opportunity to repay the Service for saving his brother's life. He'd located the powerless plane and, using his fishing nets, had tugged the plane, a bobbing cork at the end of a string on a wild ride, out of the storm's path. Durt and his two rescued poachers were transported to the Anchorage medical center.

Today, only a few minutes before, he was given a hero's welcome. Harry's was packed with well-wishers. He'd already told his story more than he cared to, but, he reminded himself, this was what he'd asked for.

What he really needed, he thought, was to find the right words to thank Jake for saving him from the icy north Pacific waters. He leaned closer to Jake as he sipped his ale. "Look, uh, I—" The right words weren't there for him. He didn't want to say something stupid, but he felt he had to say something.

Jake looked at him over his own ale and nodded his head. "Don't worry about it, kid. I'd have done it for anyone in here. It's what we do for each other. You're a real hero."

That couldn't be right, Durt thought. He was leaning in toward Jake, keeping his voice low as if someone might notice that he wasn't the hero they were talking him up to be. "You saved me. You're the hero. I was an idiot. I failed. I thought I could take on the storm. It was just me versus the storm."

Jake nodded slowly and kept his voice low. "I see." He leaned in himself to keep the conversation private, just below the constant buzz of the crowd. "Look, Durt. If you rescue folk or you don't rescue folk, that's beside the point. The real hero is a guy who makes the decision to use everything he got to go and make it happen. Nobody woulda said nuthin' if you decided not to fly that rescue. I'm thinkin' you probably went outside the damn Service safety standards. It don't take no guts to crash into the ocean. Takes guts to make the decision to go out and give it your best and say, to hell with the standards. I can do this, you think. To tell the truth, I think you're just like me. I never met a challenge I wasn't ready to step up to."

Durt was following, but not really comprehending. He nodded his head trying to make sense of it.

Jake seemed to sense his confusion. "Look, let's just say that I didn't make it in time. That you died out there. When we did find you. And we would, of course, we'd be having this same celebration. We're a different breed up north here, Durt. You might think you failed, but you're wrong."

He reached out and grabbed Durt by the jacket, pulling him even closer, "And it wasn't you versus the storm. It was us, all of us, versus Alaska. Never think you're in anything alone up here.

We're all in this together. This party here today ain't really 'bout you. I mean it is, but it's more 'bout all of us. The whole community. Mark my words. One day, Alaska will kill each one of us, but as long as we keep an eye on each other, we'll live—and drink" he said, raising his ale in a salute, "another day."

Durt understood. Almost. He took another sip of ale and allowed Jake's words to sink in.

I never met a challenge I wasn't ready to step up to.

Then he had another thought and looked at Jake in realization. "But they're poachers. I risked everything for poachers!"

It was Jake's turn to smile. "They didn't tell you?"

"Tell me what?"

Jake used his eyes to motion across the table. Durt followed his gaze to the bearded VIP who now gave him that same gaze. The calm one he'd used before when they'd faced death together in the plane. Unlike the rest of the table who were engaged in one animated conversation or another, he was quiet, watching Durt with a cool amusement.

Now he smiled. "I didn't get the chance to properly introduce myself. I'm Nalan. Nalan Rush."

The name sounded familiar. But from where? Better to keep it professional, he thought. If he were a poacher, then it was no longer a Durt problem. His father would be the one to take on that responsibility. "Welcome back, Mr. Rush."

Rush smiled. "No Mr. Rush for me. That was my father. I'm Nalan, but most folks call me Rush. I wanted to say thank you for taking what everyone knows was a pretty big risk in coming to get us. I owe you one."

Great, thought Durt, everybody owes me one. CJ especially. More than one, in fact. He was about to reply when two things happened simultaneously. First, he was pounded on the back. He stood and whipped around instinctively ready to swing. Ready to take on whoever had startled him. It was CJ and their mutual friend, Lefty, beers in hands and grins on faces. He felt his right fist clench and his teeth grind, then checked himself and relaxed, starting his own half smile; although, he thought for a second, that polishing CJs jaw with that right hook might feel pretty good right then.

CJ had his typical CJ smirk on his face. He was shaking his head as if in wonder. "Legendary, man. That was just legendary."

Lefty piled on. "Yeah man. That was something else." Then he added under his breath, "She wants to see you, you know."

"She, who?" asked Durt, more out of reflex than anything else, although he knew exactly who *She* was.

He didn't hear Lefty's answer because then the second thing happened. He remembered where he knew the name, Nalan Rush. It had been right in front of him. Nev's chrome faceplate in the plane said "Nevada" across the front of it in red letters, but in script near the bottom was the inscription, "Rush." This was that Rush. Nalan Rush was a Senior Vice President of TransComm, the commercial spaceship building corporation. He'd done the design and development work for a lot of tech things. Nev was one of them.

He caught his breath. "Give me a couple minutes, guys," he said to the pair through his stunned realization. "I'll catch up with you in a few."

He turned around and sat back down at the table. He knew what he had to say, even though he knew he didn't want to.

"Dad, you know they were poaching, right?

His father had killed people for less. Just part of the Service, he'd say. Try not to get too caught up in it. It'll eat you alive. But his father wasn't surprised or angry or any of the things Durt expected him to be. In fact, he was smiling. "Look, I know you think this is CJ's fault, but CJ didn't know either until they were airborne. Even then, things would have gone fine. Except for that storm. He did the only thing he knew. He called you. One of the best pilots we've had in three generations. Maybe more. I have no idea where you got the skills. Guess you were just born with them." His father emptied his standard glass of Kentucky and motioned for another with a wave. "Rush already worked it out with the Park Service. Not our place to disagree."

The donations, thought Durt, of course. They were wealthy poachers. He looked at Rush in a bit of a different light now, a mix of awe and contempt.

Rush seemed to read his mind. "It's not what you think."

"No?"

"We're working on a motor control device. It's a new field technology. It's a locally controlled field, kind of like gravity, but on a micro level. You know, a personal level. We're hoping one day to replace the awkward phase between losing a limb and having another one grown. We're still in the development stage. My tech wanted to see if it worked on animals, big animals specifically. He's brilliant, even if eccentric. He wanted to be able to walk right up to a dangerous animal without worrying about being attacked."

"Like a bear."

"Exactly."

Now he was starting to relate. He reached up with his hand to touch the bandage that covered his own bear attack wound. It seemed different somehow than when he'd placed it on the island. He was sure they'd changed it at the medical center. "Guess it didn't work as planned?"

Rush shook his head. "Not quite. Cut out at a critical moment. Bear took his hand off."

Durt shuddered. It wasn't making sense to him. "But I saw—"

"You thought you saw," interrupted Rush, "a guy trying to take a bear-head trophy. What you actually saw was a guy trying to get his hand back."

"And I—"

"You saved his life, actually, but you left his hand on the island. In the bear."

Durt was stunned.

"It's OK. We'll grow him a new one, but he'll be handless for a few months until it develops."

It still amazed Durt what medical science was capable of, but he didn't have anything to say. He'd misread the whole situation. "I've got to apologize. I didn't know."

"You did what you did, and we're all alive because of it. No apologies necessary. I'd stay away from him, though. He's the kind of guy who holds a grudge." Rush sipped his own ale. "I'm not, though. You've got some real skills. I'm thankful you were there, and that you're here. And I mean it. I owe you, so if you ever want to fly for TransComm," he said with a wink, "We've got plenty of places to fly that aren't into the ocean."

Durt nodded his acknowledgment. Maybe this was a lucky break after all.

Rush continued. "Come to think of it. Have you ever been to the Pacific Raceway? We've got a corporate team and pilots that fly for us. If you'd ever want to see a race and meet the ground crew, I can make that happen."

Durt couldn't disguise the enthusiasm in his expression. His eyes popped open. He'd actually been to the raceway a couple of times. Once with CJ.

Beside him, his father laughed. "One thing at a time, Durt. You've still got the rest of your duty tour to finish."

Damn. He'd almost forgotten. Hero or legend or whatever, because he was alive and fit for duty, he'd have another couple of weeks based in the cabin before he'd be free to do anything.

There was something about a close call with death that made you review your priorities.

"Sure," he said, somewhat half-heartedly. "Of course."

He stood, his ale glass now empty. "Thanks, Mr.—" Rush's eyes interrupted him. "I mean, Rush. I'm on duty until the end of the month. But I'd love to come down and see the races." He thought for a moment. "Will I need some type of special authorization?"

Again, Rush shook his head with a smile as if explaining things to people from Alaska was speaking a different language. "Our little mishap has already grown out of proportion across

TransComm. Your name is on everyone's lips, and you're the one guy everyone wants to meet. You show up on race day? Trust me, you won't be disappointed."

Now it was Durt's turn to smile. He didn't have to say anything. He just smiled.

"And I wasn't kidding about the job." Rush looked around at the mass of Harry's patrons. "You've got a lot of people who depend on you up here, Durt, but if you ever want to fly for TransComm, just say the word."

Rush's words were barely audible above the noise in the bar, but Durt understood them perfectly. He raised a hand in thanks to Rush and gave Jake a shoulder punch and wink of thanks as he turned to make his way toward CJ and Lefty. And Her.

Maybe he would take a job at TransComm, he thought. Maybe. But Dad had said it, and it was true enough. First things first.

* * *

The cabin looked different somehow. Certainly, it was the same cabin. Maybe it was the fact that Durt wasn't looking at it from its wooden floor, the gash from a bear claw ripped across his face. He involuntarily touched his still-bandaged face. This morning the cabin seemed less like a refuge or a castle and more like a prison. Maybe it was because his perspective and focus were still on last night. The drinking and dancing. The girl. The pleasure. The disappointment.

"You'd think they'd come up with a cure for the hangover," he said to the empty cabin, then realized they had done exactly that as he took another hit from his cigarette and felt the familiar internal buzz. His movements were slow and his thoughts even slower. Even cigarettes had their limitations.

Buzz raised his ears in curiosity. As always, up for anything.

Cigarette in the corner of his mouth, and a haze in his mind, he threw more wood into the stove. "Maybe later, Buzz. I just don't have the energy right now."

This morning, Buzz didn't whine or complain or insist when Durt didn't choose outside rather than inside chores first. He was always ready to go outside, but Buzz had made the same rounds at Harry's that he had and seemed content to move a bit slower than usual this morning, too.

They'd flown back in the early morning hours, their take-off lit by harbor lights and landing on the lake lit by the dawn's crimson rays. The storm had passed, leaving the season's first snow and a reminder that another was likely on its way.

He had cooking and cleaning this morning and then hunting duties this afternoon. Durt figured that might not be the most efficient, but that was really all he was up for. Presuming, of course, there were no additional rescue calls. Duty and chores aside, he had something else to think about. The offer.

Would he be considered a traitor were he to leave the Park Service community he'd grown up with, or would they encourage something like that? Maybe they'd be happy for the local boy. Flying for TransComm seemed like a dream too far. TransComm flew around the world. And to the Moon and beyond, too. He shook his head in wonder as he thought about it. The Moon.

But then there was Kim. Kim was the girl every guy in the state wanted. Easy on the eyes. OK, who was he kidding? Drop-dead gorgeous. Rich. A body to—

He shook his head, finished the cigarette and tossed the remains into the stove.

He thanked God for the body. God had been generous when he'd created Kim, and in turn, he supposed, generous also to him last night. A sight-seeing tour that began with dancing and finished with a naked playground. Wow. He'd been in disbelief until they'd finished, sweaty and spent. And then it happened. He was surprised at his own reaction as much as he'd been surprised to hear her say it.

They'd known each other for years, but nothing more than a few words here and there. A wave, a nod, a smile maybe. All fueled his desire for her—and that of many others, too. And it wasn't just the way she talked, she actually had a pleasant, almost sultry voice. No, it was what she said. As they lay there side-by-side, she'd wanted to talk. Absolutely exhausted, he was happy to listen, her voice a pleasant melody of conversation that lulled him into an almost trance state. But it had only gone on this way for a couple of minutes before he became aware of what she was saying and what it meant.

And then it was over. It was a pity and a shame, and something he'd never even considered. Maybe he was just being stupid. He could hear every other guy on the planet shouting at him and the top of their collective lungs, *So what?*

But for him, it made a difference.

She just wasn't that smart. The things she talked about were inconsequential. Talk of schoolgirls. Of hair and make-up and jealous boyfriends. Cupid's arrow had somehow gone in wrong. He didn't feel the warmth of love and comfort. He felt the chill of incompatibility. These were not conversations he could have with her. This was not someone who could see and feel and love the same things he loved. He couldn't envision himself making a life, pieced together with these types of talks. Then he thought he heard laughing. He figured it was probably God because he heard the same laugh this morning. It was like drinking cheap whiskey. Like his father. It seemed exciting at first, but then the nasty aftertaste killed the whole experience, and the hangover followed you around like a moping 12-year-old girl.

He figured she'd be a reason to stay, but after last night. No, he corrected himself, after early this morning, she was just the opposite. But it wasn't just her. Even the duties here were sometimes close to unbearable. He'd have to go out and shoot deer this afternoon. An increasing deer population meant an increase in the bear population and the Park Service had strict standards that were enforced and managed by its on-site staff. Him.

He understood its importance, but it didn't sit right with him. He cringed and hated himself every time he pulled the trigger on a defenseless animal. Even the bears. Who was he? He certainly wasn't God, or he'd be laughing at himself. Even people. He'd not killed anyone yet in the line of duty like his father had done, but dreaded the day when it came down to it.

The coffee on top of the stove sweetened the aroma of wood in the cabin, and he poured a fresh cup before making his way toward the bathroom. Buzz looked up from his prone post by the stove to verify Durt wasn't headed outside. Satisfied, he settled his nose back onto his paws.

The bathroom mirror was just that, a mirror. It wasn't a camera and video screen that showed him a high-def pic of himself and offered a full menu of data and entertainment while he washed and shaved. Just glass with a reflective backing. If he squinted his eyes a little, he could make the flesh-colored bandage on his face disappear. And yes, it wasn't the shrink bandage from his medkit, it was something different. From the medical center. It had been a few days, and he wanted to have a quick peek at what his scar was going to look like. Maybe it would be badass. Legends had to look the part, right?

He was surprised at how easily he was able to move the edges and peel it down. It was just like skin. Or at least what he thought skin would feel like. He tested a little bit, just to see if he could reattach it if he took it off. He let go of the peeled up edge, and it plopped back in place just where it had been before. Amazing.

But what happened next turned out to be the actual amazing part. He peeled away the bandage completely and stared in disbelief. There was no scar. He ran his fingertips over where he knew the scar had been as he'd crawled on the floor looking for a cigarette. Nothing. Well, not nothing, actually, because he did need a shave. Only one possibility. Rush had done this. He knew the technology existed to have this type of surgery done, but never imagined he'd have the need or have the money to be the recipient of such a service. He felt his cheek again as he walked to retrieve the hot water from the stove top.

Back in the bathroom, he shaved off his stubble and reexamined his cheek, moving as close to the mirror as he could to look for some sign of the surgery. Nothing. Smooth and pink and pristine. It was no longer a scar. It was now an invitation. Rush had offered, and now the decision was his. He'd done what he set out to do from here a few days ago, and he'd have a hard time paying for a drink at Harry's for quite some time now. But here was an open invitation to see the world. Maybe even beyond.

He made his decision. Who was he to say no?

[7]
QUESTIONS

TUCK STASHED his vest in the cruiser and moved his badge to his front pocket. Newton was a slippery place, and a little precaution was probably warranted. Boy wonder loses badge on the street? That would certainly take his cred down a step or two. He smiled at the thought. Certainly, it was possible, but not today. Things were getting interesting now. He shed his jacket, too, preferring the simplicity of his black T-shirt. No title. No weapon. No official vest. Yes, now he looked like the rest of Newton. He could observe Newton from the inside. Move with its people. Listen to its streets.

He walked aimlessly, absorbing the city's energy. There was a hunger inside him, a mental hunger to sort things out, to find some answers to the big question from within the smaller ones he'd asked himself. Newton ignored him. But not for long. He wasn't sure how long he walked, but when he realized his hunger was something more than mental, he found himself only a pair of blocks from the crime scene. He'd been propositioned for drugs, weapons, and most recently, what was described as a once-in-lifetime apartment opportunity. He was pretty sure it was an unspoken invitation to a beat-down and robbery, and were he not so hungry, he'd have gone ahead and accepted the invitation. In recent weeks, his combat scenarios had all been simulations. He made a mental note to come back and check it out once he'd put this thing to bed.

He hadn't been offered any sex propositions yet, but he figured those would come soon enough. He wasn't wrong, and when it did, he deflected the hooker's advances and asked directions for the best road-kill. He knew nothing got killed on any moon roads and the only animals that made it to the Moon on a regular basis were the rats and the cockroaches. Nonetheless, street food was affectionately known as roadkill, a joke about its manufactured origins. The evening was approaching and a wafting smorgasbord of scents assaulted him with an invitation that was unique to Newton. The mix of origins and ethnicities applied to food as much as crimes, and right now, he was tired of the second and ready for the first. Some of it was downright delicious, if you could mentally ignore the fact that it was pretty much a mass of chemicals. Tuck had no issue with that. That's all he and everyone else amounted to anyway, he thought, a mass of chemicals.

The evening was coming on, and the city began to transform itself. The bright signs absent during the daytime hours now emerged to change the face of Newton. Plenty of things to do in the evening here. Tattoos, food, dancing. A rainbow of red, blue and green invitations flashed their gaudy advertisements. What he was looking for, though, wouldn't be there in lights. But all he'd had to do was ask.

He followed the directions to a street vendor selling Meat-on-a-Stick. It wasn't the worst he ever had, and after the first one, he developed enough of a taste for it that he opted for a second and a few words. "Just superb," he told the guy between bites. "What do you call it?"

The guy was short, slim and fast, his black hair slicked back on his head. A sales smile pasted on his face, he nodded to the fading sign on the side of his mobile food truck he'd first seen a few minutes before. "Is meat-on-a-stick."

Conversation dead before it started, he had little hope for productive information but decided to try anyway. "What about that hassle up the street today?"

The guy's hands seemed to work independently of his face and his mouth. They continued to prep and serve the meat sticks to his regular customers. Many of them just handed him emoney from their wristcomms and took the stick from him with nothing more than a nod of acknowledgment. Apparently, the wrong words around a new face could spell trouble. Maybe his cover wasn't as good as he'd like it to be.

"Which hassle?" asked the vendor.

Fair enough, thought Tuck. A place like this? Probably a valid question.

"Headless body."

Meat-on-a-stick shook his head, and his smile melted to a sad expression. "Copernicus." The word was difficult for him to say, and his street pronunciation was off, but his intent was clear. "It not for everyone. Many, many folk they come here. Maybe they should not."

His speech choppy and heavily accented, he extended a hand with a stick and wrist-bumped a short woman in a small hat for the sale, and with the confirmation sales beep, let it go. "Everybody want something for nothing. No such thing. Sometimes that lesson," he pointed a meat stick at Tuck as if to make a point, "hard to learn."

The guy was right about that, he thought. This whole city was full of them. "Thanks," he said as he finished off his second and turned to rejoin the flow of foot traffic. "That's some good stick."

Tuck headed back toward the cruiser. The guy was right. There were a lot of hard lessons to learn here in Newton. The question was, what type of deception risked imprisonment and death? It had to be something big. Small crimes here were widespread and non-stop. Murder, though, and mutilation, elevated the crime to a whole new level. The question was, what was the motivation? It wasn't a single, personal issue. The crimes were too unconnected for that. No, somewhere there was a reason for it, a motivation that explained it. He just hadn't been able to piece it together yet.

Normally, this far into a case, he'd have it cold. He'd be able to see behind the actions, no matter how twisted they might be. But right now the only thing that made sense was the nonsensical serial killer theory, and that was a lot less of a theory and a lot more of an excuse. He argued it backward and forward with himself as he walked. The only thing that made sense, at this point, of course, was something that didn't pass his innate sense of what qualified as a motive. Maybe he was trying too hard. He thought the walk in Newton might have passed for the mental break he was looking for. Now that he thought about it, maybe he *would* go back and have a look at that apartment.

Whatever he thought his walk might inspire mentally in his mind turned out not to be the case. His walk had turned into more of the same. The same questions. The same thoughts. Inside and outside. Forward and backward. He agreed with himself on one thing. There just wasn't enough data in front of him yet. So that was it. Back to the vid screens and the Kick, and then he'd see what he could turn up.

By the time he'd retraced his steps to the spot on the street where they'd landed earlier, the crime scene had reset itself. Returned to its normal routines. No headless corpse. Business as usual.

Then he did a double-take.

There was something off. The ass-end of the ME vehicle was back in the same spot that it was parked in before. Odd, he thought to himself. He wondered what they missed. Had they brought Carter back?

The two ME reps were not the same as the two who had come previously. They had the same vests and the same markings. But it was two men this time, neither of whom wore little hats. Instead, they wore expressions of uncertainty.

He pulled the badge out of his pocket and held it up. "Hey

there," he announced. "Agent Tuck. LUNASEC. What did you miss?"

"I'm Will. This is Duncan," said the first who motioned to the second. "Looks like we missed the whole thing. What did you do with the body?"

Tuck shook his head, partly in wonder and partly in disgust at the ME's inability to do its job right. "No, wrong answer. Question is, what did *you* do with the body? Your reps. Rhonda and Kandi picked them up. I'm the on-scene investigator. I had a look and released the body to them."

The explanation didn't clear up their confused expressions. "Look pal, I don't know what you're talking about. Ain't nobody else on ME duty today. Just us. Me and Dunk. Maybe I better call the ME."

"Maybe you better," Tuck advised. "IDs?"

A chill began to crawl over Tuck as he read the offered badges. They were valid. Maybe he needed to call the ME, too. What he really needed to do was get back to the cruiser and pull up the Kick. This could mean a number of things. None of them good. Then he smiled with a realization. In spite of this complication, the trip to Newton hadn't been a complete bust after all.

* * *

Tuck punched in his override code and jacked the cruiser a thousand meters over Newton, probably more abruptly than he needed to. He figured he had time, but he couldn't be sure. He'd intended to pull up the Kick remotely, but there were some things, chief among them his full concentration, that he just couldn't find in the driver's seat of a police cruiser. As Newton dropped away beneath him he locked his destination and tried the ME's comm-link. By now, it was full-on dark, with the city lights below winking at him and the simulated stars above doing the same. He figured getting the ME herself at this hour was a gamble, so he was surprised when she picked up fairly quickly, her familiar face on the comm-screen showing a set jaw and narrowed eyes. If she were working late, there was an issue, and he had a pretty good idea what it was.

"Tuck. I thought I might hear from you."

They weren't really on a first-name basis. She was head of a powerful agency, and he was… What was the right word? He was a cop. A pretty decent one, but a cop still the same, so he was surprised at the familiarity. But it seemed right. Something big was going down, apparently, and she was already anticipating the next move. The over-familiarity told him that he was a part of that move, too. It wasn't an issue for him. He always insisted that folks drop the officer from Officer Tuck anyway, and no one called him by his first name. At any rate, it confirmed what he already felt in his gut. Things were not as they should be.

"Ma'am?" he responded, hoping for a little more insight into the ME's concerns.

He got his wish. "Look, I can't say a lot right now, but I've got an issue on staff here, and—" she looked away briefly, as did Tuck at the same time, to verify the green encryption bar was engaged, and their privacy was assured.

"Let me guess. Rhonda and Kandi aren't yours."

"Who?"

"What about Will and Dunk?"

She leaned toward to the screen, her whispered voice barely audible as if she could confound eavesdropper's ability to crack their privacy wall with murmured conversation. Tuck watched her head nod on the cruiser screen. "Will and Dunk are ME staff. But there are some odd things in my records here that I can't explain. And something else. My Kick access has been quirky this afternoon. Once I get in, it works fine, but it's like it doesn't like my credentials. I understand certs need to be current, but they're supposed to be done after-hours. They're not supposed to interfere with our operations. Our work. But it's been nothing but a pain in the ass today. I thought maybe you'd have some answers."

"I wish I did, but all I have are more questions."

"You found another one today, didn't you?"

He closed his eyes. He wasn't getting to the bottom of anything. "Listen, ma'am. I'm on my way back from Newton now. Let me ask you something. Have you seen a cop named Carter today?"

"Description?"

"Well, he's—"

He stopped short, second-guessing himself. Maybe Carter was fine. He'd probably already knocked off and was heading home. But if that were true, Carter would have given him an update on the disposition of the evidence. The body. Truth was, he'd heard nothing, and his repeated comm requests had gone unheeded. His badge hadn't shown in his initial Kick review, which, although concerning, wasn't unprecedented. He needed to get back and pull up his chip tracker at HQ. Disappearing ME staff was one thing, but disappearing cops was something else, and at this point, he had no idea who he could trust.

He shook his head. "No, never mind."

Then he had a second thought. "Ma'am. How late will you be there?"

She answered with a simple shake of her head. "Hard to tell."

"Let me check in at HQ," That's what he started to say, but before he was able to get it out, his wristcomm went dead. He couldn't tell if it was her comms or his that was the issue, but it didn't matter. Dropped comms like this was something that just didn't happen here. He had no idea where Carter was. In fact, now that he thought about it, based on their incident on the way to the crime scene, he wasn't sure now that Carter wasn't a part of the problem. Maybe the plan was to be stuck in traffic and give the fake removal team the opportunity to pull the evidence out before it became official. Maybe they weren't supposed to get there early and Carter was involved.

The more he thought about it, the less he understood. There was one thing he did understand, and that was the cruiser's top speed. He found it and kept it there. He had no time to lose now.

* * *

The Kick looked the same as it always did, with only two minor decorative touches serving as a reminder to their discovery a few hours before. Tuck's LUNASEC coffee cup sat on the console, still half full; the bag of sugar cookies beside it asking to be eaten. He obliged. He cringed as he tossed the remaining coffee, a shame in his eyes. A waste. Were it earlier, he'd have downed it, cold or not, but right now he needed something stronger. He set the wall in motion to roll back to the point where he and Carter had arrived in Newton and selected a recent donation of Scotch. It wasn't the best or even his usual brand, but it was closest, and right now, that was good enough. He poured a drink into his just-emptied cup and checked out the video search process.

It was right because it had to be. It was the surveillance system. But it was all wrong. Tuck put the cup down and used his hand motions to swap angles and roll back the video action in front of him. He shook his head.

Was this the right Newton street corner?

He watched the crowd on the street, and he watched himself raise his badge and disperse the crowd.

Where the hell was the ME's vehicle? And where were the two female ME reps with the small hats?

He did a quick video scrub back and forth, high-speed, making the crowd move backward and forward at ridiculously fast speeds. He kept his eyes on what he knew to be true with his own eyes—the corner where the ME vehicle had come and gone. He watched it twice. Then three times. Like he couldn't believe what he was seeing, and seeing it again would explain the disconnect. Of course, it didn't.

He brought the Kick to a full stop and sipped from his cup, trying to get his mind around the significance of what he was watching.

"It's just not possible," he whispered to himself, shaking his head in wonder.

He stared at the frozen screen for another minute, soaking in the realization of what it meant. The only theory that had made any kind of sense this afternoon was that this was the work of some demented serial killer, which wasn't a fully functional theory, he thought, only a placeholder waiting for something more plausible. And here it was.

In a kind of round-about way, it might still be classified as a serial killer, but this killer was likely not demented. This killer had protection. This killer was being shielded by someone at the highest level of lunar leadership. The ability to manipulate surveillance video was something beyond his own ability. Something he'd never even considered before. Something like this had serious, far-reaching implications. The whole lunar justice system relied on the infallibility of the evidence offered by the Kick.

But there was a dead, headless body, and this was not the first one, so in that sense, this was a serial killing. The real question now, he realized, was what these bodies represented. What were they hiding? What secrets could they tell?

Something knocked at the back of Tuck's mind. It was at that point he realized his own mistake. Not that he could have known. But he realized it now, the pit dropping in his stomach and a cold sweat reminding him that anyone with this kind of power would stop at nothing to keep it a secret, given what he'd just witnessed. And, given what he'd just witnessed, was there any reason that he might not be the next headless, handless victim? He couldn't think of one.

There was that knocking again. But this knocking wasn't in his mind. This was on the secure door to the Kick. His eyes flashed to the security camera in the hallway outside. He was right, they'd wasted no time. He hadn't recognized the knock, but he immediately recognized the knocker. It was Mick. Mick had never, to his knowledge, been to the Kick. He spent most of his time at the gym, and he was huge. Even without the gym-enhanced muscles, this guy's DNA gave him an intimidating stature.

He pressed the intercom link on the console. The security

system offered video and holographic comms as well, but that was all lost on Mick, whose brains were, like the majority of the police force here, somewhere other than in his head.

"Yes?"

The response was clear, but monotone as if he'd been instructed to play it cool and not give his intentions away but wasn't quite sure how to do that. "Chief wants to see you upstairs. Pronto."

"OK. Who'd you bring with you?"

"Um. Nobody. Just me. Mick." He was lying. Behind Mick stood two additional lunkheads Tuck didn't know. About the same size and body shape of Mick. He'd seen them around, but they weren't investigative cops. They'd never asked him for help on any cases like pretty much the rest of the force had. Probably worked directly for the Chief, he thought. That confirmed two things. First, Mick was pretty much an idiot. He didn't guess Tuck could see him because he'd used the intercom only. There was something else.

And this was the second thing. He was in some serious trouble. If he "went up to see the Chief," he knew he wasn't coming back. He didn't think his cop status would save him from a similar or worse fate than the body on the sidewalk. They had motive enough to kill, the means to do it, and the ability, based on his most recent discovery, to cover it up. He knew they were up to something, even if he wasn't sure what that something was. And now they knew that he knew it, hence the escort party.

The Kick was a secure environment. No question about that. No back doors. No handy windows. No, if he was going out, he had to go through three of the biggest guys in Copernicus who had specific instructions, he was sure, to make sure he went upstairs to talk to the Chief. In spite of his substantial personal combat skills, his ability to take out the three of them was suspect in his mind, so he'd have to take an alternate tack. A different strategy. He needed something fast.

The knock came again.

"Hang on, Mick," he said into the intercom in a stall for time, "Let me buzz you in."

Tuck watched him on the screen. He nodded and searched the door in front of him for some type of latch. Of course, the Kick being what it was, didn't have one. Access was granted only to those with secure credentials or from those already inside. He took another sip from his cup and had a thought. Maybe it would work. He could open the door from the console, but that's not the position he wanted. He walked to the door and pressed the secure access panel to pop the door open.

Coffee cup in one hand, a big grin on his face, he welcomed Mick into the Kick.

"Hey, Mick, C'mon in. Want some coffee?"

Mick looked at him with an odd, confused look as if drinking coffee after dark was some kind of crazy talk. "Uh, no."

Tuck's expression turned quickly cross. "Hey, I thought you said you were alone. What's going on?"

Caught in his lie, Mick was momentarily taken off guard. "Well, I—"

This wasn't part of the strict instructions he'd been given, thought Tuck. Good. "Hey guys, it doesn't matter. C'mon in. I was just taking a break anyway. You've got to check out these cookies I got today. They're something else."

The three entered the Kick, but Mick still wasn't sure. "Chief says you gotta go see him now."

"Sure, I'll go see him, Mick. You bet. Got a couple things of my own I need to discuss with him."

Mick looked both puzzled and relieved. Apparently, he'd expected a fight. Especially from a guy like Tuck.

Tuck motioned with his coffee cup to the console. "Full bag right there in front of you," he said to the closest guy.

The guy was about to take the step that would cost Tuck a lot more than a bag of cookies when he caught sight of the green and black label. It stopped him in his tracks. The cookies were a specialty that he couldn't really afford but apparently had a weakness for. He grabbed the cookie bag for a closer look. "Hey Dub," he said with a smile to his muscle-bound colleague. "Check it out."

He took a pair of cookies and tossed the bag. It was the moment Tuck had hoped for. His invitation into the Kick had been taken by the security team as that of an oblivious mark, but he'd displayed his ignorance with careful intent. He'd positioned himself closest to the door, and, bag in the air, he slipped his hand into his pocket, his fingertips touching his badge.

The bag never reached its intended destination. Tuck activated the badge's piercing crowd control feature, and the pain and confusion in their eyes caused by the screaming sound was followed immediately by six hands covering six ears in an attempt to escape the painful sound waves.

Tuck locked the badge's piercing sonic siren, then dropped it to the floor as he exited the Kick's door and closed it behind him, leaving all three writhing in pain as he sprinted to the manual stairwell.

He knew he had only seconds until they realized they could pull out and activate their own badges for relief and retrieve and secure his, presuming, of course, they'd carried their badges on their person as was required. He knew sometimes they got sloppy. For his sake, he was hoping they'd all been sloppy. The truth was he judged he needed about 20 seconds. That would get him off the floor and two stories up to the garage where he'd pick up the cruiser again. He presumed they'd give a foot chase instead of using the power of the Kick to activate alarms and security protocols. They were a lot more physical than mental, and without the knowledge or training, the Kick to them was about as useful as their badges, had they not remembered them.

Luck was with him. HQ was pretty deserted by this time of the evening, and it wasn't that uncommon at any hour to see a cop running for his cruiser. He passed a couple of people, but neither paid him any attention. Just another cop on his way to some emergency they didn't care about.

He blasted out of the front entrance he'd just come in a short time before. He punched in his override code, shot skyward, and sucked in a big breath of relief. Two out of three, he thought to himself. Only one left, and that was really a matter of timing. LUNASEC had two ways of tracking its population. Three ways for cops. The first was his badge, something the ordinary citizen didn't have to worry about. Second, the vehicle. If you were in a vehicle, LUNASEC knew where you were. Easy. And third, the trackers. Left forearm. Implant.

While the first two were always on, under the law, LUNASEC needed reasonable suspicion before a lunar citizen could be tracked. If someone went missing, they could be found. Escaped criminal? Tracked down. So it would take them some time. He figured about fifteen minutes, for them to report, tell their story, get the surveillance system to tell them he was no longer in the building, although the system would insist he was because that's where his badge would be. Then they'd move to track the cruiser, but that would give them nothing. Finally, they'd move to the personal tracking system, type in their request and justification, wait for and get authorization. He'd do the whole thing in under five, but that was his talent. Not theirs. Theirs would include a lot of yelling and a couple of screw-ups.

He set the cruiser down in midtown and took little notice of the clicking sound the cruiser's self-locking hatch made as he sprinted away from it.

[8]
SEATTLE

SEATTLE TRAFFIC WAS RIDICULOUS. Just like always. Durt had almost forgotten what traffic was like down here. Being the only thing with wings for miles around was something you just got used to when flying in Alaska. And it wasn't like he'd never been here before, but this was the first time he'd been the pilot of his own plane here. He usually took commercial transport or traveled with a friend. Either way, he wasn't in the pilot seat and had paid it little attention.

Today he had to pay attention. The park service had some docks on the other side of Puget Sound where he could tie up for the night, but he was really ready for a bit of nightlife tonight, which was not something you said in the same sentence as the national park.

Most of the traffic had remote transponders that directed traffic in the most expedient way. It was like no one knew how to fly anymore. Just auto-drones remotely operated by traffic servers. Calm and orderly with fundamental disregard for any planned time schedule. Transit times varied, scaled to the volume of traffic traveling in or out of the city. He could see the city and even make out its signature twin Space Needles. But traffic hung like a swarming cloud around Seattle, a mass of vehicles ferrying inhabitants and cargo to wherever they needed to be.

Where he needed to be was tied up at his destination, a multi-story marina on Lake Union. But where he was, and where he'd been for the last half hour was flying over Puget Sound—flying in circles between Everett and Vancouver Island. He couldn't remotely synch to the city's traffic server as his red plane was an artifact in this day and age. There were provisions for planes like his, ancient prop-driven things that required an actual pilot with flying skills to fly it. The provision said he had to wait his turn for a slot time. Once assigned, of course, it would be a piece of cake. No time at all. In the meantime, however, what it meant was flying in circles and eating his fingernails.

He was impatient as always, even though it was Nev who was doing the flying. Her voice was sympathetic. "You want to fly for a while, Durt?"

He did want to fly, but he didn't want to fly a holding pattern. He wanted to fly into downtown Seattle and moor his plane on Lake Union. He wanted to meet a few girls, have some drinks and fall asleep in the divine comfort of a hotel bed. "How many more ahead of us?"

"Two, Durt. Still two. The same number as when you asked a minute ago."

Realizing his tone and her quirky nature, he chose to apologize. Otherwise, he knew he'd be flying in circles with Nev cutting out and leaving him with the manual controls. She could be a bitch sometimes. That was the best way he knew how to describe it, even though he knew it was just an artifact of her personality program. "Sorry, Nev. Just impatient. You're doing a fine job."

"Thank you Durt, you're too kind."

"That's me. The kind one."

"One." Nev's response was flat.

It was hard to keep up with Nev. "One what?"

"One plane ahead of us, Durt. We're almost there."

And she was right. On their next round turn above Puget Sound, they got the green light and the vector coordinates. The flight path was clear as they approached the Seattle skyline, but it didn't feel like it. Air traffic crowded ahead and on both sides of the red float plane. It was thick and constant. Durt knew that all of the movement was remotely coordinated and that it posed little threat to his flight path, but he could feel the weight of the movement—he felt the solid, decorated walls of every type of aircraft he could imagine pressing in on his psychic vector. North of the city center the vector dropped him out of the mass of flying transports. He didn't remember it being this thick, but he'd had the poor luck to time his arrival at peak traffic time, and he mentally congratulated himself for his immaculate timing. He knew Nev would have something similar to say, and he cut her audio in anticipation. He wasn't here to berate himself or to be berated by his virtual companion, even if he deserved it.

Below him, the University District beckoned.

Welcome to Seattle, Durt.

It looked inviting, but not as inviting as Lake Union with its multi-story waterfront living and, of course, his chosen destination, the LakeEdge Inn. Its waterside locale certainly exceeded his financial means, but the Forest Service had an R & R contract here, and he had a few days coming, thanks to his most recent tour of duty in the park.

He'd told himself he was going to take the job here with TransComm, but he told himself a lot of things. In the end, he was still a rescue pilot off duty for a few days. He still wasn't sure if Rush had been serious or if it was just something offhand he'd said. He'd saved his life, he thought, that was the one thing he knew for sure, but that was his job. His sworn duty.

He sighed. He'd just have to play it by ear.

He landed easily and maneuvered his archaic float plane carefully between the sleek modern vessels that crowded the water's edge in the shadow of the LakeEdge Inn. He picked up one of the inn's private mooring buoys, and before he could grab his jacket and his bag from behind his seat, he was already being hailed from the water.

He judged the skinny water taxi driver a few years younger than himself, the tattoo on the side of his face reflecting some kind of sea monster. The taxi driver extended his hand to take Durt's bag. "Just the one bag, then?"

"That's it. I'll be here for the weekend. Oh, and I need to get out to Kent in the morning."

His driver eyed him curiously, taking a second look at his plane. "Races?" There was a doubtful tone to his voice.

Durt smiled. "Yep."

He started to say something else when his face changed drastically. Gone was dubious, replaced now with a dawning expression of recognition. "Wait a minute. You're the guy, aren't you? You're, oh, what's your name?"

Durt was surprised. He hadn't told anyone outside of the oncoming watch at the cabin that he was headed here to Seattle. Maybe it was mistaken identity. Maybe the taxi driver thought he was someone else.

"Bart Larson," said the taxi driver, then shook his head, searching his memory. "No. That's not it."

"Durt?"

"Yes! Durt Larson. They said you might show up!"

The driver was almost beside himself now with excitement.

Durt was still perplexed. *How in the hell?*

The driver extended his hand again. "My name's Calvin. And mister Larson—"

"Call me Durt."

"Durt," he said, his tone oddly starstruck. "It's a real pleasure to meet you."

Durt shook the extended hand and stepped down into the water taxi.

Calvin couldn't seem to lose his ear-to-ear grin. "Man, you don't even know, do you?"

The Inn towered above them as Calvin steered them toward the landing. "Know what?"

"Your story. Your rescue. It's all over the Net. You're freaking famous, man. When they said you might show up here, I thought it was a bunch of crap. But," he shook his head in apparent wonder, "now I don't even know what to say. If I was old enough, I'd buy you a drink."

This was not what he'd counted on, thought Durt. He'd just wanted to see the races and meet some of the mechanics. Somebody's life was about to change. He was pretty sure it was his.

* * *

The pit area for the day's races was already airborne. Floating a hundred meters above the gathered crowd, Durt remembered the saucer-like shape he'd seen on a previous visit with its elevated hangar bays and the hum of its continuous pre-race activities. It looked different from this angle, he thought, as they approached in the TransComm shuttle they'd taken over from Seattle.

Next to him, Kel piloted the craft easily as if she'd done it all her life. He figured she had a last name, but she hadn't mentioned it when she'd introduced herself.

Hi, I'm Kel. Welcome to Seattle. I'll be your escort while you're down here this time.

She'd extended a hand in greeting, a shy, tentative hand and had what seemed to be a nervous giggle when he accepted it and shook it warmly. He knew it was a standard company-directed introduction, but he'd been just as smitten with her as she'd pretended to be with him. Even now, a day later, he couldn't keep his eyes off her. Her sharp features and hazel eyes had an expression about them that seemed to hold back more than they let on. *I know something you don't*, they whispered. She wore her hair short, like a man. But there was no mistaking her for a man. Not today. Not any day.

He redirected his gaze to watch their approach as the pit saucer grew larger before them.

Actually, he thought, it looked less like a saucer from this point of view and more of a giant silver tire with hundreds of holes in it. From this distance, the crew vehicles buzzing in and out of them looked tiny, but it gave him a sense of size and perspective he hadn't had before. The hulking object served as both the start of the races and the finish, and its impressive size grew larger by the second as they approached.

He looked over at Kel. What was more impressive? he asked himself. Was it that he was being flown personally to this raceway's exclusive pre-race staging area, or was it the girl herself? Woman, he corrected himself. She was no girl. She wore the Transcomm racing outfit, which in his mind, should have been more practical than it actually looked to be, but he admitted to himself, it was well-suited to her role, especially if that role were to impress company guests. It fit her well-formed curves tightly, a bright silver diagonal stripe that crossed the navy blue of her uniform jacket. Add in the faux shoulder pads, and she looked more like a fantasy warrior than part of a race crew or a tour escort.

Kel, the woman, paid no attention to him. She had her hands full. She announced their arrival and picked up the appropriate vector for the TransComm hangar. TransComm certainly had the ability to automate a trip like this, but for whatever reason, she chose to do it manually.

Then he realized what that reason was. "You race, too. Don't you?"

She glanced over at him with a kind of half-smile on her face, her hands on the console, continuing to guide the shuttle. "Now and then."

He smiled and nodded. Now and then, he thought. He didn't follow the racing circuit that closely, but if he did, he bet himself he'd find her name, if that was the name she raced under, near the top of the list.

"Are you racing today?"

She shook her head a negative, eyeing him as if he had a third eye. "Today? No. Not today."

Again, his ignorance of the race culture had prompted the question. What kind of idiot did she think he was? Probably should have checked the race schedule so he could at least hold down a reasonable conversation. But last night at the hotel, his new-found fame had attracted a small mob, and all they'd wanted to talk about was Alaska. And him. A couple things he knew something about. He realized, now that he thought about it, that they were near the end of race season. In fact, maybe today was the final race. He hadn't planned it. He hadn't even thought about it. All he'd thought about was escaping from the cabin and the cold. He smiled. Things just kept getting better.

TransComm had claimed the top advertising spot on the now-airborne circular structure, its name repeating itself continuously, a giant TransComm ribbon wrapped around the uppermost level —the only level that wasn't constructed with continually repeating arches that allowed access for shuttles, support vehicles, and the racers themselves, to the structure's interior. The dark support columns between the arches stood in stark contrast to its bright, metallic exterior.

Kel guided them into the top-level hangar and toward the buzz of activity around a pair of planes. Sleek, metallic and fast-looking, they reeked of speed and excitement.

Durt knew the racing rules well enough. Their power plants were the same. All the racers were. Those were the rules. The designs were similar but unique to the sponsoring organization, and the design team dynamics were close enough that winners shifted almost every race. The TRI-PAC was a three-legged race with the crucial differences in leads usually shifting at each of its corners of the triangular course. The winning pilot was the one who judged the velocities the best. The one who could cut corners the fastest. Too fast? Overshoot on the far side. Too slow? Just the opposite. Either way, poor timing lost pilots their positions. The more experience, the easier it became to find the sweet spot. He'd seen the turns. They all looked wrong. Like planes stacked one on top of the other, but at incredible speeds.

Then midway through the race, they would swarm back to their respective pits, change planes, and finish the race. It didn't really matter when the swap was made. Just that it was completed.

Kel touched down, and activity in the TransComm pit came to a standstill. The shuttle extended two steps automatically, and Durt stepped down to the pit deck. The roof above that served both as the race start and finish point, sheltered the fall sunlight, but through the open bays on this level, he could make out the local Pacific Northwest countryside. In the background, he could hear distant sounds of the pre-race activity, but the TransComm team before him was gawking. Silent. As if they'd seen a ghost and didn't quite know what to do.

Kel broke the silence with her announcement, simple and direct. "Durt, this is the team. Guys, Durt."

Durt noted that the team was a fairly even mix of male and female mechanics and flight engineers. But he only had an instant before their silence dissolved in a mad rush to surround him. He was as unprepared for the reception as he had been the night before at the hotel. They pounded him on the back. They shook his hand. A slim woman kissed him on the cheek, another directly on the lips. A giant of a mechanic with a beard and goofy smile gave him an excited bear hug. Apparently embarrassed his enthusiasm had gotten the better of him, the big guy stepped back and looked around to see if anyone noticed, but the rest were all too busy fawning over Durt. The famous guy.

Kel gave him a bit of space, but then seemed to realize something and stepped between him and the crowd that had become too friendly. She raised her hands, calling for calm. "Give it a rest people. Durt's here all day, and I think he'd be more than happy to hang out a bit, but don't you have a race to win?"

The effect was instantaneous. The crowd again went silent,

taking a moment to redirect its focus, then again burst into action, moving quickly, he presumed, to their assigned tasks around the pit area.

Only three of them remained stationary, Durt and Kel, who watched the preparation symphony in progress, and crew chief, Becca, a taller woman with dark, close-cropped hair and worried brown eyes. Half her attention was on the team activity, the other half scanning the pit's open bays as if looking for a missing piece. Each team member had assigned tasks to complete. Some had digi-pads they presented to Becca. She reviewed, confirmed with her fingers, then returned them to their follow-on tasks.

For Durt, it was a practiced team, working over their preflights. Sensors. Controls. Pressures. The guts of the planes were on display and under scrutiny. Everything had to be ready. He was impressed with the level of checks and reviews in their practiced coordination. It was like an odd dance. Just the right amount of info at the right time to Becca. He was about to ask Kel about the team, but her attention was not on the team, it was on Becca.

"Becca, what is it?" asked Kel.

Becca signed off on another pre-flight and muttered one word. "Pilot."

Presumably, the pilot played an intimate role in team prep, thought Durt, and once she said it, he realized, that with all the mechanics' activity, that was the one thing he'd missed. They didn't have a pilot readying for take-off.

Becca seemed to share that same thought, her worried gaze transforming instantly as a shuttle maneuvered inside the roofed bay and moved toward their area. But it wasn't the expression of relief Durt expected. It was more scorn and annoyance.

Kel whispered to him. "Darron Daniels"

Durt shook his head like he couldn't believe it. "*THE* Darron Daniels?" he heard himself say stupidly. "Double-Dee?"

Daniels was one of the most prolific pilots in the history of these races. Twenty years or so now he'd been racking up wins.

Durt found it hard to believe he hadn't done a little more research into the race today, but it didn't matter. He had a front-row seat now.

Daniels' image sold perfumes and sports gear and cars and who knew what else. Durt didn't care much about that, but his skill as a pilot was legendary. Something he'd grown up with. Someone he idolized. While Durt was open-mouthed as Daniels stepped down from the shuttle, the rest of the crew didn't seem to even notice. He walked with a grin and shot Kel a wink as he sauntered over to Becca.

Unlike Durt, Becca didn't seem impressed with Daniels' approach or fame. No, he decided, she seemed distinctly annoyed. They spoke together in low tones until he watched her throw her head back in anger. "You're drunk!" she exclaimed in an incredulous tone.

Daniels looked older than he'd appeared in the advertising commercials Durt remembered and seemed surprised as if showing up drunk to fly on race day was something that was done on a regular basis. He shook his head at his crew chief, a sardonic half-grin on his face framing a condescending attitude that a parent might take with a child. They were close enough that Durt didn't have to strain to overhear the conversation.

"Look," Becca hissed at him. "Once upon a time, this was all about you. But that was then. Now, I have..." she stopped and corrected herself. "No. *We* have too much to lose in fielding a drunk pilot. You put yourself, your team, and all of the other pilots at risk."

Daniels rolled his eyes and pushed her aside. "Stand aside, woman. I could win this race, eyes closed." He strode past her and started toward the planes.

Becca, hands on her hips, stopped him in his tracks with three words. The first two were spoken slowly and clearly, but the final one was screamed. A scream of rage and frustration.

"You...are...GROUNDED!"

Durt watched, amazed. Could she do that? Daniels stopped

mid-stride and turned slowly, a half-smile on his face as if he couldn't believe what he'd just heard. "Seriously?"

But it wasn't just Daniels who stopped in his tracks. It was like every pit crew member was suddenly frozen and watched in rapt silence. No more testing or prep work. All stop. All waiting for Becca's next words.

Her eyes were narrow now. "Grounded," she repeated.

Did she actually have the power to do that? Durt again wondered. He wasn't sure. Was it possible that a lowly on-site crew chief like Becca could order around the famous Double D? His flight suit and his hair. Even his shoes said she couldn't. But Daniels' own response answered the question for him.

Daniels took on a more serious tone. "Look, you don't want to do that."

She shrugged. "You could be right."

He was whispering now as he turned and took a step toward her. "I'll have your job." He nodded to the crew. "Theirs, too."

"You could be right on that, too."

"So just close your eyes, and let me win another race."

She shook her head. "Negative. My pilots don't drink and fly. And that's just what I'm going to tell TransComm."

Daniels was blinking now. Blinking and sneering. "Do you have any idea what a grounding to could do to me?" It seemed to Durt he was trying to keep it a whisper, and it started out as one, but a few words in, his eyes turned wild, and his sentence ended in a screech.

Becca kept a level eye with him, shaking her head, a strict expression with a touch of sadness. "I didn't do a thing to you. You did it to yourself."

Daniels stared at her, still in a state of seeming disbelief. Money and fame usually had a way of bending the rules. Durt wondered if Daniels might try and negotiate something more. He couldn't give her fame. Well, not anymore anyway than she'd be giving herself by grounding Double-D. Maybe he'd offer her money. It even looked like Daniels was thinking about it. He wondered what Daniels saw in those dark eyes.

Apparently, he'd seen nothing but determination. He stomped back to his shuttle. "Good luck with the race," he shouted back at the stunned pit crew before his lift rotated and zoomed him off the pit deck.

The collective crowd stared in silence at the departing craft.

* * *

The pit crew floor exploded in a cacophony of surprise and confusion. Durt looked first at Kel and then at Becca for clarity. He understood what had just happened. What he didn't understand was what came next. Becca was no help. Head down, silhouetted against the backdrop of one of the pit's arched openings, she held her hand over her ear to mask the crew's excited jabbering. She was already in deep conversation with someone. Higher authority, he presumed.

He turned to Kel. "What about you? You could fly it, right?"

Kel made a little half smile, as if she'd already figured out what Becca had in mind. She didn't say a word. She didn't have to. She motioned in Becca's direction.

Becca was nodding. She seemed reassured, Durt thought. Then she did something unexpected. She smiled. No longer essential to her communication, she lowered her cupped hand and motioned Kel over.

"I want to split the race," she said after a deep breath. "Rush agrees."

Kel's grin was now unrestrained. "I thought that's what you might do, given the opportunity."

Durt was confused as the two of them turned to him simultaneously. "What? What did I do?" he asked, confused.

The pair said nothing for a moment, and then it struck him. He was part of their plan.

I'm in. Of course I'm in, but how in the hell could I help? I have no clue.

Becca's answer didn't help much. "Durt Larson. I'd like to offer you a position with TransComm."

Durt shook his head in disbelief. Here they were, minutes before the race he'd come to see, and she was talking career opportunities?

"What are you talking about? You have a race to run, don't you? Maybe we talk about this later?"

Becca lost the smile in a heartbeat and pressed her lips together. "Right you are. We do have a race to run, but we also have a company to run. You're a pilot with—"

The rest of the sentence was smothered by Durt's realization. For whatever cockeyed reason, she'd cooked up a plan that included him flying a TransComm racer. He snapped his attention back to her and caught the rest of the sentence.

"—useless. Unless you're a TransComm employee, we'd be disqualified."

His response was laced with disbelief. "But I'm a single engine pilot," he protested. "I'd be of no real use to you and the team."

Kel jumped in, apparently reading the frustration beginning to creep into Becca's voice and features.

"Look, Durt. You're a Net star. Today, everyone knows your name and your story. By next week, they'll have forgotten about you and moved on to some other amazing story. But this week, it's you. As far as flying, you can come in last place. Maybe it's even better for us if you do. More views mean more airtime for TransComm racers. That's where the money is."

He was still processing it. "You want me," he said, looking stupidly in the direction of the sleek jets, "to fly those?"

Becca responded first. "One of them. Kel will be the anchor pilot to finish the race.

Maybe this was a practical joke. Rush having fun with him. "Are you sure?"

In unison, both women shouted it at him. "YES!"

Now he understood. He laughed at what he realized was no joke, raising his arms in helpless surrender, "Sounds like a perfectly ridiculous idea, but I'm in. We don't have any time. What do I need to know?"

Becca grabbed his wrist, placing his palm on her digitab. "Do you accept a position to fly as a pilot for TransComm?"

He felt the heat and the smoothness under his palm. He nodded. "Yes," he said and confirmed the offer.

"That's good enough for now to meet race standards," said Becca. "We'll make it official after the Handoff."

Durt turned in wonder to look at the powerful pair of jets now calling his name from the center of the pit floor. How in the hell was he going to learn their complexities? In a few minutes?

A screech tore at his senses, and he jumped instinctively, realizing Becca had whistled her crew to attention, her arms over her head motioning them in. "Huddle!" she shouted. It was a shout meant for the now-attentive crew that actually hurt his ears.

They were immediately surrounded. Becca wasted no time, and the crew seemed used to quick changes in strategy. A collective gasp escaped from the crew when Durt's assignment as their new pilot made its way into their senses, but they were as familiar with the company business interests as they were with racing itself, and, with a couple of exceptions rectified by whispered explanations, the crew immediately understood.

Becca took the lead, directing actions with a sharp tongue and as few words as possible. Her first target was Durt. "OK, listen up. Standard flight controls. Only real difference is the dual propulsion system. One for maneuvering and one for racing. Big control on your right swaps omni-directional field control propulsion with racing propulsion. You'll only use it twice. Once to start and once to pit. Flight helmet has pit control comms. I'll be with you for the whole leg. You've seen races, so you know how they line up." She didn't stop to even allow him to acknowledge he'd heard. He had to keep up. This was her world now. She shouted at the team. "I want all tweaks reset to factory."

The "got it" response came from somewhere in the middle of the crowd, but it didn't slow her down at all.

"I need parameter alarms widened to allow for a novice pilot, and we've got twenty minutes. I want ten of those spent on the fam-vids. I know he's a pilot, but he's required to see those things. Get him in a helmet and get him connected to me." The crew scattered even as she punctuated her orders with an unnecessary command. "Do it *now*, people."

Kel pushed him toward the nearest plane. Someone shoved a helmet into his hands and ran off just as quickly. He felt out of control. His head swam for a minute. Then he had an idea. "Kel, is the racer connected to the Net?"

She gave him the same look as she had on their way into the Pit. Like she couldn't believe it was something he didn't know. She closed her eyes momentarily and shook her head as she answered. "Yes...Yes, of course. All of the terrain and race info is—"

That was all he needed to know. He nodded and cut off her explanation, squeezing her hand. "Thanks."

Placing the helmet on his head, he climbed into the cockpit. The hatch sealed out the frantic crew activity outside. He closed his eyes for a moment reveling in the silence until he heard Becca's voice in his ear. He scanned the console and the controls before him. They were simple and standard, and he was immediately familiar with all of them.

He knew deep in his heart he had no chance in hell to win this. But then he stopped and remembered Jake.

I never met a challenge I wasn't ready to step up to.

It was true, he realized. He didn't have a chance to fly this thing expertly his first time out. But he knew someone who did. He found the one switch on the console he was looking for, flipped it on, and took off his helmet.

[9]
TRACKER

THE VOICE SOUNDED INCREDULOUS. "What do you mean, *he disappeared?* How is that even possible?"

The voice was not that of a man used to hearing things he didn't agree with.

An awkward silence followed as The Crow chose his words more carefully this time. A more precise answer might take some of the pressure off. Relieve some of the sting. "The system shows him still in the headquarters building," he explained. "Apparently, he dropped his badge during his escape."

"Are you sure about that?"

The Crow thought about it for a minute. Standing in Trans-Comm's central security center, he admired the tech. It was better tech than the *Sec* in LUNASEC that supposedly represented cutting-edge security, and he was at home in this fishbowl of visual information. It was 360 degrees of pretty much everything that happened in the Moon's only city. All that activity was reflected or accessible here. The screen updates said Tuck's badge had been recovered in The Kick, and from an outsider' s point of view, he knew that meant Tuck could be anywhere—including in that same building. But security had shown Tuck—or at least someone who looked like him—leave the building in a police cruiser. The cruiser would be fairly easy to track, but knowing how he'd left the building, the frantic sprints and jumps, said a lot more about the situation than the mere fact he'd left the building. The Crow figured the fugitive wouldn't stick with the vehicle for long, so he'd jumped forward in the process, moving directly to locate Tuck's personal tracker.

"Yeah, pretty sure," he replied.

A short silence followed while the update was processed. "Well then, get a bead on his personal tracker."

Tines of anger and annoyance scraped through The Crow. Were the comments from one of his own staff, he might have done something about it. But that was not an option. He had to be professional. He had to be courteous. Say the wrong thing, and he could lose his position. Maybe more.

He swallowed his anger and replied evenly. "I'm working that now. It's not an automatic process. We've got to port his package to the Gen-pop tracker." It was like explaining things to a kid. All the kid really needed to know was that the issue was being worked. What was really happening was the questions were interrupting his concentration. Distracting him from what he already knew he had to do. Truthfully, TransComm shouldn't have access to LUNASEC's official systems, but because TransComm had better tech, their combined system and collaborative agreement extended its power and reach significantly further than either of the two independent systems could.

A distinct ding came from somewhere in the wall of screens before him in the security office.

"That it?" he asked the technician in front of him, but he needn't have bothered. A 3D image of Tuck's head floated over the console, rotating slowly, numbers and symbols of the various lunar position zones whizzing by next to it as the system searched for Tuck's personal tracker.

The voice in his ear was trying to rush the process again, an insistent reminder. "Well, where is he?"

The numbers continued to whiz, and The Crow had a sinking feeling. He had to give him something. He had to make some progress. He muted his communicator and redirected his technician. "Find the cruiser."

The technician didn't say a word, but responded with his left hand, reaching for an adjacent console that brought up a second simultaneous search.

The Crow un-muted. "Searching now," he advised, "should only be a couple minutes." But his eyes told him a different story. Tuck's head continued its rotation, but the numbers were now repeating themselves. His worst fears materialized. The system had searched Copernicus' population in its entirety and found no sign of the rogue cop. And now it was starting over, probably running diagnostics on itself at the same time to ensure its busted search was not a result of its own shortcomings.

His technician shook his head as if to confirm they wouldn't likely find Tuck this way but nodded to the cruiser search request.

The numbers of their second search had stopped and now stood stationary with a lunar grid location. The floating image of the cruiser now shrank as the tracker translated its numbers into a map display and pinpointed its downtown location. As he'd surmised, Tuck had abandoned the vehicle. At least that was something. "Got it. Cruiser is downtown. Sending a unit now. Will advise as soon as I have an updated status."

He clicked off. He didn't need the intimidation and the veiled threats he was sure would follow. He could hear the one-sided conversation in his mind.

It's one cop. One. You have a fully capable security staff and the latest tracking technology money can buy. But all of that is useless if you don't have the mental facilities to manage it. I'll have your head if I have to come down there and do it myself.

The berating went on and on. He'd heard it time and time again, but in his current position, he had to keep his mouth shut and nod in agreement. He didn't need the same verbal dress down he'd heard so many times before. What he needed was to find the damn rogue cop. If he could produce him, all of the rest of this wouldn't matter in the least. And if he couldn't? He pushed it from his mind. He didn't even want to think about that right now.

* * *

The ME's eyes were tired, but her features reflected a mix of recognition and astonishment. She wasn't used to being surprised. Tuck knew she was Elizabeth Day, Medical Examiner. Word on the street was Ms. Day was not to be surprised, a personal directive she impressed on her staff, a staff who took great pains observe it. Add to that fact that, especially in Copernicus, where the whole place was one big technology puzzle, no one ever went to see anyone in person. Not that it was impossible. People did it all the time for a meal or a date. It was just impractical for business. In fact, this was the first time he'd been inside the ME's office in person. He'd communicated and sat in this room virtually, but had never actually set foot in this office. So the fact that he'd come here in person was something of a surprise in itself.

Then there was the other thing. Tuck had talked his way past the guard who should have done the announcing. He'd been badge-less, thanks to his stunt back in the Kick, but with his extensive network of favors and friends, he knew a good percentage of the downtown security professionals. Some were former cops. Some were friends of cops. He knew them from sparring at the gym or chatting randomly about cases or races. Some he'd helped out as favors, others just because it was always interesting to find a crack in a case. They'd help him break cases that were a little too complex for his less motivated colleagues. Somehow today, he'd accidentally pissed off the gods of luck and fortune, but the day was waning, and apparently so was his ill luck. When he'd sprinted in, he knew his wild eyes and frantic pace would raise the suspicion of any guard worth his pay, but when he put eyes on the guard with his finger to his lips, he realized he'd get quick access. No questions asked. The guy's face was familiar and the guy had recognized him and waved him through. He guessed there were some things afoot at the ME's office as well. The ME might have been surprised to see him in person, but the guy wasn't. He got waved right on through, his finger still to his lips for stealth and silence as an advisory to anyone else who might see him and automatically raise an alarm.

Now as he stood before her, panting a bit, he watched her quick intake of breath, a precursor, he figured, to an exclamation and the inevitable demanded explanation. He didn't wait a second longer. His finger went back to his lips, and he grabbed her hand and dragged her toward the ME information center. She came willingly if awkwardly, her stylish shoes not helping her control her stumbling gait.

The ME Comm Center looked like his—but better. Classier. Tuck was sure it was just as practical as The Kick, but while he'd gotten the base model, she'd gotten a model from the top shelf. Artwork hung artistically here and there, highlighted by pastel accents. It even smelled expensive, although he wasn't quite sure what scent floated subtly in the room. Still short of breath, he had little time to explain why his window of time was about to expire. "Look, ME, you're not going to believe this. I barely believe it myself, but—"

It was an odd stare. Like she understood what he said, but was still processing the facts in her mind.

"First, call me Liz," the ME said.

Tuck obeyed as he recounted his day and his discovery of the revised video, then his subsequent realization of what it meant. Her head began to disagree with the whole notion of what she was hearing. The motion was slow but deliberate. He was communicating, but he couldn't tell if she didn't understand or didn't believe what she was hearing. Her denial was obvious, he thought, in one form or another.

Durt glanced quickly at his wristcomm. "We've only got a couple more minutes. Quickly, log in. You may not believe me, and I truly understand that, but I'll show you." He could hear an uncharacteristic tremor in his own voice as he spoke. "I'll show you, and you can decide for yourself."

She reached out slowly, her palm press bringing up an authorization screen and a welcome message in her Kick. She then swept the same palm toward him as if to say, *Your show, Tuck. Impress me.*

Without a word, he did just as he'd done a short time before in the Kick. He manipulated the surveillance wall back to Newton earlier in the day.

"Watch this."

Now she was a bit more interested. "OK, that's you," she said, following the action on the screen, "and who? Your partner?"

He nodded. "It's Carter. You haven't seen him here, have you? He was supposed to be on his way here, last time I saw him."

Her look was one of concern, but clearly, she didn't recognize him. Again, he zoomed the footage forward in time, and the Newton crowd on the screen jerked in double-speed movements.

"There's the body, and you're dispersing the crowd." She suddenly held up her hand to signal a stop. "Wait. What's that?"

She was right. It was something he'd missed before. A small hooded figure darted out of the restaurant and crouched over the body. "You're right. Pickpocket, maybe?"

She shook her head. "I don't think so. Look again, just slower."

The figure rolled the body slightly on its side and then retreated quickly back where it had come from. "Looks almost like a kid, doesn't it?"

"Got scared, maybe?"

The scene rolled forward as she continued, "OK, The body's still there. You're talking with Carter and some of the crowd. Now you're just talking to yourself."

"That's the thing." He froze the screen. "There were two ME reps there I was talking to."

She looked at him doubtfully.

"Keep watching," he pressed, "Anything about the crowd that seems off now?"

"No."

He traced a straight blue line across the screen as if it were a review of some sporting event. "Look, they seem to be getting out of the way for someone or something, but there's nothing there."

She still wasn't convinced. "OK. Maybe."

"Here's the kicker. First, by this time, the body has already been moved to the truck."

"No. It's still there. I can see it."

He froze the screen again and turned to her, using a hand to emphasize his point. "No, Liz, I'm telling you what happened, not what you're seeing."

He wasn't sure how she'd take to being called by her first name, but she seemed to take little notice. Good, he thought, she's all in. "Keep watching. Now I send Carter with the two of them. And there's me. Leaving."

"You just left the body on the sidewalk like that?"

"I'm telling you, by this time, the body was gone. Already moved to the ME truck."

"The one that's not there."

"Exactly."

She shook her head. He realized what she was thinking.

"Keep watching. I sent Carter with them. Now, they can't just make Carter disappear into a van that's not there. And they can't not take Carter with them, because I asked him to go. So they manipulated him out of the video. Pretty clever, actually. Check it out." He pointed at the screen, following Carter's image. "If you weren't looking for it, you'd miss it. Here's Carter walking toward them. He walks around the corner and then disappears from sight as he goes to get into the vehicle."

"So?"

"We freeze it there. Got the time code? OK, now look at it from the opposite angle."

The camera panned in three dimensions over the shapes of the frozen crowd below to a camera from the other side of the building.

He turned to look the ME in the eye. "Now Carter just turned the corner, right? He's out of sight from the other viewpoint. Check out the time. Yes, he should be visible right there."

"I don't see him."

"I don't either." He paused "He's not there. He's vanished. Now let's pan back, but slowly, keeping our same surveillance angle."

Figures in the crowd moved, but in slow motion, as if in a dream.

She gasped as she saw it. "Oh my God. There it is. He turns the corner of the building and disappears."

"Check out the time, Tuck," he whispered in a conversation to himself, stealing a glance at his wristcomm. "Check out the time."

She ignored him, but her puzzled look began to transform into one of fear and understanding as she continued to watch the screen.

He read her well. He pushed his seat back from the console and motioned her toward it. "You have to do something for me."

She said nothing but swallowed and nodded. Anyone with the authority and know-how to manipulate the official surveillance data in this way spelled peril for both of them.

He watched the realization transform her face. "I'm going to read you some characters. They'll seem random, but I need you to trust me."

Again, she nodded, and he dictated a string of seemingly random numbers and letters. The screen popped open a dialog asking for grid numbers.

"Pull up the map," he prompted.

In an instant, a three-dimensional map of the city filled the wall screen.

"Now, find a train. A southbound one."

She zoomed in and hovered over the bright blue wireframes. The the whole city pulsed with activity and vehicles in motion.

"There," he almost shouted, pointing. It was a train in motion. Six cars, it looked like.

As the target cursor moved around the screen, numbers zipped by in the dialogue box. She swapped her bunched fingers into an open palm and landed the cursor on one of the center cars.

He smiled in admiration. "Nice shot!"

They watched together now as the cursor shifted into an ID profile. It was him. Marlin Tuck, a 3D model of his head rotating, connected with a thin red line to the shrinking wireframe train as she zoomed the system out for a wider city view.

Her open-mouthed stare spoke volumes. She turned to look at him, straight on.

"No. That's not possible."

He smiled slightly. "It won't last for long. The system will self-resolve in a couple of minutes. Facial verification will identify it as an anomaly and remove it from the system. But this is what should be popping up at HQ now."

"Then what?"

"Well, they should immediately dispatch a unit to the next stop to intercept the train."

"And then?"

"Within a couple minutes, there will be a new sighting. Some other part of town—and then another. And another."

"But the system will eliminate all of those," she protested.

"Yes, but it will give me some cover time. Inside here," he said, motioning to the control room around them, "like a number of places in Copernicus, we're invisible to the system. Only a couple of ways to beat the tracker implants."

By now he could tell she was totally on board with him. "What if we cut it out of you?"

He shook his head in a brisk negative response "Too risky here. You need to stay out of this. And I don't want to cut it out. But I do want them to *think* I did. They have to think I'm either dead, had surgery, or I'm off Copernicus. Then they'll stop looking for me."

He checked his wrist again and leaned toward her. He didn't have much time. "Now, I've got an idea. Do you ever drive a company vehicle home?

She looked curious. His random questions still weren't allowing her to follow his logic or reveal his plan. "Sometimes," she admitted. "It's not against policy, but I don't usually do it."

"Look, I'm rogue now. If you're with me, we have to go now. If you're not, I totally understand. I have no idea how high or how deep this goes. Right now, I need a lift, and I need to involve as few people as possible."

"Where?" she whispered.

"Near the spaceport"

She made a face. "Ugh, edge of Newton, yes? What do you need there?"

He stood up abruptly and grabbed her hand again. She didn't complain. "Just a little something I need to pick up." He winked. "I like to think of it as a hidden gem."

* * *

"Got him!" The Crow raised his arms in a quick victory salute to no one in particular and kicked his feet against the floor, sliding his console seat back into the center of the control room. His smile re-shaped the dark tattoo of a crow in flight on the left side of his face. He'd sent his tech off on an open-ended break and now had the place to himself. He worked much better this way.

It was an exclamation partly of relief and partly of personal accomplishment. He didn't really know what penalty might ensue from the veiled threats he'd become used to by now. There was talk, of course, but no one seemed to have the real inside story on what happened to those whose performance was judged marginal. Or worse. He'd seen a few weak players during his time in The Seat. He recognized their type the minute they walked in. They talked big, then couldn't or didn't deliver. That was it. They stopped showing up for their shifts. No explanation. No one dared to ask.

In this environment, you minded your own business. He had no idea if the threat to *come down there and do it myself* had ever been carried out. Were he a betting man—and he was—he'd bet not. The commands he got from that voice were never insightful. They never told him anything he didn't already know or wasn't already doing. That was probably the most annoying part. But it did say something about his skills.

He remembered the first day he'd walked into this place. Then and now, it was a bad-ass place to work, but before he started, he'd known virtually nothing about it. Part-time musician and full-time bullshit artist, he'd struggled on Earth to make any kind of acceptable living with his innate talents. Most of the work seemed beneath him, and there was so much competition. So many people could do it better than he could that he found most of his successes on or near the edge of the law. He saw and took opportunities no one else would. Then on a lark, he'd come to Copernicus and discovered something about the disposition of its transient workforce. With a few exceptions, he could characterize their talent as average at best. No need to be brilliant or talented here. All you had to do was what you were told, and things usually worked out fine.

By nature, he was quick to bore and easy to discourage, but all that shit disappeared here. After only a few hours in training, he'd known this position—this seat—was his calling. Those talents that restrained him on Earth distinguished him here. For him, it was like playing a giant, complex keyboard. It seemed to just come to him. Others came and failed and left. He stayed. It was visual and fascinating and addictive. Sometimes he couldn't wait to get back to his shift and back on the board.

The pay was decent, although he admitted to himself that he'd probably do it for free. It was the constant fear of unknown consequences that ate at him from time to time. That fear had diminished over the past few months as he'd come to realize he was one of the organization's top board ops. TransComm was addicted to him as much as—maybe more so—than he was addicted to their board and its lifestyle. Then the voice came. The fear from its constant intimidation changed everything. Mutated it into a sour taste in his mouth that spoiled the best part of an op. He was less afraid now but took pains to remain professional. The truth was, a bit of fear seemed to pull something out of him. Inspirations now and again that he had no idea were there in the first place.

He allowed only a moment for his mental victory dance before advising dispatch of the quarry sighting. "Dispatch. Central. Tango is southbound on train one-niner-seven. Third car. Looks likes next stop is Woodmont Place. Request intercept. This is high-pri. Don't fuck it up."

The reply was curt. No emotion. "Roger Central."

He took a deep breath and let the oxygen wash through him. He'd steal a smoke in a few—once this thing was resolved. He wasn't a cop, but TransComm had better stuff than cops did. He figured they probably had just as many rules. One of those rules, he knew, was that you didn't smoke in Central. Not because of the smoke. Because of the distraction. You needed both hands and all your fingers at the ready. There'd be plenty of time to smoke later.

There was something at the back of his mind on this one. He'd been as surprised as anyone when the Tango had popped as Marlin Tuck. Tuck's face rotated on the screen in front of him. He'd met Tuck once. A friend of a friend. This was the guy. The master. The Crow was an apt pupil, but Tuck was a master.

How did he get himself on the wrong side of the board?

What if he were in that situation, he wondered. Would he know enough to be able to evade a rundown? He shrugged to himself. Probably not. TransComm managed a dense network of cameras and sensors with control nodes across its breadth. His was one of many, but it was also one of the go-to nodes. You want TransComm results? You get The Crow.

Tuck must have gone too far, he thought. Maybe he talked back. Maybe he failed. He found it hard to believe, but anything was possible. The mighty Tuck. Fallen. That was OK with him. More need for his talent. More space at the top.

On the screen, a new message popped up. He shook his head in disbelief.

Was the system jacked-up again?

[10]
TRI-PAC

"Durt? Durt? Listen up. Can you hear me?"

Becca bounced uncontrollably up and down on her toes as she tapped the commlink in her ear and looked sideways at Kel who now stood beside her. Impatience buzzed through her like lightning. "Comm system check, Kel," she snapped. "I'm not getting anything from him."

Becca's voice was tight. "Can anything else possibly go wrong this morning?"

Kel had less at stake and was measurably calmer. She tapped the pit status board in front of her. "Nominal status. No errors." She picked up her own status query. "Pit, we've got broken comms. Give me a visual status on the pilot."

The answer came back directly. "He's watching the fam-vid. It's up on his screen now."

"We can't reach him."

The response was rich with pit wisdom. "Leave him be. He needs his concentration now. You'll have the whole race to talk to him."

"Not if there's a technical problem."

"No technical problem, Kel. He's taken his helmet off."

"Listen up. Chief says—"

Becca interrupted Kel with a hand on her shoulder. "No, leave him. They're right." She ran both hands back through her tied-back hair, breathed in, then exhaled slowly. "He's smart. He's taking a deep breath. Maybe that's what we all need to do."

Inside the cockpit, Durt found who he was looking for.

The soft female voice spoke through the tight cabin around him. "Durt, I thought you'd forgotten about me."

He feigned surprise. "Forgotten about you? Nev, I could never do that."

"Yeah, right."

"I didn't know if this would work or not, but it seemed logical that with Net connectivity that I should be able to access you from anywhere on the Net."

"Well, this time you were right."

Nev's voice shifted into its curious mode. "Oh, did we get a new plane?"

Durt smiled at the question. "I wish. No, just borrowing this one this morning. I've been asked to race it."

Nev's reply was tart. "You don't know anything about racing."

"You're absolutely right. That's why you're here."

"But I don't know anything about racing, either. It's not part of my programming."

"Nev, I only have a few minutes here. So here's what I need."

"You want me to fly the plane, don't you?"

"No. I don't need a driver. I need bumpers. Parameters. You racing? That would throw the race right out the window. No, what I need is a compilation of average speeds and trajectories over this race course. Then I need you to set up safety parameters so I can stay on track. No way I can win, but I can fly, and if I'm not dead last, that would be some kind of a bonus for me."

"Is that it?"

"One other thing. I need those bumpers to be visible only to me. No one outside the cockpit. Can you do that?"

There was a pause. "Well, this is the standard 3100-Charlie console, but most of it's been bypassed or disabled. Very little sophistication here as far as navigation. Looks like they've made this less of a vehicle and more of a rocket with a seat inside."

This made him smile. "You got it, then?"

"Oh, I got it mister. It's you I'm worried about."

"Why me?"

"You're human. That's why."

She certainly had him there.

"Nev, now about those routes and—"

"Already got them. Now watch your heads-up display. I'm superimposing over your video. All standard trajectories are between those two blue vertical lines. Red top signal, got it?"

A red triangle flashed the top of his screen. "Yep. Is that speed?"

"Correct. Watch that one closely. You'll bump into it now and again, just because you are who you are. Just bump it though. The harder you bump it, the narrower your blue roads will be. In other words, the harder it will be for you to stay on course."

"That's it?"

"Done. What else?"

In the back of his mind, he knew what the pit crew wanted him to be doing. Watching the video. "Anything on the video that makes this different from other plane controls, aside from what you already told me?"

"No, Durt. Controls are the same, but you better not forget to buckle your harness. Secure it fully and correctly."

"Now, that is sweet. Thinking about my safety. I was taking you for a hard-ass today."

"Oh, you'd like that wouldn't you?"

"What do you mean?"

"If you're not fully harnessed, you get no power at the green light. Pretty much, you're stuck at the starting line. Last car in the race."

"I don't need any help with that. I'll find my own way there fast enough. Was that on the video I was supposed to be watching?"

She gave him one of his own replies. "Yep."

"I should watch it, then."

"Too late, you talked too much already."

Durt looked down at his safety harness, half of it on either side of him. Nothing complicated, but certainly something that might be overlooked by a rookie pilot. He snugged it around himself and a thin green line lit up across the bottom of his pilot display. He did need to check in with the pit crew, but he had another question first. "Any hints on the Net about killer starts?"

"Just take it easy. It's like Seattle traffic for the first minute. You know, you've watched these things before. Each pilot has her own preference for maneuvering, so you'll have plenty of options to open this thing up after that. Pace them all until Mt. Ranier. That's where you'll lose them."

He was surprised. "No way."

"Trust me. You will. You'll overshoot the first one, then undershoot the second. After that you should have a feel for it. No offense. Stats show that everyone does it their first time out. As far as I can tell, anyway."

He was about to protest when she interrupted again.

"Listen, I think you better put your helmet back on or you're going to get fired. And then," she said in her typical Nev fashion, "the only thing you'll be flying is your thumb."

Maybe Becca had to do it for legal reasons, or maybe she underestimated his experience as a pilot, but nothing of what she told him before the starting line helped tell him anything more of value. He might as well have just left his helmet on the seat beside him, he thought to himself, as he lifted off and moved his plane toward its starting position.

* * *

The sea of heads moved in waves. His was one of them. Kel, his tour guide from the morning, was not. She had gone her own way after the race. Durt imagined she probably had her own post-race ritual, and baby-sitting a newcomer wasn't part of it. He couldn't blame her for that. This girl was nice, too, but he couldn't even remember her name at the moment.

No, he shook his head in answer to the girl's question, he didn't come here often. He could have yelled his answer for all the good it would have done. Durt brought no wristcomm. No money. Shit like that would all disappear here, anyway. He had nothing but a buzz and a growing sense of claustrophobia. And somehow, he wasn't quite sure how, he had a drink in his hand. Well, half a drink anyway, after all the bouncing around.

The music was everywhere on the Seattle rooftop. The bass and drums pounded in his ears as the excited, sweaty bodies bounced off one another, his included. The cool November dampness and the overcast and now black sky above felt good. Glowing and flashing lights from the clothing and costumes entertained his eyes, a brilliant rainbow, frozen solid and broken into a thousand pieces that now floated amid the choppy ocean of rooftop humanity in motion.

Yes, he nodded his head at the girl's follow-up question, he had been at the races today. He took a closer look. She was well formed and smiling and in constant motion. Her blonde hair was a loose-styled braid that tossed to and fro with the motion of the crowd. Her motion. Her body was lithe and her blue eyes were hopeful. She was looking for something tonight. He was pretty sure he knew what that was, and he was looking for something, too. He wasn't sure it was her, but he could have done a lot worse. He could be stuck in that prison of a cabin in the middle of nowhere. Maybe he'd see what she had in mind.

He felt a hand slip into his non-drink-holding hand. He turned and instantly smiled. That's what he'd been waiting for. She tugged at his arm, and he followed awkwardly, squeezing his way through the human wall. A quick step, a pause, and a side step. In an unbalanced moment, what remained of his drink splashed across a guy's lighted, naked chest. The green flashing lights looked like they might be embedded in the flesh, but the chest was in a constant swaying dance motion, and he couldn't say for sure. The dancer yelled in surprise, but shut up quickly as his partner, also naked to the waist in similar lighted decor, improvised a bending move to lick up what was left of the spill. He wondered if they might conduct their waking lives in dance moves. They looked practiced and continued on as if nothing had happened. His fascinated eyes watched the pair as his arm again was pulled away. The pair were obscured by other dancers and swallowed by the crowd as he stumbled backward and caught up with himself. And her. He moved as delicately as he could without either plowing into dancers or losing the grip of the slim fingers he held onto. Tightly, but not too tightly. She pulled him to the edge of the crowd and up against the safety railing that served as the border between rooftop dancing humans and the hundreds of feet of empty space between them and the water streets 70 floors below. The aroma of Seattle was an odd mix of industry and ocean, and a waft of city air from below blew up into their faces, dissipating the damp atmosphere of smoke and sweat and perfume that engulfed them and the rooftop rave.

He still couldn't believe his luck. He'd been thinking about Kel at the races after his respectable mid-race change-out, but after the race, she'd disappeared with her friends and well-wishers. At just the right time, this perfect girl had shown up, and they'd made an instant connection. She was excited and sweating, and she was kissing him. Again. He closed his eyes and reveled. Yes. Maybe it was time to get out on his own. He had plenty of skills. He could get used to a life like this. Maybe dancing your life away might be something he could get good at. Develop some moves. He opened his eyes to take another look at her. Just to make sure he wasn't fooling himself. Over her shoulder in the distance, the twin Space Needles of the Seattle's Spaceport glowed in the developing mist. He raised his head, communing with the darkness above, and the night's mist cooled his face. He started his own slow, twirling dance move, losing himself in the music. His head up, he moved away from the rail and back toward the crowd. Life in the big city was good.

And then it wasn't.

"Well, well, well. Who do we have here?"

Durt didn't recognize the face, but he did recognize the intent. He'd been kissed, hugged, and shaken hands with a lot of folks he didn't know. Fans and friends. People who hoped his new-found fame might rub off on them. But the man who stood before them wasn't one of those. His face was a sneer, and his tone was a dare. "If it isn't the famous hick from the sticks."

Durt turned to look at the girl, just to check if she was in peril, too. But she was gone.

His new friend who stood before him now wasn't bigger than he was, in spite of his bravado, but there were four additional reasons Durt took as the cause of his attitude. Two of those reasons now stood on either side of him, and he didn't have to see the third to know it stood behind him. The fourth reason was as clear as a sunny Alaskan day in June. His right fist was adorned with something metallic. Durt had come here to dance and to celebrate, but it was clear they had a different dance in mind. One on his face.

His metal-knuckled tormentor leaned in to be understood over the noise. Durt wasn't sure what he'd eaten, but his breath was close enough to smell its foul odor. "Word of advice, Larson? Go back to Alaska. It's a lot safer."

To Durt, it seemed that line was likely their cue. Three would restrain, and this one would deliver the metallic message to his face. Problem was, the noise level was high enough so they had to rely on visual instead of audible cues. Their other problem had nothing to do with their environment, but their preparation. They hadn't done any. They weren't practiced martial artists. They were pretenders. Thugs. To his right, hands were still in their pockets. To his left, a cigarette dangled from a pair fingers with a gaze that was paying attention to something it shouldn't have. He couldn't see behind him, but he'd already judged his aggressors. Their prey was supposed to surrender and take the beating. While he hadn't done well against a surprised bear on his porch, he wasn't raising his hands in surrender to anyone. Now he was the bear. If he had anything to say about it, they'd be a lot more surprised than him.

When it came, the swing was quick, Durt had to give him credit for that. But as predicted, the thugs were more surprised than he was. He'd already envisioned the swing and his counter move. He ducked down and to the right, the metal knuckles flashing by his cheek. In the same instant, he raised his left hand and caught the just-missed wrist. When he stood up, his right palm smashed into the elbow, and he heard two sounds above the crowd, first a sickening crack of the bone, followed instantaneously by a shrill scream of surprise and pain. His brass-knuckle bravado dissolved into a whimper as he fell helpless away from Durt, his face a portrait of disbelief.

The guy's crew was almost as surprised as he was. Their role here, Durt figured, was not as attackers, but as restrainers. They would hold. He would beat. Faced now with a script change, they moved toward him but paused momentarily on either side of him, uncertain now what the next move should be. Clearly, they hadn't rehearsed this scenario.

Durt didn't even need to turn to understand the third was moving at speed for a restraining bear hug from behind. He read it in their eyes. Before the fourth had even hit the floor, Durt was already in a downward motion again, this time to his knee. It was the combined velocity of the rear assailant's lunge and his next upward thrust that connected the tip of his elbow with the solar plexus behind him. He heard the satisfying sound of air woof out behind him, and as he twisted to face his bent-over attacker, he brought a quick knee to the face that made a cracking sound. It was the nose, he presumed, as the third reason stumbled backward and to the roof's pavement floor on his back, blood already beginning to color his face.

Four on one had been pretty good odds for the crew. Two on

one, however, especially after that display, no longer seemed like such a sure thing, and the remaining two quickly disappeared into the crowd. He watched them scamper away, then turned to deal with the instigator. But he was gone, too.

Durt nodded with a smile and looked at the sky, feeling once again the cool mist and trying to clear his head. In the distance, the twin space needles stood where they had before, but in his mind now, something had changed. The girl he'd been so enamored with a minute before had disappeared, too, and he realized to his disappointment that she was probably a part of the ruse as well.

He'd been duped into this. He hadn't taken the beating as they intended, so he certainly wasn't taking any advice he got from this lot. He also wondered what would come next. But he didn't wonder for long. The hands that grasped his from behind weren't hesitant. They were sure, and they were practiced. When they spun him around, he already knew who he'd have to face. Yes, there would be some explaining to do. And it wouldn't be anyone from TransComm. This time it was going to be the SPD. The Seattle Police.

[11]
ROSE

Liz was smart. Tuck wasn't quite sure what she did and didn't know, but somehow she'd divined his escape strategy. By this time of the evening, the standard ME activity in the vehicle garage had ceased for the day. He made a quick visual inventory as they approached. No empty spaces. None out on emergency calls. The vehicles were lined up perfectly, eight white executive sedans side-by-side and two medical transport trucks—at least one of which he'd seen earlier that day.

Liz went directly to the truck on the end, sliding up its rear hatch and motioning him inside. She said nothing as she closed it behind him.

A normal person might have been hesitant to stretch out on the hover gurney, usually reserved for the dead. Truthfully, he told himself, on a normal day he would likely be hesitant, too. But today had been no normal day, and it wasn't over yet. He stretched his legs out in relative comfort, hoping in the back of his mind that this ride wouldn't be a premonition of his actual demise.

An odd stench floated through the truck's enclosed compartment. It wasn't of rotting flesh as he'd always imagined it would be, even though he knew that was ridiculous with today's technology. There was always a part of his imagination that allowed childish presuppositions until they were put to rest with an actual face-to-face experience.

The insides of the truck were lined with shelves filled with various tools and devices, few of which he was familiar with, and few, judging by their look, that ever saw much action. Their collective composite construction smelled a lot less like death and a lot more like new manufacturing, an ever-present smell in a developing city. In here, though, that smell meant trouble, and that's just where his thoughts lay. Trouble had come knocking today, and he had answered willingly.

What now, he asked himself, would be his next move? His timing was somewhat critical but certainly doable. He'd carried with him his virtual programmed escape hatch for some time now. It was a classic feint and dodge. His multiple virtual appearances were the feints. Throw in the proprietary agency rights of the Copernicus surveillance agreements, which meant that certain locations were off-limits to partner agencies, and he had his dodge. TransComm protected its trade secrets; LUNASEC protected its ongoing investigations; and the ME shielded its death inquiries. They'd be searching for his personal tracker by now, but inside this truck, the only screens that would reveal his actual presence would be in the ME Kick. For TransComm and LUNASEC, as long as he stayed in here, he remained invisible.

He hadn't developed his plan because he'd sensed any trouble. It was just that anyone in law enforcement developed a sense and a need for contingency plans and backdoors. The smart ones, anyway. It was a part of his profession and a part of his nature. Like a fire in a building. You might go in, but you never went into anything blind. You always had a Plan B; an alternate strategy.

He did have a way out, but then what? Still too soon to tell, he told himself. Need more information. But you couldn't get more information if you were in a jail cell, or worse, maybe dead in the back of an ME truck. He smiled incidentally at the irony and reminded himself not to get too far ahead of himself. He needed to be present in the present, not day-dreaming of some future contingency.

He took a deep breath and focused on the hum of the truck. It wasn't an uncomfortable ride. Not that a corpse would complain, of course. He felt the slight incline of their descent and instinctively grabbed the rails on either side of his temporary corpse couch. But the landing was smooth and when the ME truck touched down, it seemed too soon. He sat up and got to his feet.

Within a moment, Liz opened the rear hatch, her face still pressed with concern. "Are you sure you know what you're doing?"

Her voice was a whisper. She stood before him, not yielding until she no longer had a choice. She'd guessed some of what his escape plan was made of but apparently hadn't put it all together. While it might not make a difference, were she accused and grilled for what she knew, her truthful responses to the random pieces she had figured out might help protect her. He hoped with all his soul that it wouldn't come to that. He had some level of confidence it wouldn't. This was Copernicus, after all.

He smiled at her, beaming what little confidence he did have, "For both our sakes, I hope so."

"Can't you tell me what's going on?"

"I think you've figured out what I'm doing. I've told you what I know. More than that at this point is just supposition. And," he looked at her worried face more closely, "I want to involve you as little as possible."

He stepped closer to her, and she gave him a little more room to exit the truck. "What I do know is that in a few minutes, this place is going to be crawling with LUNASEC folks, and when that happens, I don't want to be here. Make sense?"

She nodded but said nothing.

"I'll be right back," he whispered into her ear. "Trust me. You won't be disappointed."

Favors went a long way around here, he thought, and he'd done a lot of them. Today was not a day for doing favors, though, but for collecting one. He was back within a couple of minutes, and her expression told him that he was right on the money. He gave her the single rose, and it took her breath away. She was mesmerized. Embarrassed almost. A single emerald rose in all its finery and delicacy. It sparkled—its transparency reflecting the city lights from the edge of Newton.

"Tuck, I can't—"

He put his finger to her lips, silencing her protest and pressing into her. "Take it. My gift to you."

It was a beautifully handcrafted specimen, a unique sculpture formed from the dust of some lunar mining effort. She was right. It was exquisite. And expensive. She couldn't take her eyes off of it.

"We should go."

She looked him directly in the eye, a new, wondrous expression on her face. "Where do you need me to take you?"

"The Boer recycler."

"My God. You're serious."

"It's the only way."

"You'll never make it out there."

"Pretty much also what I'm in for here if we don't get moving. Just back me up to the exit gate. I'll take it from there."

She closed her eyes for a moment, then nodded as if envisioning the trip in her mind.

"Thank you," she said, pressing the rose to her chest, to his surprise, kissing him in the same instant. He realized suddenly that he had no idea if maybe she wasn't in the same kind of trouble he was in. Maybe worse. That would certainly explain why she, Elizabeth Day, the ME, was so willing to help. She looked him directly in the eye, and he saw yearning. Her grey eyes bordered on the edge of blue, and through her veil of worry, he saw something more. A glimmer of faith, maybe. "I just hope you know what you're doing," she said. "If anyone can do it, it's you."

He nodded in thanks as she pushed him back through the hatch. He hoped she was right.

By the time he found his spot on the gurney, they were already airborne.

* * *

The Crow held his breath. It was Tuck. There he was again. Was it another ruse, he wondered, or had Tuck's luck just run out?

Logically, it made sense. In spite of the ghost appearances all over the city, Tuck's initial direction was southbound. Now, in fact, this second appearance, the second of what might possibly be another round of random appearances, made a direct logical line south. The edge of Newton. Which, for all practical purposes, he thought, was where someone might go to disappear.

He'd already advised LUNASEC and dispatched and recalled TransComm's own security team for the initial appearance. Now he waited hesitantly for the system either to resolve this one as a phantom or to confirm that it was actually him.

One hand hovered over the console at the ready to initiate the command. The other drummed an impatient rhythm on the side of his seat. "Stay or go, Tuck," he chanted to himself. No one else was around to hear him, and he couldn't pull the trigger until he was sure one way or another. "Stay or go. Is it you, or isn't it? Just another ghost?"

He leaned toward the screen's blinking location on the blue-lined map before him. "Wait a minute." He knew this place. He'd been there before, and he closed his eyes, remembering. At once it came to him. He slammed his hand into the console.

"Dispatch. Central. Tango south. Komarov Corner."

The response was not what he expected and not what should have happened, according to TransComm protocol. What should have happened was a security team acknowledgement and a security vehicle dispatch without delay. That was just taking care of business. Apparently, they'd seen the same ghosts he'd seen and presumed this was just another one.

"Central. Dispatch. Really, Dispatch?" The tone was not one of action as it should have been, but one of skepticism.

What they hadn't figured out and probably would never figure out was who this guy was, and why he was running. They'd already been dispatched and recalled and were probably getting a good laugh at the escape hack Tuck had just performed. He himself didn't know the answer to the second question, but he knew that Tuck knew the system and was having great luck in evading capture. What he'd just realized was that, were he in Tuck's shoes and wanted to evade and disappear, that's exactly where he would go, too.

It was illegal as hell, but if he was going to disappear, the first move he'd make would be to get that tracker cut out of him. Komarov Corner had a number of services, but in his world, Komarov Corner was famous for one thing in particular. Tattoos. And not just tattoos, but quickie facelifts. They were cheap and temporary, but popular, especially with middle-aged women trying to show they weren't, and with older women trying to show they were. What they did have there were precision surgical tools. Just what you might need to cut a personal tracker out of you. Plus location, he reminded himself. It was near Newton where you could buy pretty much any service or favor you could dream up.

"Yes, really!" he shouted. "Move it."

The lifeless monotone response returned. "Roger, Central."

Then another realization crossed his mind. It wasn't just the edge of Newton that made it the perfect position. It was only a few minutes from the spaceport. If he were returning to Earth or heading out of the system, that would be the perfect way to disappear. Virtually impossible to find without the implanted tracker.

Before him, the system reflected dispatch's compliance with his order. Three cars moved south, and information about each driver reflected on the screen. Their movement wasn't lackadaisical like the initial response. No, they moved quickly. As quickly as their vehicles allowed. But already he realized that it didn't matter. No matter how quickly they moved toward the signal from that personal tracker, he knew they wouldn't be in time. No, he told himself, with the realization now that it wasn't just any personal tracker, but Tuck's personal tracker and anyone who has the genius ability to program an escape plan within the system itself wouldn't be caught on such a simpleton oversight like this. No, he decided, this, too, had to be part of the plan.

The screen confirmed his suspicions shortly. Three-quarters of the way to Komarov Corner and the personal tracker winked out. Suddenly blank. No signal. He could picture the small delicate instrument's removal and destruction. Probably on the floor. No, Tuck knew exactly how fast the cruisers could go and how much time he'd have before being accosted and arrested. He was one step ahead.

He watched as the three vehicles slowed, then banked for the return. He didn't have to say anything to dispatch. They'd been ghosted twice. He doubted if they'd make a third run, even if he demanded it.

But he wasn't done yet. Now that he had an exact location, he could roll back the security cams to that time and location and see what Tuck was actually up to. Left to itself, the system would consider him disappeared. It was a machine. It didn't care if that wasn't really possible. But he did care, he thought, as he manipulated the view in front of him.

"The beauty of redundant systems," he said aloud to himself. When no one else was around, he liked to have conversations with himself. He was quite talented at berating himself when he screwed up but now wasn't that time. His self-congratulations spurred his mood as he zeroed in on Komarov Corner.

"There we are, location-wise. Now, let's roll back the time."

His finger commands obeyed his voice, "Not too much," he continued.

What he saw surprised and disappointed him. He was going

to have a story to tell, but it wouldn't be the one he wanted. No, this one was going to be Tuck's story. It was a story of an escape plan well executed. Tuck had thought this one through. Were it not for the fact that now he had to make a phone call; confirm he'd officially lost his prey; and that Tuck was now in the wind, he'd have stood up and applauded. As it stood, though, he didn't feel much like it. On the screens before him, the surveillance cameras for the local service area at Komarov Corner were sending him a field of flashing red messages. All of them he'd counted on to tell him the rest of the story were disabled.

"Impressive, Tuck," he said quietly to no one but himself. "Impressive."

* * *

As he expected, the gate was silent and abandoned this late. And it wasn't actually at the Boer recycler, but that was its nearest landmark. Tuck caught a glimpse of the dimly lit reactor hulk in his peripheral vision as he leaped from the truck's hatch and into the opening of the gate, the outer receptacle of the gate's environmental barrier.

For inhabitants of Copernicus, this was the edge of the universe. The gate to the unfinished outer world. Here were areas of the lunar settlement planned for construction and expansion. It had its own protective field, its atmosphere separate and distinct from that of the city. It had construction equipment bots and the essential service mechanics and technicians. What it didn't have was surveillance.

No one was there to greet him. No security. No guards. None were needed. With two exceptions—the races and the construction companies—nobody ever wanted to go beyond the dome. Nothing out here but sand and rock.

Red safety lights lit the interior of the gate as if to warn him of the danger he was about to put himself in. He pressed his palm against the control switch and felt a sudden pang of loneliness as he watched the descending airlock gate block out the lights of the Copernicus' night. He took a deep breath and imagined himself again sitting face-to-face with Liz as he watched the ME truck lift off. His disappearing act had worked as planned, but he didn't feel much like celebrating. He felt exhausted. The fear and excitement of the escape now drained out of him, he was left with a world of uncertainty ahead. Sure, he'd escaped the grasp of imprisonment or worse. And for what? For using his brain?

A surge of anger jolted his mind back into action as the gate to the outside raised before him and threw a new spectrum of light into the gate's tunnel. He walked out of the gate and into the void. Outside, the moonscape was devoid of any movement or human presence. The landscape was a stark black and white and bore no correlation whatsoever to the dome's artificially controlled day and night cycle that reflected life on Earth. Above him, the actual stars, not the fake rendered ones displayed by Copernicus's protective field, winked their bleak greeting.

He squinted as the bright lunar light reflected off the sandy surface before him and silhouetted an uneven horizon of construction projects in progress in the distance. He wondered ultimately if the entire surface of the Moon might one day be covered. One giant Moon city. He reasoned it was probably technically possible, but it would require a huge growth in Earth's demand for manufacturing to make it financially possible. Right now, demand was pretty stable with slow sustained growth.

To his left, traces of the racers who passed through here on a regular basis were evident. To his right, surface displacement was evident, too, but less so. The construction techs were few in number, both in people and vehicles. He turned in a complete circle as he walked to gauge his bearings, and a brisk pace brought him to a good-sized pair of familiar rocks that served both as a windbreak and as a marker for his cache. As undisturbed as when he'd left it, he uncovered a composite storage container beneath a few inches of lunar sand within a few minutes. He palmed the lock and pulled out the coat and go-bag that would sustain him out here for ten days.

He hefted the pack and surveyed the final leg of his plan. Between the horizon and where he stood now, he made out a haphazard group of buildings. They didn't seem to be organized in any logical fashion. It was more like they were dumped in a pile and abandoned to be made use of later. He presumed these were the temporary living quarters for the construction crews, and what he had hoped might serve as a temporary refuge. With no construction in progress now, he figured they'd be empty but should have a water supply. He left the remaining water containers inside his cache box, then re-covered it. He might have to come back for them, but he hoped not.

His destination wasn't too far off, and Tuck judged the distance a 20-minute walk. Moon rocks crunched under his feet as he set off in that direction. The environment, while sealed, had yet to have its ambient temperature control units installed. It did pick up a good deal of radiant heat from the city dome, but he could feel the temperature drop as he began to put some distance between himself and the gate. He shivered and pulled the light coat tighter around himself. Next time, he decided, he'd stash a heavier one. For now, he'd count on his quick pace to stave off the deepening lunar chill.

Life here was different. Not just different because of the environment. The opportunity here attracted a different breed of lunar employee. Work here was a high-wage proposition, but that was a direct result of its higher risk. The government kept its hands off employee management here beyond the dome. It had a contract with the construction company that ensured its schedules were met. That was the city's primary concern. All others were overlooked.

Sure, of course, it was corrupt. No one would ever argue that point, he told himself. But it had been corrupted for so long that there were no alternate expectations. Out here, you bought a position with your future earnings. It was possible to pay off the buy-in within a year or so, but few had enough discipline to do so.

Bets on the races out here and their other games of chance made most of them little more than life-long indentured servants. He was certain each of them bemoaned this status on a regular basis, but it was no secret that a buy-in was usually for life, and that endless circle of routine that began with work, touched drinking and gambling and finished with work again was the routine that expanded the human existence on the Moon. A few got rich. Most slaved away at the expansion effort. Some died. But some always died. With Earth's life-extending medical progress and risk engineered out of most every facet of life, there was a good level of attraction to places like this. There was always a sense of purpose and danger here. You didn't find good money and a lifestyle like this in too many places. It made for a tight-knit group. If you weren't one of them, they knew it immediately. They could be befriended, but they weren't for sale, and they wouldn't be intimidated by anyone.

As he got closer to the building complex, a flash of color at the base of the buildings began to emerge from the monochrome scene before him. Cars, he thought. These were the cars they raced on the weekends after they'd finished their construction progress for the week. Looked like the place wasn't empty.

When he could, he liked to come out on the weekends and watch the races. He didn't gamble like the rest, as that really wasn't in his nature, but he was fascinated with the ingenuity of the pit crews who regularly outdid one another with hardware and software tweaks to their racers—not to mention their cross-team sabotage.

He'd made a few friends and shared a few laughs, but it had been a while since he'd been here. He hoped those laughs might translate into something more. In fact, he was banking on it. This was a different world. The Earth-like illusions that he'd grown used to in his daily routines lay shattered now with the reality of what lay just beneath the veneer of technology in which they lived, worked and sometimes died.

But dying was not in his plan today. He made his way past a pair of cars parked randomly at the base of the buildings, one a brilliant orange, the other a charcoal black that matched the sky above. While the vehicles were situated at what seemed to be the front of the complex, its entrance was not. He made his way between two perpendicular buildings that, side-by-side, created a shadow-filled walkway toward what he took to be the place's actual entrance. It was a porch. Littered with boots, tools and the discarded wrappers of food and drink, its appearance matched the lackadaisical feeling of the structure itself. Apparently, their cleaning service hadn't been through this week. Or ever, for that matter.

Tuck walked up the porch's four steps, set his pack down and knocked on the door. As he did, he sensed a part of the shadow detach itself and move up behind him. A cold blade nudged the side of his neck.

[12]
JAIL

THE CELL in city lockup was as clean as Durt expected a jail cell might look, with a bed, a toilet, a table and two chairs. No door, of course. Some things were different down here in the city. Bars still kept what detainees there were in Alaska. This jail was more high-tech. Some type of a selective force field allowed everyone access, but only those authorized by the system could leave. Guards. Security. Lawyers. Those, he figured, who might occupy the second seat in the cell.

He'd glimpsed other prisoners in the block as he'd come in, and he could hear them moving about now and again. The smell of cigarettes and vomit and urine floated in the air, even though each cell had its own private toilet. Apparently, alcohol indulgence and overindulgence were as common here as in Alaska. Not everything was different. Not even in the big city.

Durt's mind was full of second thoughts. He sat, then stretched out on the bed. Its surface was hard and smooth, and he couldn't imagine sleeping here for any extended period of time. Well, he thought, what now? He might call someone to get him out of here, but who would he call? He couldn't call Alaska. No one was coming down here to spring him. Certainly not after he turned his back on them in favor or his own personal pursuits.

He'd stepped into something a lot bigger than himself here. Right into the middle of it. He kicked himself. Why on Earth had he thought that flying the race would be a good idea? He was certain that's what the scuffle was all about. Hired hands to scare him off. He wasn't scared of hired hands. His concern was police.

One or two he could have taken care of himself, he thought, but four or five? Hardly. It was going to be their five words against his one. A rave on a rooftop? He doubted if security footage actually existed. And even if it did, it would show him taking a couple of shots. He'd hit first, which surprised the rooftop thug. The second one, too. But the third and forth had plenty of time to escape. He'd looked for help, but apparently, the thugs were well enough known that no one was willing to cross them with a statement to the Police. At least that's what he'd discerned from the police questions and the subsequent discussions he'd overheard on his way here. He'd listened and kept his mouth shut.

It was as if he were invisible. The rest of the crowd had turned their backs on him. They were at a party. They didn't want to be involved. As much as the attack disappointed him, and as desperate as he was for a friend, he knew he couldn't argue with the collective crowd decision to not be involved. And his pretty and faithful escort? She'd disappeared, too. Nowhere to be seen.

He got it. He was on his own. Out of his element. He'd lucked into his fame and that had been yesterday, but it sure as hell wasn't helping today.

His wrists were sore from his restraints, and his arrest processing left him now, he realized, exhausted. Alone with his thoughts and the scent of disgust he'd rather forget, he lay back on the bed and gazed at the seamless white ceiling overhead. He closed his eyes, trying to plot his next step. Some legend he was, he thought. A day in Seattle, and he'd already been arrested.

He must have dozed off. His mouth was a desert, and the hard bed was no comfort. He added a now-aching back to his inventory of ills. After a few moments of self-assessment, he realized he wasn't alone in the cell. His peripheral vision caught the form of someone seated at the table.

"Attorney?" he asked, without much enthusiasm, still gazing at the ceiling.

"Attorney? Sure. I'm your attorney."

He stretched and sat up, a painful effort that left him squinting, his muscles complaining in discomfort. As he focused on his attorney-to-be, a glimmer of recognition flashed in his mind. He stood up and walked stiffly to the empty chair, but as he did, his mind processed that glimmer and a shiver of guilt and fear ran through him. It wasn't his attorney. It wasn't anyone's attorney. It was the man Rush had warned him to stay away from. Simms. The guy without the hand. He hesitated in mid-step as the recognition came back to him.

Simms smiled, but it wasn't a pleasant smile.

He had no idea how to explain the misunderstanding that had separated this man from his hand, so he just started. to "Look, I am so sorry. I had no idea that..."

Simms raised a hand and silenced his attempt at an apology. But it wasn't a hand. It was a temporary claw, affixed to the stump where his hand had once been.

"No need for an apology. I know what you were trying to do."

Durt let out a sigh of relief. Maybe Rush was wrong. Maybe Simms was a reasonable guy.

But the next sentence upheld Rush's warning. "But that doesn't help me in the least. I'm missing a part of myself. And you took it from me. You understand I can't just let that be."

Truthfully, Durt couldn't see why not and was about to say so when he noticed the knife on the table between them. It wasn't just any knife. It looked like the same knife that he'd used to try to cut off the bear's head. He sat down and stared at it. But something else was off, too.

"Funny thing about the security system today," Simms said. "Some kind of maintenance issue. Not to worry. It'll be back in operation shortly."

This, he thought, was what Rush was talking about. Like some kind of news update from the psycho ward. He suddenly realized what it was about the environment that tickled at his still half-asleep brain. The sounds of the other prisoners moving about. There weren't any. Nothing but silence now. He craned his neck to see if he could see someone else and realized they must have evacuated the entire cell block while he'd slept. Who was this guy, anyway?

He swallowed hard as it dawned on him what was about to happen. He tried to swallow his fear. "Jesus, Simms. You can't cut me."

Simms smiled again. This time it was more a smile of actual amusement. "Oh, I'm not going to cut you."

He stood up and walked half-way around the table, patting Durt on the back. "No, I have plans for you. I think you're exactly the person I'm looking for. But first, before we talk plans, you need to learn something about me. You did save my life. I admit that, so I owe you a debt of gratitude, but as I said before, you took something from me also, so that, in my mind, needs to be put back into balance. They will wonder, though, how you were able to sneak a knife into your cell here, especially a knife like this."

Durt watched as Simms picked up the knife and turned it over. In Alaska, the huge knife had a multitude of uses, although cutting off the head of a protected species was not one of them. Here in jail though, none of those uses seemed practical, and the implication of what the word balance meant to Simms was uncertain.

"No, Larson. I'm not going to cut your hand off. If that's what your creative mind was thinking. No, you're going to do it all by yourself."

Again, the words made the intent no clearer than before. But then it happened. As if his hand had taken on a mind of its own, Durt reached out and picked up the knife, himself. He looked Simms straight in the eye with disbelief. Simms' smile was now broad. Durt felt his left hand slammed onto the table, and his right, wielding the knife, moving toward it. It was beyond his control. Something was forcing his hands and arms to move. He strained against them, but it was no use. He was powerless. He watched in horror as he placed the knife on his own left wrist and began to apply pressure.

Simms was laughing now. And the laugh seemed to release the control Durt felt on his hands and arms. But just as quickly it was back, and he watched as the tip of the knife moved toward his face, then the corner of his right eye. "Maybe not a hand." Simms was having a discussion with himself now. "Maybe an eye would be better."

Durt strained against the control, but it was no use. He could feel the sharp tip dig into the top of his cheek, and a trickle of blood ran down its side. "No. No!" he began to shout, disbelieving what was happening. Was he going to take out his own eye?

Then Simms relented, apparently deciding against the eye, and opting for a deep gash across the cheek instead. Now dripping with blood, Durt watched himself replace the bloodied knife back in the center of the table. He still had no motion control. He was paralyzed. Frozen stiff.

He watched Simms stand up, his smile gone. Placing a hand on his shoulder again, Durt listened as the voice whispered in his ear. "We're not done, Larson. Not by a long shot. Just having some fun now. But don't think this makes us even. I've got more in store for you. Plenty, in fact. Be seeing you real soon."

Then he was gone. In an instant, Durt's strength returned, and he clapped his hand over his face, stemming his blood as it dripped onto the table in front of him.

* * *

The blood flow abated after a few minutes.

But what to do now?

He couldn't call anybody, he thought to himself. He didn't

have anybody to call. In the woods, even after he'd been mauled by a surprised bear, he'd had the ability to drag himself back to safety and rescue himself. This was a different world. In jail. He couldn't ask anyone back home for help, although they'd be happy to give it. They'd welcome him back after only a few days in the real world. Ha, he thought again. Some legend.

No, that was not going to happen. He wouldn't call anyone. This wasn't his world. No, it was something beyond his expectations. He'd battled the coldest and strongest Alaska could throw at him, and it hadn't phased him. It made him stronger and smarter. But not here. The city monsters were far worse than any monsters he'd faced down in the north.

He was as sick of himself today as he'd been full of himself yesterday at the race.

Maybe Dad was right. Maybe Alaska is my destiny.

But that was bullshit, too. If he was going to be a man, he was going to have to put all this baby crap behind him, he thought, So he got cut. So what? He got cut all the time. What happens after a bear mauls you? You kill him or you stay away from him. Either would be considered a wise play. The worst part was, he had no idea who he was up against. He didn't know the rules of the game. He was out of his element in the city, so he had two choices. Leave or learn.

Right now, neither seemed like much of a choice. But when Rush entered the cell a few minutes later, he'd made up his mind.

"Look…sir," he told Rush. "I'm afraid I made a mistake coming down here." He closed his eyes and plowed ahead. "The more I think about it, the more I think I'm not cut out for this environment. I had some big dreams, but I just don't think I have the stomach to become the cutthroat I need to be to survive here in the city."

Rush's face, as always, was curious. Impassive.

"I think my father was right," Durt continued. "And you know it hurts me to say that. I thought I felt something else inside of me. You know, some destiny I was meant for, but I'm in the city one day. Just one, and already I'm on the wrong side of the law. I've never set foot inside a jail cell as a prisoner, and I never want to again."

He shook his head, his self-disgust boiling over. "And if that makes me a hick, then I guess that's just who I am. I'm just sorry I couldn't have been a better guest while I was here, so I apologize for that. I guess I'll get back to doing what I'm used to. The thing I'm good at."

This time, Rush raised his hands. "Hang on, Durt. Not so fast."

He pulled up the other chair and sat down across the table. "If that's what you really want, I won't stand in your way. It's really up to you. But you're wrong. You do have something special." Then he smiled. "Aside from saving my life, of course."

Durt said nothing but returned a bit of the smile.

"Here's the reality of the situation as we sit here today," said Rush. "First we didn't win the race yesterday. But I didn't really expect to. But thanks to your flying skills and your willingness to put yourself out there like you did—that and your new-found fame on the Net—we doubled our viewership overnight with your beginner's run. Not bad for your first time out, by the way. I trust you enjoyed our toys."

Durt's smile did broaden at the memory, but he checked it as the pain from his cheek flared. He wasn't quite sure where Rush was going with this.

"Second, you know you weren't allowed to fly yesterday until you became part of the company. When we were sitting across the table from one another in Alaska, I asked you if you wanted a job. Yesterday, you signed on to fly. Today, you want to go home? If you took the time to read the terms of the contract—"

Durt shut his eyes and he shook his head as he realized he had no idea what he'd signed himself up for. Nobody read those terms. Except, of course, those folks who had written them and those, after the fact, those trying to get out of them.

"You signed on to fly," he continued. "Not as a full-time racer, but as a full-time transport pilot. You're scheduled to fly a load to the Moon at the end of the month. So, I'm betting you'll want to get back to your hotel, pronto; get your things squared away and get your transport quals completed. I'll leave it to you to find our training facility in Kennewick. I wouldn't want you to miss your first delivery to the Moon."

This time, Durt couldn't keep his mouth shut. But he didn't know what to say either. He'd forgotten all about the contract. Indecision paralyzed him.

"I…ah—" was all he could get out.

Rush seemed to understand his conflict, and he watched Rush stroke his beard with mild amusement. "At the same time, I do owe you a substantial debt, so if you are hard over on heading back north again, I'll make sure you won't be bound by the terms of the contract. You tell me."

He stared across the cell's table at Rush. In spite of his self-doubt, Rush was right. He was under contract, and in fact, it was a contract he'd dreamed of. Things had gotten a bit messy last night, but that was his own fault. It was too many things at once. In its own way, the city seemed just as unforgiving as the Alaskan wilderness. Maybe he just needed a little more experience. And that, he thought, was what Rush was really offering him.

Rush was now looking down at the table and seemed to see for the first time the blood, still wet on its surface. "Oh, one more thing. Sucker punching an innocent bystander didn't sound like your style, so I asked the investigating officer to look a little deeper. The rooftop cameras from last night had been disabled, but she was able to track down a couple of eyewitnesses who told a different story than the one that landed you here.

"So, I'm free to go?"

"You are. She should be here any time now to make it official."

Rush stood up, but just as quickly bent over. When he stood again, his expression had changed from a calm confidence to one of surprise. He'd retrieved the knife from the floor. He inspected it slowly. "You know," he said in a slow, measured tone, examining Simms' knife as if he were rediscovering something familiar to him. "And I've probably said this before. There are some people—even some people in our company—that you just want to stay away from."

He looked up at Durt. "You know what I'm talking about, right?"

He nodded. The burning in his cheek was a grim reminder. He knew exactly what he was talking about. He considered for a moment recounting to Rush the story of Simms' visit. But then he thought better of it. This was not a conflict between Rush and Simms, and there was no reason to bring Rush into this. No, this was something he could take care of himself. He thought about it for a minute. If he could survive an angry North Pacific storm and a mauling by a bear, he could certainly handle a vindictive little son-of-a-bitch like Simms. He'd just have to stop underestimating him.

Rush pocketed the knife and turned to leave, "You've got a pretty tight schedule, Durt, so I'll leave you to it. Look me up when you get back."

Durt couldn't tell if he was serious or if that was just his nonchalant farewell. What he did know was that he would have been wasting his breath on a story about Simms. He was certain Rush already knew.

[13]

OUTSIDE

THE BLADE WAS cold and hard. It made him shiver as it touched his neck. But it wasn't there for long. Tuck dropped and spun, knocking the shadow fighter off the elevated porch and back into the shadows on the other side.

Tuck back-flipped off the porch he'd just climbed, folding quickly into a fighting stance, ready for a hand-to-hand battle with whomever or whatever had come up behind him. At first he heard nothing. He shifted his head slightly to make a full survey of the scene before him. He had neither familiarity with the structure nor an unobstructed view to anticipate much of anything. Nothing moved. He watched in silence.

When he did hear something, he was surprised. In hand-to-hand combat, surprises can be fatal. What he heard, however, was not. It was a clang and a groan. The blade-wielder, apparently, had been knocked out in the fall, temporarily anyway, and had found something with his head, something metallic and unforgiving, as he regained consciousness. The next sound he heard was also surprising. Laughter. Muffled at first. But then louder and with more clarity. A female voice.

Confused but alert, Tuck felt the coldness of the lunar landscape seep into his bones as the adrenaline-induced sweat now evaporated and dampened the inside of his jacket. Behind, on the other side of the un-railed porch he'd just jumped from, he watched a face appear. It wasn't a happy face. In fact, it looked as if it were about to cry.

A sudden flash of light illuminated the porch area as the door opened. The harsh security light cast its broad beam across his attacker's face, resolving it into clear focus and making them both squint. The man brought up his arm to shield his eyes, and Tuck watched a laughing, athletic female emerge from the interior of the structure. Her curly dark hair sat close on her skull. She indeed was the source of the laughter.

"Whoa, it's freezing out here," she said, wrapping her arms around herself, a laugh still on her breath. She looked down at the dwelling's now broken-looking guard. "Nice work, Waldo. Looks like you really put the fear of God into this one, didn't you?"

Then, she turned to face Tuck, "And just who might you be?"

He dropped his fighting stance and gripped his now-shivering arms,"Marlin Tuck," he said, trying to keep his voice steady. "Nice to meet you."

She smirked a little. "Yes, it *is* nice to meet me, isn't it? Sorry about Waldo here."

"Walter," croaked the sentry's voice, "the name's Walter."

She ignored him and continued. "Only real fun we get around here. Sorry. Anyway, come in. I'm Trina. We've been expecting you."

He shook his head in wonder.

How could they have been expecting him?

"That's…not…possible," he said, his shivering now out of control, but he didn't hesitate at the invitation. He stepped up onto the porch again, hefted his pack, and followed the woman inside.

"Out here, anything's possible." She said as she eyed him more closely. "You must be frozen solid."

He was colder than he had anticipated, he admitted to himself, but as he stepped inside the entrance, he felt a warm blast of air.

He stood and stared. His mind found it impossible to believe what his eyes told him was true.

While the outside of the structure was decidedly industrial, a pile of what he was certain was large shipping or transport containers, the inside was a different world. The floor was paved with a smooth, reflective surface. Marble, he presumed. The walls were built of rough-hewn stone. The long narrow shape of the interior seemed to approximate the size of the exterior structure, but at its far end stood a great fireplace. He could feel its heat from where he stood. To his left, squared decorative columns supported arches spanning the hall's length, leaving a walkway between them and an exterior stone wall. A single arched window offered a view to the outside. He stared at it, transfixed. It wasn't the Moon's surface over which he'd just walked. It was a field with a mountain range visible beyond.

In the center of the hall sat a long banquet table with seating for maybe 20 guests, around which sat a group, much fewer than 20, Tuck noted, engaged in an intense discussion. Wall torches and a grand candelabra above the table cast a dim, flickering light over the group's conversation.

Here, on the outskirts of everything modern, inside a haphazard pile of industrial containers lay some of the finest fantasy rendering he'd ever seen. He was speechless.

Trina returned from the other end of the hall carrying an animal skin, a second draped over her shoulders. She motioned for him to leave his pack by the door and offered it to him. "This should help," she said, and tossed the second fur to the one she'd called Waldo. The skin had absorbed and retained some of the heat from the fire, and Tuck felt immediate relief from his bone-chilling walk.

The men and women seated around the table spoke in low tones and gave no acknowledgment of his presence if they were aware of it.

Trina took care of that. "Ladies and gentlemen, I present Marlin Tuck."

The only thing missing was an official banner and a triad of trumpeters.

The conversation went immediately silent. All stood in unison.

"LUNASEC's Tuck." It was more a statement than a question.

How many Tucks could there be, he wondered. "The same," he replied.

The table deferred to its head, a tall, older man who had called out Tuck's true identity. His skin was dark, and his beard was gray, but his brown eyes were bright. His clothing was unlike the standard lunar attire. It was loose rather than tight and looked much more like a robe than anything else. Tuck marveled at his height as he approached, his large hand extended in greeting. More than two meters tall, Tuck estimated.

"I see you have met Trina and Walter. I *am* sorry about the reception. We put him up to that. We did not believe he would actually take this wager that we had put before him."

He introduced himself as Anton. He had a unique way of talking, Tuck noted. Slow and measured.

Now Tuck smiled. "No harm intended, of course. Just reflexes."

Walter had made his way to the table and was holding his hand to his head over what Tuck was sure would be a nice bruise soon. He was grinning now. "Told you I could do it."

Anton nodded in assent. "Welcome to the outside, Marlin Tuck."

"Call me Tuck."

Anton introduced the group, and each stood and shook Tuck's hand, and while he heard the names, he was curious. "I've spent some time watching the races, but I've got to be honest with you, I don't recognize any of your faces, and this whole place here," he said, motioning to the hall with both hands, "It doesn't seem much at all like I thought it would be."

Anton turned to his colleagues around the table. "Do you hear that? That is what I call success."

Tuck was suddenly unsure of his new environment.

Who was this team, if not the racers he thought he could befriend?

"I mean, you're United Construction—UNICON, right?" he asked.

"Yes," responded Anton, "but that probably deserves clarification." He turned back to the table. "Bren, do you want to explain?"

One of the group, a petite woman with dark hair pulled into a braid in the back, waved a dismissive hand.

Anton took a deep breath and motioned to an empty chair at the table which Tuck willingly took.

"At one time, United Construction held great sway in Earth's North American construction industry. When Bren's grandfather and great-grandfather owned and operated it, it was a city-building company. Copernicus was its downfall. That lunar contract brought with it new opportunities and new directions. At a certain point, the company board of directors saw fit to shift the company focus. That meant new management. Huge capital investments here without corporate experience or structure behind them accomplished two goals." He paused before continuing and cast a sideways glance at Bren. "Neither of them positive. First, the new operation met minimum contract and subcontract standards." He shrugged as if there were worse crimes. "And second, they siphoned off huge chunks for their own personal enrichment."

That sounded more like the UNICON he knew, Tuck thought.

"They commissioned some weak programmers to move some ground around, strong-armed city inspectors to verify non-existent progress, then demanded contract officials continue progress payments. The majority of their time and effort took a new focus: racing and gambling—on company time, mind you—while their competitors expanded. The single reason this group did not fail sooner was that in its expansion phase, Copernicus had a tremendous amount of funding behind it. The money flowed and Copernicus grew."

Anton now raised a finger as he spoke, "At a certain point,

however, the next generation of Copernicus city engineers realized they were not receiving services to the level of their investments. As you well know, law enforcement has little influence out here and no legal jurisdiction. Finally, the city just gave up. At a certain point, however, it re-developed its real need for expansion, but they had no one there—no one out here—they might rely on. So they re-bid the contract."

Tuck was incredulous. "And it was awarded to UNICON, again?"

Anton held up his hands. "Patience, Tuck. Patience. Allow me to finish."

"Actually, at first the city was unable to get any company to submit a bid. The rumor held that newcomer investments would be physically taken by the incumbent." He shrugged. "I do not know if that is true or not, but it is certainly possible. Anyway, for years, no one took the bid. Then we came along."

"What made the difference?"

"We had an alternative aim in mind. Some of us wanted to restore UNICON's position as a leader in construction, even though none of us were employees. Keep in mind that we are not construction engineers, but programmers and entrepreneurs. We needed space, and we require privacy. You see what we've done with this transport container?"

He winked at Tuck. "Later, I will show you more. It is breakthrough research in molecular manipulation, and it is our concept of how we could change the world—the human race. It is not easy, but we needed an empty canvas we might use to perfect our...what should I call them? Our offerings, maybe? This contract offered the perfect opportunity. We sold everything we owned collectively and some of what we did not. We paid the majority of it to the staff for their silence and their inability, under contract, to return here. The amount for their departure turned out to be significantly less than expected." He smiled ruefully. "But we also purchased the rights to the company name, which, as it happened, was significantly greater than we anticipated. We negotiated it for Bren, and we required the privacy their previous ill behavior had guaranteed. You understand. We should have no level of expected performance."

He put his hand on Tuck's forearm. "Your comment which expressed surprise to see that you knew no one here tells us that our strategy is a success. In the opinion of The Inside, The Outside —we, in other words—are still considered a band of criminals. We actually endeavor to keep up that facade. That status is useful to us."

"What about the city officials," asked Tuck. "What's their take on this?"

Anton looked up at the group who responded with a chorus of muffled laughs. "I am not sure the city officials understand what has happened, but we have revealed our initial, revised projections and demonstrated some new capabilities. They have a much higher level of confidence in UNICON now than they ever have before. We are convinced they will leave us in peace."

Tuck had a sudden thought. Was this too convenient? Was it a setup? Had he found the exact thing they'd wanted him to find? Had he been bugged or tracked? On second thought, he decided after a moment, probably not. They wouldn't waste time. No, if this group had been with the one that had chased him, they'd have nabbed him as soon as he made contact. It was a nagging gut feeling. It was true, he thought, he was somewhat paranoid, but that paranoia had kept him in one piece. He'd trusted his instincts and was still standing.

He gazed around the great table at the group. "You don't get many visitors out here, then do you?"

"Not for a long time. Then two in as many days," said Anton.

Tuck was intrigued. Maybe they'd sent someone ahead—just in case. His guard was up. "Really? Someone from the city?"

Anton motioned to Trina. "Do us a favor and see if Clue might join us. He might relish a bit of conversation."

"Clue?" asked Tuck, "That's his name?"

"Nickname. We called him that because he has none. He knows not his own name."

Trina disappeared through a door at the other end of the room and returned in a couple minutes with Clue.

Tuck caught his breath as Trina led Clue back to the table. He knew Clue's real name. It wasn't Clue. It was Carter.

* * *

It was certainly Carter, but in his current state, it didn't even really look like him. Gone were the man's unique mannerisms that defined him and marked him as one of the few cops who Tuck assessed worthy of the title. Even though *Cop* was more a nickname than a real name, the energy and insight that went into becoming one—an officer whose duty it was to uphold the law and defend the rights of society's citizens—was significant. And there just weren't that many who, in Tuck's opinion anyway, warranted the title or position they were paid for. For reasons he knew well, within the lunar jurisdiction, that held true more than he liked to admit. And now, today anyway, there was one less cop worthy of his title.

Carter's standard winks, nods, and wrinkles of worry or concern, always a feature of his inquisitive mind, were now starkly absent, as was any recognition of himself or the environment around him. Like Tuck, Carter was wrapped in animal fur—manufactured animal fur, Tuck thought—and yes, his blank stare did match his latest nickname, Clue.

"What's happened to him?" asked Tuck with a tinge of wonder and fear in his voice.

Anton shrugged, "We are unsure. Maybe exposure. But we believe otherwise. We believe he was drugged."

"Drugged and released," said Tuck to himself under his breath. That actually made sense. If you asked LUNASEC, the official line was there were no drugs on the Moon. That was also the official line taken by the Syndicate, the city's top official, and the Copernicus business community that stood behind him, but Tuck knew better. That clean reputation helped bring new laborers, entrepreneurs and upstanding, socially responsible businesses into the community. Down on Earth, drugs had become such an integral part of the culture that a drug-free zone had become reasonably appealing. Of course, Tuck knew, it was a giant lie. The major portion of crimes and cases he took on could be traced back, directly or indirectly, to drug use and drug abuse. Even his current case had the potential for a drug-centric explanation, although, to date, he hadn't been able to come up with one. This, of course, didn't make it less plausible that eventually, it might.

"Orenz?"

Anton nodded in agreement. "That is what Trina has surmised. *A bit too much, I'm afraid.* I believe those were her words."

Tuck nodded in silence. There were other drugs, too, he knew, but if it was drugs, and it was Copernicus, it was a good bet it would turn out to be Orenz or one of its many derivatives. The wonder drug, or that's what they called it, anyway. It was a wonder to him that more of its users didn't end up like this.

Anton raised his eyebrows in a questioning glance. "What is your opinion, Tuck? Will he stay like this?"

"Hard to tell. It depends on the dosage and how the individual reacts to it. I've seen full recoveries, partials, and—like he is now—basket cases. We've just got to hope for the best. I don't think his dosage was that high. If they'd wanted him to OD, there'd be no reason for them to dump him out here."

Tuck slipped easily into his sleuth mode. "No, I think they knew exactly what they were doing. I think it was their intention for him to wander off in a stupor, become hypothermic and then just lay down and die. Out here, could be years before he was found. Add to that the fact they probably believed that UNICON wouldn't look on a badged police officer with friendly eyes, and it spells careful conspiracy, not a thug-planned murder attempt. Looks a little too careful and clever to be anything else."

Anton rubbed his chin as he thought. "So, two fellows show up here on the same day, one with his brains about him and the other without. It seems odd, does it not?"

Tuck offered a slight smile. "You have no idea how odd my last day has been."

The group at the table who, until now, had talked in low voices and whispers became suddenly silent.

Taking a deep breath and the presumed invitation to share, Tuck recounted his day, from their discovery of the headless corpse in The Kick to their separation in Newton and his subsequent escape. When he was done, the group remained silent.

"So, it is a coincidence," Tuck continued, "but not as big as you'd think. You know as well as I do about the city's four external dome gates, but three are not what you'd call common knowledge. We know about them because of the work we do. Most folks, if they know of any, only know of this one."

Anton finished his sentence for him. "Because of the races."

Tuck agreed. "Because of the races."

"You, I presume, came to find us because you believed we were—" He struggled for the right words. "The racers."

Tuck nodded in agreement as Anton reasoned. "And you are welcome to stay on as if we were the same. I am curious. According to your tale, you might have escaped and returned to Earth. Or gone on to Midway. What convinced you to stay here in spite of all that heat?"

It was a good question. It was one Tuck had asked himself a couple of times already. And he had an answer. "Look, I'm a cop. And a good one. When I discovered that LUNASEC, the organization I've dedicated my life to, has become, or is in the process of becoming, something else, I had to ask myself a question. What kind of cop would I be if I ran away? Plus, who's to say that wouldn't be exactly what they wanted?" He looked up at the group in earnest. "I tell you this. It's tough when you don't have a clue about who you can trust. The city here needs to be able to trust LUNASEC. Now they can't. But now that I know they can't,

I've become a liability." He looked over at Carter. "We've both become liabilities. And Carter here is living proof. I came here to find a refuge. Carter? Well, he didn't know it, but he came here to die."

He looked hopefully at Anton. "Anything you might be able to do for him?"

Anton gave him what he took to be a helpless look. "Sorry. Not really our area of expertise."

It was the answer Tuck expected. He nodded in understanding. "These people." He shook his head. "Whoever they are, they're good. They're very good. I just need to find a way to be better."

[14]
TRANSCOMM

They called it Orientation. It wasn't, really. It was more like torture, thought Durt. For the odd assortment of TransComm newcomers who sat through the two weeks of day-long sessions, a requirement for new pilots and flight crew, torture had been the general consensus. Like him, dressed in TransComm-issued flight attire, they, too, had a different vision of what a lunar pilot would do the first day of work. But they'd all endured it and walked away with marginally more knowledge than when they started.

Durt presumed the requirement behind the classroom sessions was a legal one. The fact they'd all agreed to assume responsibility for knowing and understanding everything they'd witnessed? That was a hint, but the fact they'd all palmed their legal signatures—swearing to it—made it quite clear. Durt wasn't too worried about the legal implications behind it all. The virtual instructors had pointed out on numerous occasions that all of this information would be available to them from their onboard consoles. On-demand. The only item of value Durt took from that was to make a mental note of its menu location and to verify it was accessible by voice command.

Easy. If I have a voice, I have a lawyer. Or a lawsuit, anyway.

But that was behind him now as the TransComm shuttle

zipped him south from the training complex toward the spaceport. Outside, the sky to the east was clear and cloudless. The sun was up and melting off some of the chill now. His recently-issued wristcomm told him the temperature outside was just above the freezing mark and that no significant precipitation—snow he presumed—was forecast in the next five days.

While less sparsely populated than the west coast, the spaceport operational footprint here east of the Cascade Range included facilities for transport, storage, repair, and of course the living facilities for the huge population that manned these and the seemingly endless number of commercial food and personal service offerings the spaceport supported. What had once been an open, arid landscape was now carpeted in a 31st-century version of construction and development. Anything that wasn't Park Service or farmland in the United Americas was mostly covered by human development and interaction. It gave him a clearer idea of why his work in Alaska was viewed as such an anomaly in the eyes of city folks. The landscape here was claustrophobic.

He strained to see ahead. They should be approaching the hangars now. His wristcomm gave him a directional signal and an ETA. Another 10 minutes. It was hard to believe how big the place was. When the shuttle finally dropped him at his stop, a polite female voice announced, "TransComm Commercial Transport Hangars," and reminded him not to leave any personal belongings on the train. He grabbed his duffel and noticed that his ETA reset once he stepped onto the Spaceport's pavement.

It would be another hike through the maze of similar-looking hangar buildings that seemed to go on forever before he could come to—

What was the name of the ship? All I have here is a number. 63996.

It didn't really matter, he knew, although he hadn't thought about it before. Durt Larson. Spaceship Pilot. Captain of the 63996? No, he decided, that couldn't be right, but he couldn't help but smile at the thought.

The air was crisp, and it was good to get out and walk a while after being cooped up in training torture sessions for days. To its credit, the wristcomm was right on the money. He checked it again as he walked into the open bay of a hangar that looked, to his eyes anyway, like all the rest. He was sure there was some coding system that would allow him to find this without the assistance of the wristcomm, but that hadn't been a part of orientation that he could remember. Not that it mattered. He'd started in the yellow section, walked through what must have been a corner of the green, and then crossed into blue, the color of the current section. He noticed occasional foot traffic, and flights crisscrossed overhead, but mainly he kept his eyes on his wrist as he walked. The buildings had standard numbers on the outside identifying them, but none of the numbers corresponded to the ship number he was assigned to. In this new environment, it was one of the many things that didn't make immediate sense to him, but this puzzle was quickly forgotten as his wrist buzzed once.

Before him sat his ship. It was a standard transport hull form with *TransComm* emblazoned on its fuselage. Farther back, smaller and in black, were its hull numbers. 63996. At one time the hull had been white, but it's work as a transport ship had turned it somewhat off-white. It wasn't sleek, and he knew it wasn't fast, but it was a ship. A spaceship. He gave himself another full minute, just to enjoy the sight, before making his way up the access ladder and through the open hatch.

Inside, he took an immediate right into the cockpit. He'd seen virtual images of it during orientation, but seeing it in person was something altogether different. This was real. This was happening. The cockpit was empty, its two seats sat before a complex array of controls and readouts. His pilot seat was on the left. From here, he'd have access to the navigation and maneuvering controls. On the right was the engineering console. TransComm transports were run with two-person teams, a pilot and an engineer. The third member of the flight triad was virtual. The console itself.

Satisfied, he turned and retraced his steps past the open hatch.

Habitation quarters were here on this level. An access door on either side of the ship led to the staterooms. He presumed his would correspond to his seat in the cockpit. The pressure seal opened effortlessly, and the empty stateroom confirmed it. It was spartan and practical. He tossed his duffel onto the bed, which, while not luxurious, looked a hell of a lot more comfortable than the one the Seattle police had provided.

The pressure door closed behind him as he exited, and he descended to the lower level in search of his engineer. He had no idea who he'd be stuck with on this ship. Man or woman? Moody or feisty? The only thing he did hope for was an engineer with experience. Someone he could rely on. Someone he could learn from. Someone he could trust.

Forward on the second level was the galley, and aft were the guts of the ship. Its propulsion drives and field generators.

"Hello?" he called out. "Anybody here?"

At first, he heard nothing, but after a moment, footsteps announced the ship's engineer.

He was tall, but not ridiculously so. He was broad and strong, and his width filled every millimeter of the flight suit he wore. A red racing cap with the TransComm team logo hid a few thin wisps of hair, and in his left hand he carried gloves Durt recognized as the type used for high voltage work.

"Durt Larson. Pilot. Reporting aboard," he said, extending his hand.

The engineer eyed him curiously. "Durt Larson?"

"The very same."

A light seemed to go off in his mind and his eyes widened. "The Durt Larson who flew in last week's TRI-PAC?"

Durt nodded.

"Damn," he exclaimed and quickly extended his hand. "Hell of a race for your first time out. Welcome aboard." He was grinning now. "I'm Truman."

* * *

This wasn't the time for talking. Truman said they had an evening slot time, most of which would be eaten up with pre-launch maintenance checks. "Six" as he affectionately called the ship—her first number—had received some upgraded components, and they were, in Truman's descriptive assessment, giving the rest of the engineering plant some hiccups.

Not to worry, he'd said. It wasn't unusual, and this was the way he worked best. Alone and under pressure. Once underway, there would be plenty of time to waste with gab.

The word, *underway* made Durt shiver with anticipation.

Underway for the Moon.

He still found it hard to believe that it could actually happen, but he was living it as they spoke. He was standing inside a lunar-bound transport. He struggled to keep what he knew would be a goofy grin off his face until he was by himself again.

Truman had the engineering duties and Durt took on the inventory. Within a couple of hours he was intimately familiar with the TransComm software, its digi-tab interface, and the cargo on the third level they would transport to the Moon.

It actually was only a small part of the material they'd transport. The cargo deck held special orders and standard supplies. The bulk of what they'd take to the Moon was many times larger than the ship itself. They called it *material*. But it was garbage. It was everything thrown away or recycled, from consumer goods to chunks of buildings, vehicles or bridges. Pretty much everything that was used here on Earth became junk at some point and was returned to the Moon for re-manufacturing.

He'd stashed his gear in his stateroom and put in a call to Harry's on the off-chance that his father might be around. He wasn't, but he could hear cheering from his friends and colleagues in the background. He smiled and promised to call as soon as he could.

He was in the cockpit reviewing the assigned route ahead of them and familiarizing himself with the console when a courier popped his head through the hatch.

"Delivery for Truman. Is that you?"

Durt didn't break his concentration and motioned with his thumb inverted. "Lower deck in Engineering," he told the courier. "Red cap. You can't miss him."

He checked his wristcomm. They only had about 30 minutes to take-off if they were going to make their slot time, and he was just about to go below and check on their status when Truman appeared and plopped down in the seat next to him. He checked the engineering console. "Perfect timing," he said, turning quickly to Durt. "Let's go."

Durt had been waiting all day to say it. "Engineering system check and status," he said, making use of the voice control feature. The nav screens before him shifted immediately. Truman flipped two switches and sat back. The engineering status screens flipped by about six times faster than he could keep track of as the entire ship was reviewed and certified for flight.

Durt took the navigation controls into his hands, ready for take-off through the now-open hangar roof above them. The controls didn't move. They were stuck solid. He struggled with them momentarily and shot a sideways glance at Truman.

Truman was laughing. "I bet you'd really like to take this baby for a cruise, wouldn't you?"

Durt felt sheepish. He'd reverted to pilot mode. In the transport, he didn't need to steer. It was all auto-vectored. His role was to ride and monitor and be there to override in case of an emergency. "Yep. Guess I just got carried away."

"Human errors cost money. They don't allow a lot of that around here. Just watch and enjoy. Any anomalies in the inventory?"

Durt shook his head. "Nope. We're good. Just need a load now."

It was a mental shift for Durt. Piloting in Alaska had always been about weather and actual piloting. Here, it seemed, he'd become something less. A passenger with an inventory and a left-hand seat in a lunar transport. But he was going to the Moon. He smiled. That made all the difference.

As expected, the pick-up was *nominal* as the soulless onboard computer continued to report. Six's trek across the North American continent was unimpeded, and they completed their material docking and pick-up as scheduled and met their slot time.

As they made their ascent, Durt decided this moon trip was the most boring exciting trip he'd ever flown. Lights from their jump point, then the region, and finally the continent receded beneath them. Durt was fascinated. Truman was pleasant, answering some standard questions about their route and about Six, but tired soon. Durt couldn't blame him. Truman had worked his ass off and, with a tip of his cap, retreated to his stateroom.

Durt presumed one day this experience might become mundane. But, he decided, it certainly wouldn't be today, nor would it be any time in the immediate future.

* * *

Durt had been awake for hours. It wasn't that he was used to waking up at this hour, and who even knew what hour it was back home in Alaska? He had that odd moment of displacement when he woke. He snapped his head from side to side, his brain frantically processing the foreign surroundings. He could be anywhere. It had taken him a moment to swim through the half-conscious daze of waking to realize just where that anywhere was. Literally, he thought, it was a world away from where he'd been when he woke up yesterday.

Coffee in hand, courtesy of the onboard galley, he'd made another tour of the ship, partly to stretch his legs and partly to remind himself of where he was.

The stark, smooth walls inside of Six were certainly a departure from the interior of his retro rescue plane that, he presumed, still floated on Lake Union. TransComm had agreed to transport it back to Alaska as part of his employment agreement, and he wondered who might be the next in line to inherit his second-best friend.

He wandered aimlessly for a half-hour or so, sipping and exploring until he found himself back in his pilot seat. He stared at the growing orb and the speck on its surface that represented their destination. He knew the moon settlement was not nearly the size of Alaska—maybe a quarter its size, he guessed—and not all of it was inhabited. The portion that was inhabited, however, was as densely populated as any major metropolitan zone on Earth. Certainly, from this distance, it had looked puny when compared to the larger landscape of the Moon itself but had grown quickly over the hours as they approached and now filled the better part of the cockpit screen.

"That's some sight, isn't it?" It was Truman. Flight suit. Never ending coffee cup. Racing cap.

"It's amazing."

Copernicus. The lunar city. Its atmospheric retaining field was opaque, so it was impossible to make out any detail on the surface, but he detected a slight glow that seemed to pulse as the activity from within, its factories and transport and lunar life in general, gave off millions of points of reflected light. It filled him with a sense of exploration and discovery. Something totally different from pulling dumbasses out of the mountains.

He was aching to do a fly-about, but he knew they were on a vector and a schedule. He caught a shadow of movement against the backdrop of the glowing lunar base, "What's that?" he asked Truman who now sat beside him.

"Material delivery. Just like us. Probably 20 minutes ahead."

Of course. He shook his head in understanding.

It was the never-ending line of recycling and manufacturing. The Earth consumed. The Moon made and re-made.

Truman did a quick systems check at his console. Satisfied, he settled back again to monitor the auto-vector approach.

"You straightened out that last-minute component pretty quickly. Nothing like being right on time, eh?"

Truman turned and gave him a blank look. "What?"

"You know, the one the courier delivered just before lift-off. It didn't seem to hold up anything."

"Courier?" Truman asked again with real or feigned surprise.

"Sure. Two cases. I saw you stashed them on the second deck. I just need to get them into the inventory. I didn't have the energy to do it last night."

"Look, I didn't have anything delivered, and I certainly didn't stash anything." Then he changed his expression slightly. "Although—"

A thought had occurred to him. "Keep in mind that once in a while we get last-minute taskings. Special delivery requests, I guess you'd call them. One thing you'll learn here. It's never standard. There's always a twist."

He glanced at the engineering status again, then stood up. "C'mon, let's go have a look."

It was immediately clear which cases didn't belong. The standard shipping containers, color-coded for their contents and destinations were stacked as perfectly as when Durt had completed his inventory. The newcomers were a pair of black containers, probably as high as his knee, Durt estimated. They looked like cases that a family might take on vacation, were it not for their color and the evident cipher lock on the one side.

Truman pressed his palm into the side to examine the contents, but a thin red locking alert light signaled its refusal to open for Truman. He shrugged and tried the second case. Same result. He shook his head. "Not the first time a last-minute shipment has come without instructions. It's OK. We'll double-check our landing instructions. If there's no update, and we don't get any update by the time we're done with the unload, we'll log it in and turn it over to Central. They'll be able to track it down."

It seemed logical to Durt. All of this was new to him, so he was learning and relying on Truman's experience.

They had a busy day ahead of them, Truman told him. It included the standard large material dump; unloading of the majority of their smaller transport cargo; and a few express deliveries. All needed to be completed before they could call it a day. They still had a few hours before they'd get started, and he should catch some more sleep if he could.

"Look, I know you've been dying to do some actual flying since you stepped on board here," Truman said, shaking his head with a grin, "But today's not your day. Only ones who get off the grid here are cops and medics. Actual emergencies. Everything else and everybody else just wait in line. We'll see some sights here, but the majority of those things we'll see as we're locked to the vector grid with thousands of our fellow drivers." He shrugged. "You'll get used to it."

Durt watched Truman's face change suddenly as a new thought occurred to him.

"You know what I do have, though. I've got an idea that you just might like. We've got some time here for the next couple of days. I think we might be able to catch a race or two."

Racing. On the Moon?

"You're kidding me, right? I had no idea that was even possible."

"It doesn't really make headline news on Earth. Pretty big on the Net, though. It's just local stuff. Local rules. Underground racing and betting. Nothing like we've got on Earth. You just might get a kick out of it."

Durt smiled. "I think you might just be right."

"Call me if you need me," Truman said as he descended to the engineering deck.

Durt's attention fell back to the cases. They were nice, and they looked expensive. He placed his hand in the palm cipher just to see what it would feel like. He watched for the red warning stripe, but it wasn't there. No, the stripe now was green, and an audible click followed as the case unlocked in response to his palm ID.

Curious, he opened the case. What he saw made him shiver. Not from cold but from fear. This was a special delivery, alright, but it wasn't for someone in Copernicus. It was cyphered for his palm. Not Truman's. This one was for him. For Durt Larson. This was certainly, in Truman's words, a twist. Inside were sealed packs. Hundreds of them, it looked like. He was no doctor, but he knew drugs when he saw them.

Welcome to the Moon, Durt. You're screwed.

No, he changed his mind. This wasn't a special delivery. This was different. This was a setup. It was a setup, and literally, his palm print was all over it.

[15]
SIX

Durt didn't get much sleep. Back in his stateroom, he spent the better part of the next few hours obsessing over his latest discovery. Trust was huge, and he knew the real element here was an answer to the question about who he could trust. The answer was always disappointing. No one. Sometimes not even himself. It was only after the rap on his stateroom door and the entrance of a curious Truman that he realized he had managed to get some sleep.

"Jesus, you look like a monkey's grandma," Truman said, his voice matter-of-fact.

Durt tried to think of something to say, but as he examined his walking-dead reflection over the stateroom sink, he had to agree with Truman. He did look like hell. His eyes were black holes, and the crimson scar itched like a wool sweater in July and looked as bad as it felt. He said nothing.

"What's the story with the—"

Truman motioned to his face, unsure of the right words. To this point, he'd been polite and not inquired about the scar, but apparently couldn't contain his curiosity any longer.

"Long story," said Durt. The remnants of his uneasy sleep

engulfed him and fogged his thoughts. He could barely walk, much less recount his long story.

Truman's nod said he understood.

Durt shuffled past Truman toward the galley's scent of coffee and his presumed salvation.

"Looks like you've still got some adjusting to do," Truman continued, as he poured another cup for himself. "Space travel messes with you more than you'd think. Even if there doesn't seem to be a reason for it."

"Thank God for coffee," replied Durt, raising his now full cup in a toast.

Truman followed suit, raising his own cup. "Amen."

"So what's first on our schedule for today? We drop this big load of trash somewhere?"

"Nope. First things first. Off-loading of the second deck cargo you inventoried."

"Wouldn't it make sense to make the big dump first? You know, get that out of the way?"

Truman regarded him narrowly. "Well," he said slowly, "maybe from our perspective. But we're not running the show here. Maybe a hundred of our colleagues are on the same route, flying transports just like us. Not really about our convenience. More like priorities. Plenty of material here. No shortage of that. Our priorities are our supplies and special orders. We've got about half an hour now before inventory and off-load. I know they covered this in orientation."

"Of course," said Durt, voice still tinged with the remnants of his uneasy sleep, trying to remember what else he'd forgotten about those sessions. "And then?"

"Then we wait. We wait our turn. Our place in the queue, you know. That'll take at least a couple hours." He examined Durt over his coffee cup. "Might be a good time for you to catch up on your console duties. Then the giant cargo dump."

"Can I see it?"

"What?"

"Our material load."

Truman shot him a look of curiosity, sharing his own slow start on the morning. Then his expression changed, apparently remembering that it was all new to Durt. "Not like that you won't."

Before Durt could respond, he realized in his half-awake state, that he'd stripped off his flight suit in his effort to get some sleep and now stood in his underwear.

Truman smiled.

Durt shook his head in an attempt to throw off the daze he felt. A few minutes later, he fished a cigarette out of his flight suit pocket and lit it as they descended to the third deck. A faint outline and a pair of shallow indentations in the engineering deck, pressed simultaneously, opened into a hatch, and access stairs descended to what looked like an observation deck below.

"I never would have seen that if I hadn't been looking for it. Good thing I didn't step on it."

Truman shook his head. "It doesn't really work like that. It's weight sensitive, so standing puts too much weight on the hatch. Doesn't do anything more than not stepping on it."

One hand on the now-elevated access hatch, Truman motioned to Durt to descend.

"I never really come down here," continued Truman. "I mean, I could, and I might need to in an emergency, but it's never happened to me. I've always got my hands full with our field generators."

"How long have you been flying with this ship?"

Truman thought about it for a minute. "Almost five years now. First job, and," he added with a smile, "the only job I'll ever need."

They descended the access stairs onto the deck below, and Durt was immediately impressed with the immensity of their cargo. He shook his head in wonder and exhaled the healing smoke of his cigarette, his sense of awe and the cigarette buzz now coursing its way through his body.

Truman watched his expression with a bit of a smile. "It's a lot bigger than you thought it would be, isn't it?"

The expanse stretched out in front of them. A giant pile of composite building material. Buildings and cars and roads. The bow of a ship poked its nose vertically out of the surface. A section of a bridge lay directly below them and stretched out into the sea of rubble before it, just waiting for renewal and recycling. All of this material—their load—was ready for remanufacturing. Just waiting to be transformed into something new, then transported back to Earth.

"It just looks like numbers and readouts in the cockpit," said Durt, almost reverently. "I guess I didn't realize the scale of what we are doing. Our little ship generators hold all this together, don't they?"

Truman gave him what he took to be a reproachful glance. "Our generators are anything but little."

He was still amazed. "It's like a mosquito carrying a basketball."

Truman agreed. "And then some."

The rest of the morning went as Truman had said. He monitored their navigated vector as they flew to the designated coordinates. The inventory bot came aboard, reviewed their color-coded cargo, and proceeded directly to its off-loading duties.

The two suitcases that were delivered aboard last minute, however, weren't touched, and he kept his mouth shut about his discovery from the previous night. He was warier now. He knew he wasn't as savvy as he needed to be, but he was not one to repeat the same mistake twice. The big city had taught him a couple of things. Critical things. He remembered the girl from the rooftop rave. She'd appeared at just the right time, and she'd taken him to the rave. Then promptly disappeared. It was too convenient. He hoped this wasn't a similar instance of convenience. For now, he'd just play dumb. He'd give himself a little more time to decide who should and who shouldn't be trusted.

"What about these other two?" he asked Truman, indicating the cases, "They weren't a part of the inventory."

Truman shrugged. "Like I said. It happens sometimes. If we don't have an update by the time we finish with the material offload, we'll turn them into dispatch. They'll match up sooner or later. Who knows? Maybe we'll get to do a little sight-seeing this afternoon."

Durt nodded in understanding and changed the subject. "I was surprised to see the inventory automated with bots. I suppose that's standard, isn't it?

"Yep. By the book. S-O-P. Standard Operating Procedure."

"Hard to figure why they even need us anymore."

"Actually, that's deliberate. It's all part of what they call Redundant Design."

That seemed less than clear to Durt. "Design?"

"Sure. Would you trust a bot to make life and death decisions for you or your family?"

"No way."

"Course not. Nobody would. There's a real distrust of bots by people. That's why it makes sense. It's a two-tier security system. Bots carry and repeat data as they've been programmed, and humans double-check it. Make sure they're not fooled by a piece of metal."

Durt protested. "But bots can be hacked,"

"So can people, but those good at hacking one usually aren't good at hacking the other. Distrust makes it a good system."

"Does it work?"

"It must. Otherwise, they'd think up something else to occupy our time."

And that, decided Durt, was absolutely the truth. Distrust was his word of the day. Inventory complete, they monitored Six as the auto-vectors navigated her into her assigned place in the queue for their material off-load.

Durt yawned. And then again. His restless night was catching up with him.

Truman motioned to the rear with his thumb. "I've got this. Catch a nooner. I'll call you if I need you."

Durt nodded. "Thanks." He could use a few winks, he thought as he made his way out of the cockpit and back toward his stateroom.

* * *

Durt was back in his cockpit seat 90 minutes later. He was refreshed and awake. Ready for anything. What he found, though, looked pretty much the same as it had when he left. In the engineering seat beside him, Truman was engrossed in what seemed like a random display of shifting engineering readout screens.

"How much longer?" he asked his engineer.

Truman looked up from his screens as if surprised to find him there, although he'd been sitting there for a number of minutes. "Oh…hey," he said, shaking his head. "Sorry. I must have zoned out." He looked Durt over. "You look better. That's good. Like I said before, space travel can and will mess with you like you'd never expect."

Durt nodded to the engineering readouts on the screen before them, "What's all this?"

"Just running some system checks and tests on the new components. If I find a problem, it's best that I do it here where we can do something about it ourselves, rather than somewhere out there. In between."

Durt saw the coldness of space in his gaze.

"You know." Truman motioned with his head, "Somewhere out there."

Durt shivered involuntarily. Just the thought of being stranded in space made him nervous.

"That ever happen?"

"Not to me."

While that was some comfort—that his engineer was so thorough—the vision of Six floating helplessly in the void between civilizations was a dose of space travel reality he understood but chose to ignore. Even more reason, he thought, to become much better acquainted with Six and her systems. Without saying another word, he pulled up the massive inventory of documentation on the ship's navigation and controls, making mental and actual electronic notes as he browsed.

"Oh," said Truman, pausing between engineering screen transitions, "We did get a delivery notification for those two cases. That's good news. Looks like we'll be making a personal delivery today. You'll get a tour." He paused for a second, then smiled. "No, make that a *detour* of Copernicus."

Durt turned to look directly at Truman. He tried to read something in the eyes. Or in the expression.

Was Truman a part of the setup he was walking into? Or was he as unaware as he seemed to be?

Presently, Six was second and then, finally, at the front of the material dump queue. The closer they got, the more impressive the view became. It was all truly orderly. They could make out what were in effect the giant jaws of the recycling facility, scooping out huge mouthfuls of the mix of discarded material ready for recycling and reforming. Truman explained that a field beneath the massive rubble moved the material that lay on top of it slowly toward the recyclers like a giant glacier.

Six was vectored to a specific dump location. While the size of their own load had been impressive to him, the seeming ocean of rubble that spread out before them had to be measured in square kilometers and it stretched to the edge of the visible horizon.

"What's it all for?" whispered Durt.

Truman gave him a look as if he couldn't be that stupid. "Construction and renewal," he said slowly.

"I know, but it can't just be for Earth. There's so much."

"Ah," said Truman, now seeming to understand. "Earth. Midway. Some to the Asteroids."

That, he thought, made more sense. He'd forgotten about the worlds on the other side of the hyper-gate.

"Don't they have their own recyclers there?"

"Not yet. I'm not sure they ever will. Not really their business. Most of their components are made right here and transported. It takes a huge amount of investment and technology. I suppose one day, maybe, the need will outweigh what they can make and ship here, but for now, it's cheaper for Midway to buy and ship than to try and set up their own op. Plus," he said after a pause, "you know there's a second hyper-gate in the Midway system."

"Sure. Everybody knows that. But there's nothing there. No habitable system."

Truman smiled slightly. "You'd be surprised."

Durt wasn't sure what he meant and, interrupted by Six's proximity alarm advising of their impending drop, he didn't bother to ask for clarification.

When it came, the actual dump was an anti-climax. The field generators loosened their grip and Six's load landed on its designated target. Durt felt the field shift, just slight motion in his stomach like the feeling you got in a quickly descending elevator or in a float plane on a dive toward one of Alaska's lakes. He smiled, remembering Buzz howling in delight. The job complete, the case delivery instructions had been auto programmed into the nav-system, and with a new destination, Durt pulled up their transit route. A colorful three-dimensional map outlined their intended path in blue, a route that led from their current location in the industrial southeast to the more sparsely populated northwest corner. Then a follow-on return route to their lodging near the center of the map.

Truman whistled. "Wow."

"What?"

"Nice neighborhood. That makes more sense now."

"What does?"

"Rich folks get whatever they want as soon as they want. Package must be something special."

Durt eyed him closely. Was Truman playing with him, he

wondered, or just reflecting what he'd come to understand as his standard scornful nature? Again, he couldn't be sure.

While the traffic beneath the lunar dome was a brand new experience to Durt, it was uncannily reflective of his experience in Seattle a few weeks before. Traffic is traffic, he thought, but here, it absolutely had a new twist. The lunar landscape, while distinctly metropolitan in nature was somehow more exotic. Unlike the basic structure of cities in the Americas, and he supposed, from around the world which had their roots in thousands of years of existence. Here, everything was more recent. Hundreds of years, not thousands. The city's lines were a lot cleaner, its structures a lot more reflective of their current age than the dressed-up versions of cities he'd seen pictures of that kept expanding, tearing down, and reinventing themselves.

"It just seems so much like Earth, you know?" he said off-handedly to Truman.

Truman agreed. "That's the intention."

"Intention?"

"They put a lot of dough and brainpower into making it as Earth-like as possible. If it actually looked and felt like the Moon, not too many folks would even think about living here. Damn amazing what the micro fields can do—aside from what we do, you know."

Durt had never really thought about it that way. He'd always wanted to come to the Moon just because it was here. He hadn't really thought about what it would be like to stay or live here. But it made sense. The city scenes flashed by as they made their way north. He had imagined the barren lunar surface as a backdrop to the city. Truman was probably right. It would be an odd, ghastly place without the city's engineered science with its stately skyscrapers rising above its communities and lush parks. Life on the Moon would be one long, ugly day.

Their trip seemed to last longer than it should have. The northern section of the city beneath the lunar dome lost much of the density of its downtown neighbors. They'd moved from distinctly industrial, through modern urban and now, as he watched from his external view screens, the communities had become more rural. Traffic was much lighter, too.

Truman sensed his impatience. "Almost there."

"What's this neighborhood called?"

"Greenville."

Durt laughed out loud. "You're kidding me. All that sophistication and science that went into creating this place, and that's the best they could come up with?"

Beneath them, the roads had turned to forest, and shortly they descended slightly, circled, still on auto-vector, and settled, landing in a broad multi-acre clearing in the forest.

Durt caught his breath. Before them lay one of the biggest houses he'd ever seen. No, he corrected himself. It wasn't a house. It was a castle.

* * *

The ship dropped them directly in front of what could only be the residence's front door, although it looked more like a gate than a door.

Truman looked at him with a questioning glance.

Durt waved him off. "I've got this. Any special directions?"

Truman ignored his comment. "These cases, they were directed to me, weren't they? According to you, anyway."

"There were two of us onboard. And they had no idea who I was."

"It's OK, Durt, I need to stretch my legs anyway." He winked. "Later, I'll show you how we really stretch our legs up here."

Durt was curious. "Do you have to hand it off to someone in person?"

"Sometimes. But only if the instructions say so. I'm guessing this is a lower-priority delivery, even if it was last minute. Delivery instructions didn't really say anything. The address was the only thing of substance."

Durt watched Truman on the view screen as he exited the ship and approached the door. Truman waited and seemed to look around for someone, maybe expecting a response to his knock on the huge door. No one came. He stood there for a few minutes, just to make sure, then left the cases by themselves on the covered stone landing.

"How will they know it's been delivered?" asked Durt after Truman had returned to his flight seat, and the ship lifted off.

"It's all in the video system. Six's video feeds are synced with TransComm's system, which in turn, is, with few exceptions, synched to LUNASEC—that's a good part of the Copernicus' police force," he explained. Durt nodded in understanding, thankful for the explanation. He continued to realize, law enforcement aside, how differently things worked here.

"No way they'd miss that," continued Truman, especially in this neighborhood. If there's one thing that's sacred here, it's that video surveillance system that runs all the time on pretty much everything here. A lot more valuable, I guess, if you have something to lose."

"True enough."

"One other thing. The name on the door. You know whose place this is?"

Durt didn't and said so.

"Some guy name Rush. One of TransComm's big shots." He saw the shocked expression on Durt's features. "Wait a minute." A realization crossed Truman's face. "You *do* know who he is, don't you?" He paused for a second and Durt watched him put two things together. "That's right, now it's coming back. You're the guy who pulled his ass out of a jam in Alaska. I'd forgotten. Sorry." He thought about it for a minute. "Who knows? Maybe you guys will hang out here on the weekends."

"It's not really like that," Durt explained but knew he wouldn't get too far explaining it to Truman. "But I do think it's what landed me this job here. That, I'm pretty sure of."

"So you save his life, and he gives you a crappy job."

"I like this job," said Durt, smiling. Then his eyes narrowed. "So far anyway."

Truman was wearing a wry grin. "Just messing with you, man," he said. "I like it, too."

Outside, their assigned vector on the return trip was becoming busier and more crowded as they approached the city.

"What about you, Truman? I'm guessing you didn't save a high-ranking company official to get this job."

"You're right about that. I barely finished school." Truman looked up with a grin. "I mean, it wasn't like I couldn't do the school work, but I couldn't really see the point of where it would get me. You know, memorizing those dates from history. That crap had already happened. How in the world could it possibly help me in the future? The math and physics weren't hard, but it was all so…

His voice trailed off, and he left the sentence unfinished. He squinted, his eyes searching upward for the right word.

"Impractical, I guess," he continued. "No way I was going to be a professor. Not really my style," he said with a laugh, seeming to consider the thought of himself as a professor. "Anyway, when I wasn't in school, I would hang around the racing crowd. We didn't do a lot of racing, but we sure talked about it a lot. We had a few old cars. You know, the crappy ones our parents didn't care much about. Turns out, I have a gift for understanding engines and propulsion. I have no idea how or why I got it. I just do. Natural talent, I guess. Anyway, after school and on weekends when we weren't too busy talking about what we'd do if we had money or cars, we'd race those crappy little vehicles."

Outside, the lunar traffic held plenty of similar types of crappy cars. Their pace was slower now, and it dawned on Durt that the majority of the cars out there weren't racing anywhere. Nobody raced around here. Like their own transport, these cars were all slaved to a master traffic model that ensured the ultimate safety of its users. Made for people and domestic transport. No guts. Utility vehicles, mostly. Law enforcement? Emergency? That was probably it. That was one thing they'd drilled into him in training. No violators. No exceptions.

Truman was still talking about racing, "So we had a lot of stupid ideas, and I mean a lot. You know? When you got nothing, You got nothing to lose. But one of those stupid ideas had some potential, and we were stupid enough to swap out some modified parts and test our theory."

Now he had a big stupid grin on his face. "And we kicked some ass!" he said, holding on to the s-sound in ass much longer than normal. For effect. "The actual race was the goofiest thing ever, but it did well enough to get noticed. By the end of the racing season, it wasn't just another crappy car we raced. It was a funded TransComm racer.

Durt was impressed. "That's some fancy footwork. So, did they buy you off to steal your secret?"

"Nope. They made me an offer I couldn't refuse. They'd give me a job if I could win them races."

"You won a few, didn't you?"

He shook his head. "You have no idea what it's like to be so comfortable with failure that success doesn't make any sense, even when you start to get a taste of it."

"So how did you wind up here?"

"Don't know if you guessed it or not. I'm not much of a people person."

Durt raised his eyebrows to feign surprise. Truman might be a little rough around the edges, but he certainly wasn't stupid. "Well, I didn't want to say anything."

Truman waved a hand at him. "Why should I mind? I know it better than anyone. Engines and propulsion systems, I get. Make an adjustment? You get a logical response. People?" He shook his head. "Anybody's guess. That's my experience, anyway."

"So faster cars wasn't enough?"

"Nothing is ever enough. They wanted to turn me into something I wasn't. I'm a great mechanic, but because I suck at the people stuff, I got the next best thing."

"Next best?"

"Best for me, actually.

"You got a system all to yourself."

Truman nodded his agreement. "I fly around here like I'm all by myself. Nobody asks me any questions or makes me talk to classes or audiences. They monitor and record pretty much everything I do. Sometimes they swipe my ideas." He shrugged. "I could care less. They see and learn from all of my successes and failures. But I know, deep down, you know, that if I screw up something, it's my ass, not theirs that's stuck out there in the middle of the void with an expiration date on my forehead. Put me in the air or on the ground with an engine, and I'm in heaven. Lock me into a project, and I forget to eat or even sleep. Truth is, I just don't see myself doing anything else. Ever."

"What about your family?"

Truman made a sound in the back of his throat. It wasn't vocalized, but Durt understood it to be a sarcastic laugh. "I was never good enough for them. Now, it probably wouldn't make a difference."

Durt was about to protest when Truman let out a low whistle. He rechecked the viewscreens he'd been partially watching for the duration of their return trip. There were now security alerts all over the screen. They had turned off the main vector and were approaching a large high-rise building close to the downtown sector. "That our place for the night?"

Truman confirmed with a nod. "Looks like they've got some kind of security alert going on here. That's a mix of TransComm and LUNASEC alerts. They're looking for somebody."

Durt's thoughts flew immediately to the two cases they'd just delivered. He had a sinking feeling. He didn't know for sure, but he had a pretty good idea of who they were looking for.

[16]
DOME

MOST OF THE time Durt was right. And most of the time, that was OK. But once in a while he hated being right, and this was one of those times.

By the time Six docked on the hotel's rooftop, the transport ship was surrounded. LUNASEC and TransComm vehicles stood at odd angles, and Durt assessed the armed force as a mix of official and commercial security forces.

Truman was as surprised as Durt hoped he might be. If this was the frame job he suspected it was, which seemed more likely by the minute—and Truman was part of it—then he must have been an active player all along. While he admitted to himself that he certainly didn't know Truman well, what he did know told him that Truman would have to be a spectacular actor to have pulled off that character for the entirety of their just-completed trip.

But Truman's current expression was not one of a player or a collaborator. Some things you just can't hide, thought Durt, unless you're a sociopath, and his money was straight up on a non-sociopathic engineer with no kind of acting skills.

Annoyance and curiosity intermingled on Truman's face as he addressed the nearest security guard whose uniform sported the unmistakable LUNASEC emblem. Arms out in a questioning gesture and eyes narrow under his red cap, Truman's voice was sharp. "What on the lunar surface are you looking for?"

"Durt Larson?" came the name and the question in the same abbreviated sentence.

Truman, now supremely annoyed, didn't answer the question directly. Tired and hungry as he was, he had no apparent intention of offering to help them discover whatever it was they needed to discover."What's the problem?"

The security officer put his hand out as if to grab and restrain Truman, but his arm was interrupted in mid-reach by a sharp whistle from behind.

Durt grimaced as he spotted the whistler, a now-familiar face among the small crowd of security staff.

Simms.

While the remainder of the team held weapons, Simms did not. He stood, hands in pockets, and observed. Actually, hand in pocket, Durt noted. Simms stance appeared casual, but his carefully positions stump looked for all the world like it had an attached hand inside his pocket. A couple more pieces fell into place for Durt, and now it made a little more sense. He spoke up. "I'm Durt Larson," he told the officer. "What seems to be the problem?"

The officer reset and redirected his reach after a nod from Simms, reading his lines directly from the security script he recited by heart. "Durt Larson, you are under arrest for suspected trafficking in illegal substances."

Durt tried to look as surprised as Truman and wasn't sure he pulled it off. He thought it funny that drugs weren't just called drugs. Maybe that was beneath them. Made them feel better to have some fancy legal words to make the arrest more dignified. He tried his confused look. "Illegal what?"

The officer began to explain in greater legal detail, but Truman spoke up, quietly but firmly. "Officer, with all due respect, we'll need to see the evidence behind this charge. You know the drill. What's your source of information?"

The officer was short, and as he sized up Truman, a head taller than him, his expression reflected the realization that Truman knew the law. According to the badge he wore on his uniform and the words that followed, the officer did, too. "It was an—" he paused a minute to make a tentative glance and Simms before continuing in an almost swallowed lower tone of voice, "an anonymous source."

"Of course it was." Truman's sarcasm was clear. "But as a sworn officer of the law here, you need more than that to take a private citizen into custody."

With a nod of his own, the man reached into his uniform jacket, produced a digi-tab, and made a couple of simple finger motions on its surface. "See for yourself," he said, handing the screen to Truman.

Durt watched Truman's annoyed skepticism shift immediately to surprise before he was able to recover. Truman shrugged. "So we delivered a couple of cases. So what? Special delivery. Last-minute crap. We do it all the time."

He turned now to stare directly down into the LUNASEC face, "What's…the…problem?"

The officer continued evenly. "We have it on good authority—"

"Whose authority?" Truman interrupted, nodding in Simms' direction. "His?"

"We have it on good authority," he said again, "that these cases contain a delivery of Orenz. You know that's a crime, right?"

Truman said nothing.

Another, presumably more senior, LUNASEC officer spoke up from behind. "It's a war we've been fighting for years, pal, but we've finally made little progress. Now, our director, he needs some progress, and we like him and want to help him out, so the two of you are about to make his day."

"It's OK," interjected Durt. He eyed Simms for a moment, and the smirking expression he saw said it all. "You say we delivered some cases. What makes you think they're mine or that we even have access to them?" He paused for a minute and then answered his own question. "Oh, that's right. Your anonymous source."

The officer looked at one of his teammates and motioned to one of the LUNASEC cruisers near them. The guy popped the rear hatch and pulled out two cases.

Truman stepped forward. "Yeah, that looks like them. Delivered to us in Kennewick. Dropped off a bit more recently in Greenville. Courier service for me. They didn't come with documentation, and I tried the palm cipher, but not coded for me. Here, I'll show you," he said moving forward to recreate what he'd done prior to their departure.

"No. Not you. Him," the officer said, motioning to Durt.

It looked for all the world to Durt like the security officer was just trying to do his job. And that was good, he thought. "Look," Durt said suddenly, "I'm tired and pretty hungry, too. Any chance we could do this a bit later?"

The response was almost apologetic. "Sorry. I need to take care of this now." It was the first LUNASEC officer. "You understand that if the cipher is yours, and these cases contain Orenz, that you'll need to come with me."

Durt nodded his assent. "I assure you. I haven't broken any laws here." Stepping forward, he offered his hand and placed his palm in the case's slight indentation. He looked up at Simms before he did, and saw that Simms had changed his expression from a smirk to an open-mouthed expression of feigned surprise. Simms was mocking him.

There was an audible pop as before, and the first case's lock yielded.

The officer went for handcuffs, but Durt reached for the case and opened it, laying it out on the floor.

The officer froze in place as he saw the contents of the case. A jacket. A pair of boots. A toolbox. A few other random objects were packed in there, too.

Durt reached over and opened the second case, the twin of the first. Again, it yielded, and its contents were similar. He looked up with his own fake expression of surprise. "Well, shoot. I guess this is my stuff. Not sure what I would have done without it. Thanks. Thanks for bringing it back. I guess I owe you one."

Truman looked as confused as the rest of the security team looking on.

Durt raised his head to meet Simms' gaze. Gone was the mockery. Gone was the bravado. In its place on his face were lines of anger and determination. Somehow revenge was involved, Durt presumed. He realized now this thing he had with Simms wasn't over by a long shot. He needed something better than this, a better plan. Something with enough impact to put this behind him.

Simms wasn't giving up that easily, but he'd already made his impression on the crowd. Now he just sounded pitiful. A desperate man. "Search the ship," he said. "They must have hidden it inside. C'mon, LUNASEC. Do your job."

That did it. The officer who, just the minute before, had reached for handcuffs now looked Durt, then Truman, and then Durt again—in the eye. He said nothing. He turned on his heel and paced directly toward Simms. Durt could hear the curt conversation. He had no probable cause to search the ship, he said, and based on the quality of his last piece of information, had no confidence in its basis of fact. Waste of his time. Simms was TransComm, this was a TransComm ship. He could do his own searching. He signaled his crew and the LUNASEC team climbed back into their cruisers, leaving TransComm to its own uncomfortable confrontation.

Truman took a couple steps forward. "You got the authority to search if you want, I guess. You break anything that ain't already broken, I'm gonna have a problem with you."

Simms turned on his sickly sweet tone. "Truman. It won't be necessary," he said for the benefit of his security team, then dropped his voice to a whisper, "but don't think for a minute this is over."

Truman acknowledged the comment with a nod, "You'll have to do better than this."

Durt had shoved his stuff back into the cases and was now tossing them back into Six's cargo hatch. "Can we go now?"

They left Simms fuming and, Durt figured, plotting. He knew who was behind this now, which made things a lot simpler. At the same time, remembering what Rush had told him, things were a lot more dangerous now, too.

* * *

The Dome was both a name and a symbol. The graphic sign over the entrance to the main restaurant in TransComm's hotel facility read, *The Dome.* But they'd done some work with the typography so the letter D in Dome lay on its back, creating its own little dome.

Durt stepped ahead of Truman to activate the sensor that opened the Dome's entrance doors, but Truman's hand on his shoulder interrupted him. Truman didn't say anything but nodded at him. It took him a second to realize that Truman was suggesting he toss the cigarette now hanging from his mouth. He started to protest, but thought better of it and tossed the half-finished smoke into the atomizer on his right.

"It's a fancy place," said Truman simply. Beside them, what was left of the cigarette disintegrated with a woofing noise.

"But it's healthy," protested Durt.

Truman smiled as he opened the door to The Dome. "You'll thank me later."

Truman was right, thought Durt. So right. The scent of the thousand meals he'd dreamed of eating when he was stuck in the cabin and then in space combined now to welcome him to a new world of dining. He licked his lips, and in his mind, he was already eating before they sat down.

The inside of the restaurant was indeed a dome, its ceiling paneled with what looked to be actual wood, though he knew it couldn't be. Their booth looked simple, but the form-fitting seat that was not too soft made him smile immediately.

Truman did the same. "I thought you might like it."

Durt found it hard to describe what he was feeling and kept his mouth shut. Following what looked to be a well-practiced signal, two frosty glasses of ale were quickly delivered to the table.

Truman winked at him. "You'll have plenty of time to smoke later. For now, enjoy this."

As Durt sipped the cool froth, he closed his eyes. Around him, the rumble of mealtime conversations was punctuated with commands and replies from the busy kitchen. This wasn't just some protein manufacturing plant. Actual food prep was underway here.

Truman read his expression. "This is one of the perks. Aside from flying, you know. TransComm knows how to treat its pilots and crew."

Truman wasn't kidding. He could really get used to this, he thought.

Within a minute, a waitress made her way to their table.

"You," she said with a wink at Truman, "I know." She turned to Durt. "You, on the other hand, I've never seen in here before. I'm Tania. First time?"

She was much too pretty to be a waitress, he thought, but then back in Alaska, Kim had been much too pretty, too. She was blessed and cursed by her looks. But he wasn't here to ogle women. He was here to eat, so he smiled and introduced himself. "Durt Larson. Yep, first-timer. What do you recommend?"

She was a flirty type. "I recommend you come back and see me as often as you can. I think you're going to like just about everything here." She pointed to their table. "Menus are at your fingertips."

When he gave her a curious look, she pressed her palm into

the center of the table and it turned into a digital screen. With a flip of her wrist, she scrolled through a delicious-looking list of options.

He looked up at Truman with an inquiring eye.

Truman wasn't looking at the menu. He was looking at Tania.

"Yes. I know what you want Truman," she said. "You should try something else once in a while."

He shrugged. "I may someday. But not today." He turned back to Durt. "No need to choose carefully. There are no bad choices."

Durt watched the food scroll by beneath his fingertips on the table. "What are you having, Truman?"

Tania answered for him. "Truman's having a rare steak with crispy fries and two eggs."

Durt looked quickly at Truman to verify.

"She knows me pretty well."

Even though he had a virtual kitchen in front of him, the way she said it painted a picture in his mind he couldn't resist. "I'll have the same."

Tania was taken aback for a moment then responded in a playful jest, "Suit yourself, Durt Larson. I give you a break as it's your first time. Next time? Be more inventive."

With a wink, she was back to her floor, her kitchen and her other serving duties. Hers was a practiced dance of restaurant service. She knew exactly what she was doing. Placing. Removing. Flirting. Durt smiled, watching her flit about the Dome and following her enchanting movements as if it were a performance.

He returned his gaze to Truman, but his engineer's demeanor had shifted. His face was all business, and he reached under the table and activated the opaque privacy screens on the table. The restaurant noise went immediately silent, and they were ensconced in a small, table-sized dome that served as a sound barrier.

Truman's face was one of concern and curiosity. "What did you do?"

"I ordered the same thing you did."

Truman rolled his eyes. "No. Not that." He leaned in toward Durt and whispered as if he didn't trust the integrity of the privacy screens. "I saw the video of us making the drop. You know what I saw?"

"A video of you walking the cases to the door?"

"That's what I expected to see. No, I saw a video of *you* walking the cases to the door."

Durt narrowed his eyes and pointed to himself, not understanding clearly what Truman had said. "Me?"

"Yes, you." It was as if he was still trying to get his mind around it. "I know two things now" he said in a low voice. "First, it didn't happen that way, and second, I know that security video was legit. You know what that means?"

Durt nodded because he did know. In security circles, the municipal security system access was sacred. And the ability to manipulate it? Not just criminal, but treasonous. It was a crime against the state.

Truman continued. "Now, for whatever reason, whoever has that level of control also has it in for you. So, I ask the question again. What did you do?"

"Oh, that. You didn't hear?" he said, playing off the dread he felt, his finger absently scrolling through the surprisingly long menu of options on the table-screen menu. "I thought that story was common knowledge to pretty much every TransComm employee."

"In case you haven't been paying attention, I'm not every TransComm employee. If it doesn't have anything to do with my ship or my job, I tend to ignore it. Of the million things I don't pay attention to, that is one of them."

"Fair enough," said Durt.

As quickly as he could, he recounted his Kodiak Island rescue and the subsequent threats. And the scar.

When he was done, Truman shook his head in wonder. "But you saved his life, if I follow the story correctly."

"That's true. But he doesn't really see it that way. I mean, I guess I could be dead now, so that's something. But apparently he has something else in mind for me. Right now, I get the sense that he's just playing with me. Why? I have no idea whatsoever."

Truman was thoughtful again. "Where did you put them? The cases, I mean. Are they on the ship?"

Durt looked him in the eye. "I'm betting you don't really want to know, do you?" He had a sudden realization. If Simms had hacked the Copernicus surveillance system, he could potentially hear every word they said. He motioned with his eyes to the side of the booth where he presumed the hidden mic would be placed.

Truman didn't say anything for a second, then winked in understanding. "No, I guess not."

"Look, there has to be someone we can advise. I mean, think about that security officer. He didn't seem to like Simms any more than we did."

Truman agreed. "That's true. Simms probably has some influence with LUNASEC. Maybe an inside security contact, but it may be minimal."

"It must be. A secret like this would virtually impossible to keep. But we can't just walk into any LUNASEC station and make this accusation. Who would believe us?"

"Something else we need to think about," muttered Truman. "He was sure those cases were packed with Orenz."

"And?"

"And nothing. First, in order for any charges to stick, it had to be genuine Orenz. And second, the price for those two cases must be ridiculous. I'm betting it was their standard shipment."

"What is Orenz anyway?"

Truman eyed him doubtfully."You really don't know?"

Durt made a helpless shrug. "Certainly not something we use in Alaska."

"It's a derivative of a veterinary medicine. It allows you to stay awake for months at a time. Without side effects."

"That doesn't sound like something I'd pay for."

"Maybe not, but you're not on contract. You're on salary."

Durt wasn't understanding. "What's the diff?"

"Lots of people come here to pay off debts they ran up on Earth. Others are just looking for an adventure or a job. Everybody has their reasons. But with Orenz, say you're on contract for a year. You can work off your bill in half that time and be back on Earth six months later. Manufacturing is an around-the-clock thing here, so lunar manufacturers turn a blind eye. TransComm transports it. Only law enforcement is at war with it."

"I thought there were no side effects? Should be licensed."

"Actually, in rare cases, I've heard there are side effects. You know us, nothing gets government approved until a baby can eat it. Probably affected some Senator's kid. Who knows? Anyway, it's lucrative, but as of today, it's still illegal."

Durt shivered and felt a cold sweat break out. He absently brushed his hand over the now-throbbing scar on his cheek. He realized what Truman said was true. "They're not going to let it go, are they? You don't just steal a drug dealer's stash and walk away, do you?" He answered his own question. "No, you don't. And now," he said, looking up at Truman, "Now, you're in my mess, too. Maybe you and I should just split up. Safer for you."

Truman shook his head vigorously. "Nope. No way. You're fine until they get the cases back. So, I'm with you. With what we both know now, I'm just as much a liability as you are. No," he said with certainty, "we stick this one out together."

"And when they get the Orenz back?"

"*If* they get the Orenz back," corrected Truman.

"*If* they get the Orenz back, then what?"

Truman response was flat. "Then we're dead. The both of us."

Durt thought. Hard. He thought about crashing into the freezing North Pacific. He thought about being mauled by a bear. It could be that Copernicus was a new culture for him. It could be he was the new kid in town. But there was one thing that he wasn't going to do. He wasn't going to lie down and take it. He admitted that one day he might die on the Moon. But it wasn't going to be today or anytime soon. And it certainly wasn't going to be at the hands of a smug little son-of-a-bitch named Simms.

I never met a challenge I wasn't ready to step up to.

"That's exactly what he wants us to think," Durt told Truman. "But it's not true."

"What are you talking about?"

"Simms has a lot of power, but it's not legitimate. I've looked into his eyes. His power is intimidation. He's a bully. And that only works if we allow it to work. He uses his power secretly and cleverly. But that doesn't change the fact that what he's done, and what he continues to do, are crimes punishable by prison. Or death."

He watched Truman's head nod in agreement. "So, what are you thinking?"

"I think the right people have to see the right evidence at the right time."

"Sounds like a fairy tale."

"I think—"

A knock outside their booth interrupted his response. Before he could say another word, Truman deactivated the privacy screen. Standing there, with two plates overflowing with fries and two of the biggest steaks he'd seen in his life, stood Tania. He wasn't quite sure how she'd knocked, but waitress talents didn't stop his mouth from watering or his eyes from bulging.

"You boys have plenty of time for talking when you're done," Tania said as she placed the plates in front of them. "Careful, they're hot. Enjoy. Call me if you need anything else." Like before, she flitted away.

Durt stared. It was like he'd never seen food before. Certainly, he'd never eaten in a place like this.

"You were saying?" asked Truman.

Durt looked quickly around to see if they should raise the screen again.

Truman waved away the thought with a motion of his fork. "Doesn't matter anyway. He's listening or he's not."

Again, Truman was right. "We need some help," said Durt. "I don't know who the right person is, but we need more intel than what we have right now. We need hard evidence, and we need to disappear. I never laid down for anything in my life, and I'm not starting now." He looked up from his plate and into Truman's eyes. "How much time do you think we have?"

Truman's eyes had a faraway look. "I don't like that little shit any more than you do, but I didn't come in here to leave early. I'd say we have enough time to eat. Even a condemned man deserves a last meal, right?"

He examined his steak carefully as if it were a work of art, then cut into it and a smile returned to his face. "Then I know a guy—maybe two—who might be able to help."

[17]
UNICON

The silence was momentary. What had been a hushed conversation now became an outright belligerent one. They were arguing and pointing, and Tuck found it difficult to follow. He turned to look up at Anton standing beside him for the possibility of some help. Some explanation. Anton's eyes were locked into the conversation, but he turned momentarily, noting Tuck's confusion. Without averting his gaze, Anton pulled a pair of glasses from his robe, offered them to Tuck, then turned back to the conversation.

Tuck was unsure how the glasses would help explain what he was witnessing or how they might help decode the jabbering crowd, but as he slipped them on, he understood immediately. The glasses offered no magnification but revealed instead a spectrum of light not visible to the naked eye. It was clear the focus of their conversation was a virtually rendered display positioned slightly above the banquet table. The renders were not solid, and as he moved to the right and away from Anton, he could see through them to those seated on the other side of the table. No one else at the table wore glasses, and he presumed they used ocular inserts.

The rendered objects floating above the table were primarily in white, with some in primary colors. Some yellows, reds, and blues revealed themselves as he shifted his point of view. The forms weren't organic, but rather simple geometric shapes. He didn't recognize what they were or what they might represent, so he moved back to his original spot next to Anton in an attempt to see the shapes from Anton's perspective. It didn't help.

Suddenly the display changed from simple shapes to a rendering that he did recognize. The yammering voices went silent. An aerial view of the complex in which he stood was now displayed above the table. Unlike the previous view, this display was unmistakably organic and crystal clear. He could make out fine details on the cars parked out front, and as the point of view expanded, he saw the dark wall of the dome's field and the dome gate he'd come through earlier. The view panned in a 360-degree angle, paused and then abruptly returned to the geometric display.

"External Security?" asked Tuck.

Anton said nothing but confirmed Tuck's assessment with a nod.

So that's how they knew I was coming.

He watched for another minute before his curiosity got the better of him. He leaned closer to Anton. "What is all this?"

The table conversation continued, but Anton spoke an aside to him. "This is what we bought."

"From UNICON?" Durt asked. He paused for a second to clarify. "I mean the old UNICON?"

"Exactly."

"It looks like a kid's game."

"That is what we thought, as well. The problem is, it was sold to us as the software interface for the construction equipment that came with the sale."

No way they bought this sight unseen, Tuck thought. "Didn't you demo it?"

Next to him, Anton rolled his eyes as if it were the stupidest of questions, with a bit of embarrassment rolled in. Tuck figured it might be the fact that the low-tech thugs they'd bought it from had swindled them with some high-tech sleight-of-hand. "Of course we did. And it worked without defect for the duration of the demonstration."

Tuck kept his mouth shut. He didn't want to be in the business of offending his host. Apparently, though, their business sense didn't match their technical expertise. He looked back at the shapes before him. The group seemed to be insisting to one another that the key to unlocking the software lay somewhere in the game. Some combination of shapes in a certain order. Ironically, the game itself seemed to be a child's game of construction, using shapes to excavate and build particular structures in a simplistic three-dimensional world. He turned to Anton. "I think it's a misdirect."

"What is?"

"The game. I don't think it's the key." Tuck had another thought. "Did you take possession of the original source code as part of the deal?"

"That is actually difficult to say," said Anton with a wistful smile, "We have some code they have provided, but we are hesitant to use it after we were locked out. We no longer trust that, at this point, it would do anything positive. We anticipated they would observe the accord we negotiated, and that this was merely an affectionate manner of jesting with us. To amuse us, perhaps, as we are programmers by trade."

"And?" asked Tuck, prompting a response.

"And to our dismay, we have been amused for far too long."

"Go back to the original manufacturer?"

"Out of business."

"Of course they are. Sounds more and more like a dirty trick than anything else. Why would they do this unless—"

Anton started to speak, but Tuck cut him off with a raised palm as another thought occurred to him. "Who was your legal advisor? Who reviewed your agreement?"

Anton looked over at the table as Bren raised her gaze and her hand. "It was me. They asked me to do it because of my interest in regaining my family name for the company."

Tuck asked the obvious question. "Are you an attorney?"

Bren laughed out loud. "Hardly. No, I'm a programmer like everyone else here."

"I presume you read it. Was there something, maybe, that might be misinterpreted? In a legal sense, I mean."

Bren closed her eyes for a moment before answering. "You're not terribly familiar with contracts, are you?"

Tuck had to admit he wasn't with a shake of his head, but he said nothing, presuming the question to be rhetorical. Copernicus contracts were tricky. Not only did they include all the legal local requirements, he knew, but they also fell under Earth jurisdictions in the higher courts. It was never a cake walk, and most of the time, there were loopholes you could fly a transport through. He'd been a witness to some of these examples in his law enforcement role, and it was usually such a complex interpretation of whatever law was in question, his tendency was to take whatever legal counsel he received from a qualified attorney at face value. But this was different.

"Is it possible to pull up a copy of the contract?" he asked Anton.

"For all the good it will do," said Bren with a tinge of sarcasm, "It's probably more than 100,000 words. What, in your learned opinion, might we expect to find?"

Tuck ignored her mocking, two-syllable *learn-ed* pronunciation and motioned to the hall they were sitting in. "I presume that because you have the ability to build this, the creation of additional construction equipment is possible, too?"

Anton was thoughtful, but Bren was quick to catch on to Tuck's line of thinking and was already scrolling through what he presumed was their company archive.

In spite of Anton's thoughtful pause, his narrow look betrayed his growing suspicion and distaste for the deal they'd made. "Yes. We do have the capability to design and build exactly that, but the effort at design, testing and rendering all take time and effort. Effort, in our collective opinion, that is better spent pressing forward on our current programming than working backward on something that should only be a password away."

Tuck understood but wasn't convinced. "I'm not so sure. I could be way off, but I'm betting they made it easy for you to contact them, probably through a local attorney here in Copernicus."

Bren gave him a sideways look. "How did you know that?"

"Here's what I'm thinking. I would bet that somewhere in that contract that you signed is a clause. Probably well hidden, but in there someplace, that authorizes them to return—if you invite them."

Anton was perplexed. "I do not understand. For what reason would they try and come back?"

Tuck smiled. It was refreshing once in a while to see an unfettered trust in the universe. It was unfounded usually, but a nice change of pace, nonetheless. "I would lay you solid odds that that group of thugs you dealt with—fairly and squarely in your opinion—are now on Earth, living it up on some beach on the money you gave them. This," he said, motioning to the screen before them "is most likely a trap. Or a series of traps that will enable them to return—and legally, no less—to the Moon. When they get here, I think they'd most likely resume their old habits. They wouldn't buy it back. They'd just take it. Without law enforcement to help you out here beyond the dome, there'd be no one to stop them."

Anton stared blankly at him as if he couldn't believe the truth of what he was hearing.

Bren spent the next few minutes in silence, her fingers manipulating the search function with practiced finger motions. Text flew over the table at a tremendous speed. No one said anything. Finally, the text stopped its continuous speed scrolling and Bren interrupted the silence with a low whistle. "Wow. There it is.

Really just in the middle of nowhere." She highlighted the text for the group.

Tuck read the words, squinting with discomfort as he read them. "Man, I hate being right sometimes." He looked at Bren. "How did you find it? It doesn't look anything like the text that surrounds it."

"I tried to think of legal text that might be used to describe what you were talking about. I tried searches for the word *return* and for the word *software,* but there were just too many instances. Then I tried *contingency,* right here in the middle of the standard disclosures, a place where there shouldn't be any contingencies, and here it is."

"So you are right, but what now? What does it mean?" asked Anton, his concern now evident. "We still have no software, and should we try and activate it, you believe it might enable their return and leave us with nothing?"

"I think it's likely their plan is to return. Maybe even sell this whole thing again. To someone else, you know—at least I wouldn't put it past them. And if that's true, I bet the actual software is still here, but not accessible the way they demonstrated. It would be through some other way. Some backdoor that would allow them to pick up right where they left off."

Like Anton, the rest group at the table was stunned into silence.

It was Bren who finally asked the question. "Any ideas?"

Tuck thought about it for a minute. With the adrenaline now gone, the warmth of the fire and the fur over his shoulders were having their intended effect, and he realized suddenly, in the middle of his conversation, that he needed two things. He was hungry. Only now did he realize how much time had passed since his meat-on-a-stick in Newton. He yawned involuntarily, then winked at her. "No guarantees. But yes, I do have an idea."

She seemed to understand exactly what it was he needed. "Good. But first things first. You need something to eat, and then—"

She left the sentence unfinished. "Well, why don't you sleep on it? Maybe you can come up with two ideas."

* * *

Tuck couldn't be sure. The dinner was fabulous. What he wasn't sure about was whether it was a result of the preparation, the ingredients, or his own relief at arriving at the end of his odd day in one piece. The subsequent sleep was likewise glorious, and he'd woken with a renewed sense of energy.

The long hall had a different look to it. The backdrop visible through the side window wasn't the lunar surface, but at the same time, it wasn't the open field he'd seen the night before. This morning he could feel the breath of a breeze outside on his skin, and he could see an oceanside scene with rolling waves and beach grasses waving in the wind. This was some type of programming. The objects in the hall remained the same, although the fireplace was no longer lit.

He sipped the offered coffee and took a deep breath. He hadn't come up with a second idea as Bren had suggested, but he wouldn't let on about that. At least not until the first one failed. And he hoped it wouldn't.

Based on their initial reception from the previous day, the current UNICON group seemed willing enough to put him up and keep him out of harm's way. His status as a law-skirting fugitive didn't seem to have much impact on them. The same standard seemed to apply to their thought process. Outside the dome meant outside the law. Out here, a man's word was the law. They had their own reasons, but from what he understood from yesterday, their aims were not to break the law but to keep their unique programming ideas under wraps from their competition, and based on what he'd seen already, it was certainly something worth protecting. While he was grateful for their voiced acceptance, he didn't trust it much. Primarily, he thought, because it came from the group rather than from an individual. Groups were hard to control and virtually impossible to predict, so this morning, he told himself, he needed a win. He needed something to cement this new relationship and ensure an ongoing friendship. He needed them to be in his debt.

Some of the group from the previous evening had joined them, but not all. Anton and Bren sat with them, talking occasionally with the others, but clearly waiting for his lead.

They greeted him with hopeful eyes as he approached the table, and he led with self-confidence. He surprised even himself when he sounded a lot more confident than he felt as he asked his initial question. "You didn't happen to record your closing sale with the other UNICON did you?"

Anton and Bren stared at him for a moment and then at one another. They shook their heads in unison.

That avenue a dead end, he tried another approach. "No problem. Who actually sat in on the deal when the terms were discussed, and they demo'd the system?"

Bren answered. "It was me, Anton and Walt."

"Was it here in this room?"

"Yes," said Bren, "but it didn't look like this. This was the best they could offer for a conference room. There weren't chairs or tables. It was more like containers strewn around the place. Some had rations in them. Others had parts. For their vehicles, maybe." She wasn't sure and thought about it for a minute, trying to visualize the room as it had been. "They had a heater, too, but it didn't work very well. I just remember it was really cold, but it didn't seem to bother them."

Anton agreed. "It was a mess. It was more a junk pile than anything else. A work area for mechanics. The view screen they used for the demo was placed in the center of the room." He stepped toward the table and motioned with his hands. "In the center here where this table is today."

Tuck's hand was on his chin visualizing the scene for himself. "So, the three of you." He grabbed one of the chairs and looked at

Bren. "I think it might help you remember if we do some re-creation here. Where were you sitting?"

"I wasn't," said Bren. "It was disgusting in here. She moved a few paces to her right. "I stood here."

"What about you?" he asked Anton. "Were you standing, too?"

"I was not. I took a seat and remained there. I believed it would be a friendlier interaction if I sat. Because of my height," he explained.

"And Walt?" He looked around the group and realized Walt was not among them.

Anton looked over at Trina who had until now watched the conversation with disinterest from behind her coffee cup. "Trina, would you be a dear and fetch Walter?"

Trina lowered her cup. "Sure," she said. Tuck expected her to set it down on the table and go look for Walt. While she did set the cup down, aside from her eyes rolling, she didn't move an inch from her position.

"WALDO!" she screamed at the top of her voice, the sound a piercing arrow through their collective eardrums and the peaceful morning. "GET YOUR ASS IN HERE."

Anton looked annoyed, and Bren smiled, but it worked. Within a few seconds, a fuming Walt appeared, "Walter. It's Walter," he said, scurrying into the hall. "Is that so hard to—"

He stopped in mid-sentence, seeing the group.

Trina sported a half-smile as she went back to her coffee, and Tuck motioned him over.

"Walt, we're re-creating the day we made the deal with the old UNICON. Do you remember where you were when you made the deal? Were you sitting or standing?"

Walt's face took on a thoughtful look. He nodded his head as he looked at the table. "Yes. Sure I do. I was sitting right next to Anton."

Tuck pushed one of the chairs toward him. "Go ahead and move this to where you were sitting and have a seat."

Walt nodded and complied.

"Now, what about the old UNICON reps? How many were there?"

Walt, apparently the group's designated corporate memory, now took the lead. "Two. The leader, Bike, and his tech."

Tuck wasn't sure he'd heard the name right. "Did you say, Mike?"

"No." Walt shook his head. "No, it was Bike." He was adamant. "With a *B*. But that's funny. We asked the same question. I think it kind of pissed him off. You know, like everybody he met asked that same question. Anyway, his tech wasn't introduced to us, and she didn't say a word the whole time. Bike did all the talking."

"Go on."

Walt shrugged. "We explained it was our plan to rebuild the company into the respected construction giant it used to be. Bike seemed like an understanding sort. Anton outlined our requirements. The biggest one was they had to agree to depart and not return to the Moon. Now, he didn't say it, but it seemed to me like Bike and his crew were already in the process of leaving. Like they were liquidating everything. You know, selling all the stuff they didn't need."

Tuck looked at Anton and then at Bren. "You two have the same feeling?"

Both nodded in agreement.

"Then what?"

"Then nothing," continued Walt. "They did the demo on the equipment. We agreed on the price for the equipment and the copyright. Signed the contract, transferred the funds, and they left. Their contact attorney is some big shot in downtown Copernicus—you know, in a high-rise office and all that. We had 24 hours to change our minds on the contract."

"But you didn't call them on it, did you?"

"We did not." It was Anton in a low voice. "But for the first couple of days, we had no reason to call. Like I said, it worked without defect. We experimented with the controls and came up with a strategy for reprogramming them. Then we wake up one morning, and it is this game. This ridiculous game. We have spent our energy now for the last few weeks to see how we could transform this pile of rubble, but those weeks was time wasted not moving forward, and now we are—"

He paused, trying to think of the right word.

Bren answered for him. "Now we are screwed. That's what we are. We need to come up with something soon, or we're going to burn through what capital we have left. This is not what we had in mind when we made the deal."

Tuck visualized the scene as it had played out. He wondered what in the name of space he could see that hadn't already been thought through. But then again, their expertise was in programming. They didn't have a suspicious brain in the bunch, except maybe his were he to be counted in the bunch.

"You bought smoke. That's what you bought," he told the group. "Smoke and maybe a couple of mirrors, too."

Bren looked at him with a frown. "That's your great idea? Smoke?"

He repeated himself. "You bought smoke. So, let's see it."

The group stared at him like he was speaking gibberish.

"Look, I'm betting that they didn't use the same interface you're using, did they?"

Walt looked momentarily confused, then understood. "You're right. They had a portable container with old-school components. I checked it out, but it was basically trash. No firmware embedded. I thought it was really a retro way to control their displays. Plus, it was nasty. I mean I thought I might catch something. You know, some infection or something like that."

Tuck looked at him, now with renewed interest. "Where is it now?"

"I threw it out."

"You what?" screeched Bren in an incredulous tone.

"I figured we didn't need that ancient crap. This," he said patting the table proudly, "works much better."

Tuck felt a sinking feeling. If Walt had destroyed their backdoor, then maybe he couldn't help. He knew his own well-being depended on their success, and that he still needed a win, as he'd thought earlier.

This wasn't good news at all.

Bren looked at Tuck. "That, Tuck, is an incredible idea." She turned to Walt. "You go and get that right now. If it's damaged, I'll have you outside on guard duty day and night."

Walt said nothing and hurried off.

Tuck was surprised. "You mean it's not destroyed?"

"Destroyed? Why would we destroy it? No. Walt's a hoarder. He has a pile of crap four meters tall out back. He says he keeps it just in case." Acid seemed to drip from her voice as she said the last few words. "He's part of the team. He's invaluable sometimes. But he *is* a major pain in the ass. Sorry about that. Anyway, that's a lot better idea than any of the ones that we've come up with."

Walt returned within a few minutes lugging a battered case. He set it on the table and opened it up. The inside looked almost as dilapidated as its outside. The container held a pair of controllers, a screen built into the case's cover and a manual keyboard with more than a few keys missing.

Walt looked up at him hopefully. "Just give me a minute, he said, "and I'll get the interface set up."

"One other thing," said Tuck. "I need you to go through Carter's things."

"Carter?" asked Anton. "Who is this Carter you speak of?"

"He's the guy you call Clue."

Anton nodded as he remembered and looked at Trina. Tuck expected more grief from Trina, but apparently, her coffee had done its job. "Sure," she said. "What do you need?"

"Bring me his badge."

[18]

THE KEY

THE BADGE WAS GENUINE. When Trina handed it to him, Tuck knew —just by its weight. He'd confiscated a number of fakes in his time, but this one wasn't. This was official issue. It had been a long time since—

He thought about it.

Hell, he couldn't even remember a time when his own badge wasn't within arm's reach. He'd only been without it for a day or so now, but he felt naked. Thinking about his badge, first lying on the deck of the Kick and now probably sitting on the Director's desk, it was calling his name. A small, insistent voice in the back of his mind, it urged him to return—to face whatever kind of a resolution awaited him. Yes, he answered himself, he'd go back. Yes, he *would* have that badge back. All in good time. Heads would roll on this one. But he had to be careful, he reminded himself. The timing had to be right. He had to make sure one of those heads wasn't his.

"Excellent. Thanks, Trina," he said, running his thumb over the contours of the metallic badge. "Any change?"

She squinted and shrugged. "I can't really tell. He's sleeping like a baby. I think that's good."

With a little bit of luck, Carter would sleep it off. He wasn't sure how long it would take as everyone reacted a bit differently, and he had no idea what kind of a dose he'd been given. "Thanks. Just keep an eye on him, will you? He's a good man."

Trina's response was sincere. At least as sincere, he thought, as a sarcastic soul like Trina could be. "Sure thing, Tuck."

The others now watched him expectantly, curious how a LUNASEC security badge could do anything more than make him feel good. He understood their doubt. He, himself, shared that doubt but pressed blindly forward. Even if he found nothing, part of the exercise from his point of view was to ensure he'd looked under every rock. Exhausted every possibility. Were it easy, they'd have it opened by now, and they'd have no use for him. This was an opportunity. His opportunity. In truth, all he really had to do was explore some of the approaches they hadn't yet tried. Impress for success. Even if he failed, he figured, his collaborative attempt should cement his relationship with them, and at a minimum, secure shelter here from his LUNASEC issues. At least until he could figure something out. At the same time, should he make a breakthrough, that would be even better. He'd feel a lot more confident in asking for the return of a favor, something by this point, he realized, he was going to have to ask for anyway.

He pressed the back of the badge and moved it over the sorry-looking monitor case. "Alright, folks. Here goes nothing."

The group said nothing but responded with the sound of shuffling feet as they crowded tightly behind him, jostling for position and peering over his shoulder. He moved the badge slowly, hovering just above the tabletop case.

The group let out a collective gasp.

Beneath the badge's illumination, the concentrations of human residue—the sweat, the dirt, the invisible skin cells left behind as a calling card by its human operator—glowed blue. Walt had been right about the potential for catching something from this. He wondered if it had ever been cleaned at all. Of the system's two controllers, the left showed almost no blue tint, while its twin on the right was engulfed; it looked as if it were painted blue.

Mental note. Right-handed tech.

The flat screen mounted in the lid of the case was likewise finger-painted in blue, he noted, but his real focus was on the keyboard. The blue glow showed its operator had used the keyboard fairly extensively, with all keys—at least the ones that weren't missing—but had favored a few in particular. He wondered about the missing keys, then had an idea. "Does this thing come off, do you think?" he asked no one in particular.

Walt responded with a shrug. "Who knows. Let's give it a try." He reached into the open case, running his fingers around its edges, looking for some unevenness in the surface. Some clue that might allow the keyboard and controller assembly to be lifted out. He found nothing, and his face reflected his disappointment.

Tuck moved aside, allowing Walt more room to stand directly in front of the case. "Go ahead. Try again," he told Walt. "Slowly. Deliberately."

Walt nodded. "Got it." He started again, placing both hands at the top of the inside case and running his index fingers, one on either side, in a small channel that ran between the edge of the case and the keyboard and controller assemblies. He did it slowly as Tuck suggested and when the fingers got to the middle of the case, one on each side, he stopped suddenly. "Hey," he said with a smile.

"Indentations?"

He shook his head. "Nope. Bumps. You know, like a rough area."

"Symmetrical?"

"Feels like it."

"Try pushing."

Walt leaned forward with his push, but nothing happened."

"Nothing," he complained.

Tuck frowned. "Try tapping."

Walt tapped the right side a couple of times.

"No. Do it together. Right and left. At the same time."

Walt nodded and tapped a single, deliberate tap with both index fingers.

Nothing happened.

Worry flooded the back of Tuck's mind.

In frustration, Walt was tapping again. Tapping and talking to the case. "C'mon, you witch, open up."

Tuck heard an audible click and looked at Walt in surprise. "What did you do?"

Walt was as perplexed as well. "No clue," he said, raising his hands in surprise.

Anton had watched in silence, but understood how they'd accidentally found their way in."Multi-tap. It was the multi-tap."

Depressed handholds appeared on either side, and Walt lifted out the top component and placed it next to the case, peering inside with a hopeful gaze. Again, disappointment showed on his face.

Tuck ignored it. As he'd expected, inside the empty case was a tray containing five odd-shaped pieces, each about the size of a fingertip.

"What the hell are those?" asked Walt.

Tuck said nothing but picked up the five pieces and motioned with his head to Walt.

Walt understood, and with a careful touch, replaced the keyboard and controllers back in the case.

The group whispered in understanding, watching, as Tuck placed each of the five missing keys back in their proper positions on the keyboard. Again, he picked up the badge and floated it above the keyboard.

The keys glowed in response. He observed the pattern of use carefully for a few moments before placing the badge back on the tabletop and looking up at the group.

This time he had the full story, and he had something else. He had a smile to go with it.

* * *

What does it mean?

They were all thinking it, but none in the group was asking it out loud. It was pride. Professional pride. They had to figure it out for themselves.

Tuck understood. Again, he took the badge and floated it slowly over the case's keyboard. He moved to the side to stretch his reach to the back of the case, giving those behind him a better view. They pressed against one another, stretching to see what Tuck had seen and make sense of it for themselves.

At first, they merely stared, watching in silence as the hovering badge and the varying degrees of blue residues glowed beneath it. Anton saw it first and chuckled. The collective group look first at him, then back to the keyboard. He looked up at them. First Trina, then Bren saw the pattern and broke into their respective smiles. Still no one spoke.

Walt was the last one. "I don't get it," he complained. "I see it but I don't understand—"

He stopped in mid-sentence, staring at the brighter glow from two of the keys. In a way, they were symmetrical, each one in the center keyboard row and each one midway between the center and the keyboard's edge. He, too, joined the group with his smile. "A two-key cypher," he said under his breath. "How about that?"

Tuck looked up at Anton. "Do you want to do the honors?"

"No, I think we are all in agreement," said Anton, "We have been chasing our tails in the wrong part of the puzzle. All of us were convinced that it would be a software puzzle, not a mechanical latch. I am impressed, Tuck," he said with a bow of his head. "No, the honor is yours."

Tuck verified it with the rest of the group who all nodded their heads in unison.

"OK," he said, reaching out with both hands and pressing the two keys simultaneously "let's see what this sleight of hand is all about."

Nothing happened.

Tuck began to sweat. “C’mon,” he hissed at the case as Walt had before him.

He waited impatiently for some sign that the system was responding.

Still nothing.

Anxiety welling within him, he began a series of taps, still using the same keys. First just once. Then twice, then continuously with increasing tempo and frustration.

Anton laid a hand on his shoulder. “It’s OK, Tuck.”

Tuck continued hammering the keys.

How could he have been wrong? The evidence was there. This should work.

“Jesus, Dude. Give it a rest,” said Trina. “That didn’t work any better than our guesses.”

Defeated, Tuck finally gave in, and the tapping keys went silent. “It should work,” he whispered repeatedly to himself. “It should work.”

They weren’t angry. Tuck got that. He’d come up with an angle they hadn’t thought of. Problem was, it wasn’t the right one, and they weren’t any closer now than when he’d first stepped through their door.

“It was a good guess,” said Anton, in his resonant tone. “Superb, in fact. And certainly worth the time to spend exploring all angles. You came at it from a wholly different perspective. You do not find fresh solutions without doing that, and I must say that the group of us here—we are, as a general rule, single-minded. We know now what we must do. It is ugly, and it is inelegant, but now we have work to do.”

Tuck had a sudden thought. “What did you say?”

“I said we’ve got some work to do now. Reprogramming. Recoding the software.”

Tuck shook his head. “No, before that. You said I came at it from a wholly different perspective.

Anton nodded. “Yes, I did say—”

Tuck cut him off with a wave of his hand as he turned back to Walt. It was rude, but the inspiration, if it was the right one, he thought, would cover for him.

"Take it off again."

Walt understood and with a quick hand movement, removed the case's top component that held the keyboard as before, lifting it free of the case.

"Flip it over."

Walt squinted, perplexed, but complied and inverted it, then set it down on the table beside the case.

Tuck hovered the badge over the now inverted surface. The edges glowed with blue smudges where Walt, and presumably, those before him, left their fingertip marks. But nothing in the center.

"Damn," said Tuck under his breath.

Almost doesn't work. You won't ever know you're right until you're exactly right.

They stared at one another for longer than seemed comfortable to Tuck. He watched their collective faces. He'd let them down. They seemed less disappointed in the fact that they still didn't have access to their software and more disappointed for him. For his failure. That his inspiration showed promise then petered out. It was a good crowd here that he'd bumped into, he thought. A day ago, he'd been on top of Copernicus. Then, in a single incident, he'd lost pretty much everything. Just like that. Bam. If there was something to be thankful for, it was that his new hosts seemed genuine. It wasn't like his fellow cops who stopped by the Kick on a predictably frequent basis. They all wanted something. For themselves. It wasn't really friendship. There was respect, and there was deference, but friendship? He'd almost forgotten what it was was like to have a real friend. And that was something worthwhile.

There has to be a way. Even if I can't think of it right now.

"What about this?" asked Walt. He was still screwing with the control board when another audible click caught his attention.

The keyboard came off in his hands, the stand-alone rectangle now in Walt's possession.

With a string of failures, Tuck was almost hesitant to try. He was full of failures today and didn't relish another disappointment. He didn't need to say anything. Walt seemed to understand that he was looking for something on the bottom side of the keyboard and promptly flipped it over and offer it up like a waiter might offer a plate in a restaurant.

He deliberately raised the badge again and floated it centimeters above the keyboard's inverted underside. He caught his breath. Two stripes of blue began in the center on the bottom of each side of the keyboard and arced outward.

Walt wasn't looking at the keyboard. Walt was staring at his face. "What does it mean? What are they?"

Tuck felt a smile spread across his face that he couldn't stop. He no longer had control of it.

"Thumbprints."

Walt had not yet put the blue glows together."Thumbprints?" The curiosity in his voice was clear.

Tuck nodded. His smile turned into a short laugh. "Let me demonstrate." He took the keyboard, placing his middle fingers on the appropriate keys and using his thumbs to squeeze from behind the now elevated the keyboard in front of him.

"Fuck you. Fuck you all," he said.

The group was astounded at first.

"That's what UNICON is telling you," he continued. "This is the smoke that you bought."

Their silence was broken by a short "Ha!" from Trina as it became clear to her. "You're flipping us off."

"No," he corrected, "UNICON is flipping you off."

It doesn't matter who you are, you can't ever escape your true nature.

Part ego. Part irreverence, he thought. Their arrogance had blinded their security standards. It wasn't easy, but clearly, it wasn't impossible to breach, either.

No longer silent, the group began to talk all at once. Tuck was parading among them in a circle, the keyboard in front of him flipping them all off.

"Whoa." The voice was deep. Anton. But he wasn't looking at Tuck's antics. His gaze was on the screen in the case. The displayed three-word message on the screen was clear.

Tuck whispered it to himself as he read it. "Welcome back, Bike."

* * *

The group exploded in celebration. Shouting, they pounded Tuck on the back and pulled him into an improvised circular dance in the center of the room. It only lasted a minute or so, but the expression of joy was so sudden and profound, it seemed much longer. Only one remained silent. Bren now stood before him, and with tears in her eyes, embraced him tightly. "Thank you," she whispered into his ear before kissing him on the cheek.

He wasn't sure what to say. In the end he said nothing, just nodded and smiled. The gratitude in her eyes told him that he didn't have to say anything more. He'd done enough.

Anton's raised hands scraped the ceiling and brought the impromptu celebration to an abrupt halt. "Alright. I am as happy as each of you are, but now we have work to do." All eyes turned to him as he directed the group, a musical conductor coordinating an orchestra's performance. "Walt. Convert that security mech into something that will work with our interface. But do it quickly. I need your mind back on the race and surveillance as soon as possible. Bren, take a team and inspect the cars. Do a visual with the actual equipment again. Keen eyes, mind you. We're going to use them, not just inventory them this time. We need to make sure there are no other *transactional* surprises."

Bren's eyes narrowed at Anton's emphasis on the word transactional and nodded vigorously, already on her way out the door, a pair of younger team members in tow.

Anton shifted his gaze to Trina. "We need another external security view specifically for the equipment. Rig that; see that lunch is underway. Then you're on forward scout duty."

She responded immediately, but not to Anton. She was already heading out of the room, presumably to whatever food prep area they had. "Waldo. I need access to that interface as soon as you have it rigged," she said over her shoulder. She turned to Anton, still walking, but backward now as she talked. "And I'll need Tuck with me."

Walt, at the keyboard, shook his head, his fingers banging with annoyance on the keyboard. "Why is it so hard to get my name right?"

Anton turned to Tuck. "I hate to impose, but you could really help us understand the races. It's in our best interest to pass ourselves off as the old UNICON."

"Because of the broadcast?"

Anton nodded. "I don't even know what's possible, and after what you've done for us here—"

"Look, I don't know what I can do, but yes. Sure. I'm in."

Anton smiled, placing his large slim hand on Tuck's shoulder, a sign of thanks. He didn't say anything, but he didn't have to.

[19]

MICAN

THE SCREEN in the lift displayed the number 14 as they exited. Durt figured it was the 14th level, but as he and Truman walked through the entrance doors, he guessed the high, looming space before them was more likely the 14th through the 20th levels.

Durt presumed they'd be visiting LUNASEC to look for help, and he'd seen the directional advisories with LUNASEC signs pointing them in that direction. Truman, however, had taken them on a detour. They stood now in the TransComm repair hangar attached to the hotel, and as they gazed at the far end of the facility, he saw an opening to the city beyond, a sliver of Copernicus skyline. He hadn't noticed the facility from the air as they'd approached, but with Copernicus construction sometimes as dense vertically as it was horizontally, he didn't wonder that it didn't stick out in his mind.

A frenzy of activity across the hanger floor melded into a mechanical symphony of work, and components of aircraft, some of which he recognized, stood propped at various angles as circuits and surfaces were replaced or refurbished. The tail structure of a ship stood above the rest near the center of the hangar as if the craft had crashed vertically into the hangar floor, leaving only its elevated tail visible. To Durt, it looked like an odd mechanical forest squirrel, poking its head above the rest to survey the hangar activity. The scent of composite manufacturing here was strong—like he'd just stepped into a brand new ship. Here and there, a bright flash of color stood out, but the hangar, like the aircraft and components it housed, was primarily a gray-black tone.

Truman leaned in and raised his voice slightly. "TransComm doesn't manufacture its own aircraft, but it does repair them."

A slight, trim woman with a TransComm cap approached them, a questioning gaze on her face that quickly shifted with recognition. "Truman!" she said with a huge smile as she embraced him. "And who have you brought with you?"

"Angela, Durt. Durt, Angela."

Durt shook her extended hand in a polite greeting. Her voice was difficult to make out, but he read her lips. "Nice to meet you," she said.

"Likewise."

Apparently, Angela was used to few word conversations here where noise, speed, and efficiency were all part of the hangar's environment. "Mican?" she asked Truman.

He nodded.

She pointed toward the back of the hangar, then turned abruptly and returned to her work. Truman nodded. He knew where to go.

Durt followed.

The hangar activity was a mixture of human and bot labor, and what had initially looked like a random scattering of projects across the deck now revealed itself as something much more practical. Each major repair project sat on its own individual repair deck that fit together with others seamlessly like a puzzle. Durt watched as a project, apparently complete, floated above the deck and then receded away from them 50 meters or so, at which point the floor shifted appropriately to make space for its next step. Along the way, shouts and waves from the techs on the floor greeted them. Bold yellow lines marked an unmoving path between the various hangar sectors which they followed for a good five minutes before coming to the section Truman was looking for.

He followed Truman, and they stepped out of the main walkway and up onto a platform that supported what looked like a solid, circular black wall about three meters high. Truman found an opening, and they stepped inside. A mass of display screens covered the inside of the wall and illuminated the covered interior. Gone was the incessant rumble of repair activity. A single control seat at the rotunda's center rotated slowly and stopped, concentration evident on the face of its occupant. He looked up, and the face melted into a smile of recognition.

"Truman!"

"Hey, Mican. Was in the area. Thought I'd drop by."

Mican looked a lot like Truman, Durt thought. A bit smaller, and his face a bit more animated, but there was a definite similarity. They could be brothers. Mican stood up from his control seat and came over to greet them.

"Great. I'm glad you did. This thing's driving me batty."

Truman smiled. "Something new?"

"Nah. Same thing as always. Making sure our hardware keeps up with their software." He shook his head in apparent frustration. "You know, as individuals, we're brilliant, but as an organization, sometimes we're pretty stupid."

He extended his hand. "Sorry about that," he apologized to Durt. "I'm Mican. Nice to meet you." He looked a little closer at Durt and whistled. "Wicked scar. What happened?"

"Long story. I'm Durt. Durt Larson."

Mican froze. He repeated the name as if he weren't sure exactly how to pronounce it. "Durt Larson? *The* Durt Larson?"

Durt shot a questioning glance at Truman for clarification. He wondered if maybe there was another Durt Larson they knew.

Truman smiled. "Yep. He's the one."

Mican was still shaking Durt's hand, and he continued to do

so, as if he'd forgotten exactly what he was doing. "Man. It's my pleasure to meet you, sir."

Durt realized Mican must be one of Truman's racing friends and had likely watched his TRIPAC adventure.

"No *sir*, Mican. Just Durt."

Mican was still pumping his hand. "Of course. Sure thing, Durt. You know what? You guys, if you're done with your drop, you should come out with me tonight."

"Out?" asked Durt. "Out where?"

Mican had given up the hand-shaking but remained over-animated as he spoke. "The races, man. Oh, boy, you should see what we have in store for those UNICON stone draggers."

Durt looked at him skeptically. "Races tonight? I thought they were set for the weekend."

Truman half-smiled but said nothing.

Durt shot a sideways glance at his wristcomm, realizing the week had slipped away. Somehow, it was Saturday already. He shook his head. The moon jump *was* messing with his sense of time, just as Truman had said.

"Yes, of course," said Mican with an enthusiastic nod of agreement. "The races are tomorrow, but our team goes out the night before. You know. Few test runs. Good for the driver." He paused for a moment. "OK. Good for the ego, too," he admitted with a smile. "So whadaya say? Are you with me?"

Truman looked at Durt and started to answer, but Mican held up a finger in a wait signal. He touched the finger of his other hand to his ear, apparently listening to some communication. His eyes shifted quickly from excitement to concern. He leaned in. "Someone here asking about you. Some company bigwig." He shook his head. "No, I didn't get that," he said, holding up his finger again as he listened. "OK," he said with a nod. "Yes, I've got it." He returned his look to Truman. "Guy with one hand?"

Truman grimaced.

Mican's face looked as if he'd suddenly made the connection. "It's not Simms is it?"

Durt was surprised, but Mican was TransComm. It made sense that if he knew about the race, he'd heard about the other thing, too. He confirmed with a nod.

"Look," said Truman, his eyes wide and sincere. "We don't need you to be involved. This won't likely be good news."

Mican nodded, his eyes gazing upward as he listened. "Thanks."

He looked at the pair of them. "Angela told him you'd come by and were coming back later. I'm presuming you don't want to talk to him."

Mican looked as if he already knew the answer. "I wanted to show you this anyway. It's a new project we're working. But now I have another reason. Two reasons." he said and motioned for them to follow him to the back of his monitoring rotunda.

He pressed one of the display screens, and the section slid to the right, revealing a descending staircase. "Go on down. Have a look around."

He looked at Durt with a smile. "You still owe me a long story. I'll be with you in a few minutes to hear it."

* * *

Green safety lights inset low into the sides of a descending stairwell beckoned. On the twelfth step, if he'd counted right, Durt noticed the step down was marginally longer than the previous step. So was the next. He felt a bit of lightness in his stomach, like the sudden lift of riding a high-speed elevator, but it passed quickly, and he shook it off. Behind him, he heard Truman catch a surprised breath, apparently feeling the same sensation. He wondered if it might be the effect of one of the TransComm projects they were working on the floor. He watched his step, and with Truman behind him, the pair made their way carefully but deliberately down the oddly constructed stairs. Durt counted a total of five longer steps before the steps regained their original height.

Another six steps brought them to a landing and a dimly lit door. He turned briefly to see Truman signaling him on with a shooing motion of his hands.

Durt shrugged, opened the door and stepped through. Now he caught his breath. As they walked forward, he thought for a second his eyes were playing tricks on him. It looked for all the world as if they were standing and walking, in fact, on the ceiling of the level below. Above them now, he could make out a few desks, some stacked equipment and notably, upside-down doors and windows.

He turned to look at Truman who'd come to the same conclusion. "Is this weird or what?"

"We're on the ceiling." It wasn't a question. It was a statement. But it was clear from his tone that he was as surprised as Durt was. In front of them now was a video screen with a low table and a few chairs arranged in a semi-circle around it.

"C'mon," Durt said, grabbing Truman by the sleeve. "Check it out."

On the screen now, he saw a man sitting in a console chair. He could make out the images of screens behind him, and he realized who they were watching. "Mican," he said to himself in wonder.

Truman walked up and took a seat. He was almost laughing as he turned to Durt and motioned for him to sit down, too. "This is so like Mican. I'm betting he's going to put on a show for us."

Durt was still at odds with his vertical perception that they were—somehow—standing and now, as he took his seat, sitting, on the ceiling. "I'd heard they were working on something like this, but this is my first time experiencing it."

"Mine, too."

"How do they do it?"

"Gravitational field manipulation."

It rolled off his tongue. He said it as if it was something he said every day. Actually, Durt thought, as a ship's engineer, he just might.

"But what about—"

Truman interrupted his question with a raised hand and a renewed interest in the screen. Simms. His missing hand was his unique signature. They didn't have an audio feed, but they could get a pretty good summary, just through the interpretation of the body language. Mican stood greeting him, shaking his right and only hand. Simms was saying something and shaking his head. Some form of explanation. Simms took a moment to digest what he heard, then took a full 360-degree turn, checking out the various update screens in Mican's rotunda. He asked something else, and Mican nodded and shrugged.

Durt waited. He knew it was coming. Typical Simms. Predictable. Simms leaned in to whisper something to Mican. His last word. His threat.

Mican said nothing but watched Simms depart, then moved his gaze to the security screens.

After a minute, Mican walked through the door and joined them on the ceiling. He wore a big smile. "Man, that guy has some issues."

"Keep your distance from him," Durt warned him, repeating the advice Rush had given him.

Mican took one of the extra seats set around the screen, looking at him curiously. "That's the guy in the long story, right?"

"Simms," said Durt, agreeing. "TransComm management. I should have left him on the beach."

"Why didn't you?" asked Mican. "Seems like a perfect candidate for it."

"Not really my style. I'm a rescue pilot, and that's what I do. You need rescuing? I rescue. Even if you are a major jerk. You still get rescued."

"Yeah, that's the tale I heard. But what really happened?"

As best and efficiently as he could recall, Durt recounted a play-by-play recap of that day in Alaska: the bear, the storm, the landing and almost fatal crash.

Mican listened intently. "Wow," he said when Durt had finished. "You saved his life, and he still has it in for you?"

"That's what I said," said Truman.

"Then I was right," said Mican with a knowing nod. "He does have issues. He'll have his hand back soon enough, I'm sure. You're right. He is some kind of TransComm manager. No idea what he does, but if you pal around with Rush, you're somebody. I've heard of him but never met him. Before today, anyway."

Durt allowed that everything Mican said was true. "He just can't seem to get over the fact that his hand is missing, and that I'm the one to blame for it. He has this idea that there's some specific punishment I deserve, but I gotta tell you, I have no idea what that is. But what I do know." He looked over at Truman and corrected himself. "What we *both* know. Is that he is into something or some *things* he shouldn't be." He looked up at Mican and nodded at the screen in front of them. "What did he ask you?"

"He was certain you were here. I played stupid and told him exactly what Angela told him. That'd you'd been here until just a few minutes ago, and he'd just missed you. If he hurried, he might be able to catch you. At first, he didn't want to believe me. I think he was about to insist that you were here, but there's no way he could know that. Unless—"

He paused, and his eyes narrowed. "Unless he has access to the personal tracker system—which legally he can't have. He almost came out and said it, but he caught himself. No way he could admit something like that to me without creating trouble for himself."

"Then he threatened you, didn't he?" asked Durt.

"Sure did. But it wasn't a very impressive threat. I managed to keep a straight face, but I almost laughed. I'm sure by now he's on his way or has already checked in for an update. But when he checks for your trackers, he won't find you."

"Why not?" asked Truman. "We were standing only a few feet below him."

"It's not how the system works. He wouldn't have a personal tracker monitor on him. He'd have a comm device and a man on the inside. Probably one of the security board ops guys with access. Anyway," he motioned to their ceiling position, "this project plays havoc with the trackers. They're quirky anyway, but this grav project we're working zaps them like nobody's business."

"So we're invisible?" asked Truman.

Mican nodded. "Until midnight, anyway. That's when they re-push patches and updates. Everyone in Copernicus gets refreshed. Then you'll pop back in as if you were never gone."

Durt took a deep breath. "Don't underestimate him," he advised Mican. "Just steer clear. Somebody with the connections and influence he has? Trouble. Here's something else. He has more than access to the tracker system. He has the ability to access and manipulate LUNASEC security video."

Mican was skeptical and shook his head, dismissing the thought. "No way."

Truman then related their experience from earlier in the day and the video the officer had shown him.

Mican was dumbfounded. "You've stumbled into some pretty serious shit." Then his face broke into a grin. "But stick with me. I seem to stumble into something all the time. Stumbling in is easy. Stumbling out? Sometimes, not so much, but one way or another, I always do."

Durt was checking out the level above them. Or actually, below them. "So, what is this anyway?"

"This is what I wanted to show you. It's called Modular Gravity. The Casinos have had it on Midway and use it to help create their shows and amusements. Multiple fields of gravity can exist beside each other. At TransComm here, we've ignored their commercial applications because—"

He paused for a moment. "Because. Well, to tell you the truth, I don't know why. Maybe it's just opportunity. Anyway, we're working a major construction project on the other side of the second Midway system hyper-gate. We're redesigning transport ships and may even include this in updates to our current fleet."

"New Manhattan?" asked Truman.

Mican was surprised. "You've heard about it?"

"Just word of mouth. Engineer community is pretty sure they'll have to expand their existing fleet if this thing goes forward."

"Well, I don't know where you heard it. Doesn't matter. It's probably true."

Durt had his eye fixed on the level overhead as a door opened and an employee walked into—and onto—the ceiling above. "How is that possible?" he asked in wonder.

"That level has gravity, just like we do," said Mican. "In fact, if you had a big enough ladder, you could actually climb out of our gravitational field and into that one."

"What, then I'd fall up?"

"That's what it would look like to us from here," said Mican, "But if you were standing where that guy is, it would look like you'd taken a serious fall down."

Durt whistled. "My eyes see it, but don't believe it. That's something else."

Mican brought them back. "So, are you guys in? Races tonight?"

Durt couldn't think of a better place to be. He looked at Truman. He, apparently, was thinking the same thing. They did need to disappear for a while.

Truman winked at him in reply. "Oh yeah. We're in."

* * *

No question about it, the car was fast. But its speed was fleeting. Durt sat in the rear, the forward thrust slamming him back into his seat as they exited the rear hangar opening. Below them the cityscape of Copernicus expanded, the city's texture a fascinating mix of geometric urban architecture, punctuated here and there with sometimes practical and sometimes artistic tower structures standing watch. A few seconds later, the force relinquished its grip on him. He shoved his head forward and saw the grinning faces of Mican and Truman.

"What the hell just happened? That was great. For a minute."

Mican turned his head from the driver's seat, still grinning. "We call it efficiency. Can't believe you're not familiar with it yet."

So that was it, he remembered, surprised he'd forgotten so quickly. It was the city itself that took control of their vehicle as soon as its transponders came into range, assessed destination coordinates, and routed it properly. He now could guess why the racing sport was so popular. No rules. No limits.

The blazing speed of their take-off and the emotion of being inside a race vehicle again had apparently given him temporary amnesia. Maybe it was too many new experiences all at once. Or the jump. Of course, it was the city itself in all of its efficient glory, he thought. But the force of the car that bucked against Copernicus' Earth-like gravity, even if it was engineered gravity, gave him the rush of adrenaline he remembered from Alaska. Buzz would be howling now as they dove to a rescue, or as he sometimes did, just for fun.

"Nothing like a little punch to get you going and keep you on your toes," said Mican from the driver's seat.

"Or on my ass."

The city now had them in its grips, and they moved methodically above it, their vector and speed integrated with the thousands of others now airborne over the downtown structures. It was a dancing swarm of synchronized movement, sometimes more dense, sometimes less. Durt could see faces in some of the other vehicles as they passed on their way to their individual destinations. A few returned the gaze. Most were otherwise occupied.

He leaned forward again. "Look, Mican. This is pretty decent of you. I know you're sticking your neck out here, and that's more than I could ask of anyone. But we don't know how well connected Simms is, or what he's got up his sleeve. I can't ask you to complicate your life just because of something I did."

Mican let out a short laugh and turned to look at Truman. "That's rich." He shook his head in apparent wonder. "Truman, where'd you get this guy?"

Truman said nothing.

"Look, kid. First of all, I heard your story. If I believe it—and I do 'cause you got no reason to lie—then it wasn't anything you did that made him come after you. You saved his life. If it wasn't for you, his scrawny little ass would be nothin' but a pile of bones on a beach in the North Pacific. No, what you are is an opportunity, and guys like him? They take advantage of every opportunity that comes their way. I don't think he wants to kill you. If he wanted that, you'd be dead now."

There was some truth to that, Durt thought. He recalled the sickening fear he'd felt and how Simms had controlled him in the jail cell. He'd initially gone for the hand with the big knife. And then—for whatever reason—had pulled back and just cut his face. His cheek throbbed just thinking about it.

"No, I think he wants you to suffer, and he wants to be the cause of it. You know, like he has to balance things out. He's got some kind of a twisted mind, and he's also got some kind of power. But keep in mind, based on what he told me and what he didn't, it can't be absolute power. You know what I mean?"

Durt was following and nodded. That was the same point he'd made to Truman.

"Personally? I think he's got a secret. All this stuff," Mican said, motioning with both his hands in the air, "all these things that he's able to do, is being done through someone else. Not him, right? Also, all this power that he's got working for him? It has to be for a reason. You see that he respects the force of LUNASEC and even the TransComm chain of authority. No, I don't know what he's got going on, but anyone with that much power and that much at stake is, in my way of thinking, in a pretty dicey situation."

From that perspective, it did make sense, thought Durt. He wondered if maybe he wasn't as bad off as he'd figured before.

"Another thing. Don't you go thinking this is your fault. That's pretty noble of you to try and take credit for it, but the way I see it, it's not really about you. Here at TransComm, we have a pretty good thing going on. Ain't that right, Truman?"

"Pretty great, I'd say."

"Got that right. And for me? Even if that *we* doesn't go beyond the three of us," he paused for a moment to clarify himself. "well maybe a few others I could think of, too. But even if that's how many folks are actually affected by this so-called secret, it's got consequences far beyond you, friend. So, yeah, I'm in. All in. It's not about you, it's about us. All of us."

Durt had heard that line before. Something tickled the back of his mind.

What was it?

Then he remembered. They weren't the exact words, but they were pretty close. They were Jake's words. From Harry's bar.

Never think you're in anything alone up here.

"Maybe you're right, Mican, but maybe I'm not getting everything you're saying. We're on the run here, and you seem a little too happy about it."

"Too happy?" This time Mican laughed out loud. "Too happy? What's not to be happy about? I got Durt fucking Larson in my car, and we're headed out to take on some low-life knuckleheaded stone kissers who think they can race. Man, I haven't had this much fun in a *long* time."

He was beaming.

[20]
SCOUT

THE SEA OF TRANQUILITY was as barren as Tuck remembered it. It seemed that way in pictures and in vids. In person, it was even more so. Stark. Sterile. Their conversation wasn't much different. Tuck, by nature, wasn't much of a talker, and today anyway, Trina was even less of a talker than he was. She seemed preoccupied, but as head of security, he was sure that was often the case.

They'd taken one of the cars inherited with their UNICON purchase. He'd seen the cars before, race vehicles from the consistent and semi-successful racers. The old UNICON team weren't very creative with the vehicles and relied more on their intimidation and dirty tricks. That's what made them unavoidably watchable. The new team made some mods, and he wasn't sure what they all were, but the most obvious was the color. All the old UNICON vehicles were black. It was their trademarked UNICON look and style. Not anymore. Trina had taken the vehicle with the bright orange tint that had first caught his attention. He wondered as they sped above the lunar surface whether the loud color that stood in stark contrast to the monochromatic blacks and grays that whizzed by outside was the best choice for forward scouting work. He kept his mouth shut. As he had previously surmised, they seemed to be better programmers than they were spies—or racers.

He turned his attention back to their progress. It was the speed that grabbed him. Exhilarating. Speeds he'd only seen remotely on the network. Within the city, he could go off-grid in emergencies, but speeds like this were a new sensation. It felt like he was breaking the law, even though he knew inside of himself that he was the law. This was why the races were so popular, he thought. Even if you couldn't go fast yourself, you had the experience with the onboard cameras. Still, all those times he'd watched from the Kick. It wasn't the same—not even close—to doing it yourself. In person.

"I know what you're thinking," said Trina in one of her rare, vocalized comments. "But the color doesn't really matter out here. If there is somebody out here, we'll see them electronically long before they see us."

While he liked her confidence, he wasn't convinced what she said was accurate. "If you have sensors, and they have sensors, wouldn't you see each other at the same time?"

Trina kept her gaze straight ahead on the flat surface that stretched before them. "Technically, yes. It's just that we wouldn't be recognized."

He turned and gave her a narrow look. They must be really bad spies, he thought. Maybe even delusional. "Not recognized?"

She maintained her forward gaze but betrayed a slight smile. "You're probably thinking that we don't have a clue about what we're doing here. And in some cases, you'd be right. The races for instance." Now she turned to look him in the eye. "That's where your talent comes in. We've got a talented crew, but we're out of our element in racing. So, yes. You'd be right on the money to think we don't know what we're doing." She tapped him on the thigh. "We're counting on you. But when it comes to energy manipulation and deception, we've got a good, solid game. The orange? Doesn't matter one way or another. I just like it. The part that matters is the coating we applied. It captures and retransmits modified transponder signals."

She moved her arm in an arc, indicating the lunar horizon. "Any electronic snoopers out there? They don't see an orange racing vehicle. On their screens we look like a mobile surveillance camera, a lone ranger out in search of who knows what?" She turned to look at him again. "So yes, you'd be right to presume we'd be seen. But thanks to our micro-manipulation techniques," she said, patting the console of the vehicle as if it were her pet, "we'd be dismissed just as quickly. Identified. Logged. Dismissed."

Tuck was impressed and nodded in understanding.

The pair went silent again, each retreating into private thoughts, fears, and suspicions. After a time—and Tuck wasn't really paying attention to how much time had passed—a white dot appeared on the lunar horizon. Out here he was rather enjoying a break from his timed, disciplined existence in the Kick. At first, it was insignificant. Without an object for scale comparison, its size was impossible to judge. Gradually, however, it grew larger until he was able to recognize it as a giant pile of moon rocks. He looked to Trina for confirmation.

"The Pin," said Trina simply.

"The Pin," Tuck repeated to himself. He didn't need an explanation. The Pin was the turning point in the races. There were no fancy turns, no ongoing driving or racing challenges. This was it. There was the start, the Pin, and the finish. That was it. From a racer's standpoint, the approach and turn to the Pin won or lost the race, all other things being equal. The challenge and the intrigue of this race, however, as he well knew, was that all other things were *not* equal. It wasn't really about driving fast, although that was a part of it. What it was really about was following the mantra of race fans. He knew the chant by heart. He'd heard it repeated before, during and after every race he'd ever watched.

The first and only rule is there ain't no rules.

A thousand times. It wasn't proper grammar, but there was

something about its outlaw feel that attracted the wild side of every race fan. Sure, it was about driving fast, but what it was really about was driving fast and cheating. More race viewers spelled more money, and it was money that made the world—and the Moon—go around, he thought. Centuries of engineering had worked the risk out of most earthly pursuits. Lunar pursuits, too. Even hyper-gate jumps to the distant Midway system and beyond were remarkably safe. Everything was so damn safe that a race like this tickled some of the more primal human cravings for excitement and deception. The races didn't usually disappoint.

As part of the pre-race preps, camera droids made their way up from Copernicus the evening before for trials and maybe some pre-race shenanigans. In fact, he thought, checking his wrist-comm, the first ones should be due around the starting line soon.

Trina slowed the orange racer, setting it down right next to the white rock pile that was the Pin. Opening the driver's hatch, she exited and stretched with a satisfied groan. Tuck followed suit. The stretch wasn't required, but it did feel good.

Trina pulled a container from the racer's rear hatch and placed in neatly inside a crevice in the rock pile.

"There," she said in a satisfied tone. "That ought to do it." She checked her wristcomm and motioned with her head to Tuck. "We gotta make tracks. You wanna drive back?"

He was surprised but jumped at the offer. "Oh, hell yes." She didn't have to ask twice. He slipped into the driver's seat, swung the vehicle around and felt the force as it responded to his controls. Grinning, he slammed them both back in their seats as he headed the racer for home.

Once they reached terminal velocity and the adrenaline wore off, Tuck had a moment to rethink what they'd just done. "Wouldn't it have been just as easy to drone that thing out here?"

Again, Trina wore her I-have-a-secret smile. "This one was Waldo's idea."

"Walt?" asked Tuck.

She winked at him and shrugged, but didn't respond to his

query, continuing her train of thought. "It's actually pretty clever. His plan is to re-position the Pin."

That certainly would be a trick, he thought, *if* they could pull it off, but he wasn't quite sure how they could. "Wouldn't that throw the race? I mean, for both teams, not just theirs."

"That's the clever part. He's not really going to move the Pin, he's just going to erase it from their screens and put in another one just over the visible edge of the lunar horizon. You know. Closer. So they wouldn't actually finish the race."

Tuck began to understand. "Still, wouldn't it be more effective to transport that via drone?"

"We thought it would be less risky this way," she explained, "Drones have their own payload and their own signature. They also have their own unique speed capabilities. We haven't yet been able to code a coating that worked well enough to imitate one. Drones fall into a separate, actually quite particular, aviation category, based on their use as delivery vehicles. The delivery guilds have done a clever job of protecting the base components of delivery drones that give their transponders a unique signature." She shrugged. "That's what Waldo says anyway. Has a lot to do with their ability to represent the interests of their services."

Tuck understood. A drone delivery would be both identified and then suspicious. A trick discovered before it was even performed. As executed though, it looked as if a random electronic camera had flown out to the Pin for some pre-race images. The package would serve its designated purpose, then after the race was over and eyes were no longer on the Pin, they could drone it home at leisure.

Well played, Walt.

* * *

They weren't shouting, but pretty close. The full group, again gathered around the banquet table arguing and pointing, went suddenly silent as Tuck and Trina reentered the now familiar banquet hall.

"Oh, yeah," sang Trina to the group with a strut in her step. "We delivered."

The crowd called out a few kudos of appreciation, then immediately returned to its animated discussion.

As he remembered from his first entrance, to his unadorned eyes, they looked like a group arguing among themselves, but not really addressing one another. He fished the glasses out of his jacket as he and Trina approached.

Tuck presumed that Walt had been busy in their absence, porting the digital contents of the dilapidated video case into their preferred method of review and manipulation.

He wasn't wrong. But, at the same time, he wasn't prepared for the sight that greeted him.

Above the table floated two distinct towers of data, one at each end. Actually, the first one couldn't really be called a tower . It was more of a small pile. It sat at the head of the table near where Anton stood, dwarfed in comparison with the huge columns at the opposite end of the table where Bren sat, her eyes now on Tuck with what looked like a pleading request for an explanation. It looked like a giant game of high-stakes poker, Anton with a paltry few chips left to his name, and Bren winning as if she were on a once-in-a-lifetime streak. Tuck noticed another key difference as he looked closer. While the pile was small, it was also static. It sat quietly. Immobile. The data towers, on the other hand, were anything but. They moved as if they were alive. They maintained their structural parameters, but it looked like a glowing mass of crawling things. Like they were made of busy, colored ants—all moving to some end.

"What am I looking at?" Tuck asked.

Walt looked up, his eyes bright, and his response energized by his discovery. "It's the contents of the case. Check it out." He motioned to the small pile. "That's the construction software and the full extent of what they programmed the machines to do."

Tuck shook his head. "Looks like almost nothing."

Walt nodded quickly. "Exactly. Whatever they were using this for, it certainly wasn't construction. Some of us think it's corporate data. You know, financials. Each tower of data there has maybe the operating status, the credits and debits of a single large corporation. You know, updating their transactions in real time." He stopped for a moment, fixing his gaze on Tuck. "What do you think?"

Tuck was thoughtful. "I don't know. Could be. I don't think that's it, though. I've seen financial data before. Sure doesn't look like this."

He examined the display more closely. Big, square columns, their exteriors blanketed in continuous motion, the holograms rendering a rich visual reflection of . . . .Well, he wasn't quite sure what it was tracking, but it certainly reflected an organized and coordinated operation. As he moved around, he saw other columns within the group. He eyed them with curiosity. The majority were green, but a pair of smaller columns with a yellow-gold tone were tucked in between the forest of green columns, and then two large purple columns that stood behind, completed the inventory. He also noticed a marginal difference between the columns. Aside from their color and varying height differences, there was something more. In most of the green columns the movement of its glowing ant-like components was active and moving, most had continuous movement in the column's upper sections with the lower portions solid and static. One, however, was in the same state as the smaller pile next to Anton. It was solid and completely still. No movement from within.

"Sorry," he told the group "I haven't seen anything like this before. Afraid I can't be of much help."

Next to him, Trina was staring hard at the data displays. She hadn't said anything, but her eyes were full of disbelief. "Algorithms," she whispered.

All conversations suddenly stopped.

"Algorithms?" asked Anton from the head of the table, " Algorithms to what purpose?"

Trina's voice sounded somehow lost. Like she saw it and didn't believe what she was seeing.

"This is bad. Very bad."

"What is it?" asked Anton again, the urgency now obvious in his more demanding tone.

It seemed to snap her back from her wandering trance. "Clearly, they're used for lots of things, she said. But in the security world, they're used pretty much for one thing." She swallowed. "They probably *are* corporate. Or maybe government. I can't say." She shook her head. "Either way, it's no good. In the security world, we use these algorithms for code-breaking. And now," she said, shaking her head, "Now, they're going to blame it on us."

Tuck tilted his head in curiosity, not so much about Trina's comment, but more about her body language. She couldn't stand still. It was like she had to pee but had no place to go. She paced and muttered, still shaking her head, then paced some more. He realized that she'd been doing this since they'd returned, but with the columns and the questions, he'd not paid much attention.

"We have to go," she repeated yet again. "Let's go now."

Tuck found it hard to believe that Trina's impatience wasn't dampened by the discovery they now stared at in wonder, its movement and colors mesmerizing them all. Except, of course, Trina. Actually, he thought to himself, she's the only one who's able to maintain focus. Responsible for security, their new-found discovery might not amount to anything without the cover story the race would provide. Maybe she was the only one among the group able to put enough mental distance between their new discovery and their planned deception.

Tuck wasn't alone in his observation. "You are correct. We must move quickly," Anton said, now towering above the rest, his hands raised in an effort to maintain control. "Let us stop with our suppositions for the present time. We have other issues to consider."

He went into full-on director's mode and turned to Trina. "Trina. Take the first car. Take out their lead racer. Mican, I believe his name is. I do not know how you will do it, but take him out. Out of the race." He looked uncertain for a moment "Mican. Yes, I believe that is correct. The remainder of the crew is incidental." He shot a quick look at Tuck.

Tuck nodded his confirmation that Anton had indeed called the name properly. Race fans knew the name. He knew the name. "The others seem to show up now and again," Tuck confirmed. "He is the constant."

Trina needed nothing more. She nodded and without another word, turned on her heel, making tracks for the race site, the banging door marking her exit.

Tuck, however, had caught the gist of what Trina suggested. It made a lot more sense to him now. "So that's what they're up to."

"UNICON?" asked Walt.

"Yes UNICON, and if I'm right, I'm afraid they might want their name back."

This time it was Bren who raised the question, her voice shrill and suspicious. "What? What are you talking about?"

"Here's what I think," said Tuck, moving about slightly to examine the data columns from different angles. "I think these color schemes have to do with categories. Maybe categories of location."

"What, like on Earth?" asked Walt.

"Could be. But I think maybe bigger. I think the green probably represent organizations on Earth. Gold? Just because of the size. I'm thinking that's here in Copernicus."

"Purple?" asked Walt. "Look at the size of those things."

"I was thinking about that, and I'm thinking only one thing makes sense. Only one thing could have that much impact. Midway. Midway has got to be the purple. Two purple pots of gold."

"Midway?" asked Walt. "What would they want with that giant amusement park?"

The silence that followed was not one of wondering, but one of wonder. They all knew there was one thing on Midway with that type of power. The answer was clear, but no one spoke.

"Casinos." The voice came from the far end of the hall. It was familiar but, at the same time out of place. Tuck's head swiveled in surprise.

[21]
THE PIN

MICAN WHISTLED. "THAT'S HUGE," he said with a disbelieving shake of his head. "A real step forward for them."

The race jackets Mican had provided now served a dual purpose, warmth and camouflage. They'd spent the night before outside the Copernicus dome, setting up the race tents, racing, and enjoying the mental freedom of being off-grid. In Copernicus, the ambient temperature was comfortable enough with his TransComm flight-suit, and the race tents had their own environmental controls, but out here the chill of the lunar surface made Durt shiver, and he could feel that chill as he breathed it in. The jacket was a little too big for him, and he pulled it tighter around his shoulders to maintain as much of his body heat as possible.

"A real step forward? What do you mean?" he asked Mican. Across the flat of the surface, they watched the bright orange vehicle scream by just above the surface, kicking up a dust rooster behind it as it tore south.

Beside him, Mican and Truman wore similar jackets, and the three of them sat on what looked to be the surface of the Moon. In actuality, they sat on the roof of Mican's vehicle. They'd been sitting in this lunar crater for at least a couple hours now. The crater was not a very deep one, Mican had told them, but a crater, nonetheless, within the Sea of Tranquility filled with sand. According to Mican, some of the craters were filled with moon sand that was more than two kilometers deep. This was nothing like that, but it had enough sand for their purpose now, which was to hide the vehicle. He said the sand here had a dangerous habit of acting like quicksand, with heavier objects sinking through it like mud or water. The grav field that enabled them to breathe here also gave them their gravity, but with TransComm's recent research and development in field manipulation, Mican had rigged a tweak to his car that allowed him to modify its grav field enough to allow it to sink a few feet into the lunar sand before returning local gravity.

For now, they sat on its roof, their butts warmed by the vehicle and the rest protected and disguised. It was the first time he'd tried to look like a moon rock, but there had been a lot of firsts over the past few days.

"UNICON usually rigs some booby trap in this area. Just after the Pin when we're on the home stretch. They are dangerous, but if we know where they are we can avoid them. That alternate detour vector loses us seconds in time, and sometimes the race as a result, but in the end, we're in one piece."

The element of danger surprised and intrigued Durt. He looked at Truman who, apparently, had read his thoughts and nodded with a smile. "Nothing is worth anything if there's no risk. They play for keeps out here."

Mican continued. "Spend some time out here, and we get to find out where they put it and watch out for it. Part of our strategy. We've lost racers because we didn't pay attention before."

"But this is something new?"

Mican extended the digi-tab he used to control his vehicle. On it, Durt read the displayed transponder identification. It seemed wrong. "It says it's a camera."

Mican nodded. "That's the step forward. If we were sitting back at the start gate and relying on our remote sensors, we wouldn't have given this a second look. Just another camera on the prowl for images. But this? This is sophisticated. This is a real hack. They've disguised an entire car to reflect a camera signature. Looks like they may have some new talent on the team."

Durt read the concern on his face and a thought occurred to him. "Wouldn't they have seen us, too? I mean, electronically?"

Mican patted the warm roof of the vehicle beneath them. "Thanks to the optimization of our transponder scanners, they limit their field of search to surface and above-surface."

"What, they can't scan sub-surface?"

"Sure, it's possible, but it's a different system. And," he said raising a finger, "it's more expensive to produce. You don't normally go looking underground for potential collision targets. So all commercial vehicles are equipped without that feature. Which makes my car," he said with a smile, "invisible."

"So they didn't stop here. Where did they stop?" asked Truman.

"The Pin," said Mican. "According to this camera vector, they stopped right at the Pin."

Durt asked the question. "And what does that mean?"

Mican shrugged, "Could mean anything. Won't know until I see it."

"But, wouldn't that reveal our position? We're not walking up there." He shot a quizzical look at Mican. "Are we?"

Mican checked his wrist comm. "You got that right. That *would* reveal our position. Keep in mind, a healthy dose of suspicion is critical. Everything else is timing."

Durt watched Truman's expression change to one of understanding as the realization came to him. But Durt was still in the dark. "What is it?"

Mican deferred the answer to Truman with a nod as he stood up and motioned them to follow his lead. They stepped off the roof and onto the moon itself. "We'd better give it about 10 meters or we'll be buried in the sand as well."

Durt shook his head and quickened his step. "Not good."

Mican agreed. "Not good at all."

Durt turned to Truman as they walked."So what's with the timing thing?"

"By this time, the course will be covered with cameras and cars of all kinds. Pre-race is in a few hours, and there are plenty of fans who bring their own vehicles up and speed them around. It'll look like a circus. No one will be looking for race tricks in that crowd. It gives us cover."

Mican motioned them to a stop, turned and with a few fingered motions on his digi-tab, coaxed the car into motion. Durt felt the microgravitational shift in his stomach and watched as the car came up out of the sand, nose first, then executed a circular turn that brought it up to within a few feet of where they stood. It must have had an up-angle to its in-sand position, Durt figured, and just moving it forward allowed it to exit its sandy hiding place.

Mican was all business now. "They always have a surprise for us. Let's go have a look and see what this one is."

* * *

"What the hell is it?"

At a glance, it was difficult to tell it was even there. It was a pile of rocks, and the container looked pretty much like a rock. If they hadn't known or suspected something was there in the first place, they'd have overlooked it completely. Durt stepped forward to pick it up and examine it more closely. Truman restrained him with a hand on his arm. The grip was tight. His voice was short and sharp. "Ho!"

Beside him, Mican nodded with a quick motion of his head. "Good call, Truman." He paused for a moment as Durt looked at him in confusion.

"What?" Durt asked, his tone almost indignant. "It's just a box."

Mican's reply was soft. Almost as if he were reciting poetry. "Know thine enemy."

"*Just a box* could blow off your hands," said Truman.

Mican agreed. "Or your head."

Durt turned and observed the box again, this time with growing curiosity and respect. It wasn't that big of a box and certainly didn't look threatening. Its shading and texture looked almost as if it had been manufactured specifically to fit in there. Maybe that was the point. He thought about it. No, he decided, it wasn't practical. Low probability of anyone stepping out and randomly looking—much less, picking up—the rock-like container. No, the only way someone might happen across this would be if they were actually looking for it. Like they were. Unless. He stopped again for a moment. If the orange car knew it had been spotted, this could be a trap. Based on what Mican had said earlier, the races were for keeps.

The first and only rule is there ain't no rules.

He struggled with his impulses for a few seconds. Should he disregard safety for a closer look? It was a struggle for him. Safety was the primary rule of survival when it came to flying rescue missions. If you wanted to fly again, you learned lessons from others who'd flown before you. He was about to follow his own advice when the image of an arm with no hand flashed through his mind and turned his stomach. He stood still, paralyzed by the thought for a moment, then took a respectful step backward and looked over at Mican.

"It's a race, Durt. Just a race."

In an instant, Durt's attitude shifted. It wasn't just a race. Nothing up here was just for entertainment. Not for him, anyway. He was sick of being pushed around by some demented psycho. No, it wasn't life and death, but he couldn't walk around scared of everything. He had to stop running at some point and face what he was running from.

"Aw, fuck it," Durt growled, angry more at his own inability to resolve the situation he'd created. His movement was quick and abrupt. The pair behind him first scrambled to grab him, then realizing they couldn't, beat a hasty retreat. They scrambled and stumbled in jerky off-balance motions, then dove face-first into the gritty landscape, their hands covering their heads.

Durt lifted it gingerly. It was a curious shape but had nowhere near the mass a rock should have. It was light in his hands, and he tossed it into the air like an odd-shaped basketball and caught it again. One of the two behind him, and he wasn't sure who, yelled out sharply as he tossed it up, but was quickly silenced. The result, Durt presumed, of a second duck-and-cover move, the yelling mouth muffled by its proximity to the sand.

He examined it, more closely this time, turning it in his hands to check for any cracks or crevices that might offer the opportunity to open it and examine its contents.

Mican was dusting off his coat and cursing. "Damn fool. You could have killed all of us."

Truman just shook his head in silence as if he couldn't believe what had just happened.

"Not with this," Durt said, placing the container back into its crevice within the rocks. "It's not a bomb, and there's not a visible opening so we can see what's inside. I don't know what it is. What I do know is that if you're going to trap an animal, you don't hide the trap where the prey won't walk. You put it directly in their path. Curiosity does the rest. You don't disguise a trap and set it where it won't be found. Makes no sense."

While they couldn't disagree with his logic, it didn't seem to lighten their mood.

Maybe they just needed a little encouragement. "Nice diving technique, boys," he said with a deadpan smile. "Based on that, I'm guessing this is not one of their old tricks. An addition to their inventory?"

Truman was stone-faced.

Mican, however, did respond, if only with a half-smile and a nod of agreement. "Something's going on. First the car. Now this? This puts a whole new face on the race. I've got to pay attention to this one."

Mican had stopped talking to them and retreated into a

conversation with himself. "New wrinkles? New strategy. Watch yourself, Mican." He checked his wristcomm and frowned. "Something's wrong. Should be a crowd here by now," he said, scanning the lunar horizon.

The three of them stared south in silence. Mican was right. But he wasn't right for another few minutes. He shook his head and paced and then dug the digi-tab out of the vehicle.

"There we are," he muttered to the digi-tab. "Come to Mican."

Durt checked the horizon again, and this time he saw it. It wasn't a vehicle. It was a dust cloud. More like a fleet. The white dust of the Sea of Tranquility rose and billowed and reflected its shifting shape, announcing the arrival of the pre-racers.

At first, they were only specs beneath the great cloud, but within a minute he could see the mass of northbound racers. He guessed 20. Maybe 30 of them. He stood in awe as he now felt their arrival rumble the sand and rocks beneath his feet.

Mican, his concerns now either gone or disguised was back in form. He was nodding and motioning them back into their vehicle.

"Move it, gents. Let's kick up some dust of our own."

They moved in unison, understanding immediately Mican's intent.

"They'll see us heading back from the Pin. It's our cover," he said over his shoulder as Durt jumped in first and heard the hatch close behind him.

"Plus," he added with a smirk, "the exposure is good for business."

* * *

The day before, the starting line had looked pretty much like every other location in the Sea of Tranquility not currently occupied by Copernicus. Dull. Black and white. Monotone. In fact, as Mican reminded him, before they'd set up their tents and equipment yesterday, the only unique features here were the the positioning numbers of the vehicle's LPS readout.

Now, it stood transformed. Activity was chaotic with colorful tech tents erected, and arriving vehicles scattered haphazardly here and there. Across the newly erected compound spread the mass of fans, a crawling frenzy like ants on a dropped snack. Durt estimated the food, drug and race vendors probably equaled the number of race fans, a mass of humanity drinking it all in. Feeding off one another's excitement.

He found the scene eerily surrealistic. The crowd looked as if it were a living organism, engaged in a weekend stage performance. If he focused on the larger view, the edges of the crowd moved and swayed with the arrival of new fans and vehicles, and if he moved his focus closer, the groups within the groups worked on their own performances. It was almost like the rooftop rave in Seattle had reformed itself here. That hadn't ended so well for him, he remembered. He hoped this would turn out better.

It was a little circus city. Within their risk-averse society existed an underlying longing for it. This was one of its regularly scheduled manifestations. Drugs and alcohol of every sort imaginable made their way here, their vendors hawking them as freely as if they were watches or sushi. This was one of their many stops —some legal. Others not.

Outside the dome? Outside the law.

Once you exited Copernicus proper, you were pretty much on your own as far as law enforcement went. At least that's what Durt had heard. He confirmed it to himself as he picked his way through the crowd. They'd parked the racer next to its twin, their backup, in the main team tent erected by Mican's team that served as the team's pit garage. Mican had a long list of system checks, and Durt understood immediately Truman wouldn't budge from his side until they were completed. He watched with interest for some time, then without interest for a longer time. What he really wanted to see was the crowd, and of course, to check out their competition.

Who was behind the orange car? Why had Mican been so impressed with it?

Finally, he couldn't help himself, and without a word, set off to check out the race scene. Free-flowing vices were pervasive and had a way of attracting their own sideshows. Whores and gambling usually went hand-in hand—plenty of options for poor decision making, he thought. Fights seemed to break out spontaneously around him, and where there was a fight, a crowd surged, and money went down.

To the winners, the spoils.

Not so much to the winners of these fights, who it appeared, were usually satisfied with bragging rights. But the winners of the bets had a full spectrum of vice available to them; their winnings returned quickly to the crowd.

Around him, the tide of the crowd ebbed and flowed as he pressed forward through the ocean of race fanatics. He saw a woman whose hair jutted out and formed a ball three times the size of her head. She was talking with a man whose head was half shaved. Where there should have been hair was a bald, colorful scalp decorated with a tattoo of a crow. Another woman wore a skin-tight dress that wasn't a dress at all, he realized, as they passed in the crowd. She was as naked as the day she was born, and the dress was painted directly on her skin. He shivered inside his race jacket just thinking about it. Based on the offers he got for women, drugs, and a few things he didn't even know existed, it was certainly possible the vendors outnumbered the race fans.

The sights and sounds of the crowd blurred his sense of time, but ultimately he was successful in both hanging on to his money and arriving at his desired destination.

Up close, the competition's racer looked similar to Mican's. Its hatches were open for inspection, and it drew its own crowd. They stood, talked, laughed, argued on and around the racer, but their conversations and their focus were not that of the vehicle itself, but of the race and of racing in general. They spoke their own race language, referring to races, racers and racing terms with ease and with speed. While he caught bits and pieces, he was hard-pressed to make much sense of any of it. He wasn't unfamiliar with the concept of these races, and he'd seen a few but had nothing more than a passing interest during his off-duty time in Seattle.

A hand touched his arm. "You like it?" It was a friendly voice from a tall, attractive female.

He looked at her for a moment taking in her smile and her hospitality before returning his gaze to the racer. "It's something else," he breathed.

His duty as a rescue pilot had always given him a certain type of privilege and notoriety. Something he'd become used to. What it hadn't given him was deep pockets and the ability to do anything more than lust over vehicles like these. He knew it couldn't dive and roll like his crimson rescue plane, but it was a speeding bullet, nonetheless. Its form. Its shape. Its very nature called to him.

"You want to sit in the driver's seat?"

He almost couldn't believe she'd asked. He couldn't say no. In fact, he realized, he was so excited he couldn't say anything. He nodded vigorously.

She smiled at his enthusiasm. Apparently a rare thing, he judged, as she guided him forward. She stopped short and looked at her wrist. "Sorry," she said, "I have to take this. Go on." She motioned to the pilot seat, then stepped back. "Have a seat. See what you think."

The inside of the racer was markedly different from Mican's, maybe as much as Mican's was different from the flyer he'd piloted in the TRI-PAC back in Kent. He felt the controls and noted their positions. It was a lot cruder on the inside than it had appeared from the outside, but he was sure this car would easily slam his lungs and his guts into the seat behind him. He smiled as he gripped the controls and settled in for an imaginary race.

It was over before it started as the woman reappeared. "Like it?" she asked as if she could already read the answer on his face.

"Oh, very much so. Something about sitting here changes your whole perspective." He looked up at her. "And not just on driving. Know what I mean?"

She said nothing, but nodded slowly as if she knew exactly what he meant.

She extended her hand in greeting as he climbed out of the car. "I'm Trina. Nice to meet you."

Her hand was smooth and cool to the touch and the sensation had an immediate impact on him. Attraction? Trust? Lust? He couldn't be sure as he looked into her eyes. "Likewise," he responded. "Durt. Durt Larson."

The reaction was not what he expected. There was no polite smile. No wink or welcome opening to additional conversation. Her response was an undisguised open-mouthed stare. And it wasn't just her. The crowd around the racer went immediately silent, too.

"What?" asked an incredulous voice. "What did you just say?" It was a young man, about his age. He was dressed in what looked like some commercial designer's ripoff of a pilot's uniform. It wasn't a practical uniform, but it wasn't cheap either. Probably had his own racer. Just for fun, Durt thought.

He repeated his name slowly, realizing again the power of his unrequested and somewhat, in his opinion, awkward fame. "I'm Durt Larson."

In a rhythm he'd now become used to, a moment of silence was followed by an instant of recognition, then a mob of pawing and gawking arms. Instant best friends—to his dismay. He tried to be as gracious as possible. He answered a few select questions. Someone produced a marking pen and he signed some arms, a couple shoulders and even an exposed breast before he felt Trina's insistent tug on his arm, which he obeyed gratefully, following as she pulled him past security and into the opposing team's race tent.

She found a couple of chairs somewhat away from the buzz of activity surrounding the team's primary vehicle inside the tent.

This one wasn't orange either, he noted. Same shade of black as the one outside.

"Thanks," he said. "I'm not really good at being a celebrity."

"So it's true then? You're Durt Larson? TransComm's Durt Larson?"

"In the flesh."

Now her smile returned. "Now, isn't this a nice bit of luck?"

He wasn't sure why she'd call it luck. There wasn't anything remarkably lucky about it—unless, of course, she'd taken an instant liking to him. Maybe there was some benefit to his instant fame.

"I have to apologize," she continued, "I don't know much about you."

He shrugged. "Not much to know. First time to the Moon. First time to one of these races. What else do you want to know?"

She stood quickly and held up a finger, motioning him to wait. "Please, just wait there. Two seconds. I'll be right back. Don't go anywhere. Promise?"

He held up both hands in a gesture of surrender. "Sure. Sure. Whatever you say."

It did take longer than her promised two seconds, but not much. Before he could think about making his way through the crowd and back to Mican's tent, she was back with a bottle of champagne and a pair of glasses.

Now, he thought, here *was* a bit of luck. Yes, a nice bit. She'd been right.

"What's that for?" he teased, "Shouldn't you wait until after the race before you start celebrating?"

She handed him a glass, popped the bottle's cork with an agile, deft motion, and he watched the bubbles fizz as she poured the golden liquid. "Not every day I meet a celebrity. Don't worry," she added in a mock undertone. "There's plenty more, so we can celebrate after we win, too."

Her eyes sparkled with her jest, nearly as much as the champagne, and he raised his glass to touch hers. "Here's to winning," he said, "whatever course that takes."

"Clever." She winked. "I'll drink to that."

They spent the next minutes sipping, walking and talking. He was impressed with the level of tech that they'd carried and set up on site here, knowing only hours before the only thing here was lunar sand and expectations.

She was walking him through the race monitoring system when he felt the champagne hit. He didn't remember drinking that much, but when he glanced over at the bottle, he realized little remained.

She caught his gaze and his elbow."You OK? You look a little dazed."

He shook his head and tried to shake off the sudden wave of exhaustion that seemed to have dropped on him like a heavy blanket.

She was sympathetic. "I forgot. First time, right? Don't worry. It happens to a lot of first-timers." She grabbed the front of his coat and looked him straight in the face. "What you need is some strong coffee."

As before, she stood before him and motioned with her finger to wait right where he was.

"Two seconds. I'll be right back."

Again, he said nothing. His nod spoke for him. He hoped coffee would do the trick, and then he really had to get back to the other tent. He sat back and tried to watch the monitor that displayed a view of the crowd outside. Was Truman out there, too? Of course, she wasn't back in two seconds. And there was something else. He wasn't quite sure if he'd heard it right. The Net was broadcasting a story about Nalan Rush. He thought it said suicide. He tried to get up and move closer to the monitors, but he couldn't. What remained of his energy and his will to do anything but close his eyes dissipated completely. He'd had jet lag before, but this sapped his strength something fierce.

He tried to muster some kind of anger. He wondered if maybe

that could kick-start some adrenaline. Then he thought about standing up, but he couldn't do either.

Trina was back and he felt her face close to his. "Hey, Durt? You OK? You don't look so good."

She had coffee, but he didn't care anymore. He tried to speak. To respond. It was like he was being crushed. He fought it, but only momentarily. No use. He gave in and closed his eyes.

[22]
AWAKE

THE GROUP TURNED in unison to see Carter walking toward them.

His face was visibly strained and his movements slow, but his eyes were clear.

"Hey, Clue," said Walt, his tone one of friendly recognition.

"Carter," corrected Tuck. "Friends, this is a colleague of mine. Officer Carter."

He turned back to face the now-ambulatory Carter. Tuck had a million questions for him but realized this wasn't the time. "Welcome back, Carter. You look like—" He stopped. No need to be overly concerned or overly crude. "Ah—"

He paused and started again. "We could use your help."

Carter read his mind. "Look, we can catch up with all the happy horse shit later. Tell me about this."

Somewhere, Carter had picked up a spare pair of glasses and now stood shoulder to shoulder with the rest of the group.

Tuck wasn't unfriendly, but priorities were priorities. "Not now, Carter." He turned to Anton. "Trina's right. We haven't got much time left. By now, curious faces are sniffing around the starting line, hungry for pre-race tidbits. Odds are we'll miss the pre-interview session."

Anton's raised eyebrows queried Walt. "Car color. How long to revert it to its original black shade?"

Trina was gone, but Tuck could still hear her unspoken protest defending her orange choice. Anton faltered momentarily as a thought crossed his face. "She did not take the orange vehicle, did she?"

Walt's half smile told the whole story. In a flash of motion, his fingers swapped the data columns for the exterior overhead surveillance view, the bright orange of the racer serving as the colorful centerpiece to the blacks and whites of the lunar surface. He had his issues with Trina, but it was respect Tuck detected in his response. "No, she's smarter than that." Already his fingers moved in synch with Anton's direction. "On it," he said. "Shouldn't be long now."

Tuck nodded. "That should give us a few minutes," he turned back to Carter, offering a cigarette from the case he'd pulled out of his pocket. As a general rule, Tuck didn't smoke, but a decent cop prepped for contingencies, and he was a decent cop. Carter nodded without emotion, slipped a cigarette behind his ear, then lit a second with the case before returning it to Tuck.

Tuck nodded with satisfaction and began to summarize the string of events that had taken place since their paths separated in Newton.

Carter listened to it all, taking it in word by word. He hadn't been fully awake when he'd wandered out of the back, but he seemed to savor each word he heard, his mind considering and assessing its syllables and deciphering its meaning in context. When he did speak, it was only a word or two, an assent or a confirmation of understanding. Tuck brought him up to speed on his discovery, his suspicions, and the host group that now offered them both shelter and a challenge.

When he was done, Carter remained as silent as he had before, lit his second cigarette, and turned his focus to the colored data display before the group. Like Tuck, he peered at it from all angles, noting its variations and similarities. In spite of the time factor they faced, the group did not interrupt his inspection, allowing him his silence to contemplate and offer his opinion.

The only sounds in the hall now were the subtle sighs and internal exclamations Walt made to himself as he worked through the data manipulation that would replace the color scheme of the racers. That and the distant sound of ocean waves coming through the virtual window along the side of the hall. The constant discussion had masked the sound before, but now as they watched Carter expectantly, Tuck noted that the exterior beach scene from the morning remained, with only the warmer tones and longer shades of a late afternoon sun reminding them of the passing day.

"Algorithms?"

"Yes," replied Tuck to Carter's one-word question. "That's what Trina thinks."

"I think she's right. Looks like they've cracked one already."

"What?" interjected Anton who still stood above the rest of the seated crowd, looking down on the data from a higher perspective. "How is it possible to tell?"

"Just a guess. But check out that medium-sized block," he said pointing to a green stack in the center. "See it? The one that's not moving?"

Murmurs of recognition came from the group. Tuck had noted it, too. If these were code-breakers, then maybe the movement noted progress as Carter suggested. The majority of the green columns were at least partially completed with the upper portions active and alive with motion. But one of them was not.

Tuck let out a low whistle as the realization of what that meant revealed itself to him. "That's where they are. That's what they're doing."

"They who?" asked Bren.

"They, the old UNICON. They're not vacationing. They're on a job. They're testing out their new key."

"That's just not possible," said Bren.

Carter disagreed. "Actually, it's very possible. It makes sense, too. With a key in hand, they wouldn't need this cover story anymore here. They could sell it and move on."

Bren clarified. "No. We talked with them. Interacted with them. No way they're that sophisticated."

"Criminal elements rarely are," said Carter. "It's not their standard method of operating."

Tuck concurred with Carter. "Based on what you told us, Bren, their primary tool is intimidation. No reason intimidation wouldn't work on a locksmith. But a scheme of this size? They could do some real damage."

"My God," said Anton, now understanding the gravity of their discovery.

Bren was adamant. "It doesn't matter how. We've got to stop them."

Anton shook his head. "We cannot," he said in his deep, measured voice. "We have neither the authority nor the ability to do anything but watch them at this point."

Bren stared at him, mouth open, apparently not wanting to believe that was the case. As she did, the data image in front of them faltered, froze, then disappeared altogether, leaving only the small, stunted pile of data in front of Anton visible.

Carter shook his head in confusion. "What the hell was that?"

Walt, still engrossed with his racer mods, looked up at the distraction and made some adjustments. Within a few seconds, the data columns flickered back to life.

"Walt, can you access those data columns?" asked Tuck.

Walt looked at him momentarily, then returned his focus to his racer programming. "It happened before, too," he replied, his voice answering the question, but his fingers continuing on task. He took a quick look at his wristcomm then returned to his program without looking up. "I'm recording an image of it, but that's all I've been able to do." He nodded his head at the other end of the table. "That little pile over there? That's local data. We have access to that now—thanks to you. This other big stuff? I can see, but I can't touch. No data files here, just the images of what you see."

"Walt, we're programmers," said Bren from the end of the table. "If anybody can crack those codes, it should be us. Our team."

With a few abrupt swipes of his hands, he stopped his active movements, raising his hands above his head, partly in victory, Tuck figured, and partly just to stretch the limbs he'd given full use of to finish. "We're back in black!" he announced with a flourish, as he slapped his raised hands down on the table. He took a deep breath, then turned to address Bren's question. "Yes, Bren. If these were local data files, I have no doubt we'd be able to pull them out. You're right. But this case is not a data storage unit. That's not how it works. This is something else.

Again, Carter was the first to understand. "If it's not a data storage unit, there's only one thing it can be," seeming impressed with the technology. "It's got to be a data receiving unit."

* * *

The orange car now black, Walt lost no time in pressing forward with the race review. Tuck had little idea what they might expect to find. He knew from experience that TransComm team's tricks and deceptions were usually subtle, although effective, much like Walt's idea to virtually move the Pin. What they needed was something from previous races that gave the deceptive appearance that this was, in fact, the same UNICON team.

Walt's eyes gave a momentary pleading glance before refocusing on the floating screen before him as Tuck stood over his shoulder. A disjointed collection of race clips zipped past as Walt tried to make sense of them. Broadcasts from previous races, but not in any particular order that would make sense—to a human, anyway. Walt had put the contents of the case discoveries on hold and was now exclusively engaged in race preps.

Yes, thought Tuck, Walt had been busy. The external view screen showed the car outside no longer displayed its festive race color, but had taken on a darker tone. OK, who was he kidding? It was black as night. Barely visible. Walt had followed his race research direction but was lost now in the jumble of video clips. "What am I looking at, Tuck?" Walt asked. "I'm lost here. I pulled a bunch of vids from the cars, but I'm having a hard time piecing together the race timeline. I'm trying to make sense of them, but I don't know anything about racing."

"Three parts to each race," explained Tuck. "Two interview sessions. One before and one after. Mostly trash-talk up front and mostly gloating after." He checked his wristcomm. "First one? We're missing it right now."

Anton looked up from the other side of the table, concern on his face. "The previous UNICON crew ever do that before? Miss a pre-race event?"

The question reminded Tuck that it wasn't just a race, but a deception as well. He understood their intention was to defend their remote status and keep their projects out of sight and out of mind until they chose to unveil it, playing themselves off as the UNICON thugs. They seemed to hope it would buy them some time to experiment with their unique technology.

Walt offered his suggestion and Tuck was impressed with his ability to both participate in the conversation and continue to work the project before him. "I don't know racing, but I do know whatever we do might fool some of them. But not all of them," he said without looking away from his display.

Tuck agreed. "Walt's right. Race fanatics won't be taken in." He turned to Anton. "To answer your question, yes, they skipped the pre-race on a pretty regular basis. Nothing new."

Anton nodded in satisfaction. "What else, then?"

"I think the biggest thing was the car color." Tuck considered a moment before continuing. "I think what's missing here is a solid tie to the past races. Doesn't have to be glaring. In fact, subtle is better. That's the kind of thing the fan fanatics tend to focus on. They'll overlook big in-your-face evidence as a joke, but focus on smaller things as reflecting reality. The whole concept of the races is based on deception of one kind or another."

Walt looked at him with curiosity, his hands still in constant motion.

Anton looked down at him. "Such as?"

He gave a quick shrug. "I don't know. I wasn't at the races. I caught some of them here and there. Best thing to do? Exactly what you're doing. Let's have a quick look at the past round-ups. Walt, you can toss out the trash-talk and the actual race vids. Won't tell us much. Best place to look is those after-race summaries. If it was in the race, they'll talk about it there."

The display froze as Walt awaited direction.

Tuck had an idea. "Walt, let's go back through the last three races. You, Anton and I will each take one."

Walt put the screens in motion again, most of which dissolved. What remained was a much-simplified display with only the three screens in question remaining. "There you go. That's it," Walt said. He flashed a grin and tossed his arms up into a *V* for victory. "Last three rolling now."

"What is it that we seek?" asked Anton.

"Just pay attention to their tricks. What they did, or what they tried to do. If you're going to pull off any type of disguise, your race antics need to be similar to the previous races. When we're done, we'll pool and choose. We don't have much time, so stay quiet and focus. You're going to have to explain to me what tricks they used. Or at least, what tricks they said they used."

Each nodded in assent and leaned into the interviews. For the next few minutes, only the sounds of the on-camera interviews filled the hall. The sound was somewhat unnerving. Three interviews. One voice. That singular voice that Tuck attributed to the

UNICON leader, Bike, took up most of the screen most of the time. He hadn't done the actual racing, but he did most of the talking. It was deep with a rasp. The interviews would have been impossible to follow with that single voice overlapping itself, and only a selective focus on each of their assigned screens made it possible. Many of the words were swallowed or mispronounced. If thugs had a language, Tuck thought, this guy would have written its dictionary.

The screens stopped suddenly as Walt held up a hand for silence. "I think I have something."

Tuck looked over at Anton. "What about you. You got anything?"

Anton shook his head a negative. "Not a thing."

"Me neither. Alright, Walt. I think you've had enough great ideas to embarrass the rest of us. What is it?"

Walt tilted his head and squinted his eyes with a bit of uncertainty. "Well," he said after a pause, "Maybe it's nothing. But I was thinking. Mine here is two races ago. And this guy won't shut up about the hyper-switch. I don't know what it is, but—"

"The hyper-switch," interrupted Tuck. "Yes, I remember that one. They swapped out a bum hyper-switch for the good one during the pre-race car review. After that, it was no contest for the speed race."

"So?" asked Anton. "How does that help us?"

An idea was forming in Tuck's mind. "We need to offer them easy access to a hyper-switch."

Bren's response beside him was immediate and shrill. "And throw the race?"

Walt offered a knowing smile, nodding his head as he worked his solution.

Tuck looked across the great table at Anton with raised eyebrows.

If they were to be successful in their deception, it had to be a team effort.

Anton took the unspoken message to heart. His response was spoken to the group but directed at Bren. "Let us keep before us our primary objective," said the tall man in his measured voice. "We are *not* the old UNICON, but we must *play* the old UNICON. It matters not," he said, shaking his head, "if we win or we lose." His face reflected a sudden uncertainty, and he turned to Tuck. "They did not win or lose constantly, yes?"

"I don't know the actual stats, but based on my race knowledge, I think it was a pretty even split."

"We are the *new* UNICON," Anton continued. "We are not here to win races. We're here to change the way people think about life. About the way they live. We're here to envision miracles. And then to create them."

Bren didn't take it personally. Her thoughts were hidden, but she nodded and even betrayed a bit of a smile at the corners of her mouth.

He wasn't kidding about the miracles, Tuck thought. Had he not known better, he would have believed his senses. They insisted he was standing in the banquet hall of a seaside castle. He felt the smoothness of the floor beneath his feet, saw the imperfections in the stonework, and heard the waves come ashore through the open window.

He breathed deeply. Miracles indeed.

* * *

The team was almost there. They had a plan. They had a black car. They were missing one thing.

Anton had somehow sensed Tuck's thoughts and surveyed the group before him. Without a large pool to start with, his options were limited. "One last thing. Unless I am mistaken," said the tall man, "we require a driver."

He looked over at Walt. "What I mean—" He left his sentence unfinished and began with another thought. "Unless we program an auto course into the vehicle. That is possible, yes?"

Walt's eyebrows raised momentarily above his work, a sarcastic expression forming on his face as if to say, *And you call yourself a programmer.* But he skipped sarcasm and went directly to practical. "Not in the time we have left. Just…can't…do…it," he said in rhythm with his fingers which continued to dance as an accompaniment to the conversation.

Anton turned to Bren, his questioning expression offering her the driver's seat.

Her response was sharp and quick, "Don't look at me," she said with venom. She was indignant as if driving was below her station in life.

Anton pursed his lips, his face ambivalent seeming to consider whether to press her or not.

She narrowed her eyes and crossed her arms, withdrawing from the conversation.

Their final answer was both simple and surprising, and one none of them had considered.

"I'll drive."

It was Carter.

Tuck shook his head a negative. "No way. You can barely stand up."

Carter lit another cigarette. "I said I'll drive," he said evenly. "No standing involved."

Tuck felt his hard expression melt to a smile. Driving an outlaw car outside the dome might very well be a dream for some. Feeling the determination of Carter's response, he sensed maybe Carter, who, he remembered, was hesitant about even breaking Copernicus grid protocol for police business, might just have an untapped desire to kick it loose.

"That's it, then," said Tuck and paused as a last-minute thought crossed his mind. "Walt, toss me the badge. Never know when that might come in handy," he turned to face their newly selected pilot, "Officer Carter."

Carter now looked like he felt, Tuck thought, his face reflecting that something that had been missing before. A true cop felt naked without a badge. Almost like a hand or a foot. It went with the job.

Carter smiled in satisfaction.

Walt, already onto his next project, reached out his hand without breaking his focus. His hand patted the table where he'd last seen it. He paused for a moment, a questioning glance first at Tuck and then at his empty hand. He stood up quickly, checking his pockets and coming up empty. "Look, I'm sorry Tuck," he said, his expression sheepish. "I was carrying it around with me for a while. I didn't think it would do any harm. It just felt so—" he searched for the right word. "Powerful. I must have put it down. It's around here." His shrug was of embarrassment. "Someplace."

Tuck understood the power of a police badge and dismissed Walt's concerns with a shake of his head. "It's not important. We'll get it later. We've got a race to run. Plus," he said with a reassuring wink at Carter, "I guess Officer Carter is dead. What would a dead cop need with a badge?"

He looked quickly at Anton. "You made the ME notification, right?"

"Just as you asked," Anton confirmed, closing his eyes and reciting from memory. "Body of Copernicus police officer found outside dome. Cause of death unknown. Presume hypothermia. Request appropriate protocol."

"And the signature?"

Anton's voice was more a question than an answer. "Rosa Vidri?"

Tuck breathed in deeply. "Yes. Thank you. No response yet, right?"

Anton shook his head in silence, but Walt interrupted.

"Actually, there is something. Just popped in. ME confirms receipt of messages. Asks for coordinates and—"

He paused for a moment, his creased face trying to make sense of what was apparently an anomaly. "Does this mean anything to you? XXOXOX. Maybe some kind of unique signature or originator's code?"

Anton shrugged. "I do not know, but confirm and send our coordinates, yes?" he asked with a questioning glance in Tuck's direction.

Tuck did his best to hide his surprise, putting on a mask of feigned perplexity. "Yeah, that's probably it. Who knows? Sure, Walt. Go ahead and send them the coordinates."

Carter apparently had questions, too, but Tuck's wink held them at bay. For the moment anyway. Tuck motioned toward the door, prompting their exit. "Let's move before we miss any more of the most exciting day of your life, ghost driver."

"Walt, a little darker tint on the windows, please," he called over his shoulder as they exited the long hall. We can't very well have an image of a dead cop piloting a racer all over the Net, now can we?"

* * *

Carter took a number of test spins around the exterior of the shipping containers, a familiarization drill with the car's controls. Most vehicles were of a similar design, and because of the focus on racing and the potential for lost races that came with unnecessary complexity, this vehicle offered minimal opportunities to screw up. After the fourth turn, Tuck figured Carter was just having fun. The biggest challenge was reading the race monitor, a central console screen that gave them views, stats, navigation and race updates. Carter flipped it through its various modes as they sped toward the race.

Tuck, for the most part, ignored him.

XXOXOX?

He couldn't remember which were hugs and which were kisses, but he wasn't really surprised that the coders didn't recognize it as anything more than some type of code. That's what they did, and that's how they saw the world. But that did mean a couple of things. First, it meant that his Green Rose feint that had gotten him out of Copernicus had a bigger impact than he had hoped for. Not bad for a spur-of-the-moment, pull-it-out-of-your-ass idea. He'd needed help, and he'd turned to Liz as an impulsive shot in the dark—a colleague on the better side of law enforcement. Right on the political borderline.

He hadn't looked at it as anything more than a fair trade. His life for an expensive piece of jewelry or sculpture or whatever you'd call it. That wasn't his thing, and the only reason he'd done it was that the business next door to the tattoo place just happened to be a glass sculptor he'd been of some assistance to a couple years back. That wasn't the surprising part. In his line of work, he helped out hundreds each year. Most were uncommonly grateful. Others, he smiled to himself, the ones on the other side of the law, the ones he'd *helped put away,* weren't nearly as grateful.

No, the surprising part was that he remembered. He hadn't given it half a thought, but when he'd poked his head into the shop on a lark, the man's face and smile brought it all back. Tuck didn't even remember his name. And the rose? That hadn't even been his choice. All he'd said was—in an out-of-breath whisper —*A special rose for a special lady*. That was it. The glassmaker had offered a knowing nod and pulled out that gorgeous green rose. Its texture and sparkle dazzled him, and he'd hoped it would do the same for her. As he thought back to it all now, it seemed too distant be have been real, but apparently he'd been right. The proof was staring him in the face.

You didn't follow a cop who'd gone rogue, he reasoned. That, by all rights, was a career killer. Or worse. Her professional courtesy should have stopped at the entrance to her building. Then it should have stopped at the Med transport. After that, at the edge of the Copernicus dome. But amazingly, it hadn't. He was more than surprised, because not only had she acknowledged him, she was collaborating with him. With any luck, she wasn't alone.

This was good. Very good.

What he still couldn't figure was the headless—and handless

— corpse. That was the apparent root of the whole issue, at least from his point of view. The serial killer. Which, he was convinced, wasn't a serial killer. The problem was he didn't know what it was. It had to be a distraction. Some kind of ruse to entice the virtual public audience of the Net, and, of course, to distract a potentially troublesome police force. That part seemed to have worked pretty well, but he was sure there was a more particular motive. The timing, maybe, when the focus should be on collecting and analyzing evidence and not taking tips from news reports resulted in the generally thin, presumptuous conclusion that there was a madman at work in the city. Lots of them populated the Earth. But this was the moon. Things were better here, or, in the case of the police force, a lot worse. Few violent crimes meant few sharp detectives were required here to investigate and solve them. For the majority of them, as he often thought, duty here was its own career killer.

As it turned out, though, there was a lot more for him in Copernicus than met his initial appraisal. A few decent Earth-side cops would have quickly dried up his unique, localized talents. But as things had gone, here, his above-average closure rate on Earth made him a giant among dwarves. A magician, even.

Outside, the lunar surface looked pretty much the same as it had when they'd climbed into the racer. It was hard to judge speed by anything but the bright dust cloud they kicked up as they sped toward the starting line. Carter finally stopped fiddling with the console controls, satisfied he'd become as familiar as he needed to be and sat back in the driver's seat. Tuck watched the expression of supreme satisfaction transform his face.

Carter cocked his head at Tuck with a slight smile. "XXOXOX?"

"It's code," said Tuck without cracking a smile.

"Damn right, it's code. How did you pull that off?"

Tuck shrugged and shook his head. He told the truth. "No clue whatsoever."

"Seriously?"

"Serious as a hull breach. I recruited her to help with my emergency evade and escape plan."

Carter laughed. "Recruited? Tuck, she's the ME. You don't just *recruit* MEs. She's a damn political appointee."

"I thought the same thing, but I was at the end of my rope. I figured I'd ask. Impossible for me to tell who was and who wasn't compromised. If I was going down, I was going down big."

In spite of his previous suspicions, Carter had turned out to be a real law enforcement asset. It felt good, Tuck thought, to be held in high regard by someone you respected. Apparently, his last-ditch effort to save his own ass had somehow elevated that status, based on Carter's expression of admiration.

"You think the coders knew what it meant? Or were they just being polite?"

"Hard to tell, wasn't it?"

"Seemed genuine."

"That's what I thought, too. In their world, I think they see everything as a code."

"And they were right, too."

Tuck said nothing but smiled at the thought.

Yes, they were right.

"Accidentally or on purpose, it doesn't matter," said Carter. "That's some skill or some good fortune. Or both. And thanks to you, it looks like the best day and the worst day of my life might just be the same day. Thanks, Tuck."

"That it?"

"Yes, sorry for being so—"

"No," said Tuck, shaking his head, his gaze locked forward, "is that it?"

Carter followed his gaze to the horizon, then punched a pair of screens on the racer's console until the forward zoomed view came up. He split the low-tech, ruggedized display in two and the data identification legend confirmed that they were now on approach to the starting line. It didn't look like much on the horizon, and Tuck knew that it wasn't much, the Net just made it seem so much bigger.

Carter confirmed as well. "Yes. That *is* it." He turned back to Tuck momentarily. "But seriously. Thank you, Tuck."

"My pleasure," said Tuck, suppressing a smile. "Just drive, and we'll call it even."

[23]
THE CROW

IT WAS TRUE. He worked for the man. But it was a job, and there were a lot worse jobs to have. Copernicus had plenty to offer in the way of suck jobs. He was the Crow, wasn't he? Even if a lot of his talents were wasted, he reasoned, that would be their loss. He figured the best thing about it wasn't really the job itself, sitting in that freaking console center for the better part of his waking days, but the access it got him. And this race was one of those events that really paid for the rest of the week. This was the cake and the icing, too. He might not have had a great week, but he was going to have a great weekend. With this crowd, that was pretty much guaranteed.

Then something popped in his subconscious brain. His work had trained his eyes and brain to pick out patterns and anomalies, and in this excited, costumed crowd, those without garish clothes and make-up distinguished themselves easily. He shook his head, trying to free himself from his ever-present vigilance. It was a race jacket. One of the race crew was making his way through the crowd. For the first time, it looked like. Racers usually ignored the fans and avoided the crowds, leaving the partiers to their own tasks. Racers had duties and chores, especially this close to the start of a race, otherwise they wouldn't be here. But not this one.

This one was checking out the faces, apparently amusing himself with colors and the inventiveness of the crowd. Not that he had a problem with that. That was part of the fun. Everybody was checking everybody else out. There was, however, something unduly familiar about this one, though, and he couldn't put his mind immediately on it. Like everyone else here, he had a buzz going. He didn't really want to concentrate. It was his day off, for fuck's sake. He shouldn't have to. But his brain wouldn't leave him alone.

Finally it hit him. What was his name? *Larson, Durt Larson.* It was one of the guys on his watch list. One of the floating faces. He was tracking him, and poof, he'd just disappeared. Damn system was quirky enough that he was used to it, but here he was. In the flesh. For whatever reason, the guy had made his way here and was posing as one of the pit crew for TransComm. Said so right on his jacket. He was impressed. Had it not been for the floating face on the console he'd watched, he would have thought nothing more.

What stupid luck. On my day off, too.

But a job was a job, he thought, and maybe there was something extra in it for him. Like the rest of the crowd around him, he was dancing and swaying to the race music that seemed to surround them all. He wasn't really dancing, but unconsciously, he moved with those next to him. Now, he picked up his motion. Dancing not like he was faking it, but dancing like he meant to dance. Music was his background and his strength, and dancing to him came naturally. For a few moves, he mimicked an orange-haired female with a little talent and a lot of swing in her behind. Then he knocked off a few of his own. Each new move took him a little closer to his intended subject. As he closed in, he lifted his hands in the air and did an odd crossing and clapping move. It didn't really look that good, he admitted to himself, but it wasn't for show. It had a tactical purpose. A few seconds later he stopped and withdrew, checking his wristcomm. Sure enough, a couple of images were sharp enough to identify the coat-cloaked Larson as his person of interest. A couple more finger swipes and the image was off. Now, he thought, he could get back to focusing on what he'd come here to do. What he'd waited all week to do.

Not 30 seconds had passed before he got the callback. He knew immediately what it meant. He cursed, then composed himself. If he didn't care so much about the stupid payoff, he'd tell that arrogant son-of-a-bitch what to do with himself. But, of course, he didn't.

His wristcomm transmitted directly into his ear plant. He wondered how many times he'd heard the rants and threats. It didn't matter. This time, and maybe it was because they were beyond the dome, it sounded thinner, less threatening. He listened and shook his head in disbelief.

"Look, I just got here," he said. "Forget it. No."

Then that voice came back again. The money was good. It was too good. Too good to pass up, anyway. He cursed again. "Yeah, OK. I'll be there soon enough," he said with an edge. "Yes. Don't worry." Then he signed off.

The voice wanted him to escort Larson back downtown. It wasn't that he couldn't do it. Sure, he could do it. But Larson wasn't even aware of him, and he knew exactly where to find him after the race. The race jacket gave it away. So he took a deep breath and went back to dancing.

First dance. Then race.

He smiled.

Then, get paid.

* * *

"Seen Durt?"

Mican's head was buried inside the racer. When he pulled it out to answer Truman's question, his forehead was slick with exertion. Or excitement. Truman couldn't be sure. In spite of the chill under the exterior field dome, Mican had worked up a sweat in final preps for the race, the efficiency of his race team jacket making its own contribution to heat conservation. His response was silent and curt, a shake of his head and a shrug of his arms. Mican turned to one of the pit crew Truman hadn't met. "You seen Durt?" Mican asked.

The kid was young with big eyes and was draped in the same team jacket that looked a couple sizes too big for his skinny frame. He shot back a confused glance. "Who?"

"Larson. Durt Larson. Guy who came up here with us."

He mimicked Mican's silent shrug that said, *I have no clue what you're talking about.*

Mican dismissed him with a glance, and the kid scurried off to whatever prep task he had. "Don't worry about it, Truman. If Durt can find his way to Copernicus, he can find his way around this dump. This is all new to him. Probably over checking out the competition. Or the show."

Truman wasn't quite sure what he meant.

Mican smirked at his uncomprehending stare and nodded toward the race crowd that was quickly becoming a mob. "The freak show. The old *No Rules* standard really brings 'em out here. He's probably getting an eyeful. Quite a few earfuls as well, I would imagine. Nothing like a bit of strange scenery to turn your head inside out."

He looked at Truman more sharply. "That it?"

Truman moved closer to display what he'd hidden in his pocket. It wasn't that big, and it wasn't that impressive, but it was a hyper burst unit, and it was what he'd gone after.

Mican smiled quickly and shook his head in disbelief. "How did you do it? They usually guard their vehicles like my mother-in-law guards her cigarettes."

Now it was Truman's turn to shrug. "There was only a couple of them, and they were in the middle of what I figured was a technical discussion," he said, nodding in the direction of the mob's now-constant roar. "Freaks. No," he corrected himself, "worse. Know-it-all freaks. I was going to join, but I couldn't get a word in for anything. All the time, this little baby is just sitting there. Like it had my name on it. Calling me. What could I do? I took it."

Mican didn't seem suspicious by nature, but Truman figured he'd been to enough of these races that he'd know when suspicious was justified.

Mican said, "Something's screwy. That just doesn't happen."

Truman agreed. "Screwy's probably a good word. Did you hear?"

"Hear what?"

"So, I eavesdropped a little. You know, maybe pick up some kind of strategy we might take advantage of. You know what I hear?"

Mican's silence was tinged with annoyance. He checked his wristcomm, his mind elsewhere.

Truman continued. "Rush. Nalan Rush."

Mican's look was impassive as he closed the propulsion hatch and took the hi-jacked part from Truman, inspecting it more closely. "So? What about him?"

"Dead." It was short and final, and it got Mican's attention.

"Whaddaya mean, dead?"

Truman shrugged. "That's what they were talking about. You know who he is? Said he killed himself."

Mican's stunned expression lasted only a pair of extended seconds before he stretched his lips over his teeth and whistled sharply. It worked. In a matter of seconds the skinny kid reappeared and confirmed shortly thereafter that, in fact, Rush's death was the talk of the race camp and the top story on the Net.

"You know, we were just there," said Truman. "at his place out there in Greenville."

Mican was hard to read. Clearly, he understood what had happened, but some things were bigger than him. Bigger than the both of them. He shot a quick glance over Truman's shoulder, eyes vigilant for their competition. "I wouldn't put it past them to follow you a few minutes later. Beat you silly then take back their precious burst unit. Who was there? Did you recognize anyone? Oh…maybe—"

Truman took his meaning clearly. "Nobody I recognized. And with those guys, it's hard to tell the pretenders from the racers. Never catch one of them dead in corporate gear." He shrugged. "Maybe they're slipping. Or maybe they're just new additions to the team."

"Maybe that's what they want us to think."

Truman paused, but only for a second as he checked his own wristcomm. "Maybe we get you to the starting line, and I make myself scarce. I haven't had my ass kicked in quite some time. Maybe I could extend that a bit longer."

Mican slammed the racer's propulsion hatch shut. "Ride with me."

Truman realized his surprised features spoke for themselves. "What?" he asked curiously. "We've done all the weight calculations specific to you. I'd just slow you down."

Mican turned the link component over in his hand and held it up in front of Truman, apparently oblivious to anyone who might be watching them. "Thanks to you, we won't need to worry about speed anymore. Sounds like we may have other issues, so let's enjoy this while it lasts," he said with a quick smile. "Our burst will be sweet, I tell you. But what that means is they probably have something else in mind. Another set of tricks. These guys play rough, and they play for keeps. I've lost crew out here before. Part of the thrill, I guess." He looked Truman in the eye. "An extra set of eyes now might save the race." Again, he looked over Truman's shoulder to the crowd beyond. "Or more." With a decisive step, he rounded the racer and vaulted into the pilot seat with a practiced motion.

Truman couldn't hold back his grin as he attempted to imitate Mican's slick move into the navigator's seat. He knew the score. He loved the thrill, and in fact, he told himself, a good dose of danger made him sharper. He failed awkwardly at his seating move but beamed a smile as he adjusted his harness.

Mican swung the racer around and steered directly for the center of the supporting mob. Slowing it to a crawl, he eyed the misfit parade of race fanatics as the crowd parted, a stream of faces and hands slipping by the window. Truman scanned the crowd, hoping to spot Durt, but held out little hope. While an undecorated face would probably stand out in this sea of faces, this was only a portion of the larger outlaw crowd that now inhabited this otherwise barren piece of the lunar surface. He put it out of his mind. They'd made their transit and delivered their first load as a team, he thought to himself. They were going to make a great team. For now, he deserved to have some fun. He smiled at his own good fortune and his unprecedented view of the race that was about to unfold. The freaks now fell in behind the racer as they marched in unison toward the starting line.

The two racers sat side-by-side. Two black bugs facing off in the Sea of Tranquility, the giant white sandbox that lay before them. Two cars. No rules. One race. One winner. A birds-eye view of the scene would have shown the two vehicles dwarfed by a semi-circular carpet of human onlookers, a black ocean of supporters thick enough to blot out the white lunar surface on which they stood. Of course, no actual birds lived out here. Only mechanical ones, but that was the initial view that would broadcast over the Net to outlaw fans and the sizable community of Earth-side viewers.

Truman listened to the sound. It was familiar but different. He'd heard it countless times, but never from this close. He could feel the buzz inside of him. Anticipation. It wasn't just a race. It was a race for life and death.

Now that he was here, in the middle of it, it wasn't just the thought of it, but the experience itself. Intoxicating. He didn't know if he could go back to just watching it on the Net. He could skip the makeup and the costumes, but sitting in the car was completely different from watching a viewscreen from a bar or his ship or even from a pit tent, and for the first time, he shared a particular strain of race fever with the crowd.

Next to him, Mican had turned to stone. Truman recognized his pre-race meditation. He'd shut off his pit comms and now stared at the expanse of lunar surface before them. As a racer, Mican listened to every piece of pit chatter but rarely spoke during the race.

It was a live Net event, and Truman knew the sequence by heart. They'd start the race after the announcements and the advertisements. The crowd would do its obligatory countdown. He mouthed the words as he watched the broadcast on the racer's dash monitor.

The Net announcer kicked it off just like every other race he'd seen. "What's the first and only rule?"

The response was tremendous. He mouthed it in unison with the roaring race crowd. It was a single voice a thousand times over. It thundered across the lunar landscape, and he felt its vibration resonate in his chest.

"There ain't no rules!"

Mican came alive. That was his cue. His hands flashed across the console in his last-minute pre-flight.

An intentional pause let the power of the crowd wash over the local bystanders and the remote audience. Then the countdown began.

"Ten…nine…eight." The roar of the count continued, but now only through the dash cam. Mican sealed the racer's hatches and leaned forward slightly. His hand hovered above the console.

"Three…two…one."

Mican's hand flashed in its practiced synchronicity. Just as the car had hinted it could do for that moment in Copernicus before they'd locked into the traffic grid, the force of acceleration pressed him firmly and directly to the back of his co-pilot seat. He strained his neck to see Mican in a similar posture, sporting a grin from ear-to-ear. Outside the hatch, he was surprised to see their opponent neck and neck with them, matching their speed. It sat there just as if it were parked, even though he could see the grey blur of sand and rocks screaming beneath them. The viewports tinted dark, he couldn't make out any faces inside. It was somewhat unnerving. Like if he couldn't see anyone, maybe there wasn't anyone there. Maybe they weren't even racing against UNICON, but rather UNICON's black vehicle from hell. Great clouds of the lunar dust billowed behind them as they sped forward across the Sea of Tranquility.

Truman regained the use of his limbs as they approached their terminal velocity. Next to him, Mican shot him a look. "Ready?"

He'd seen this part so many times he couldn't remember, and on the screens he'd watched, it looked almost unreal. Like no vehicle already going that fast could possibly go any faster. But it did. And it was going to happen now. He gripped the hatch handle because it was handy. He nodded.

Mican engaged the hyper boost, and a second invisible hand slammed Truman back to the back of his seat again. It pressed against his face and his limbs were useless. Four sticks glued to a board. The power of this vehicle was simply amazing, he thought. That yearning for speed he sometimes felt while waiting impatiently in traffic and observing the wonders of a city engineered for safety was now completely satisfied. And then some. He would have shaken his head in disbelief, but it was pinned as surely as the rest of him. Gradually, the acceleration decreased, and he peered out the hatch. He smiled. No competitor sat beside them now. They were alone at terminal velocity. He checked out the rear view screen. They, literally, he realized, had left their competition in the dust.

Not that he was too surprised. It was impossible to make a hyper boost jump without a functional hyper boost link, and from its current position in Mican's jacket pocket, it hadn't been terribly effective.

His joy was short-lived, however. Mican's face no longer smiled. It now reflected attention and focused concentration.

"What happened? What is it?" he said in a whisper of concern.

Mican shook his head. "Too easy." His jaw was set. "They've got something else planned. I can feel it. This speed? Not much we can do other than continue to go fast and hope for the best. I'm taking the instruments. You watch the forward port. Shout if anything seems out of place." He repeated himself. "Out of place," and looked over at Truman for the briefest of seconds to ensure Truman understood his role. "Any. Thing."

Truman's eyes locked forward, straight out the front viewport, he nodded in silent assent. The problem was, there was nothing out there. Nothing to focus on. He froze his head like a dog might, took a deep breath, and settled in for a tense staredown with the lunar surface. He kept his eyes just below the horizon. He had no idea what danger Mican had warned of, or what it might look like. Right now, it looked like nothing. Rocks and sand and black and white. He knew behind them they left a billowing dust cloud, but at their speed, it was well behind and visible only on a toggled view screen and in his imagination. He dared not avert his gaze for fear of missing some optical or physical dirty trick. At this speed, it wouldn't take much at all to send them spinning out of control and out of the race. Seconds became minutes. He blinked repeatedly to keep his eyes clear. His neck began to ache, and his grip on the seat's sidebars was relentless. Never had he driven so fast and seen so little.

Mican's voice was low and deliberate, and Truman caught his profile with his peripheral vision locked in an unmoving stare at the sensors on the racer's instrument display. "Any time now. Straight on. Twelve o'clock."

Still nothing.

"What about now?" asked Mican.

He blinked. "Nothing." But maybe there was something. "Wait." His eyes had stared long enough that now he wasn't sure. He blinked again to make sure it wasn't just a visual artifact, something his mind had invented to relieve him of his duties. But it was marginally larger now. "Hang on." He paused for an instant to verify. "Yes, it is something. Something vertical. It's the Pin."

Beside him, Mican let out a quick sigh of relief, but his fingers were already busy configuring the racer's 180. Mican's seat extended out, creating a solid barrier between the cockpit's twin seats. They had to round the Pin and complete the second half of the race the same way they'd come. In a straight-on sprint, this was their critical, and only, maneuver. This made or broke the race.

Mican's direction was appreciated, but unneeded. "Now you hang on."

With their sizable race lead now, Truman was pretty sure they'd blown the competition out of the race. Their competition now was not the other racer, but the course itself—Mican's previous times and speed records.

The G-force of the turn surprised and paralyzed Truman. It seemed the Pin might have been close enough to touch had they traveled the same route at a crawl, but it was nothing more than a blip as they screamed by it. He wondered again for the briefest of instants what the box disguised as a stone was for, half expecting it to explode and blow them off course. Just as quickly, he forgot. He understood now the design of the side-support in his seat. The turn's crushing weight pressed them both sideways into the extended supports.

Mican's delight was clear. "WoooooоHooooo," he shouted as they rounded the turn and steered into the giant cloud of disturbed lunar dust that now whirled before them. Outside, visibility dropped to zero and Truman felt the pressure of renewed acceleration. Mican's G-force seat retracted and revealed a smiling Mican shaking his head in wonder. "I don't know what you did on the drives here, Truman, but this just could be the fastest time I've ever made on this course."

Truman was surprised as well. "I didn't do much. Couple of new patches."

Mican shrugged. "Pshaw. Couple of new patches. It's a damn magic trick, Truman. This win is all you."

While he appreciated the compliment, Truman wondered in what way the patches had enabled such a fast transit. He shrugged. It was true, though, sometimes that's the way racing was. A couple little complimentary tweaks could have an unexpected impact.

"We'll see what the diagnostics say after the race," said Truman. He suddenly had another thought. "What about visibility now? Wouldn't this be where we'd be most at risk?"

Mican nodded to confirm his fear, but said nothing, eyes glued to his console.

Still at his lookout post, Truman watched the visibility clear as their dust cloud settled, then return immediately to zero as their competition screamed past them on their way to the Pin.

Mican said, "There. Now that we've passed the other car, we're on the same return path we cleared on the way in. Double check your harness because, as you know, there ain't no rules, but trickery almost always happens on the way out. It's the speed and the potential impact to the crowd of fans on the way back. We pretty much throw our safety to the wind, but in the end, it's not the pilots or the racers who make the races what they are. It's the fans. Send a car into a crowd, and you decimate your fan base. Not good for racing. Not good for business." He looked over at Truman. "Not good for anyone."

Truman nodded in understanding. "You know what that is then, don't you?"

Mican raised his eyebrows. "What?"

"That," said Truman with a grin, "is the one rule."

[24]
TRINA

THE CROW WAS DEAD.

The body was right, but the head was on backward like a child's doll, its features frozen in a grimace of horrible realization and pain. Trina had no idea how he'd done it, but there it was. The Crow was like a broken doll, the body prone on the floor, the dead eyes of the reversed head staring up over its back at the ceiling.

She couldn't believe her eyes. She felt sick and turned away, trying to hold it together.

Simms shrugged. "Loose end."

She shook her head violently as if denial might make it go away. Change things somehow.

"Look, don't get all sentimental on me now. You knew from the beginning this was a possibility."

"You killed our best tech?" She hissed. It was both a question and an accusation encompassing her inability to wrap her mind around what he'd done.

"We'll get another one."

Trina shook her head. "Not like this one, you won't."

Simms gave her a hard look.

A sudden realization shook her confidence. She felt her chest compress and the words escaped, even though she knew she should have kept them in. Her voice was little more than a whisper. "You didn't kill him because you had to. You killed him because you *wanted* to."

Simms said nothing, his face impassive, but she understood two things. First, she was right. He had no qualms whatsoever about ending a human life. Second, the fact that he'd said nothing in return meant something, too. Maybe she was next.

He stepped toward her, and she took an involuntary step back, keeping a buffer zone between herself and the monster.

His voice was sharp. "Focus! We're almost there. Just a couple more steps, and you'll have everything we planned. Everything I promised."

She couldn't bring herself to ask the question, but she didn't have to. He rolled on as if she had anyway.

"I need you to kill Tuck."

Now she was shocked. "What? Why? What did he do?"

"Nothing, really. You know. Wrong place. Wrong time."

He said it so matter-of-factly that she cringed. Just snuff out a human life. Talk about having a bad day.

"He doesn't have to suffer," he continued. "He'll just feel a little sleepy."

She shook her head no, denying any part in a murder.

"You kill him, or I will. And you don't want that. He seems like a good type of fellow. I just won't be able to help myself. It's just that—" He thought about it for a second. "He's too smart. He knows about the video hack. He knows what it means."

Her head continued to shake a negative. "What about the rest of them?" she asked slowly.

"Them?" he laughed. It was a contemptuous, crass laugh. "No, they don't know, but don't worry. I'm going to ensure the old UNICON has reentry rights. They'll gladly take care of the rest of them as a favor. It may be that was their plan all along. That crowd doesn't know their asses from their hats. They're easy. Tuck. Now, he's the hard one."

She was uncertain. "I can't. I don't want to—"

"Of course you do," he interrupted. Now he was taunting her. "You want to, and you will. You see, the Crow here was a loner. No family. No one to look after him." He paused with a sardonic grin. "No one I could use to leverage him. So, he is exactly what I told you he was. A loose end. Nothing more."

"Is that what I am, too? A loose end?"

His smile seemed genuine to her as he explained her misunderstanding. "Sweet Trina. Of course not. You could never be a loose end. You have plenty of friends and a large extended family. They are going to be eternally grateful to you for all the help and support you're going to provide. Isn't that right?"

She caught his intention as clearly as if he'd spelled it out, letter by letter. He didn't need to kill her. The family who had been her motivation now suddenly become her vulnerability. She no longer had a choice. She belonged to him. She hated him. She hated the choices she'd made, and she hated herself for making them. She looked him straight in they eye. "I should break your skinny little neck and be done with you right now."

Simms wasn't used to being threatened and didn't take kindly to it. He needed respect. Always. His anger flared instantly, and he glared at her with contempt. "You stupid, fat bitch. I—"

He paused for an instant, but never got the chance to finish his rant. It was wrong, but apparently he couldn't help himself. She wasn't fat—far from it. And she certainly wasn't stupid. But one part of what he said was right. Exactly right. It was the part that hit him right between the eyes and then between the legs. Yes, she was a bitch. He went down. She could see him thinking about getting up. Considering it, then deciding against it. He stayed down. She actually hoped he'd get up. She could already feel the satisfaction of that final kick that would knock him out cold and leave him kissing the deck again.

As the door slid shut behind her, she considered the possibilities. She could go back and kill Simms right now. Not a bad idea, but she'd have to do it quickly while they were still alone and her killer instinct was up. She wasn't sure she could finish him off in cold blood. She paused to turn back. She held on to that thought —dead Simms eyes staring out of a gruesome death mask—a thought she'd need to save for later. She needed a lot of things, she decided. That's what led her down this path in the first place. She did have a large family, and she'd incurred a mass of debt and favors looking out for them. What she needed now was more time, which she didn't have.

Then, almost as suddenly as the realization of who Simms was and what he'd become dawned on her, she felt a wave of self-loathing.

It should never have come to this.

Even if he had gotten up now, she realized, she wouldn't have kicked him. She couldn't. She didn't want to touch him. She didn't even want to see him. She needed to assure herself that she wouldn't become a monster like him.

She presumed he remained in his groveling heap but didn't go back to check. She exited the building, climbed back into the vehicle and headed north. She knew now exactly what she had to do. For herself. For her family.

It wasn't until she'd already undocked that she changed her mind and realized what her contribution had to be. Damn the consequences. Simms was a cancer that needed removing. If not her, who? There wouldn't be another opportunity like this. She cursed repeatedly, banging her fists into the console in front of her as she re-vectored her destination. Already she could see the delicious surprise on his face. She could never truly atone, she knew, but this might be a good start.

* * *

"Hello, Durt."

Simms looked into the kid's uncomprehending eyes as his gaze made its way through the haze of Trina's knock-out potion. It was about time, he thought to himself, and so poetic, too. Sometimes the best things in life were the things you had to wait for. But even now, it wasn't great. He had a bit of time, and he figured that's all he really needed. The kid would give up the drugs, and he'd be on his way. He really needed to keep better company, better than the thick-headed lugs that currently passed for his partners in crime. They could be useful, but they certainly turned out to be a lot of extra work for him. Soon enough, he'd have to eliminate a couple to cover his tracks.

There were people, he mused, who got in his way, and there were people who failed him. People who didn't do what they said they were going to do. In a sense, that was getting in his way, too. He had no time for those unfortunate souls. No, unfortunate was probably the wrong word. It was just the way of humankind. Survival of the fittest. The strong would always prevail, and the weak would be pushed aside. Those were the rules. He didn't invent them, but he played by them, and if they chose to get in his way, that was the wrong decision—for them, anyway. A sign of weakness.

The response from the annoyingly famous Durt Larson was predictable. "I'm not saying Jack."

"Oh, I think you will," he said, then as an afterthought added a bit of explanation. "I'm not going to kill you, Durt Larson. I'm just going to take a few choice pieces off." He paused for a moment, rethinking. "No, that's not actually correct. You, Durt. You'll be the one who carves off a few pieces of yourself."

Durt's stare was blank.

"Nothing personal. Just to show you that I'm a man of conviction. You know…that I do what I say I'm going to do."

It really was a matter of willpower, Simms thought. Single-mindedness. He had the will to remove those who stood in his way. Permanently, if necessary. Usually, it was more trouble than it was worth. The first time he'd done it just to see if he could. It always surprised him how easily some submitted to their own deaths. As a general practice, he had others do his bidding, but once in a while, like today, he set aside a special case.

He reached his good hand into his pocket and watched as the fuzzy-brained Larson picked up the same knife as before. The same one he'd used in the King County jail. It seemed to tickle something in Larson's memory, and his expression distorted itself into one of dread.

This was something that would satiate his anger and remind him that his role was not to sort out right and wrong. No, his role was to thin the herd. If he could kill his adversaries this easily, then they weren't worthy adversaries. No, they were annoyances. Now, those he couldn't kill? Those were the worthy ones. Those were the ones who deserved his attention. It wasn't anybody's fault, and he took no credit or blame for any of it. Annoying punks who stood between him and his dominance had already chosen their destiny. Who was he to argue with the world? They played their parts, and he played his. That's all anyone could do. And this time, he wanted to take his time. Take his time destroying the most annoying person he'd ever met. Problem was, now that he had the kid, he didn't really have the time he needed.

"You know who you can trust, Durt? A dying man. That's who. Got nothing left to lose. So, you know what? I trust you. But that's it."

Blood was flowing, freely now, from Larson's right wrist, and Simms realized he had a narrow window while the fear of mutilation and death brought heightened focus but before the lightheadedness and confusion from blood loss compromised his interrogation. From the look in Larson's eyes, this was the time.

"This is easy, kid. We don't need to do this. Just tell me where you put the Orenz."

Larson's expression wasn't what he needed or anticipated. This was a kid. This should be easy. Easy for the kid to cave. Easy for him to get on with his business. He'd had tough customers before and usually by this time they'd be bawling like newborns. But this expression wasn't capitulation. It was defiance. Simms shook his head. He didn't have time for this, so he had to turn up the heat. Wrist number two it was. He watched Larson grimace as his blood-soaked hand took up the knife and moved its razor-sharp blade toward the pink, waiting flesh of his right arm, the wrist target visible now just below the cuff of his gray coat.

* * *

Durt stared at his hands in disbelief. Like before, he had no control of his own movements. Simms had some kind of mind control power that could control his every move. He watched in horror as he deliberately sliced through his own flesh. He caught his breath and squeezed his eyes shut as the pain seared through him, his body now drenched in sweat.

"You see, this is a win-win for me," said Simms as Durt stared in paralyzed anguish at the wink and the smile that came with the comment.

It wasn't a nice smile, and Durt shuddered.

"We're going to have fun figuring out where you stashed what you took from those cases. And I hope," he paused momentarily and tilted his head slightly. "I hope it takes you a while to remember. Not too long, mind you. I've got a schedule to keep."

Durt snarled at him suddenly, a bulldog restrained by an invisible chain. "I should have let you die on that beach."

Simms offered a thoughtful nod. "That might be true. But you didn't." He paused for a moment in thought. "Which tells me you're weak. And that, my friend, is disappointing. I like my adversaries to be worthy." Again he paused for a moment in mid-thought. "But what was I thinking? You're just a kid."

Durt resented the remark intensely, but he understood the score. He was in no position to negotiate. So he did the next best thing. He kept his mouth shut and his eyes open. The room that surrounded them was windowless and had a drab orange tint to it. He didn't know much, but he knew one thing. If this was Simms' place, then his taste was in his ass. That seemed about right. He had no idea where he was, but he knew where he wasn't. He was no longer at the races. This room looked nothing like the temporary pit tent. In fact, the place reminded him a lot of the King County jail.

What was it with this guy?

He checked himself. He wasn't physically tied up, even if he couldn't move an inch. Like the jail, the room had a table and two chairs, one of which he was sitting in.

Just listen.

This was one of those guys who loved to hear himself talk. He could never get enough of himself. Soon enough now, according to his father at least, braggarts run out of mundane things to say. He'd tire of repeating himself and at some point would start toying with riskier information. Of course, at the same time, he realized that the only plausible reason he would share that type of information was if he, himself, was no longer a threat. Or wouldn't be a threat for long.

Think assimilated. Not intimidated.

He needed to be a sponge and soak up everything Simms was willing to spill. If he survived, it would come in handy. If he didn't. Well, he didn't really want to think about that, but in that case, it wouldn't really matter anyway. It seemed ludicrous. He could survive a bear attack, a crash into the North Pacific and all number of other dangers, only to be knocked off by this weasel? The universe couldn't be that cruel.

Stop it.

He pulled himself harshly out of his downward mental spiral. Yes, eventually he was going to die, but he resolved it wouldn't be today, and it certainly wouldn't be at the hands of this gloating son of a bitch. Which meant he needed to stop daydreaming and actually listen to what Simms was saying. Listen. That's all he could do.

Sometimes people are so tickled with themselves, they'll tell you everything you need to know and then some.

That was his father talking. As Simms droned on, he realized his father might just be right.

Just listen.

"No reason, Larson. No reason at all for me to do this. Just tell me what I want to know. That's it. Easy. I'm—"

Simms stopped his relentless coaxing suddenly, cursing as he jerked his wristcomm in front of his face. "What?" he screamed.

Durt felt the pressure of Simms control release him. Thankfully, at least for a moment, he was no longer the target of Simms' fury.

The tone of his tormentor changed abruptly. He could hear the concern. The fear. "Internal affairs? From Earth?" A slight pause ensued. "No. No, don't. I'm on my way."

Durt stared in wonder at the blood seeping from his wrists. It didn't hurt, and he felt sleepy. Maybe a nap would do him good.

"You lucky son-of-a-bitch," said Simms, his voice staccato with anger and forced through clenched teeth. "I wouldn't move around too much with you all cut up like that. You might not make it. You've only got so much blood, you know. Now, I have to go out because some other dumb son-of-a-bitch can't follow simple instructions. You just sit tight. Move too much, and you'll bleed out before your time. You just think real hard about whether or not you want to see Alaska again." He leaned in closely, as he had a nasty habit of doing, and whispered. "I'd be happy to send you right home. You tell me where you're keeping my stash and maybe, just maybe, you'll make it through this thing."

Durt said nothing. He heard the door shut. He was no longer restrained by whatever Simms had used. But Simms was right, he needed to put pressure on the cuts and keep from moving. His mind and body were both retreating simultaneously. His lights were going out. So much blood. Where the hell was Truman? He should leave Truman a note. A clue. As long as Simms didn't have the Orenz, he'd stand a much better chance of survival. Once the stuff was out of his hands, his fortune shifted from adversary to liability. He needed to avoid that at all costs, but he'd need energy, and what little he had was slipping away quickly, his blood now running to the edge of the table and dripping to the floor. He pressed his wrists together and lay his head forward on the table.

His hands had already started to look odd and unfamiliar to him. He floated in and out of real and imagined plans of escape. He realized that someone now sat beside him. He didn't look up. He didn't need to.

"Hey, Jake. What are you doing here?"

"Shhhhh. You know why I'm here."

"But how did you find me here? No way you could—"

Jake's words came back to him, and he heard them as clear as a crisp October morning in Alaska.

I never met a challenge I wasn't ready to step up to.

Jake was right. He couldn't allow this minor setback to be his final story. His legend. He had to think. But the weight pressing down on him, forcing the strength from his body and the sense from his head consumed him. Something familiar tugged at the edge of his memory, and he knew he was dying. Somehow the scrawny little shit of a man he should have left on a North Pacific beach had bested him. He should get up and fight. Try and escape. Leave a message. All good ideas, he thought to himself, before the last of his energy seeped from him, and he descended into darkness.

[25]
SACRIFICE

THE RACE TOOK everything Carter had. It left him barely able to stagger back through the hall before collapsing onto his now familiar bed in the back. Tuck had no idea how long it might take to recover from the shock his system had taken. Carter insisted he was fine. He just needed a few minutes rest. Tuck trusted Carter no more than he trusted himself with medical diagnosis, but he allowed that when Carter felt well enough to move about on his own, then that's what they would do.

For now, Walt was the hero, and by all rights, the team should be in the midst of a victory celebration. Instead, the discussion at the long table, now devoid of any mid-air race renderings, focused again on the multi-colored data towers. Was it an intended robbery? A robbery maybe still in the planning stages? Certainly, they were a logical crowd, Tuck thought, but at the same time, they were guessing.

Bren was all in on the robbery theory and was adamant they address it immediately, but questions remained in her mind. "There's still one thing I don't understand. Why would they leave it open like this?" she asked.

Walt offered the answer they were all thinking. "I'm pretty

sure they didn't believe there was anyone outside their little circle who could crack their old-school access code."

Tuck made his own contribution to the theory. "I don't think they're on a beach somewhere," he said. "I think they're field testing one of these, and I bet they're planning to come back. From what I understand about them, when they want something, they take it. And when they *need* something—and I think they need this—they're not going to hold back."

"But, legally they can't!" complained Bren.

As was his style, Anton provided a more measured response. "There is a universe of illegal things they cannot do. We should not worry about those. I do worry about their next step. We have not contacted their designated attorney. I fear they will press this issue soon."

"Look, maybe you're right," Bren said in a low voice. "Say we forget legal for now. What is it they're trying to break into? If Carter is right and the purple columns are the Casinos, what are their easier targets on Earth?"

Walt was dismissive and shook his head. "No way to tell with the info we have. Besides, we don't care."

"What do you mean? Of course we care."

"Not me. I don't care a Newton's whiff. They try something? You know, a big heist, maybe. And they'll get locked up for it. No big deal. It has nothing to do with us."

Walt was a tech whiz but a strategic oaf, Tuck realized. Data was his friend. People, on the other hand, apparently along with relationships and motivations, didn't translate into his brand of data logic.

Anton raised his hand slowly. "Bren is correct. In a post-crime investigation, the presumption of guilt would fall directly on us."

Walt squinted, trying to follow the logic.

Anton's slight smile seemed to reflect a familiarity with this vein of explanatory conversation. "Think about it, Walt. Put yourself in the shoes of an investigator. Whose fingerprints would be all over a robbery of this nature? Keep in mind what we know of them, this questionable band of outlaws. While this data collection appears sophisticated, they themselves do not. Whether or not they are sophisticated, that is not the question. It is clear from this piece of technology that, by some means, they have acquired it, and while they may not be programmers, this level of tech, logically implies a partner. Those would be our fingerprints—false and unintended, of course, but ours nonetheless. Further, our strategy to masquerade as them has served as a windfall in their direction."

The group remained silent, now curious.

"We strive, now, to maintain our anonymity, and we pass ourselves off as UNICON. As we do," he said slowly, watching the comprehension make its way around the small group, "we offer ourselves up as the perfect scapegoat. We understand we are not the violent criminal element that makes up the UNICON image, but should a crime be committed that calls that relationship into question, it certainly does have something to do with us. We would, in all probability, become the investigation's prime suspect. And all that we invested in keeping our work quiet would be wasted effort."

Walt nodded now in understanding but had little to offer. "What do you suggest?"

Bren was adamant. "We need to turn this whole thing over to Copernicus law enforcement."

Anton turned to Tuck, the presumed representative of lunar law.

Tuck raised his hands in defense. "Sorry. Not your guy. Not today, anyway," he clarified. "I'm no longer law enforcement. More like outlaw enforcement right about now. But," he said with a smile, "together, I'm thinking we might be able to get your info to the right person. Before that right person comes looking for you, that is. Who knows?" he said with a wink. "You might make a new friend."

Anton nodded in assent. "We might need one."

The discussion continued. Usually in circles, but over the next half hour, they worked to sketch out a strategy that would, at least for the time being, allow Tuck and Carter to remain anonymous and outside the reach of Copernicus surveillance.

Tuck smiled to himself. Walt's tint job had done the trick at the races. Trina had manned the show car that the crowd had crawled all over, and they had raced in its twin. Walt's fake hyper-drive component had worked like a charm. It had been a fine job of deception. No one was the wiser that the winning pair were two wanna-be pilots, cops on the wrong side of the law—at least for today, anyway. And there was only one surprise bigger than the expression on the faces of the winning racers who had shorted the course, and that was his own amazement at their win.

For obvious reasons, they'd not stayed for the after-race wrap-up interviews. That would leave fans guessing for weeks, he mused, but they had monitored coverage on the racer's screens on their return trip. There was Mican, the driver Trina was supposed to take out of the race, but didn't. The co-pilot? Damn if it wasn't Truman, the same Truman who helped them out with the LUNASEC security fleet now and again. A security patch that stumped LUNASEC engineers and grounded half their cruisers was a 20-minute fix for Truman, the friend of a friend who'd come through. He owed Truman one. Watching the interview, he guessed maybe now he owed him two.

* * *

Their plan was well solidified by the time Trina made her way through the door, a crate of what Tuck guessed was champagne in both arms. She smiled and waved with a nod of her head. Hands full, she turned and disappeared into the kitchen and dining area, the door yielding to her backward bump.

Tuck turned to Anton. "Champagne?"

Anton smiled his big, slow smile. "If we know Trina, then it's only the best. I do not know where the jewels she brings here come from, and I am hesitant to ask." He looked down at Tuck for a moment, his smile shifting to a knowing nod. "I believe that it is, as in many situations, better to not ask the question if you are not in real need of its answer."

Tuck smiled. There was some truth to that, he thought.

"Hey," yelled Walt, looking up momentarily from his ceaseless data-management tasks in the direction of the door that had just closed behind Trina. "I thought you were going to take out Mican."

Trina was silent, but Bren answered the obvious question. "Whatever she did, it worked, didn't it?"

Walt was about to reply but then changed his mind.

Bren had a follow-up question, too. "What's the chatter on the Net, Walt? Have they figured it out?"

In response, Walt materialized a host of displays over the central table. Some text. Some voice. All combining to make a racket of confusion.

"Whoa there, Walt," said Tuck with a slowing motion of his hands. "Let's get a filter on that. Way too much information for us non-Net types. In truth, Tuck's years in the Kick had actually accustomed his vision and his brain to process this level of diverse visual information, but he caught the surprise and confusion in Anton's reaction.

Walt relented and lifted his hands in the air. "OK. OK. Hang on a sec." The displays dropped to three, one displaying a text feed from an online race group; the second a discussion group reviewing and offering their commentaries on the race clips; and finally, the official after-race commentary directly from the race site. It was clear the excitement level was high, and after a couple minutes of review, the spectrum of opinions from every remote corner of possibility disguised their identity, lost in the madness of analysis and explanation.

While Tuck got it right away, Bren and Anton took a bit longer. He said nothing, watching their expressions for the impact of their own analysis to sink in. Bren was first. She glanced over at Tuck whose gaze remained on Anton. She took a breath to comment, then stifled herself realizing Anton's careful, methodical assessment was still in progress. The slim giant studied the displays with an even, curious expression. Listening. Figuring. Even if it took him longer than the others, it was only by a minute or so. Slowly, but surely, his smile came back.

He raised his arms toward the small crowd, maybe too dramatically for Tuck's taste, but it seemed to fit perfectly with Anton's demeanor. "Unbridled success," he declared to the small group. He turned slowly to Walt. "That, my friend, was a nice piece of digital trickery. Let us celebrate." He nodded slightly with his head. "Music, Maestro."

Walt's face reflected an appreciation of the compliment, and Tuck felt a strong bass beat fill the hall. Outside, the beachside disappeared, replaced now with a silhouette of a city's skyline at night, rainbow streams of fireworks illuminating its individual structures. Tuck shivered at the sight. He was blown away by the artistry of the scene.

As if on cue, Trina emerged from the kitchen, an ice tub of champagne between her arms, champagne glasses dangling and clinking from between her fingers. Tuck stepped quickly to offer assistance, reaching for the glasses.

"No, no," She said with a vigorous shake of her head. "The bucket." Her voice was urgent but contained something of a smile. "Quickly, before we waste it on the floor."

Tuck moved his hands to grasp the tub, and she let out a sigh of relief. "Thanks, Tuck."

He hefted the tub to the table, and Trina plucked one of the five contained bottles, pouring carefully and offering the glasses around to each.

Trina looked up suddenly, a mid-pour detour that Tuck was certain would end up with champagne on the stone floor, and looked at Anton. "Any progress with Clue?"

Anton shrugged with the impassive expression Tuck was now familiar with. "Sleeping like a baby."

The answer satisfied Trina who shifted her focus back to the glass before her and avoided Tuck's predicted spill.

Apparently finished, she stood up. For some reason Trina had skipped Tuck, the only one now, aside from her, who didn't have a glass in hand. As he surveyed the smiling crowd, he realized she'd left two glasses, their slim crystal stems reflecting the rainbow of fireworks from the exterior window, side-by-side on the hall's great table. Her pour was deliberate as she filled first one, then the other, the amber liquid bubbling its way into its new container.

With delicate care, she placed the bottle on the table and lifted the pair of sparkling glasses. "Friends, I should like to propose a toast."

He watched her approach, the glass offered from her extended hand, and the expression on her face one of resigned satisfaction. He began to smile, but it froze midway. A sudden change came over her. Not in her voice or even in her face, but in her eyes. The celebratory music slipped easily beneath her voice as the toast continued effortlessly. Something about new friends and old, champions and the future, it was actually quite eloquent, he thought, but her soul wasn't in it. Her eyes told a different story, and he would remember those eyes for the rest of his life. As she spoke, she shifted the offered glass. She extended the other as she spoke, and he took it from her. It was curious, he thought, that the eyes and the voice should tell such different narratives, but his mind wouldn't put together the answer until it was too late. She finished her toast and raised her glass. The others, as did he, followed in unison.

He wondered for a long time later if, had he been just a bit more perceptive, he might have saved her.

She drank. It wasn't a sip, it was a drain. He watched, first frozen as understanding broke over him. The golden liquid disappeared down her throat, and the expression of resigned serenity returned to her face. It could mean only one thing. Somehow her great talent and knowledge had been turned against herself. He had no idea how or why, but he'd seen the expression before. Crime and punishment. Betrayal and atonement. The rest of the group buzzed with conversation, but she said nothing. She shook her head slowly, and he watched as the light began to fade from her eyes. He stepped forward and embraced her. Whatever the cost of her sacrifice, it was clear she'd made it on behalf of her friends. She collapsed into his arms, and he held her tightly for a few moments until he felt her muscles go slack, then lifted her gently and laid her on the table.

The music continued, then cut out abruptly as Walt realized something was amiss. The city skyline winked into darkness.

"Sooooo—"

Trina's voice wasn't a word, but a whisper.

The group focused its attention on her in an awkward, confused silence.

The whisper came again. "Soooo. . . sorry," it managed.

All eyes were on her and immediately shifted to Tuck for some explanation.

Tuck watched her eyes, eyes that reflected a sadness as she closed them. What a waste, he thought. While he understood betrayal, he couldn't fill in the blanks. Powerful forces about which he had no information had tempted then destroyed the woman. He understood the wine glass swap. He was the target. She'd protected him. But from what? Maybe protection from who was the better question. She'd overestimated herself or underestimated her adversary. He didn't know her from anyone else, and it wasn't pity he felt. Just sadness.

In a sudden movement, her eyes opened again. They were wide and staring, an apparent last-minute realization. She choked out a few words. "Tell . . .Waldo."

That was it? *Tell Waldo?* Not helpful, he thought, not at all, as far as explaining anything to anyone.

But she wasn't done. The last word was even a word. It was an exhalation. Barely audible. Her dying breath.

"Simms."

* * *

The form that used to be Trina lay on the table facing the ceiling, her still eyes open and staring. Her look was serene. Bren produced a blanket and covered her with it in silence, a tear making a meandering path down her cheek. It was as if Trina had no more troubles, and she didn't, Tuck realized. No troubles for Trina, but a wicked puzzle for the rest of them.

The silence seemed to go on for hours. The actual time was a matter of minutes, and the group, stunned by the sudden loss of Trina, was uncomfortable with their new reality, their movements furtive and uncertain. A dead body in the middle of a conversation has a way of doing that. For Tuck, who didn't know any of them well enough to presume what the others might be feeling, emotions were a jumble. He felt he should grieve, but he wasn't quite sure how. He wanted to stomp and yell and scream his anger out, but he wasn't sure who those emotions might be directed at or how the others might view his outburst. He sensed the others had similar thoughts. He needed silence to think and to reason as he always did, but somehow this was different.

Her last breath. Cims or Sims. That was the only clue she'd left them. What was she into? Tuck wondered. What had been so critical that it was worth her life? Few things, he knew, could rise to that level. Two real possibilities he considered. First, the most fundamental of human decisions. Fear and avoidance. Pain came in many forms. In his tenure at LUNASEC—even before—he'd seen the full spectrum. Fear of torture. Fear of poverty, Fear of embarrassment. It was different for each and every person. Trina didn't strike him as the fearful type, however, which left only one other possibility—that she was protecting someone. He'd seen the look in her eyes. It was a moment of decision but also a moment of surrender. Were she not dead, he certainly would be by now. Tuck presumed there were others, too. You don't sacrifice your life for someone you've just met. Unless—

The extended silence wasn't just pervasive. It was deafening.

Death had its own protocols and courtesies, but it happened so seldom to those who'd not reached their 100th birthday yet that the group was stunned into its own awkward blanket of social interaction. No one dared break the silence with the wrong word. Respect for the dead and respect for Trina kept their lips zipped. Only Bren's quiet tears and occasional sniffle expressed what they all felt.

When the silence broke, it did so all at once. Tuck uttered a wordless thought of thanks, his eyes closed, a nod to Anton.

"We have work to do, people," came the deliberate voice. "Let us not waste what Trina has gained with her sacrifice."

From silence to cacophony, the dam broke, and they all spoke at once. It wasn't really a form of communication, but more a relief valve. Exclamations, opinions, and questions all attempted to drown out the others, the shouts bumping off one another until Anton's raised hands again brought silence, but it was different now. This was an operations team used to activity. Training and habits kicked in. All eyes turned to Anton. Then to Tuck.

He took the opportunity. "Look, I've got to get back to HQ. Whatever I bumped into—if it's come to this level— has got to be teetering, and it's going to fall. No doubt about it. Right on top of you. Us," he corrected himself.

He looked at the back of the hall. The shouting had roused Carter who now made his way toward the group. He wore a look of confusion until he realized Trina was not in a meditative state, but awaiting rigor mortis. He said nothing, but Tuck watched his eyes and ears put the story together for himself as the conversations continued.

Anton was giving his crew directions. He and Bren would find the alleged attorney, then share their story—the columns, their analysis, their concerns with LUNASEC. He'd looked initially at Tuck but a silent squint reminded him of Tuck's fugitive status.

"Walt, Carter's going to need his badge to make this work"

Walt nodded, searching behind and beneath what lay before

him on the table, but finished with a helpless shrug. He started to speak, but Bren cut him off with her sharp venom.

"Jesus, Walt, if you thew it out with the rest of your crap, I will personally make you go through it with your teeth."

His mouth was open, but no words came out as he shook his head violently.

Tuck looked back at the body on the table and realized the truth of the matter. He raised his own hand. "Look, it doesn't matter." He looked at Anton quickly. It was late Sunday afternoon, Copernicus time. Tuck knew they needed all the time they could spare to track down the attorney and then get through the maze that was LUNASEC. "Go."

Bren was already at the door with an imploring gaze at Anton.

Anton nodded his assent, "Tuck, you and Carter are welcome to the other racer." He turned to his digital eyes and ears. "Walt, I need you here."

Walt seemed ready to protest, but it was clear his comprehension lagged.

Anton paused but only for a moment. "Monitor comms. We may need some remote assistance."

Walt sat down, a slow deliberate motion that reflected his disappointment. "I understand."

Tuck knew he didn't.

Anton took a deep breath, "Walt, you understand I am counting on you. As I do at all times."

Walt managed a weak smile and nodded as Anton turned on his heel, closing the distance between the table and the door in surprisingly few steps.

Tuck studied Carter for a moment. "You good?"

His face was pressed from sleep, his hair a mess, but his eyes were alert. "Tuck, we're not good. We're anything but good. We're screwed. We're outside the dome with no badges. Might as well be transients in Newton."

Tuck eyed him narrowly, moving his hand to his waist where his badge might be kept. It wasn't that Carter was that far off.

Hunted by LUNASEC and, apparently by TRANSCOM, too, they were indeed a pair of nobodies. But Carter didn't need to know that. He just needed to see things from a different perspective.

"We don't need these," Tuck said, patting what should be his badge and best friend. "We need these," Tuck pointed to his head. "Our brains are the only reason we have badges in the first place. And if we can't figure a way to put them back where they belong, we don't deserve them."

Tuck watched his expression turn from one of despair to one of resolve.

Tuck nodded with satisfaction. He liked Carter for a reason. Carter was his kind of cop. Carter liked a challenge.

Carter nodded slowly in agreement. "You're right. Yeah," he said, now with a smirk and a fresh perspective, "I'm good."

[26]
PIECES

SIMMS FELT HURRIED. And that wasn't good. Things had a way of unraveling when they were rushed. It wasn't that he hadn't anticipated some level of haste, but it meant dropping some of the more intricate details. It meant focus. Extended, consistent focus, which by the way, he thought to himself, was something that stupid Bike had none of. Imbecile. Yes, Bike had his talents. Apparently following directions was not among them. He beat his way into problems, then beat his way out. Not an elegant strategy by any means, but now and again it was practical.

The problem was that where he should be—where he needed to be—right now was headed for his ride out of Copernicus. The schedule was tight before, but now he had little time to get the location of the damn Orenz, retrieve it, then complete a list of other details that, more than likely now, just weren't going to get done. Maybe he shouldn't have offed the Crow so quickly. He shook his head as he cyphered back into his temporary office. No, The Crow was talented, but unreliability was not a talent. He'd needed to minimize the moving parts to his plan, and that had been a twofer. Reduce risk and eliminate a witness. No, it was the right move. But now it fell on him. He didn't like to operate this way, but today it was necessary. He entered the office and walked quickly past The Crow's backward-headed corpse.

Yep, I'm alibied there. No way a one-handed man could do that.

He stopped short as he opened the door to the back room. The kid was motionless, face-down on the table, his hands crossed above his head as if they were nailed to the table there. The gray coat covered most of him and the secret he was trying to pry out of him.

"Superstitious bullshit won't help you now," he said in a low voice, mostly to himself.

The kid didn't move.

He rounded the table for a closer look. The dried blood told the story. Apparently, his technique to stop the blood flow had worked well enough, just not soon enough. The mouth was open, and the open-eyed stare told him there was no way he was getting the secret out of the kid now.

He let out a high-pitched scream of frustration as he kicked the seated body. The corpse tumbled out of the chair and thumped to the floor.

Simms placed his hands on his hips.

What now?

He was stumped. But only for a minute. What he saw on the table first creased his brow with curiosity, then spread a smile across his face. There, written in blood were some characters. Some numbers and a few letters.

Guess the kid thought I'd go easy on him. Had a change of heart.

That wasn't it, he realized as he looked at Durt's still form. No, he expected to be found by his friends. This message was for them.

Stupid.

"Yes," he said aloud, "You'll be found. Bad news, though. You won't be rescued."

Ah, to be young and full of hope. Yes, he remembered. At one time, he was like that as well. What it was like to see the universe through those naive eyes.

He stood stock still for a minute. Wait, he thought, that was it. See the world through his eyes.

Right now, The kid's dead eyes were staring at the floor, but he was pretty sure their damn TransComm ship was still docked just outside the Dome restaurant where he'd seen it and had it searched.

He shook his head, kicking himself mentally.

It was there all the time. I was just looking for the wrong thing.

All that information was stored neatly in the ship's databanks. It had to be. Company policy. Wherever the kid had stashed it, the ship would help him find it. In fact, as a bonus, he might as well just take the ship to retrieve the Orenz. He lifted his wristcomm to task The Crow with moving the kid's body before he realized what he was doing. He shook his head and took a deep breath. He cared nothing for the two bodies on the office floor, aside from the fact that he would have to return here himself to clean up. But that was part of his cover. Doing things a one-handed man couldn't do. Any other one-handed man might struggle with the task, but he had it covered, and he absent-mindedly reached into his pocket to thumb his controller. His hand bumped into something else. The badge. In the rush, he'd forgotten.

"It's OK," he told himself, smiling. "Just go get the Orenz. You're back on schedule now."

With the badge, he had off-grid authorization. Authorization for a cop who might not even remember he was a cop for a while.

Thanks, Trina.

Yeah, Trina took a little convincing. She'd kicked his ass, and he probably deserved it, but she'd come around, he thought. With Tuck out of the way, she just might be worth the hassle he'd put up with. But if this worked out, even that didn't matter. He was going to disappear like he'd never been here in the first place. All part of his breakaway plan. Which, by now was in full motion and on an unstoppable timeline. He had to hurry.

He captured the letters and number on the table on his wristcomm. Even if the ship held the information he needed, he thought as he exited the office, he dreaded the time it would take to scan through the piles of data to pinpoint the stash's location. With a bit of luck, this tabletop message written in blood might just be the shortcut he needed.

* * *

Durt tried to piece together the bits and pieces of his shattered memory. What might be the ugliest shade of orange he'd ever seen now stared him in the face. His cheek was throbbing again. And cold. He was on the floor, he realized, the burning on his arms remained, reminding him of what he'd done to himself. But there were other things, too. He'd sipped something from a canteen. Or was that just wishful thinking? His throat still burned with a wicked thirst. Then Jake. Jake told him something. No, that was impossible. No, it was the woman. The one who'd poisoned him. She'd been crying. Or maybe that was the dream, too. If it was a dream, did it mean something? No, he decided, a more logical explanation was that it was all the random rambling of his tortured mind trying to put itself back together again. Who knows? he thought. Maybe this whole thing was a dream, and he'd wake up back in the cabin. More wishful thinking.

What wasn't a dream he now knew was that his eyes were open, his head was pounding and his throat was on fire. A memory suddenly flashed into his mind's vision.

"Here, take this."

It was the woman. The traitor. His downfall. She'd lifted his head, and he'd stared stupidly at her offered canteen. He drank deeply. It wasn't water, he realized. Too thick, but it was tasteless, and the act of drinking soothed his throat. He'd looked up at her, still not comprehending. She was beautiful. Maybe even more so now with tears in her eyes.

She shook her head slowly. "I'm so sorry. I have to go."

He felt her rearrange his arms on the table in front of him.

Deep inside he'd felt a warm glow. Then nothing.

The floor definitely had a manufactured odor to it. It was sharp, almost like that of a rifle discharge on a cool Alaskan morning. He admired its smooth surface. It was reflective. Not overly so but unblemished like an alpine lake on a windless day. From his foot-level viewpoint, his eye detected a slight anomaly in the smooth surface. A button, maybe? Some small object displayed itself a meter or so away. From a standing position, he might have missed it, but from this angle, the floor's reflective properties doubled its size. He examined it from a distance, not yet feeling the strength to move his frame from its current face-plant position. Funny, he thought, how discomfort could be a relative feeling. When had he ever felt comfortable lying face-down on a rock-hard anything? But it wasn't so bad. Soon enough, his curiosity got the better of him, and he attempted a ginger motion toward its satisfaction. Bad idea. The pain in his wrists made him gasp as he moved into a sitting position. He closed his eyes for a moment and took a series of deep, rapid breaths, trying to bring himself to deal with the sheets of agony that paralyzed him.

The fire in his arms subsided into a general throb, and he used his feet to slide his butt awkwardly toward his target. He extended a hand with care and found he had regained some semblance of agility. He pinched the thing between his thumb and forefinger and brought it carefully to his face for a closer inspection. His initial assessment was that of a stray component from some type of electronic gear. That seemed out of place here, as the room was devoid of any electronics. Just that stupid table and pair of chairs. It was the size of a small beetle, and it wasn't until he turned it over that he realized what it was. What it was—was impressive. Not necessarily the technology, but the size. He'd seen things like this before, but they were the size of a fist or a small book. The one for his rescue plane was the size of a human head.

It was a field generator. A miniature generator with little grasping feet on its bottom side. He shook his head in wonder. Now things made a lot more sense. His mind returned to the King County jail and that foul stench that was Simms' breath. At the time, he figured Simms had whispered in his ear for effect. To intimidate. Sure, it had worked well enough, but this explained a lot more. That was his technique. He'd threaten with his mouth and place the field generator with his hand. Once attached to the individual, he seemed to have ultimate control over body movement.

He shook his head in wonder, the burning pain forgotten for the moment as the realization dawned on him.

"I'll be damned," he said, hearing his father's exclamation in his own voice. "That's how you messed me up, and—"

A piece of something else, a memory, materialized in his mind. He knew it was true. "And that's how you killed Rush, too," he continued in a hoarse whisper to himself.

He looked up at the door, presuming it would be locked, and in a pained but deliberate motion, got to his feet to check it. Just in case. He had no idea how much time he had left, but quick movement and speed were not talents he currently possessed. To his surprise, the door opened easily, not into the building proper, but into an adjoining office.

At first glance, it looked pretty much like any other office with cabinets, a desk and a workstation. He froze. What wasn't like any other office he'd ever seen was a pair of legs extending from behind the desk. Prone on the floor, they faced down just as he had a couple of minutes before.

"Hello?" he called out. "You OK? Can you hear me?"

The boots didn't move in response, and as he edged to the other side of the office, he saw that the boots were definitely not OK. The body was face down, but the head and its now dead eyes stared straight up at the ceiling. It was a frozen, screaming grimace. Durt felt the mini field generator between his fingers and realized he wasn't its only victim. This guy had literally twisted his own head backward like a northern hawk-owl might. But this one didn't twist back. The horrid vision turned his stomach, and he closed his eyes and bowed his head with a quick motion. Deep breaths, he told himself.

Eyes closed, he realized he'd seen this guy. Half the head was shaved, the image of a great black crow tattooed on the flesh. It was one of those unforgettable images from the race crowd he wouldn't now soon forget. If this is what Simms did to his colleagues, he had a new level of urgency.

Sweat broke out on his forehead, and the odor of death now pounded a spike into his skull. His wrists throbbed, but he now had a whole new set of circumstances and motivations to work with.

"Sorry, Crow man," he apologized to the body as he opened the jacket. The inside breast pocket held what he sought. Cigarettes. He gave himself a half minute to allow the smoke to do its job. That's about what it took. With careful but firm effort, he pulled the boots and the corpse away from the workstation. Then he stood, panting. He realized he didn't really have the strength to do what he'd just done. His head spun. He took a few measured steps, walking slowly back into the back room and taking a careful seat. His eyes focused on the dried blood. His blood. He was surprised at how much there was. He realized something else, too. The letters scrawled on the tabletop were in his own script. It was his treasure map. He guessed he'd left it for Truman, but thanks to the cigarette and a pinch of mental clarity he realized it was more than that now. It was a death sentence, too. The location of the Orenz shipment was what kept him alive. If Simms got his hands on the shipment, then he—and Truman—just made the expendable list.

"Shit. Nice work, Durt," he admonished himself, shaking his head in disgust.

With his resources, Simms could find the location as fast as Truman could have. Maybe faster. Clearly, Truman hadn't found him yet, or he wouldn't still be here. He had no idea how much time he had left, but it certainly wasn't enough. He made his way back to the front office.

Based on the guy's death grimace, he guessed death had come swiftly. A second discovery confirmed Simms had been in a hurry.

The office workstation was still connected and waiting patiently for input, its virtual screen hovering above the desk.

Finally, he thought to himself, as he sat carefully and began to work a multitude of screens, a piece of good luck. He wouldn't have to remove any eyes or fingers from the body for access.

* * *

Simms had a habit of talking to himself. It seemed odd, somehow, but it was logical enough for him as few people really understood his thought process and motivations. He talked and listened at the same time. For whatever reason, it seemed to help him work through his problems.

"I'll find it just like his engineer would have found it," he muttered.

He hadn't been too surprised to find the ship in question just where it sat the day before. It looked like any other TransComm fleet transport, from its twin-berth layout to its cockpit and transport bay. Inside and outside it was the same as hundreds of others he'd been inside. Truthfully, it looked no different than when he'd had it searched. But it *was* different. He now had a much clearer idea of what to look for. He was the man. He knew it because he had a plan.

"You *are* the man, Simms!" He said aloud.

The transport's security field wasn't activated. He'd made sure of that yesterday.

Who in their right mind would want to rummage through a commercial transport vehicle?

No, he corrected himself as he walked up the transport's access ramp. Who in mid-town Copernicus would think about doing something like that? Were it in Newton, he thought, that would be different, a different story altogether. In Newton, the thing would be stripped bare of anything useful. Rendered flightless as well. No, in Newton, you had to be careful. That's when the security field paid for itself. Here, it was just another heap of scrap compared to its neighbors in the docking bays.

The pilot and co-pilot's quarters were probably cyphered, but he didn't care about them. That wasn't where he was headed. He made his way easily enough to the nav-station in the cockpit. This ship was as much his as it was anyone's. It was TransComm property, and right now, he had a need of the property. Clearly, not for company business. But if he was TransComm, then was there really a difference between his business and TransComm business? He smiled slightly as he activated the nav system and the screens popped up before him. There was something wonderfully predictable about it. The machine was built to obey and serve. Not like people. People were complicated and had this annoying habit of coming up with their own ideas. He settled back in the surprisingly comfortable seat as the startup sequence verified the ship's location and completed its system checks.

He kicked himself mentally for not thinking of this sooner. It was all here. All the places they'd been. All of their conversations.

"Alright, boss," he told himself. "Let's see what we've got."

The same thing that filled him with hope also held a serious drawback. It was all there. Days and hours of recordings and data he didn't care about. What was important? What wasn't? He hoped he wouldn't have to make too many of those choices. He synched his wrist comm with the ship's databanks and executed a universal search command. He presumed that's exactly what the kid's friends would do.

The clues were fairly generic, a seemingly random selection of letters and numbers. He wondered if the numbers might be lunar location grid info, but he was no navigator. He had people to do that for him. Well, before today, he had people. Now, not so many. It took him a few minutes to scroll through the search results. He wasn't quite sure what he was looking for, but figured he'd know it when he saw it. He sat back in the chair as the images and characters scrolled above the console in front of his hopeful eyes.

"No, no. Nothing there," he said. He shook his head at the mass of data he had before him but never averted his gaze.

It has to be in here. Someplace.

He was right. When it did come up, he knew immediately what had happened. The machine did an admirable job of filling in the blanks. It was one of the letters Larson had written that did the trick. The letter sequence was R Y 3 A, but it was the letter R, reversed, that made him look at it twice. Almost as if the kid was dyslexic. He was pretty far gone when he'd left him there, Simms reminded himself, so he didn't put anything past him, but as he inspected the screen and followed the links, he realized that RY3A referred to a Russian transport ship dumped for scrap. The databank found it and spit its contents up on the screen, the system highlighting the Cyrillic lettering on the ship's bow. It had been part of the transport's recycle dump, and a few of the additional numbers the kid had scrawled appeared near the ship. Sure enough, an image of the vessel's bow and its lunar location coordinates popped up.

Simms exclamation was sharp. "Yes!"

He didn't need his luck to last forever. But he did need it to last just a little longer. He had two primary tasks left. Presumably, he'd be able to locate the stash now. Now that he knew where to look and with a little luck, the ship's surveillance banks would show where in the ship he'd left them. The other was to clean up. He'd need to move the bodies out of that office. That was a dead giveaway and a link to him. It was a tight timeline, but he also had the ability to fly where, and as fast, as he pleased. He dug the badge out of his pocket, confirmed his destination coordinates and added his recently acquired law enforcement authorization.

He thought now, not about where he was going, but where he would be when he stepped onto his Earth-bound transport with thousands of others, his identity lost in the mix. His tracks would offer a logical explanation that Moon cops couldn't refute. Certainly, they'd have a little help from some well-placed clues. They hadn't been cheap, but then what worth anything in this day and age was? Then he'd be out. Out of the way. Out of sight. Most importantly, out of their jurisdiction. They could fight that all out among themselves. It wasn't a tough nut to crack. They'd be at it for months. Years, maybe. In the meantime, he had a few locks to crack and a few scores to even.

[27]
WARRANT

Carter steered the racer in a westerly direction. It wasn't true west as the edge of Copernicus extended out in a protective circle beyond the city limits, as did the larger exterior dome under which they now drove. It was this exterior dome that enabled city infrastructure expansion and, of course, the race they'd just won.

In a larger sense, Tuck thought, they were driving in a circle, both literally and figuratively. No matter. All part of what he'd hoped for. For years he'd done nothing but chase small-change cases. Petty thievery. Time wasters. It wasn't easy, keeping his sanity in a place that offered challenges far beneath his potential skills. But patience had paid off. Sooner or later he'd figured something like this would come looking for him. Something big. He figured the longer he waited, the bigger it would be, and that was based on nothing more than his interpretation of humanity and its ugly, consistent habits. This was his chance to bump up against a case that truly tested his resolve and his investigative powers. At some point he'd probably long for solitude—the quiet, boring existence Copernicus had offered for as long as he could remember, but now that he'd finally landed right in the middle of what he'd secretly hoped for, he couldn't help but smile. Just a little.

They'd agreed that the north access gate used by the racers was too risky, though he was certain that Bren and Anton had already used it on their way to the city's center. With the race now over, traffic through it would be non-existent for the next few days. If they wanted to paint a target on themselves, that would really be the best way. For the others, his new-found friends, a LUNASEC intervention might just help expedite their errand. They weren't fugitives. But for him and Carter, at least for today, stealth was the more practical choice.

They'd chosen instead to enter through the west gate. While this choice meant at least double their drive time, the west gate probably doubled their cover as well. This was the gate used by Copernicus officials for new construction surveys, public and promotional tours, and whatever else the city did to support its expansion efforts. Also, the city's internal traffic infrastructure favored that gate, which, in the absence of both of their badges, was the gridlock they were stuck with. Just like every other driver in Copernicus, there would be no authorized off-grid shortcuts on this trip. Once inside the dome, they'd be fused to the grid, subject to Copernicus standards of safety and mass traffic coordination. Yes, he agreed with himself, it certainly was a longer and more circuitous route, but if they could avoid suspicion and reduce the risk of a traffic stop, it might just be the faster choice.

To their left, the dome stretched skyward, a giant black structure that blocked out the stars. He knew, given a bit more distance, they'd be able to see its curvature, but this close, it looked like nothing more than a giant shadow wall. An amazing feat of engineering, Tuck mused. From the inside, the sky—day or night—seemed to go on forever. From the outside, it was just another hole in the Moon, unless you saw it from up close, and then it looked like the barrier wall it was, standing in the way of pretty much everything.

Tuck keyed the racer's console, his fingers walking the well-practiced code from memory. He knew he wasn't in the Kick, but his fingers didn't. Tesso's face popped up immediately as it always did. He had the perfect face for a duty officer. Broad with a strong jawline, his determined expression was topped by his well-groomed hair that always looked like it was trimmed that morning. His expression of determination shifted instantly. "Tuck?" he asked, confused.

Tuck ignored his surprise. "Hey, Tesso. Need some info."

Tesso's mouth worked as if trying to speak on its own until he zipped it tight and leaned toward the screen, his determination evident again, his voice low and awkward. "Hey, Tuck." He paused for a moment and swallowed. "Sorry to hear about Carter."

Tuck lost his recent memory for a moment. "Why, what do you mean?" he asked, shooting a momentary glance at his driver.

"Oh," came the voice from the other end, followed by that same uncomfortable silence. "You haven't heard yet."

Next to him, Carter was smiling. Tuck had forgotten completely about the Rosa Vidri message, and that it likely had made its way beyond its intended target. They thought Carter was dead.

"No, actually *you* haven't heard yet," he corrected Tesso. "He's sitting right here next to me." Another silence followed as Tesso processed it.

"Look, Tuck—"

He saw it from Tesso's point of view and cut him off mid-sentence. "Hang on a sec." Tesso wasn't wrong to be suspicious. Who could believe anything now? Especially given what he'd learned in the last couple of days.

He punched a couple of the buttons on the console, and the racer's screen picked up his wristcomm conversation and displayed the duty officer's hesitant expression. Tuck thumbed his wristcomm again and split the screen so they could see Carter's smiling face. The duty officer's face now broke into a grin.

"Sorry about that," said Tesso, "I couldn't tell if you were being straight with me or not. Everything 'round here's gone half-crazy."

So it wasn't just him, Tuck thought. "Like what?"

"Well, first you. You, of all people, get a warrant taken out on you. Then Carter vanishes and winds up dead. Now he's back with you. But somehow you're off grid. I just punched up our badge net, and it looks like yours is sitting right here at HQ."

"Yeah, about that—"

How was he going to get back into HQ if they were obliged to detain him?

As if on cue, the face on the screen retreated again into confusion.

"What? What is it, Tesso?"

The duty officer shook his head. "I give up. I can't figure it out. One minute I'm looking at your arrest warrant, next minute it clears, *poof*, just like that. No explanation. You know, like it never existed."

Now Tuck was smiling. A little bit of luck now and again never hurt. "Yes!" he said, clenching his fist at his small victory.

Tesso was shaking his head. "Makes no sense."

Tuck couldn't disagree. He knew the process as well or better than anyone in LUNASEC, and Tesso was right. A warrant didn't just disappear. There was a process to follow. Endorsements. Approvals. Something was, as he'd just heard, half-crazy. It did, however, agree with what they'd experienced with data and surveillance manipulation. He had no way of knowing whether he was cleared or not. Just as it had vanished, it might just as easily—and quickly—reappear. That would happen, he presumed, at the most inconvenient time to him. He had another thought.

"What about Carter? His badge. It's missing. Can you locate it?

"Sure," replied Tesso without hesitation. "I'm on it."

His face disappeared from the view screen for half a minute, presumably to assign the task to the duty staff. "Search initiated. Should have an answer shortly." He paused momentarily before shifting subjects. "I was thinking about you today, Tuck."

"Yeah, bet the warrant was hard to ignore."

"You got that right," Tesso agreed. "No, it was something else. I know you've been working that serial murder thing for a while now."

"What, you got another missing head?"

Tesso's response was slow and deliberate as if he were trying to make sense of the oddity he was describing.

"No, this one was sliced and diced. Bled out. Contacting ME to try and ID and sort it out. Want to join?"

Tuck caught a warning eye from Carter and kept his mouth shut. "Listen, Tesso. I'm coming in for my badge." He paused, searching for the right words. He didn't want to compromise Tesso's trust. He had few enough friends already. "Presuming, of course, that my warrant stays disappeared. If it doesn't, you won't see me. You can't. We'll explain everything when we get there, but you've got to trust me."

Tesso shook his head in an easy nod. "Got it, Tuck."

"Good. Glad at least someone understands."

"No, Tuck. I've got the badge. Carter's badge. It's—"

He paused and moved off screen momentarily. "Is this right?" Tesso asked an HQ colleague, his face only half visible on the monitor as he turned away for confirmation. Tesso's face came back, the screen now full, maybe too much detail in his face for comfort, his expression uncertain. "It's off-grid aboard a TransComm transport. Near the edge of the new material dumps."

"Tesso, do me a favor. Keep an eye on it. Track its movement. If it comes back to the city, and I don't care who it is, detain him until I can get there. I have a feeling about this one."

"Tuck, you know there's a warrant out for you," Tesso reminded him.

"I thought you said it cleared."

"No, I said it disappeared. I didn't say anything about it clearing. That's a whole separate protocol."

He was right, Tuck realized. Could be any of a number of

things. For now, he was just as wanted as the minute he'd skipped HQ and headed outside the dome. He had another thought.

"Look, let's do this. You know me. I want you to be my arresting officer. I'm coming in."

Now Tesso was concerned. "You sure?" he asked, his dubious expression filling the screen.

Tuck wasn't sure, but that was the best plan he had at the moment. He confirmed with a shake of his head.

"Just one thing, Tess. Whoever that imposter is—" He took a breath and looked at Carter. "Whoever it is...doesn't go anywhere until we get there."

Tesso nodded. It wasn't a convincing nod. "Sure, Tuck."

"Keep in mind, we may not be there until the morning, so—"

"It's OK, Tuck. We'll do what we need to do."

"Oh, and put your hands on my badge, too. I'll be wanting that after you take me into custody."

Tesso looked as confused as the last sentence sounded. "Tuck, I can't tell if you're brilliant or an idiot." He paused for a moment. "I hope it's the first one."

With a swipe of his hand, Tuck patched out and sat back in the racer's passenger seat.

"Brilliant idiot," he muttered to himself. Tesso wasn't wrong.

He just hoped he had enough info and luck that the half-assed plan he'd just set in motion would work.

Tuck knew the only evidence of their progress around the outside of the inner dome would be visible from above, a telltale dust cloud kicked up behind the tiny speck of a racer. They were making good speed, but only marginal time because of their chosen route. In spite of their velocity, the lack of landmarks to judge their forward movement made it seem like they sat still. The surface here was flat and the sand fine with only an occasional anomaly that flashed by the viewport. The view before them seemed like a frozen video frame with a fleeting glitch now and again. The seamless black exterior of the dome on their left hid the frenzy of activity that was the lifeblood of Copernicus, from the majesty of the downtown's architecture to the unsettled slums of Newton, the city's silent scapegoat.

The monotony of the landscape melted away some of the adrenaline Tuck had endured these past days.

Beside him, Carter's faraway look told him that while he drove the racer, he'd retreated into his own personal thoughts as well. Tuck shifted in his seat, its design one of utility rather than comfort, and once again replayed in his mind the video of the headless corpse in Newton.

There was something about it that tickled his mind, but it was just out of reach. It wasn't that he couldn't remember. No, he remembered it well. In detail. It had played continuously in his mind since he'd first reviewed and puzzled over it. There was something there he just couldn't put his finger on.

He tried again.

One of his primary presumptions was that the serial killer theory was a logical news plant, a plausible distraction. In all likelihood, its intended effect was to distract a potentially troublesome police force. Tuck smiled to himself. Yes, that was him, and to this point, it had worked pretty well. He was both attracted and distracted and was yet to make his way to the truth of the matter. The last thing a good cop should do, though, was rely on crime-solving tips from rumors and Net reports.

What the cops should be doing was analyzing evidence. Asking pointed questions. Applying experience and an inquisitive nature. No, he corrected himself, that's what he usually did. What the other cops usually did was ask him for the answer, the illogical solution. That's just what they'd become accustomed to on the Moon where things were a lot better, or in this case, a lot worse. For the police force, fewer serious crimes meant fewer opportunities for them to challenge themselves and their own wits. Here, you had to be something special to thrive in this lower crime environment.

Because the instances of crimes like this were so few, it made this one, or this recent string, rather, unique. It was this same reason that made Tuck believe the headless bodies were created distractions offering covering fire for, presumably, less violent but more lucrative crimes.

Copernicus was a city of industry. Its productivity and the fruit of its collective labors fed an insatiable and ever-increasing Earth appetite. Never a shortage of opportunities here. And crime? For the most part, it was unprofitable and bad for business. On the law enforcement side, its low quotient for challenging cases meant fewer qualified investigators were needed. Every Earth-side cop knew that duty here was a career killer.

Real or fake, the news reports had drawn public attention like nobody's business. When they agreed with the prevailing police investigations, it looked too easy for Tuck's suspicious mind. Public fascination with this phenomenon was too convenient. And when things were too easy or too hard—like now—it meant he'd missed something. What he couldn't do was place his finger on was what that something was.

He closed his eyes and let the video roll again.

The restaurant door slides open. Out stumbles the headless, handless body that then plunges face first—if it had had a face—to the sidewalk. Horrified passersby stare, scream and, initially, give it a wide berth. The street is crowded, but the foot traffic bunches and creates an impromptu gawking circle with a good two meters of space, as if whatever caused the loss of head and hands might be contagious. The crowd builds. A Newton thief darts into the open zone, kneeling behind the body, likely to relieve it of any valuables, but gets scared and disappears back into the crowd. The crowd continues to gather and in under 10 minutes, the fake MEs. Rhonda and—. He stopped. He had to switch between the actual video replay and the memory of it in his mind, because they'd never shown up on the video. He struggled for a moment visualizing the two. Kandi. That was her name. They'd cleared a path to the vehicle and—he realized something. Actually two things. First, the surprise. Not his, but hers. He remembered Kandi, who clearly wasn't the leader of the two. She saw his badge, then his face. What she hadn't seen or maybe even realized at the time was her own telltale face.

That expression now took on a new meaning for him. She hadn't expected LUNASEC to show up and interrupt whatever it was they were doing. Truthfully, Tuck told himself, he'd made a note of the expression, but dismissed it as a rookie face—what he judged to be inexperience—not too many days removed from her first one on the job. He'd felt a tinge of pity for her, a girl trying to do her job the best way she knew how. She wore that little hat on her head and was, at least in his initial assessment, a true beauty. Distracted. Not his best day. Not the assessment of a real cop, he thought to himself now. Working on the Moon had made him softer than he should be, and in retrospect, he figured those looks were the likely reason she'd been chosen for the job.

As he reviewed and surveyed her in his mind, that expression stuck out like a headless corpse. It shouldn't have been there. An ME should have expected the cops to show. Even a fake ME team would have presumed the same. Why the surprise? In reality, there weren't too many explanations. The initial one—the one he'd decided on being the most likely—was that they had inside help. They had direction from somewhere, and that Carter's inability to drive their cruiser off-grid had been an intentional delay tactic. Except for him. Tuck. He wasn't supposed to be there. Their happenstance viewing of the corpse should have been dismissed as another phantom on the net. By the time they got there, it would be nothing but a bunch of wild-ass comments on someone's virtual reality trick. Just like the one he'd used to clear the area of prying video eyes.

He shook his head and looked over at Carter, still frozen in that introspective stare. The same one he'd had for the better part of their trip. The discomfort of the seat prompted him to shift again, to no avail. His bones ached, and his mind wished for the stretches and lifts of his workout routine. Even a simple walk. He tried thinking about nothing. Then meditating. Nothing seemed to help as they drove on.

It wasn't until evening in Copernicus time that they finally approached the West gate. They watched its graphic representation on the console screen long before anything came into visual range. Carter cut their speed to an agonizing crawl a few kilometers out. Tuck's body screamed in dismay, but he suppressed the complaints. Stealth was their approach, and a giant cloud of dust from out of nowhere would bust that all to pieces.

In the end, it didn't matter. Carter pulled the racer to a stop as the structures outside the gate made an appearance as bumps on the horizon. Tuck groaned. All this work for nothing. The place was as quiet as the remainder of the lunar surface. No activity. No movement. They wouldn't fool anybody by sneaking in. For now, anyway, they were good and stuck.

Carter popped the hatch on the now-silent racer and tossed Tuck a water ration he'd retrieved from the storage area behind the seat.

Tuck caught the canister in mid-air, his mind and his muscles excited finally to react to something more than watching the bare lunar panorama that had displaced their visual senses for the better part of the day. He looked at Carter with an inquisitive glance as he sipped the water.

Carter, already outside the racer, tipped his own container skyward. "Looks like we've got plenty of time on our hands." He motioned with his head in the direction of the gate. "Let's go for a walk."

Tuck sucked in a deep breath and another drink from the container. He smiled. Carter wasn't going to have to ask twice on that one.

[28]

CLEANUP

SIMMS WAS BACK ON TRACK. Almost there. Outside the office he rubbed his his hands together as if to mentally wipe off grime from the square kilometers of garbage that remained fresh in his mind, before remembering he was missing his left hand. He swore in disgust and slammed his right hand against the plate on the wall, opening the office door. He was close to being back on a schedule, and with time running short, his realization now that he might actually make it out of Copernicus as he'd planned put a deliberate purpose in his step. The inside of the office looked exactly as he'd left it, with one key difference. The odd smell. Almost sickly sweet. He didn't usually stick around to check on the bodies of those he'd killed, so this sour scent in the air that left a foul taste on his tongue was new to him.

No time to lose, he thought, striding toward the rear office.

No, he usually delegated the dirty work, although there were times—like this one—when it was necessary to make a clean break, and he'd decided that this was the most efficient way to do it, although in retrospect, he now realized the flaw in his hastily made plans. Haste had a way of doing that. He stopped for a moment in the middle of the room and took a deep breath. He had time, he thought, but not a lot of it. He needed to keep it together. Haste was his enemy. He had no time for additional departures from his plan.

The other, more challenging task now was to move and stage the bodies. It had to be close, but not too close. He'd considered removing their heads, but that thought had come too late. He had the knife, but in his own assessment, he didn't have the time to do it properly. His detour had compressed what little time actually remained, and it didn't seem practical to do anything more than stage a simple drug deal gone wrong. He didn't need anything fancy. He presumed the scene wouldn't stand up to any type of scrutiny, but in that aspect, he didn't care. By the time they had it figured out, he'd be beyond their jurisdiction anyway.

He had a couple of ideas, but what he didn't have was a left hand, and one-handed, there was no way he could drag both bodies out of the office, to the transport lift, and on to their final resting place. Actually, he thought, that was an aspect of this plan he liked—it effectively took him off the primary suspect list. Aside from ideas, he also had leverage. The micro fieldgen offered experimental technology that could accomplish this same objective. He had two bodies. One would carry the other. He wouldn't have to worry about retro-active video forensics to cover his tracks. The surveillance system would reflect exactly what he needed it to reflect. Larson carrying The Crow on his shoulders.

To his left, the boots covering the now lifeless feet extended out from behind the desk and the emanating smell clarified slightly as he focused on its origin before his mind returned to his own plan.

Time was tight.

The range of the fieldgen was enough that he could remotely control the body carry from midway between the door and the lift. Simms thought about it and shook his head. Certainly it would be clear he was involved, should the surveillance footage roll back, and he allowed himself a smirk. He actually liked it better this way. Once he was out of Copernicus and beyond their reach, he predicted they would ultimately discover he'd been right next door to their headquarters, and they'd missed their opportunity. He visualized Larson carrying the Crow. The smuggler carrying a rival—or partner, he thought with amusement at the variety of potential police theories—before collapsing and bleeding out. It was random enough to offer a nice selection of criminal explanations, many of which would seem possible, but none of which could be.

Screw anything more complex, he decided on the spot. He'd leave them both in the lift. The lift would take them out of range, and they'd collapse there. He just had to remember to plant the knife and the drugs—maybe one on each of them—before he skipped out.

He felt the single brick of packed Orenz squeeze his chest from inside his jacket as he reached to open the office's inner door. Just in case there was any question that this was about drug smuggling, it would serve well as an unmistakeable calling card. That translated into the Orenz task force and, thanks to the added coordination, added time—something he was certainly running short of, he reminded himself yet again.

The inner room looked exactly the way he'd left it. Larson's body still lay on the floor where he'd pushed it. He pulled the fieldgen controller from his jacket pocket as a sudden thought crossed his mind. One thing *could* compromise his plan he realized. Rigor. If the kid had been dead for too long and rigor had set in, the fieldgen's muscle control would simply snap the limbs off Larson and his whole cover story. He paused in mid-step to make a quick time calculation. No, he thought, he should be OK.

It was impossible to tell exactly when the life had run out of him there on the floor. He knelt beside the body, testing his calculation by lifting and moving an arm. He smiled as it moved easily, and he slipped the knife inside the body's gray jacket. "This should keep them guessing for a while," he told the lifeless eyes that stared at nothing. "Too bad you couldn't stick around for the fun."

Satisfied, he slid backward on the hard floor and reached into his pocket for the controller. He thumbed its controller, but nothing happened. It wasn't working. Something was wrong. The paralysis field was on, but not functioning. He pulled it out and examined it, pressing its controller a second time. Again, nothing.

Something was definitely wrong.

"Damn experimental unit," he hissed to himself. "Crap thing probably fell off."

He stood up and searched the floor for the telltale button. Nothing. This was not what he needed.

He pulled on one of the body's arms and rolled it back on its side. Crawling over it, he took a closer look. Again, he couldn't see it. He shook his head, perplexed.

He glanced over at the body again, but this time he saw something that made his blood run cold.

One of the dead eyes winked.

In desperation, he quickly pointed the controller at Larson and pressed the button on the controller a third time.

This time it worked, just not as he'd intended.

The ploy worked perfectly. Almost. Durt had hatched it halfway through his second cigarette. By his third, he'd connected with Nev and could feel the healing chemical energy of the converted smoke flowing through his veins.

The concept was simple. He'd turn the tables on Simms and use his own puppet show to extract a confession for his crimes. By now, he guessed, Simms had found the drug stash and retrieved the bags of Orenz. What he couldn't do was leave a couple loose ends like himself, and apparently, the dead guy with the crow tattoo. He wondered what murder suicide narrative Simms had already have written to cover his tracks. Or maybe not. Maybe he had access to an atomizer nearby and their molecules would recycle into new Earth-bound products.

No, what he had in mind now was to use the mini fieldgen to

march this psycho, drugs in hand, directly into LUNASEC headquarters.

Explain that one, bitch.

Nev had confirmed his suspicions from the desktop monitor, locating Six's flight track and current location. Regaining his mental capacity, he'd retreated back into the inner office and, best he could, repositioned himself as before. He sprawled out on the cool, smooth floor and waited. He still felt his injuries, but the smoke had done its work, and they now became more of an annoyance than the debilitating pain that had incapacitated him before.

Nev was right. Just like always. He didn't have long to wait before Simms strode into the room. Durt had seen dead bodies before but had no way of telling whether or not his facade of a death stare could fool anyone. He hoped Simms hadn't seen enough himself to be able to tell the difference. When it came down to it, it didn't matter. Simms was preoccupied with other concerns and quickly jumped to the conclusion that, in fact, he was dead. Simms' mutterings made it easy enough to follow his thoughts. He flopped helplessly in response to Simms' prod, as he thought a recently dead body might, and as Simms searched for the small button of technology, he placed it onto Simms' right pant leg just above the ankle. Then he waited. As Simms pulled back on his knees, his puzzled face began its shift to anger. Durt was ready.

He winked at the man.

He watched with glee as the wink had its intended effect.

Simms face froze and in desperation, he punched his controller again. The fieldgen now attached and engaged, it froze him stiff in his kneeling position.

Now it was Durt's turn to smile, which, of course, he did. He plucked the controller unit from Simms' paralyzed fingers and stood up carefully. In spite of the three cigarettes he'd used to clear his head, it now spun, his vision nearly escaping him. He took a seat back on the chair where he'd nearly bled to death and just sat. He was going to need more than cigarettes. He'd need rest and food and a lot more time to recover than he had at his disposal. In front of him, Simms remained immobile on his knees, staring at the spot on the floor where Durt had just been.

He examined the controller in his hand. He had no clue how it worked, but presumed the upper control would be for the hands and arms while the lower was likely for the legs. He pressed a couple of controls, but with no immediate results. Then he watched as Simms moved. Mechanically, as if he were being forced into some kind of robot walk. Simms, the robot, turned and walked toward the door.

Durt was stumped. He'd pressed something and he wasn't sure what. He stared at the controller, trying to fiddle with the controls. It wasn't until it was too late to do anything that he realized the truth of the matter.

Simms was now at the door, his signature smirk on his face. He turned and uttered a single word, winking as he said it.

"Failsafe."

Durt heard two steps and the sound of the outer door. Instinctively, he sprang from his chair to give chase, but he had no strength. He stumbled and fell to the floor.

"Damn," Durt swore as he climbed to his feet. "Stupid, clever son of a bitch."

He didn't know if it was all an act or if the controller was programmed to release Simms after the initial freeze. That had been his failsafe. You couldn't kill the assassin with his own gun. It didn't matter how he did it. It was a master play in sleight of hand.

He was stunned. He sat and stared. For how long, he wasn't sure. Eventually, he got up and made his way back into the outer office, but the same thoughts continued to swirl about in his mind.

Simms was free. He had the drugs. He was just clever enough to pin this thing right back on him. He made his way back to the workstation. It almost didn't matter what happened now. It would be bad, and it would be his fault. All this fancy pilot shit? He could kiss that goodbye. If he wasn't headed for prison, he was at least headed home with his tail between his legs. He'd been stupid, out of his league, and he'd been beaten.

"Durt?" It was Nev on the screen in front of him. "Durt, do you want me to ground Six? I can do it remotely."

He could hear the dejection in his own voice as he waved off her offer. "Nah. Wouldn't make a bit of difference now. I'm sure he's got an alternate plan. He's going to disappear. I'll be on the hook for every questionable thing he's ever done. I don't know how, but that will be the end game. Just wait and see."

Again he sat and stared. Minutes dragged by.

"God, I'm a loser. I don't know why I thought I could survive up here," he said to no-one in particular and shook his head in disgust with himself. "He got the drugs, and he's got the ship, and somehow, some way, Durt Larson is going to be responsible for it."

Nev contradicted him. "Durt, he didn't go back to the ship."

Durt stared at the screen in front of him. "What do you mean? Of course he went back to the ship."

"No, he's gone somewhere else. Couldn't tell you where, but no one is on the ship. He'd have plenty of time to get there by now if that's where he was going."

He'd taken the ship to get the drugs, then just abandoned them?

He thought about it. If drugs were found on Six, then they'd go into LUNASEC custody. Which would screw Simms out of his delivery. Unless—. He realized another possibility. Unless LUNASEC was the dealer and intended delivery point. He thought about it. Wouldn't that be pretty? Suddenly it became all too clear. He and Truman framed for trafficking, the delivery completed and Simms free and clear. Maybe it was too perfect not to be the case. Only one thing wrong, and that was Six's logs would show Simms picking up the drugs, so it wouldn't work. Then he remembered the surveillance video had shown Durt delivering Rush the cases. If video manipulation was possible, and he'd seen the evidence with his own eyes, then removing himself from Six's databanks wouldn't be beyond the realm of possibility. But if he was doing that, then he would have gone right back and done it.

Just one more thing that didn't make any sense right now, he thought. He shook his head in wonder and lit another cigarette.

* * *

His arms ached; his head pounded and his throat burned, but by the time Truman walked through the door, Durt knew exactly why Simms had abandoned the drugs. The drugs were his net, and he was fishing. Somehow, Durt's possession of the drugs was more important than the drugs themselves.

Nev had been great about coming up with electronic solutions. She'd offered to disable the ship. That would have been sweet. He could picture Simms escaping with Six, only to find the ship unresponsive. But it was just wishful thinking. No, he thought, they had to get to some kind of law enforcement. Soon.

Durt eyed Truman with a curious look. "How did you find me?"

But he already knew. He couldn't see her, but he was certain Nev was smiling.

"Durt are you—" began Truman, then stopped in mid-sentence and eyed the two boots protruding from behind the desk. He stared in disbelief and started again, slower this time. "Holy—" He paused. "What the hell happened here?"

He didn't wait for an answer as he peered more closely at Durt. "Jesus, you look like hell, Durt."

Durt ignored his concern. "Truman. You've got to get me to LUNASEC. Fast."

"No, Durt, We've got to get you to the hospital."

Durt extended the pack of cigarettes he'd taken from the dead guy, but Truman waved them off. "Maybe later. Right now we've got more pressing issues."

"Really?"

Durt nodded. "Really. Remember Wislon Simms?"

"The guy you saved?"

"The guy I saved."

"The guy with one hand?"

"Yep."

"How in the—"

Durt knew what his question was. How could a one-handed man kidnap and transport him here? "He's clever. Not in a good way. And he had help."

Truman said nothing, his gaze returning to the boots.

Durt raised his arms, wincing as he did, to reveal his scarred wrists and arms.

Truman whistled.

"He figured out where I stashed the Orenz. I thought that would be the end of him, but I think he's left the Orenz on Six and is on his way to pin a distribution charge on us.

Truman stared at him for another moment. "OK, Durt. LUNASEC first, but then the hospital. You're not really in any shape to go anywhere. I do have a couple of LUNASEC friends." He shook his head. "I don't know if they'll be of much help to us, but we can give it a try."

As if punctuating his sentence, the building around them rumbled and shook. Only for a moment. Truman's expression reflected complete confusion. "Moonquake?" he said, shaking his head in disbelief. "That is *not* good. No way that should happen." He grabbed Durt by the coat sleeve. "We've got to get out of this building now. That means walking, and that means stairs."

Durt looked at Truman not comprehending the urgency.

"Now!" commanded Truman, dragging Durt to his feet and toward the door.

Durt obliged to the best of his ability. He'd been sitting, and the smoke had helped, but he still felt weak. He held his own as they made their way out of the building and into the street.

People streamed out of nearby buildings, the crowd buzzing and shouting. Most of them looked as confused as he felt.

Truman asked some of the others standing nearby about the quake, but it was clear none of them had any more insight than they did. The good thing was they hadn't felt any additional tremors yet.

"This ever happen before?" he asked Truman over the street noise.

Truman's expression remained perplexed. "First time for me."

Up the street, they watched as an injured woman wrapped in a blanket was escorted through the crowd. Overhead, Durt listened as emergency vehicles buzzed and hovered, apparently landing on the roof. He used Truman's shoulder to steady himself. What he really needed was a bed and sleep, but in the absence of either of those—or any immediate answers—he needed one thing. Focus. Grabbing Truman's arm, he took a hesitant step up the street.

"LUNASEC," he urged his engineer.

[29]

BIKE

Liz found it hard to breathe. The clothes she'd taken such pain to select that morning now lay strewn in strips on the floor of her examination lab. She was almost more upset with the shredded designer labels than with her own personal situation, which, she had to admit to herself, was dire. The only thing she wore now were the few strips of her beige slacks that bound her hands and feet. She'd screamed her lungs out for a good half hour, for all the good it had done. The wad of cloth jammed into her mouth that had once been underwear now gave a new, more literal meaning to taste in clothing. Her face still sticky with her tears of fear and frustration, she now looked into the leering eyes of a man who was most decidedly not from internal affairs.

She wasn't sure at first what had happened. The building shook and the floors shivered. He lost his balance and tumbled backward, his hands searching for purchase, and his eyes searching the room, trying to make sense of it. It only lasted for a few moments, but as the shaking subsided, so did his fear. He moved quickly to untie her, a move that made no logical sense to Liz. At first. Whatever happened, she realized, he was tied to her. Of course, at the moment, she was tied to the table.

She thought about it. If he was untying her, that meant he was moving her. She had no idea where that might be. She wondered if even he had an idea. It didn't look like he was in a conversational mood—if he was a guy who even had conversational moods. She didn't care. While the better part of her being had been busy withstanding the pain and fearing her own demise, the lesser, more logical part of her had worked on an escape, or at least tried to. Waiting for an opening. Thinking through contingencies. If only she could free her hands—or even a foot—she might be able to put up some resistance. If only something would distract him. Like a cramp. Or a heart attack. She sighed mentally. No such luck. That part of her brain had not dwelled on the "what-ifs" but rather on her actions, should she have the opportunity.

He'd cut her. A couple of times. They hurt like a son-of-a-bitch, but they weren't that deep. She took that to mean that he intended to take his time. That was something. She kept that in mind.

While his strength was immense and his sense about what she might choose as an escape move was uncanny, his understanding of human physiology was pretty iffy. He'd probably attended thug school to train for his intimidation and interrogation techniques. It certainly made an impression with her. But, as her nose kept reminding her, good hygiene was not one of his keener skills.

He wore the clothes of a government official, but they fit poorly. He didn't have the body to match his supposed sedentary lifestyle. Whatever he'd done to keep in shape, he'd done a lot of it. Fully dressed, she wasn't sure if it was physical or of it was the result of enhanced surgery, but he was certainly out of his element here as an inspector for Internal Affairs.

Had there been more time, she might have divined his identity and purpose, but the Internal Affairs appointment was punctual and at her own request, so by the time she'd seen him without the jacket—by the time her mind had filled in the blanks—it was too late.

At that point, though, his strength wasn't her focus. It was his approach. Meticulous, he was not, and the clothing he'd selected

—maybe from the actual inspector—had nothing to do with it. No, she thought, it was the way he handled the instruments.

Another slicing, burning pain evoked another scream into her gag.

The intense pain teared her eyes.

He smiled.

He'd bypassed the current state-of-the art lasers and scanners for the shiny, stainless steel ME kit she kept on display as just that. Display. They were never used, but she liked to have them around as a reminder of the professional legacy that preceded her work here. The occasional visitor found them fascinating. As did the current one. Of the full set, though, he only used a few, apparently unsure the actual purpose of many of them. Thank God for small favors.

She shook and screamed and shivered as he tried each one, dropping one in favor of another. He had no idea where the discarded ones lay. But she did. She knew exactly where each one had fallen. It was that little contingency tracking part of her brain that had listened, then placed each of the instruments in her mind's eye.

Her focus was currently the scalpel that lay between her ankles. She'd heard its distinct clang as he'd dropped it, and she felt its steel bump against her skin before falling on the metal table.

To get her hands on it, a number of things had to happen, and it would require a bit of play acting, but that didn't seem like a real problem. The guy didn't seem like a theatre critic. Still, she reminded herself, she needed to be somewhat subtle should the opportunity present itself. This didn't appear to be his first interrogation session.

She certainly couldn't hide the look on her face when the building shook, but he'd been otherwise engaged. Trying to keep his feet underneath him. But now her eyes were closed, her entire frame limp as a fresh cadaver. Whatever the shaking was, she couldn't figure, but he seemed to think that being tied here to the table was the wrong place for her as he worked to free her ankles from their bonds. Maybe he was going to move her.

Total relaxation.

He untied her left hand first, then her right, grasping it in a preventive move. Still, she remained limp. He brought her to a sitting position, and she flopped her head forward, a loose ball on the end of a string. With it, she flopped her loose arm forward in a purposefully awkward movement.

"Crap," he muttered to himself. "Ain't that just like a woman." She knew a scared, screaming woman could be predictably dragged and pushed, but a loose, lifeless form—like a sack of trash—required a whole different approach.

The blood he'd already spilled from her was an additional complication, making her even more difficult to grip.

The metal scalpel now lay beside her limp hand, and she understood that a missed cue would forfeit her life. She'd wet and compressed her disgusting gag enough now that she was ready to unleash everything at once. This was her chance. It wasn't much of one, but if her calculations were right, it would surprise him. That's all she needed. A couple seconds of surprise was worth a lifetime. With tongue and teeth and lungs, she spat out her panties, sucked in twin lungfuls of air and let him have it.

The scream startled him, but not as much as she'd hoped. Thankfully, it was enough of an opening. He stared at her for a second. He was still unsteady from the building shake, and his hijacked pants from the actual, portlier inspector hung loose around his trim waist and muscled thighs. She guessed she'd have enough time for a two-stroke move. She wanted both legs but never got there. The first scalpel slash made quick work of the loose hanging slacks, and the second sliced easily into his inner thigh.

He barely noticed. He grunted a single word as he backhanded her face. "Bitch," he snarled as her head snapped back from the force of his slap.

She dropped the knife on the deck and went limp again. She

felt her final bond release as he hefted her up on his shoulder. She had no idea where he planned to take her. What she did know was that her extra weight wasn't going to help him a bit. She also knew that he was about to learn a personal physiology lesson—one they didn't teach in Thug school.

* * *

"This is the guy?" Tuck wasn't so sure, even though Tesso insisted it was.

Their trek to the inner halls of Copernicus law enforcement had taken both skill and luck. For Tuck, luck came in only two flavors—good and bad—and it came in waves. Sometimes you just had to wait for it to turn. Patience, he knew, was not something he had a lot of. Carter, on the other hand, had it coming out his ears. It was Carter who'd reminded and convinced him that their luck would turn—if they'd just wait for it.

Carter turned out to be right. He could learn something from his colleague. Who knew? Carter had said. Maybe the waiting might actually work in their favor. Carter was as honest as he was patient. "We might never know," he'd said. "but let's see how it plays out. I've got a good feeling."

This time anyway, luck had come their way.

Tuck could hear the skeptical tone in his own voice now as they stood before the supposed thief of Carter's badge. "You're *sure* this is the guy?" he asked Tesso again.

The guy didn't look like a thief, although certainly his present stance—sitting next to the interview desk in restraints—did nothing to discourage that assessment. Tuck watched him interact with Tesso and a couple others. This guy didn't display any of the classic behaviors of a thief. No wild stories. No outbursts. No knocking knees and chattering teeth of a desperate criminal.

In fact, for the most part, he looked more serene than the majority of the law enforcement officers who stood or wandered through the central processing area. Even here at HQ where it might be presumed that its carefully manufactured granite columns and marble floors hosted law enforcement administration at a more sophisticated level than that of its local sub-stations, lawbreakers were interviewed, scanned, and released or booked into downtown detainment facilities until they could be processed and transported. It just seemed fancier here.

The guy was almost apologetic that they'd made a mistake. He was sorry for wasting their time, he said. They could check his records, and he'd just be on his way. In fact, Tesso advised, he'd done that very thing. He'd checked the records and the guy was right. Nothing out of the ordinary. Some mid-level manager over at TransComm.

Tuck wondered if maybe the guy had nothing to do with it, and it was his own unfulfilled need to cobble some explanation together. There were too many loose ends. Was he grasping at anything that looked like it might lead to an explanation? He took a deep breadth and looked away for a moment, clearing his mind.

Last night, it was he and Carter who had been in the explaining mode. The group of youngsters outside the west gate had been suspicious at first, too. They were not that much younger than him or Carter, but they'd yet to develop the scornful Copernicus attitude that grew on the majority of contracted folks who worked here. They were wide-eyed and full of wonder at the races. They'd been wary of opening up to a pair of strange guys who looked, acted and dressed differently. There were probably 20 of them, and they'd brought out six cars in the group, all functional beaters that were serviceable for transportation but not for the races they talked about without pause. Clearly, the vehicles had been handed down from contractor to contractor as contracts completed and they returned to Earth.

Tuck and Carter weren't used to disguising their law enforcement identities, and the group made a poor attempt to cover up what they were up to. Things shifted quickly, however, when they brought forward the racer. An hour later, a string of rides, and the promise of access at the next race turned into the perfect cover.

They'd come with six and returned with seven. They couldn't have asked for better cover. Their luck had turned.

Tuck returned his attention to the restrained man before him. There was something. His mind couldn't articulate it, but his gut warned him that something about the man didn't quite fit.

Tuck watched the questions and the conversation for a minute or so before he pulled Tesso aside again.

"So, give me particulars. What's his story?"

Tesso shook his head, his expression, thought Tuck, still not reflecting the trust he'd hoped to instill by offering himself up for arrest. "Name is Wislon. Wislon Simms," said Tesso in a low voice, turning and shielding his voice with his right hand, the hand that held what he presumed was Carter's badge, "Says he found the badge," he motioned to it with his eyes, "discarded in a TRANSCOM stairwell. Figured he'd bring it to HQ and turn it in. Only about a 5-minute walk over here."

Tuck stared at him. Tesso's uncertain face reflected exactly what he was thinking. The badge had been aboard a TransComm transport at the material dump site, so it might well have been discarded. Except for one thing. "Simms," he repeated under his breath. It wasn't an electronic component. It was a man. This unassuming man was on Trina's dying breath. He turned slowly to reassess the one-handed man.

"One other thing, Tuck," continued Tesso, "They identified the slice job," he whispered. "Internal Affairs. From Earth."

The update didn't sink in immediately. Over Tesso's shoulder, he watched the mistaken identity story and its expression of apology melt away. The suspect, this guy named Simms, was no longer watching Tesso. He now stared into Tuck's eyes. It wasn't a face of innocence, but one of determination and a certain smugness.

Now it was a different conversation, the guy's voice even and directive. "Release me now and she lives."

Tuck looked into his eyes, afraid of what they might reveal. "She who?"

"Your girlfriend."

He responded immediately before realizing the comment's intention. "I don't have a girlfriend."

Tuck's detective mind suddenly put a number of things together.

The ME. Liz. That's why he's smiling.

"Probably having some real fun with Bike now. Don't worry. He won't leave a mess. She'll just disappear." He motioned with his head toward the ceiling, "Poof!"

So, Bike was back.

Tuck's anger seethed as he brought his fury within an inch of the guy's face. "Where is she?" he hissed.

The response was nonchalant. Simms shrugged as if he had all the time in the world. "Copernicus is a big place. She could be anywhere."

Tuck backed up a step and punched up the ME staff on his wristcomm. No answer. He tried Liz direct. Still nothing.

Simms apparently couldn't help himself. His face seeped smugness from every pore.

That stupid smile.

"Look, I'm in something of a rush, and now with this mixup —" Simms trailed off in mid-sentence, eyeing Tuck for a moment. "You let me go, and I'll send you the location. You'll be a hero."

Tuck didn't buy it. Not even for a second.

She could be anywhere.

That was the clue, he thought. She could be anywhere, but she wasn't. No, if she was with Bike, then they needed Liz out of the picture. Something else, too, he realized. This Simms guy was the reason he himself was on the run. If he could get through to the ME, and Simms was TransComm, he had superpowers or—.

He thought for a minute. No, he didn't have superpowers. What he had was a partner. Someone on the inside. Tuck had never met Simms before but had a pretty good idea why he needed to vanish. Plus, the ME was an appointee. Plenty of security for a high-level player like her.

She could be anywhere.

Maybe he should let Simms go. He was probably a minor player anyway. Save Liz, then track this son of a bitch down and take him apart.

No, he thought, as something else occurred to him. Tesso's update. Internal Affairs.

Suddenly he knew where she was, and who Tesso's slice job was. He snatched Carter's badge out of Tesso's hand and ran. Time, as always, was not his friend. But this time he didn't have a choice. He flashed past reception. Past booking. Right out the main entrance and up to the roof.

* * *

He burst out of the entrance. Sprinting, he jumped into the racer only a few vehicles down. He banged the hatch shut and smacked the console with his hand to power it up. Just because he didn't fly often didn't mean he didn't know how to fly. Flying wasn't the real issue, though, Tuck thought to himself as the racer climbed almost vertically and Copernicus receded below him. He was a detective, and what he really needed was a physicist. It wasn't only the racer he'd jumped into, but a physics problem as well. The problem contained speed and velocity and material elasticity and a bunch of other variables that probably should be considered, but with him at the controls, wouldn't be.

It was Carter's badge that authorized his skyward climb, and truthfully, he had no idea if it would work or not. The limit of his mental capacity and calculation ended at his chosen solution of *climb high and dive fast.* He had no idea whether or not he'd survive or end up as a bloodstain on the Copernicus sidewalk below. Who knew? he thought, maybe his head and hands would pop off and he'd become part of the mystery he was trying to solve.

There was a time for thinking, and Tuck knew now that his was up. It was no longer a matter of physics. It was a matter of time, and he was out of it. He closed his eyes, took a deep breath and slammed the racer forward into his head-long, diagonal dive, the hand of physics pressing him backward into the racer's cockpit, the toy buildings racing toward him now at incredible speed.

An instantaneous thought flashed across his mind as he made out now his ultimate target below him.

What the hell am I doing?

He'd made a string of what he now realized were non-Tuck like decisions. The they were emotional. They were gallant, but for all he knew now, they were destined to failure because he hadn't done his homework. He thought about aborting. Pulling up. The little voice that had talked him into this now laughed at his fear and uncertainty. He thought about the ME. Liz. Was he saving her? Was he killing her? Was his logic sound, or was he just grasping at the straws of some internal fantasy he'd cooked up over the course of a 10-minute conversation?

Right or wrong. Dead or alive. It didn't matter. He was past the point of any decision other than his originally intended one.

He closed his eyes as the racer dove into the roof of the ME's building and the forces of physics did their best to tear him apart.

[30]
HEADQUARTERS

LUNASEC's criminal processing was located on the ground floor of its headquarters, smack in the middle of Copernicus' city center. Desks and questions. Jabbering. Complaining. It seemed crazy busy for a Monday morning, but after a weekend here, it made perfect sense. Were they not on the moon, Durt could swear he and Truman had just walked into Seattle's King County jail. Maybe a few more modern touches with the granite and marble, but the interior design that framed the sea of offenders and defenders of Copernicus law held an eerie similarity. His scar throbbed with the memory. Ornate but practical, with no corners on anything within reach. Rounded edges, he imagined, served as a first line of defense against inventive criminal minds. Similar layouts likely reflected generally accepted law enforcement practices—universal requirements meant universal design.

Behind the reception counter, a woman managed a layered wall of floating screens, her hands deftly assessing and directing each to its appropriate information queue. Her profile was a model of beauty with flaxen hair, high cheekbones and eyes of dark sapphire. She turned momentarily to assess them before returning to her communication management task, and Durt's heart skipped a beat. He'd only seen it for a second, but a scar that marred the left side of her face immediately put their law enforcement errand into perspective. She'd seen action someplace. Durt wondered for an instant if it was Simms' work, but it bore little resemblance to his own. It wasn't hideous. In fact in his mind, it enhanced her wicked efficiency and self-confidence.

She'd made no wasted movement and no mistake with her glancing assessment. "It's about a 15-minute wait to make a complaint," she said, her eyes still focused on her screens. She'd known they weren't cops in an instant. "You can find a seat out there," she said, nodding to the Bullpen, a twitch of her eye replacing the smile she chose not to share, knowing there weren't any seats. "Names?"

Durt glanced at his engineer who took the lead. "Truman"

"Truman what?"

Truman shook his head. "Just Truman."

She rolled her eyes and shook her head. "Freak," she said under her breath as she turned to Durt.

"What about you—"

She stopped mid-sentence and stared, if only for a second. Durt felt his face grow hot, knowing his scar was her point of focus. He needn't have worried as her face broke into an alluring smile. "What's your name?" she continued.

"Durt," he said after an unexpectedly stupid pause.

What the hell is wrong with me?

"Durt Larson," he finished.

Her large blue eyes got even larger, if that was possible. "*THE* Durt Larson?"

He nodded sheepishly without a sound.

"Well," she said, regaining some semblance of her efficient self, "That is a badass scar." It was almost a whisper. "Don't worry. They'll find you when your screen comes up. You and—"

She pretended to forget his name.

"Truman," Durt filled in.

"Right. You and Truman go take care of business, then you come right back here and tell me how you got it."

He stumbled over his words again. "It's…um…kind of a long story."

Behind her, the video wall of incoming data was reforming itself. She winked at him. "Oh, I hope so."

They moved into the crowd. The waiting area offered few seats to begin with, none of which, clearly, were empty. Durt did notice the injured blanket woman from the street sat in one, now surrounded by her own small crowd, one of which appeared to be a med tech accompanied by a waist-high medbot. Concerned faces completed the circle around her.

Durt figured on giving that crowd some space, but Truman had seen something and moved directly toward them.

"Truman?"

One of the concerned faces was now looking at them and smiling. He stood, extending a hand. "Truman. What a nice surprise." His greeting and the surprise were genuine, Durt judged. "What brings you into our zoo?"

Truman was hesitant and clearly not a smooth-talking spokesman by any means, but he said what he came to say in a few words. "Um…We've gotten ourselves into kind of a jam." He nodded at Durt. "We're hoping you might be able to help?"

"Marlin Tuck," he said, extending his hand to Durt. "Friend of Truman is a friend of mine. Call me Tuck."

"Durt Larson. Great to meet you."

As it had, really since the TRI-PAC race, his name froze Tuck where he stood. The man's eyebrows raised in another surprise, and he didn't release his grip as he turned to confirm his suspicions with Truman.

"Your friend," he began.

Truman corrected him."Pilot."

"Your pilot." Durt watched the understanding expression flow across Tuck's face as he turned back to face him. "Of course, he's your pilot." Then without skipping a beat, he addressed Durt. "So, you're with TransComm now? First trip?"

Durt confirmed with a nod as Tuck finally released his grip.

Formalities complete, Tuck was all business. "Look, Truman. You know I'll do what I can do to help, but I'm kind of in the middle of something right now." He lowered his tone, but Durt heard him nonetheless. "And Larson here, he doesn't look so good. Problems with the jump?"

Truman nodded, "Yeah. Guess you could say that."

The medic and the medbot were both busy with the woman who sat beside them. She let out a whimper as her medical aid proceeded.

"Is she going to be OK?" asked Truman.

Tuck didn't get the chance to answer, as a LUNASEC cop interrupted their conversation abruptly.

"What the fuck, Tuck? You're in some deep shit for that stunt," said the cop, his words curt and angry. "We got facilities for this. You know. *Rules*." He grimaced as he growled. "This is my watch, and you shouldn't—"

Tuck cut him off. "Tesso, you recognize her?"

Tesso's expression shifted instantaneously as he recognized the ME. "Oh, my God," he said, his face now full of concern. We have to get her to an emergency room. *Now*."

"Thanks for the concern, Tesso, but not your call."

Tesso nodded and backed off. "Sure Tuck. You just let me know what you need. I'll get the ER on standby."

Durt listened as Truman ran Tuck through a short but effective summary of their recent activity. He listened, but he already knew the story, and his eyes and mind began to wander. His gaze was without purpose at first, but he instinctively snapped his head back as his brain caught something of interest in the corner of his eye. The crowd was dense enough so that when he looked up again he lost it. He turned back to Truman's conversation, but his mind wouldn't leave him alone. It was a flash of something. Something that didn't quite process but that couldn't be ignored.

Curious, he trained his eye in the general direction, continuing to follow Truman's words. Then it happened. A large man in a bright orange shirt shifted slightly on his feet as he talked in earnest with a shorter, balding man. He recognized the clothing.

"Holy shit," he said to himself, staring at a seated Simms, his right hand cuffed to a booking chair. He grabbed Truman's sleeve.

Truman looked up and saw the same thing. "It's the guy from the parking garage."

"Simms," said Durt.

Tuck was surprised. "You know this guy?"

A slim woman with braided hair interrupted Truman's answer. She'd slipped quickly through the crowd and the edge of concern in her voice bordered on hysteria. "Tuck, what the hell happened?"

She was accompanied by one of the tallest men Durt had ever seen. It wasn't just his height that set him apart from the surrounding crowd. The man's clothing and eyes made Durt look twice. Instead of the slim-fit clothing now in style in Copernicus, he wore a robe of some sort, and his gray eyes took in the frantic energy of the crowd with a calm resolve.

"Later, Bren," Tuck told the woman, not unkindly. "Guys, this is Bren and Anton," said Tuck indicating the tall man, then turning back to them "and this is my friend Truman and the famous Durt Larson."

They smiled politely. The tall man, Anton, bowed his head in greeting, but gave no notice to the fame Tuck had attached to Durt's name.

Finally someone who is meeting me and not the story of me, thought Durt, as he returned a nod of greeting.

"So, you're familiar with my one-armed badge bandit?" Tuck asked Truman.

Truman nodded to Durt. "That's his story."

Tuck said nothing, but Durt read the urgency in his raised eyebrows and assented.

"His name is Wislon Simms. He worked for Rush, and I pulled

the two of them off a beach in the North Pacific. Rush was freezing to death and Simms was about to bleed out. His hand is probably still inside the rotting corpse of the grizzly bear we left on that beach."

Tuck was nodding and following the story. "This is the same guy?" he said, his face puzzled. "You saved his life?"

Durt shook his head, maybe a bit too cynically. "For all the good it did."

"What do you mean?"

"Rush killed himself." Durt corrected himself, "I mean all the reports on the Net say that's what happened." He nodded in Simms' direction. "Simms was behind it."

Tuck looked confused. "Rush is dead?"

"Yeah, man. It's been all over the Net," said Truman. "Constant. Where the hell have you been?"

Tuck half smiled. "Later." He turned back to Durt, urging him forward. "You pulled them off the beach. And then?"

Durt stared blankly at Tuck. He realized suddenly the pressure he felt on the one side of his chest was not internal, but external. In their rush, he'd forgotten. He now stood before a cop standing in cop central and was recounting his story. He felt hot and he began to sweat. He tried to swallow but the dryness in his throat made it difficult.

Inside his jacket, he realized, he carried Rush's murder weapon.

* * *

Durt allowed himself an inner smile, figuring an actual one at this point might be considered inappropriate. Things were looking up. His weakened condition, he realized, had likely covered his fear of discovery and blame. The LUNSEC processing area was still packed and vocal, but their small group had expanded to include an officer he presumed was Tuck's partner, Carter. Tuck related their recent activity inside and outside the dome, and with Carter and Truman filling in some blanks, they begun to fill in the answers to a number of their collective questions. When Tuck told of Trina's collaboration with Simms and subsequent death, Durt realized Trina was the one who'd taken him and ultimately saved his life with her second knock-out drink. The group was riveted as he shared his own Simms story and his discovery of the mini-fieldgen.

Tuck and Carter both now had their badges back. Based on their run-in with Simms before, Truman had suggested the director of the Orenz task force they'd advised of during their run-in be present for the arrest. Tuck agreed, and based on what Carter had suffered at the hands of Simms, suggested to Tesso that it would also be appropriate for Carter to serve as the arresting officer.

The group now occupied the open space between the woman in the blanket who remained seated and Simms, the one-armed badge bandit as Tuck had called him. Even with imminent arrest staring him in the face, Simms remained indifferent. Durt wondered if he knew something they didn't. If so, he couldn't imagine what that might be. He was isolated. They had the evidence. At Nev's insistence, they'd locked and encrypted Six's log, blocking any potential admin manipulation. In a nutshell he was done, he thought, as he stared at the seated Simms, even if the man didn't believe it himself. He allowed that Simms, in spite of his short in stature, was always long on confidence.

Simms must have felt the stare and returned it with mild curiosity. Before Durt could think about forming words to describe the emotions he felt inside, they just slipped out. "You're just plain evil," he heard himself say.

Simms shrugged. "Maybe. Maybe not. Truth is you can't really tell until you have all the pieces. But I think you're starting to get there."

Maybe returning some of Simms' confidence to him would convince him to do the explaining himself. "You made a mistake."

Simms assented. "More than one."

"You made one big one," Durt continued. "Your deceptions were intriguing. Too intriguing."

Simms said nothing.

"The harder you tried to cover up your secrets, the bigger your target was for LUNASEC.

"Maybe you're right, but it is Copernicus."

Durt was not sure what he meant by that, and Simms must have seen that in his eyes.

"You should have stayed in Alaska, kid," Simms continued. He stared past Durt at the group behind him. "Here on Copernicus, the cops are cheap. The good ones avoid assignments here like the plague. Does nothing for them. The ones who do come are second rate. Couldn't make it someplace else. Pretty good at asking questions and filing reports, and here where crimes are simple and minor, gets them decent closure rates. Good for them. But they're pretty bad at asking tough questions." He winked. "Good for me."

"Except?" prodded Durt.

"Except is right," said Simms. "Exception. There's always an exception." He again looked past Durt.

"Tuck?"

"And Carter. A pair of them."

Durt stared wordlessly. Simms was a criminal. Sooner or later he'd have been caught anyway. What he needed to know was—

Again, somehow Simms knew what he most needed to know. "You." Simms stared directly into his eyes. "You want to know about you."

Durt's expression must have communicated his question as if it were a carefully lettered advertisement.

"Afraid my motives were somewhat personal," he admitted. "But it's hard to explain to someone who hasn't lost a hand. I couldn't deal with not having my second hand."

"But you have your life."

"It doesn't work that way," said Simms shaking his head with a humorless gaze. "My body, no, my soul, needs that hand to feel complete. I don't even understand it sometimes. It demands an explanation, and the most simple one is blame. I blame you. I hate you as much as you hate me. And I guess it was just coincidence, that we needed a distraction and a scapegoat."

In a strange way it made sense to Durt.

"Your problem is that messing with the drug trade goes much deeper than that," continued Simms. "You might guess that it's Copernicus recycling and manufacturing that make the world go round, but you'd only have half the picture."

Simms was looking at him again, this time with an amused smile. "You and me? We're actually a lot alike."

Durt's face broke into an expression of immediate disagreement.

"We are," insisted Simms. "We're both at the mercy of forces beyond our own control. You want to do me a favor? Just kill me now. I'm already dead. Or I might as well be. I failed, thanks to your do-gooding and thanks to those misguided intentions, you cost me and the rest of us a lot more than just annoyance."

Durt offered a wry smile. "Glad I could be of assistance."

Simms' face darkened. "You thought you were doing something right and good. But around here, those terms are pretty flexible. I was ready to make a clean break."

"I just wanted justice."

"You probably wanted truth, too, didn't you?"

Durt couldn't deny it. He shrugged.

"Man, you have no idea what truth really is." He waited for a moment, and Durt could sense anger seething behind the man's calm cynicism. "The truth is about money and profit and keeping the business of manufacturing here going." He paused for a moment before continuing. "At any cost. And when a task force has the potential to shut the whole thing down, then something has to be done. For the greater good." He shook his head with a humorless smile. "Those are not my words, just so you understand."

"The greater good? Are you kidding me?" Durt couldn't help

himself. "You killed Rush."

Simms disagreed. "I didn't kill Rush. Rush killed Rush."

Durt opened his mouth to speak, but Simms cut him off with a raised left stump. "I know what you're going to say, so let me rephrase it for you. He looked up at the ceiling overhead, apparently searching for the right words. "Rush discovered the truth about Orenz and thought he could stop it. Thought he was better than it. You know, like above it. Morally." He focused on Durt again. "Look, I didn't have any beef with Rush. Truth be told, he was a decent man. But he was fooling himself." He paused for a second and stared into Durt's eyes. "Kind of like you. Understand, though, if I didn't have him killed, someone else would have. Could have been a lot worse for him."

"What a shame that would have been," muttered Durt.

"He's probably better off dead. A lot of us are. And if it sounds like the rant of a cornered dog—like one who's trying to talk himself out of the same corner he happily played in before—you might not be wrong. But as you're beginning to find out, things here on the Moon are not always what they seem. Nobody here died by chance. They died to save things that are important to Earth." He thought about it, then corrected himself. "Well, what the Earth says is important, anyway."

That did it. He wasn't quite sure he understood it all, but that didn't matter. He needed, once and for all, to wipe that smug attitude off Simms' face. Durt's weakness momentarily forgotten, his hunting instincts took over. In an instant the knife was in his hand and in the next it was on Simms' shackled wrist, ready to slice it off clean. "I'm gonna set you free," he snarled, inches from Simms' face.

Simms' fear was real, his eyes wide with the realization of what was about to happen, and his scream was that of a 5-year-old girl, a high-pitched shrill of terror that echoed off the granite and marble.

They sat momentarily frozen in time, the guillotine steel resting on the skin, Durt poised to release his pain and anger in a single stroke. Their eyes locked.

The scream died in Simms' throat and left the entire floor in silence.

[31]
DEPUTY

It wasn't more than a whisper from Truman, but it was accompanied by a restraining hand. "Don't do it," said Truman with a shake of his head. "Not worth it."

Durt took a deep breath. Truman was right. The cowering figure in front of him wasn't anything more to him now than a manifestation of his own anger. He nodded, stepped back, and slipped the knife back inside the jacket. He got what he needed.

He wondered if Simms might need to change his pants. Not his concern. His concentration on Simms had blocked out everything else, and he still struggled to put the pieces together. Their entire group had gathered closely around them, but now he sensed something else, too. Something different. He took another step back and looked around the floor. A cold fear tickled his neck. He was face-to-face with the bear again on the cabin's porch. Something was wrong. Aside from their group, the place had emptied. Even the woman working reception had abandoned her post. Outside their little group, only the one named Tesso remained. Durt could feel the fear he saw on Tesso's face.

The others in the group looked at one another wordlessly for an explanation.

The explanation entered the area with a purposeful stride. She was all business.

"Tesso, I said the Task Force head, not the LUNASEC deputy," said Tuck.

Tesso was nodding miserably, "I know. That's who I called."

An echo of Simms' words chilled Durt.

Messing with the drug trade goes much deeper than that.

"You—" The slim woman named Bren was pointing an accusing finger at the Deputy in disbelief as if she had more to say but couldn't get the words out.

"You?" asked Tuck

"You," Bren said, still pointing. It was almost like the woman couldn't believe what she was saying. "You and Bike. You made the deal with us."

"Yes we did," the Deputy agreed. "And now I'm ready to make another one. Pretty easy choice actually. First, none of this can be reflected in our surveillance system." She shrugged. "But that's not a problem. It won't be the first time."

Durt wasn't sure, but it looked like she winked at Tuck.

The Deputy narrowed her eyes. "So you've figured us out, have you?" she addressed the small crowd.

"It doesn't matter. In an hour, all of this will be erased. As if none of this ever happened. So say want you want. It won't matter. Here's what's going to happen. Each of you will be arrested. None will leave the building. Not sure if any of you will survive. I haven't decided yet." She paused for a moment, in thought. "I think I'll need a couple more of your heads," she mused to no one in particular. "Those segments seem so popular on the Net."

"Tesso, arrest her." It was Tuck.

Durt watched Tesso. Clearly he was scared. His eyes were wide, and his head was shaking as if to say, *No way*.

"Officer Tuck, isn't it?" said the Deputy, turning to him, a smirk on her face that looked like she'd stolen it from Simms. "None of you have the authority to arrest me. As a matter of convenience—my convenience, not yours, of course—the Director is out of the system for some much needed rest and relaxation. At my suggestion," she added needlessly. "I, and I alone, now decide what is legal and what is not."

Tuck shot a glance at Tesso who confirmed with a nod and a grimace, his open arms confirming.

"I am your legal authority." Her voice was even and toneless. "A number of you are sworn LUNASEC officers. You will discharge your duties as I direct."

The familiar fear that he'd become acquainted with during his encounters with Simms returned to paralyze Durt, and he shivered at the thought. She was just like Simms, he realized. Maybe worse.

Was this how it all ended?

He fingered the knife inside his jacket. He could hold his own in a fight, and the woman was fooling herself if she thought he'd go down without one. She, like Simms, brimmed with confidence, and he wondered what would stop him from just walking out now. He glanced toward the exit and made out something he hadn't seen before. He felt his spine tingle again with that same cold fear. He hadn't heard them come in, but there they were. Trafficbots. Silent and foreboding, he also picked out something else. Something was different about these functional pieces of repair automation that kept Copernicus' traffic infrastructure optimized. They were armed. Each silent bot held a tactical laser before it. It looked wrong, but he presumed that the same arms and servos that allowed repair work could also aim and fire a weapon. Beside him, Simms had recovered and traded in his fearful trembling for a broad smile.

Durt's survivalist mind began to map out a defensive route. The knife against his chest felt tight. The deputy woman was right. The front door wasn't an exit possibility. He didn't care about that. Just like Alaska's boulders and trees that offered cover, the desks, chairs and the deputy herself offered him shields of opportunity from potential laser fire. Exiting the building wasn't his plan. The building went up stories above, too. That meant more cover. More time. More options. He was certain the Deputy wouldn't be armed. She was just too smug for that. No, a person like that would keep her hands clean. Leave the dirty work to others. Other people. Other bots. He reached slowly inside his jacket and felt the knife. The same knife that had cut him. The same knife that had killed Rush. He felt his adrenaline rise and his fear disappear. If he was going out, he was going out on his terms. He controlled his destiny now. He fished for another cigarette and lit it. He took a deep breath and visually ran through the route before him that included dragging the deputy for a couple meters for cover. His focus was intense. So intense, he realized later, that he missed three sounds that changed everything.

The first was a series of words. Then a flash of movement and a distinctive clicking sound. Finally a laugh. A deep laugh that gradually caught on with the rest of their small group.

Durt hadn't been the only one with an escape plan, he realized.

Officer Carter had moved quickly to place the deputy in restraints.

Truman turned to him in confusion. "What just happened? What did that woman say?"

Tuck was grinning now.

"Shoot them. Shoot them all," shrieked the Deputy.

Instinctively, Durt reached for the knife and scanned the line of trafficbots for incoming fire.

None came.

"You should have paid more attention in Civics studies." It was the same voice that had laughed. The voice was deep and came from the tall man, Anton.

Durt's mouth was open, uncomprehending. His cigarette fell to the floor.

Tuck nodded in agreement. "I, for one, am glad she didn't."

Truman repeated his question. "Tuck, what the hell just happened?"

Tuck turned to explain. "I think we've discovered the root of a couple of our mysteries." He turned to Bren and Anton. "First, that thin man over there with one hand? You can lay Trina's death at his feet. I know she took her own life, but it was his doing. Believe me." He turned back. "And second, if you hadn't figured it out, this woman that I've been watching over is Copernicus' medical examiner."

The woman looked exhausted, but raised a hand and smiled weakly from within her blanket.

"She is an Earth-appointed executive and the direct representative of Earth's premier. Just like the LUNASEC director, who, for whatever reason, can't be here today. The deputy," he said motioning to the now-silent restrained woman who continued to scowl at them all, "is not. She, like the rest of us, is a civil servant, and subject to our civilian code of justice. Our medical examiner, first identified herself and then charged the deputy with treason."

"Treason?" asked Truman. "You really think she committed treason?"

Tuck shrugged. "Doesn't matter what I think. Legal experts will sort that out. Eventually. What matters is that it was a legal order. And that is why—"

He looked at the exit blocked by the traffic bots.

Truman nodded and completed the thought. "That's why we're not melted piles of flesh."

"Right. Their programming followed orders as it was designed to do."

"The deputy here seems to have over-estimated her authority," he finished.

Durt processed it all slowly. He walked to a now empty chair and just sat, the stored adrenaline of his escape plan now melting away. His body throbbed as he sat and stared and began to smile, for Simms now bore the expression of a man destroyed. He wondered if Simms might cry. The clicking sound of the restraints on the deputy had eliminated his failsafe backup plan and finally wiped the constant smirk from his face.

"One thing I don't understand," said Tuck. "Why all the focus on the headless body?"

Her voice was low, but Durt listened as the medical examiner responded. "I think I can explain that one. At least part of it anyway. Orenz does some amazing things. Things our bodies were never meant to do. Its effects are usually mitigated through the medical manipulation that accompanies the detox at the end of the contract." She paused and let the rest of them catch up. "But, once in a while. Maybe one in a thousand. Maybe even one in ten thousand, the drug trips a DNA switch that brings on Progeria." She shook her head. "From what I can tell, a wicked one, too."

Durt had no idea what it was. As he looked around the crowd, the faces told him he wasn't alone.

"Pro-ge-ria?" asked Tuck hesitantly.

Yes. It's a term for premature aging diseases. Imagine you're mid-way through your contract here and you wake up one morning, you look at yourself in your bathroom monitor and you realize you look like you're 120 years old."

"Oh my God," said Bren. "I'd kill myself."

The ME nodded. "That's what happened in a few cases. Some asked for help."

Now Tuck was putting it together, Durt could tell. "They lost their heads and hands so there wouldn't be easy identification or—

"Or reveal the secret," she finished. "That the same drugs that enable the continuous profit stream to Copernicus had the potential to destroy them, too."

"So the serial killer theory was just a LUNASEC plant? A misdirect?"

"Afraid so, Tuck," she said. "LUNASEC has kept its hands full trying to keep this under wraps."

Tuck acknowledged. "Near next to impossible with a new drug task force sniffing around," he mused. "How did you figure it out?"

She looked suddenly weak and tired, her voice frail. "Bike and I had what you might call an exchange of information. I was curious from an ME perspective, and he willingly explained." She closed her eyes. "I wasn't supposed to survive."

"Bike?" The question was clear and sharp from Bren. "Tuck, you have to do something about him," she shrieked. "Our whole enterprise depends on it."

A calmer, deeper voice followed. "I believe the medical examiner said it was an exchange of information, if I am not mistaken," said Anton. "Pray tell, what did the man learn from you?"

Her voice was almost a whisper. "A lesson in physiology. The final lesson of his life." She was shivering just thinking about it. She paused for a moment, straining to answer the question. "That you need both femoral arteries intact to live."

* * *

The fight broke out just after midnight. It wasn't unusual. In fact, for Harry's, it was only a little early.

It was the same crowd and the same stuffed bear still trying to crawl its way to the ceiling. The bar reeked of spilled beer and old cedar, of sweat, pain, joy and disappointment, but maybe above it all, Durt thought, it smelled like adventure. Alaska remained one of the Earth's great treasures, a place beyond the vast farmlands and overcrowded urban growths that continued to devour what remained. This small crowd of rough immigrants who managed and protected her was just one of thousands of similar crowds across the northern expanse. All had their own unique duties and adapted to local customs of entertainment. Here, entertainment pastimes of booze and music were only trumped by one thing, aside from the tall tales they liked to share, and that was bar fights.

The band was on a break, and the grunts and smacks of the fight now took top billing.

Unlike the Moon races where there were no rules, the rules for a bar fight at Harry's were fairly strict. Problem was, they weren't written down anywhere, and the only way to learn the fight rules was to actually get into one. In Durt's assessment, they were all stupid, but at least they were consistent. Once in a while they were about money, but more often, they were about respect—or rather lack of respect. A regular supply of newcomers looking for adventure and work made sure this form of entertainment never failed. They were the explosives, and alcohol was the fuse. Put them together with nothing better to do, and the result was predictable. Never failed.

His eyes were on the scene before him, but his mind was not. He had a couple weeks now before he and Truman had another load to run. It wasn't because they weren't ready. He'd recovered from his wounds nicely on the return trip. The jump still messed with his inner clock, but not nearly as much as on the way out. No, it was TransComm. They wanted him to be.... He thought for a moment. What was the word they'd used? *Unencumbered*. That was it. Available for any follow-up interviews after the arrest of Simms and the LUNASEC deputy. He and Truman had created quite a mess and were temporarily Earth restricted until they could get it sorted out. According to Tuck, they'd also helped prevent some kind of virtual bank heist, too. That was one they hadn't even known about. The great thing was both Tuck and Mican invited him to come out to the races and actually see one next time he was in Copernicus. He'd been half out of it but had agreed whole-heartedly. Funny, he mused, how it all worked out.

Harry, hands on her hips, watched her bar with interest as the fight crashed into a crowded table, its occupants laughing and melting into the tables behind to give them room. No, Durt corrected himself, her name was Ida. Even if everyone called her Harry, her name was Ida. Next to Ida sat Zeus. Zeus was smiling, and not just because he was tanked. He never had any cash but never needed any. A slight man with a head a bit too big for his frame, he was a master craftsman from the South and something of a sculptor with Alaska's well-protected supply of wood. From the apartment upstairs to the drink in his hand, everything went on his tab, and by the end of the week, that tab would grow to sizable proportions. Part-time handyman and full-time philosopher, Zeus spent his work week repairing and replacing the damage to the bar. Just like everything else here, there was a kind of beauty in the symbiotic way they worked it all out.

They were all there, his father included, a fresh girl on his arm and a glass that was never more than half empty, a proud smile on his face—something that, at one time, was all Durt wished for in the world. Now, however, the girl and the booze made it less genuine, even if it was tinged with sadness now and again. Funny what a few weeks away would do, he thought, now seeing his father as the rest of the bar likely did: Larson senior a good way into his next bender.

The most beautiful girl in Alaska was there, too, hanging off his every word. Kim was gorgeous as ever, but the timbre of her voice and the tilt of her smile were more that of a child than a woman. No, he thought, the change was in him. The bar was the same, but it was smaller somehow, and even the stuffed bear's post-mortem climbing prowess seemed diminished since the last time Durt was at Harry's, and that was only a few weeks back. The shaggy symbol of Alaskan wilderness reflected a cheaper, less authentic version than he remembered.

He watched them all, but their attention wasn't on him. No, it was on the fight, their faces grinning and eyes straining to see what unspoken rule might be taught and learned tonight.

No, they hadn't tamed Alaska as many of them had set out to do. Alaska wouldn't put up with that. It was more of a friendship. An on-again, off-again relationship. Some of them couldn't wait to get out, but most of them never would. Most were just too restrained by their own fears and limitations, but somehow here it was easier. Something about being in touch with the basic elements of life rather than being estranged from it, living in a virtual paradise, eating who-knows-what. Eating themselves. Eating each other. Up here Saturday night was as good as it got.

And when you got up on Sunday, you could have bacon and eggs and know they were bacon and eggs.

Yeah, at least here they were honest about it.

He felt it. Something *had* changed inside of him. He surveyed the rugged stock of Harry's patrons who'd come here from pretty much all over and realized now he had no clue of what he wanted for himself. They were all looking for adventure and something more—most of them disappointed and trying to remember what it was they were chasing, and almost none of them doing very well at it.

Then there was Jake. Jake was the exception. Jake, too, looked the same, but with Jake's words echoing through his mind and his recent application of those words, Jake had become something more to him. Jake was someone who saw in him something he didn't see in himself. Someone who knew what he wanted—and found it. Durt envied him.

I never met a challenge I wasn't ready to step up to.

Jake was here because he wanted to be here. It was in the way he looked. The way he spoke. The reverence that he held for this northern land. Alaska had called, and Jake had answered. He followed his dream by chance or by design and wound up exactly where he wanted to be. And maybe that was lucky. Durt doubted it. He figured it was more about Jake. He was one of those rare folks who embraced whatever the universe presented.

Jake looked up and returned Durt's gaze, somehow feeling that thoughtful stare. Smiling slightly, Jake offered his knowing wink. "So, gonna stick around for a while now? Big ugly world out there."

Jake was right, of course, and Durt wondered if that question was probing for another whose passion for the North matched his own. But in the short time he'd been gone, he'd seen ugly, and ugly wasn't limited to the world. And now that he'd seen it for himself, it didn't seem to bother him that much. In fact, he mused, a little ugly now and again might not be such a bad thing.

Durt answered with a noncommittal shrug and smiled at the

man he admired most here, but in his mind he already knew the truth of it.

The fight was winding down now, and Harry's seemed too small for him. He knew he was going to have a blast here with CJ for a few days. Maybe have another roll or two with Kim, as well, but right now, he needed air. He needed to feel the real Alaska around him. He stood up and whistled. He needn't have. Buzz was there as soon as he moved to stand. Ready to go. Ready for whatever.

Durt leaned over for a friendly nuzzle and looked up at Jake. "You'll look after him, won't you?"

Even if no one else understood him at Harry's, Jake did. But this time Jake was silent. Another wink and a nod confirmed that Jake read him like a topographical map. He could never deprive Buzz of everything Alaska had to offer a husky. Buzz could run. Buzz could fly. Buzz could scare off bears to his heart's content. He, however, had other ideas and dreams. His own destiny.

Outside, Alaska's chill slapped his face. Beneath his feet the snow crunched an odd rhythm in tandem with Buzz's as they walked together. Above, the dark blanket of sky above sparkled with inviting stars and the borealis. The cuts on his arms had healed nicely, even if they ached now and again. And his scar? He'd decided to keep it. Weeks ago he'd thought differently. But things *were* different now. The scar was a part of his story. A part of him.

His feet still, he welcomed the silence around him and gazed up. "It's up there someplace, Buzz."

Buzz, too, was still, listening as if he pondered the same questions.

"I just have to go find it."

DEAR READER

Thanks for reading *Durt*! I sincerely hope you liked the story.
If you didn't know, I am a self-published author. That means two things. First, I don't have a large "promotional" budget that puts me on the same footing as authors with an agent and a publishing house, so recommending *Durt* to that one friend of yours who (like me) is a sci-fi fanatic, would be a high compliment.

The second? What many readers don't realize is the most valuable contribution a reader can bestow is that of a reader's review. If you could find the time to write a few sentences about the book, it would help me tremendously. I think Durt would appreciate it, too. I hope it's positive, but honesty is appreciated, too.

Finally, if it's morning on the East Coast, there's a good chance I'm working on my next project, so to friends, Romans, and countrymen—to readers, writers, authors and Earthlings—drop me a line. I'd love to hear from you. Send your note to: james@jamesslaterbooks.com. Better yet, visit my website jamesslaterbooks.com. Check out the sequel, *Claustrom*, and subscribe to my blog. I share the stories behind the books, the book covers, and the characters living between them. And don't worry. I won't spam you. I don't have the time or energy for that. I'm a much better storyteller than a used car salesman.

Again, many thanks for reading. I look forward to hearing from you!

=James

Cover design by Sarah Hedges (sacslater@gmail.com)

Made in the USA
Coppell, TX
15 December 2019

12935085R00213